NE·
ROSTOFF
BO

by
Stella May

NEW HOPE

First edition. June 17, 2024.

Copyright © 2024 Stella May.

ISBN: 979-8224207527

Written by Stella May.

Also by Stella May

Rostoff Family Saga
New Dawn
New Hope

Upon A Time
'Till Time Do Us Part
Time & Again
No Other Time

Standalone
Rhapsody in Dreams
A Twirl In Time

Watch for more at www.StellaMayAuthor.com.

To Sharon Burke, my teacher, my Queen, my dearest friend.
Thank you for everything.

CHAPTER ONE

San Francisco, California 1995

The Rostoff household was in an uproar. The official cause – nothing less than the upcoming celebration of Peter's eighteenth birthday. The real reason, a family reunion of sorts. After five long years Dmitry Rostoff was finally coming home. To the States, to his family estate in California, *Zolotoe Selo*.

Frenzied anticipation buzzed through the formidable estate including all the staff.

Only Elizabeth remained calm and seemed unaffected. She went through each day as usual, without any interruption in her schedule, as normal as you please.

Ivan, the one servant closer to Elizabeth than any other member of the staff, took no notice of any changes in her behavior. After Peter announced that Dmitry accepted his invitation and promised to fly in for his birthday, Her Grace nodded and calmly ordered her son's rooms prepared immediately. That's it. No emotions, no objections, no reaction whatsoever.

God only knew what was really happening inside her heart. Or her head.

Ivan long ago gave up any attempt to solve the great puzzle of Elizabeth Rostoff.

He feared her, yet remained completely in awe from the moment he began to work for the Rostoffs. And foolishly and helplessly in love. Even after so many years.

Even when Elizabeth's father-in-law and her husband were still alive, Ivan never doubted the true master of the household.

Her Grace, a domineering force, a power to reckon with, Ivan loved her to distraction. He fantasized about Elizabeth every night. For more years than he remembered.

Was he obsessed with her? Probably.

And she knew it. Oh, she knew, all right! And used it. Constantly. Ruthlessly.

Sometimes he hated her. And dreamed of revenge. Other times he ached for her, wept for her, called for her from the depth of his soul.

But never once for the many years of his employment, did he question her decisions or her orders. Therefore, he remained indispensable to her with his blind obedience which he preferred to call loyalty. Whatever his Mistress wished, he hurried to execute. Always.

And so, per Elizabeth's order, Dmitry's rooms were immediately scrubbed from top to bottom, and aired. All the furniture gleamed and smelled subtly of lemon and wax. The old grandfather clock ticked seconds away, its pendulum lazily swinging, awaiting its master.

Anticipation hung in the air like a rain cloud, thick and heavy.

CHAPTER TWO

N atasha roamed through all the rooms of the suite ready for Dmitry to occupy during his visit. It became her habit over the past few days to return here and stay for a minute or so. She didn't know why this particular suite pulled her like a magnet. The fact that *he* will occupy it, sleep in the huge bed, look out of this window?

Maybe. Probably. More than likely. She drew a deep breath.

You are acting silly, Natasha. He already forgot about you.

But silly or not, she came here every day. And remembered.

Five years, Natasha mused. Five long years since she last saw him, or talked to him. She learned about him from his son Peter, Petya as she preferred to call him in Russian. From the bits and pieces of information he provided, Natasha knew about Dmitry's life in Paris, his work, his friends. But nothing about his private life. She didn't want to know. No concern of hers. *He* wasn't her concern.

Or so she tried to convince herself. Every day for the last five years.

No, really, she cared less if he found someone else. Svetlana, his true love, died a long time ago. Life should go on with or without people we love as the natural order of things.

So, why is your life going nowhere?

Oh, my life's just great!

Habitually Natasha debated with her opponent, her inner voice that recently disagreed with her too often.

I have a family, even friends. I have all I need; all the life I can handle!

Yeah? Then why are you coming to his rooms every night? Do you like torturing yourself?

I'm not! Torturing myself, that is. I just...

You just... what? Remember? Dream?

Well, yes. And what's wrong with that?

Nothing, except that dreams are cruel. You should know that.

She sighed. Yes, she should. And she has. She shouldn't even think about him, not now, not ever. Except....

So many issues bound them together.

Svetlana, the kids.

And, yes, memories.

He left five years ago without a word. Just like that. Like he never was.

She felt rejected. Betrayed. Even though she had no right to feel that way. He never said anything, never promised her anything. He never even touched her except that night in the gardens, when he held her. Close, but not close enough.

The memory of that one night haunted her for a long time. Instead of ignoring them or locking them inside, Natasha often intentionally dragged her memories from her subconscious mind, forcing herself to face them. That self-imposed torture cost her dearly, but it also helped her to accept the truth. She meant nothing to Dmitry Rostoff. Their chemistry was just a fluke born out of the shared traumatic experience. No less, no more. She accepted it, learned to live with it. But she could never forget.

Whatever happened, or rather not happened, between them five years ago didn't die a natural death. No, a brutal amputation ended everything. And like any chopped limb it throbbed and bled. Still.

When Dmitry left he stole some vital part of her that could never be replaced. No longer the same person after that and healing became impossible.

Being whole again – completely out of the question.

And Natasha accepted that. She was hurt before, cruelly. Her scars might be invisible, but they existed. Dimitry added one more scar to her collection. No big deal. She was a survivor. She'd go on and overcome.

She *was* fine. The trick – look forward—never back, a lesson she learned long ago. The past belonged to the past. Dmitry belonged to the past. Her stupid infatuation with him belonged to the past. Buried and forgotten.

Who are you kidding?

Natasha shook her head. God, why now? Why after all these years had he decided to come back? The simple answer – for his son's eighteenth birthday. She'd be more surprised if he failed to attend because Peter was the only family member Dimitry truly loved, and cared about.

She absently played with the delicate gold cross around her neck as she wandered around the room before walking to the huge Palladian window. She parted the heavy drapes and looked out.

But for once, the splendor of Elizabeth's gardens failed to grab her attention.

How on earth will she face Dimitry tomorrow? How will she be able to pretend that nothing happened between them all these years ago?

But pretend she must.

She'd rather die than give him the satisfaction of knowing he broke her heart.

God, how naïve! Pathetic. Falling in love with Dimitry was the stupidest thing she had ever done in her life.

Then again, maybe it wasn't love at all. Maybe just a crush. Maybe tomorrow she won't feel a thing and wonder what she ever saw in him. After all, she changed, grew as a person. That poor girl, devastated after her best friend's tragic death, dragged halfway around the world to another country with a helpless baby on her hands, did not exist anymore.

Natasha became a totally different person. Stronger, smarter. Older.

Her thirtieth birthday was in a couple years. And after all this time she grew into a mature woman able to take care of herself, and oversee two children. She smiled, thinking of them. Her kids, Petya and Katia, her pride, her joy, and hope. Every single day she gave thanks to God for bringing them into her life.

Natasha didn't feel cheated because she never had her own children or her own family. Those two were all the family she needed. She considered Peter and Katia her own, had great pride in them, and loved them to distraction.

She honestly forgot that she failed to carry them inside her body or give birth to them. In her heart and soul, they were hers.

And that mattered the most.

Of course, they had another living parent, their father. But that *parent* decided to be absent from their lives. Granted, not so much from Peter's. But in Katia's case...

Dammit.

For the gazillionth time, Natasha wondered why he couldn't love her. Wasn't he curious about the child he created with the woman he loved? Does he ever wonder how she looks, for goodness' sake!

How can anyone stay away from their flesh and blood for five years and not bother to call or send a birthday card? Oh, there were gifts and presents from Paris after Peter's visit with Dmitry. But Natasha knew the boy bought all of them, bless his kind heart. Dmitry never knew about all these toys and cute clothes "from Dad" which Petya usually carried in by truckloads and presented to his half-sister.

Damn the man, how could he be so cold and unforgiving?

And damn her for carrying so much, for hurting.

For remembering.

Never again, Natasha vowed with clenched fists. Never again will she let her heart be so open, so trusting, so vulnerable. Never again will she deceive herself, dreaming of happily ever after. Because no such thing existed. Period.

Svetlana's dream of love and happiness turned out to be the most tragic event of her life.

But it gave you Katia.

Interrupted by the sound of loud breathing behind her, Natasha glanced over her shoulder, and smiled.

"Well, boys, thanks for coming to fetch me." Two oversize German shepherds hovered by the threshold, lolling their tongues. Natasha expected the intruders to have shown up sooner.

"I would invite you in, but it isn't my room, you know, and anyway, it's time for me to go."

The dogs answered by thumping their tails against the polished wooden floor. Natasha stepped closer then gave each dog a head rub, all the while trying to avoid their tongues. But as always, she failed to escape their wet greetings. Frankly, she didn't try all that hard, and these two hooligans knew it. She loved and trusted the pair of trained ferocious looking guard dogs Dmitry got after an unsuccessful attempt on Katia's life. One was tan and black, the other silver grey, both sleek and massive and impressive.

But they turned to putty in Natasha's hands, not to mention Katia's. Both dogs adored their little charge, fiercely guarding her inside the house and out of it, not letting anyone except Natasha and Peter to approach the little girl. Not even her grandmother Elizabeth.

The dogs seemed to tolerate Elizabeth as their necessary evil. And only to a point. No one tricks animals, or children. She remembered Katia's first reaction to her grandmother. It has changed with years, but subtly. Katia no longer broke into hysterics nowadays whenever Elizabeth came around, but she became instantly alert and unnaturally quiet.

Same as two German shepherds.

Nope, couldn't fool animals and children.

The animals in question flanked Natasha from both sides, and fixed on her as if asking, *Where to?*

"Let's take a walk outside, boys." Both dogs turned to the direction of the staircase. She didn't have to say anything more than that, no longer must check on Katia or wonder if she should expect Peter back tonight. The calm behavior of the dogs and their easy willingness to go out with her now answered all her questions. Katia lay fast asleep on her cozy bed, and no Peter until morning. Things were as they should be. Accompanied by her four-legged escorts Natasha sighed with relief and headed for the garden forward. Pasha and Misha—ridiculous names for trained guard dogs if you asked her—appeared to be two house pets, harmless and friendly, but appearances were deceiving. Once Natasha witnessed as in a blink of an eye those two became dangerous predators.

That memorable transformation terrified her. She tensed so tight she thought her skin might split even though she knew the dogs would never turn on her. Yet under certain circumstances, Pasha and Misha were trained to kill just as easily as they trotted beside her now. But she knew in her heart they meant no harm to her or Petya, and especially not Katia. Petya had their respect, Natasha their love, but only Katia held in her small hands the dog's very souls. When their little mistress slept, like now, they followed Natasha around like two shadows.

When she needed solitude, they kept their distance. But mostly, they kept her company. Their silent presence gave her comfort. And understanding. The dogs seemed to read her moods. They also knew her whereabouts at any given time, day or night. Whenever she needed them, they ran to her side without verbal command. Their connection was almost eerie. Sometimes Natasha wondered if they communicated telepathically, for the dogs seemed to "hear" her in their minds, even at a great distance. But whatever the reason, Natasha stopped questioning it a long time ago. Grateful, she simply accepted it. Pasha and Misha helped her keep the distance between her and the household staff. Almost everybody feared the dogs, and were in awe of the uncanny communication between Natasha and them.

It brought her a grudging respect from some, and a wide berth from others, perfectly fine in her book. The dog's presence also put a stop of searching her room once and for all, thank God.

Nowadays she slept peacefully, undisturbed by prowlers or nightmares, because the dogs slept outside of hers and Katia's bedrooms, guarding them through the night.

But tonight, sleep eluded her. Natasha tossed and turned, hot one moment, cold the next. Dawn almost broke when she finally drifted into a dream where a silver-eyed man held her close to his heart and vowed never to leave her again.

CHAPTER THREE

Dmitry sat in the car, watching from a distance his mother's estate, *Zolotoe Selo*, where he was born and raised. His private plane landed at San Francisco International Airport on a clear and crispy September morning, so different from a miserable rainy weather he left behind in Paris.

He decided to drive himself. Dismissing his chauffer, Dmitry climbed behind the wheel of the Mercedes sedan, and peeled off. The drive to *Zolotoe Selo* usually took thirty-five to forty minutes. He arrived in twenty. Just before the last twist in the road that brought him to the main gates of the manor, Dmitry stopped the car, and stared ahead. The barrage of emotions he tried to suppress for five years rushed in a flood, stealing the oxygen from him. As ambushes went, this one was brutal. Vicious. Merciless.

He scanned the painfully familiar golden gates of the estate. Bitter bile abraded his throat.

Betrayal.

It hit him first, like giant fist in a solar plexus.

How could you, Mother?

Dmitry clenched his jaw, hurting, remembering. The wound of that betrayal remained fresh and throbbing. As if it happened just yesterday.

All the memories he buried long ago and forgot burst free. He escaped from here five years ago, and relocated to France. Definitely the right decision for him. Keeping his distance was a defense mechanism. Or an act of self-preservation. He survived. The business prospered under his leadership. His life returned to normal. Even though unremarkable, yet pleasant enough, content, and almost stress-free. He even began to enjoy himself.

But as soon as he stepped into San Francisco airport, his contentment shattered into little shards, and his mood plummeted. He made a mistake.

Dammit, he shouldn't have come here. But how could he not?

Yes, five years ago he vowed to never return. But fate intervened. Peter asked him to come for his eighteenth birthday.

Dmitry could ignore anything else, but not that.

Last winter, he declined the official invitation to Elizabeth's 70th birthday. Four months ago, he disregarded his daughter's sixth birthday. For him, May 25th was the anniversary of Svetlana's death, and nothing else.

Only for Peter Dmitry broke his sacred vow. Only for his son did he finally came back to the place that held so many memories. Ugly memories.

Only for Peter.

He condemned himself to the purgatory of this visit.

From afar, the manor house Dmitry christened the Mausoleum was a blurry spot. Surrounded by luscious gardens, it seemed almost serene and welcoming.

Dmitry knew better.

Maybe it was time to go back? To revisit the place he abandoned in anger? Maybe then he could let go of it—and the hurt—and get on with his life?

His best friend Vlad constantly lectured him on it. And Marie insisted that he would never heal completely if he allowed the past stay in his way. Right as always. Who should know better than her, the woman who went through hell and back, and found the strength to let go, to forgive and forget?

Thinking of Marie, his former store manager, and now a renowned artist, Dmitry smiled. She married his best friend, Vlad Albrecht, and soon became the mother to their adorable twin daughters. So much happiness filled her she all but glowed. And she deserved it. But their pasts were different.

Hers was buried long before she met Vlad. And his...Dmitry swore under his breath. His past looked him straight in the face. Lying in wait behind the walls of his mother's house, and very much alive.

Deep in his heart, Dmitry knew he should let go, to forget. To forgive.

And finally become free from the past.

But God help him, he still could not.

Five years was a long time, but apparently not long enough.

The sudden urge to make a U-turn and leave grew so strong Dmitry revved the Mercedes back to live. Then abruptly, he turned off the ignition. He cursed, raked both hands through his hair, then cursed more. In helpless rage, he brought both fists down, and hit them against the steering wheel.

No, he can't leave. He reached the point of no return.

Marie knew exactly what she talked about. He couldn't ignore his past any longer, or he'd become a fucking robot. Without untangling the knot of hatred inside of him, Dmitry stood no chance be whole again. He must face his past, must make his piece.

Only then, he will be content and completely free. And only then, he will leave this dreaded place forever, and never return.

Annoyed that his hands shook, Dmitry once again brought his car to life, then drove to the front gates of *Zolotoe Selo*, his mother's home.

His personal hell.

CHAPTER FOUR

P eter pressed his right foot on the gas pedal, accelerating faster. His new car bulleted forward like a missile. A satisfied grin spread across his face.

You are speeding, Peter's responsible half noted in a firm, stern voice.

But not dangerously, his reckless half butted in.

Peter let out a hoot of carefree laughter. He was speeding, but just enough to make the car purr like a giant kitten, and glide like a dream.

This baby can really move!

Thankfully the roads were relatively empty that early in the morning. And besides, a car with five speeds begged to fly. Exhilarated, Peter floored a little more. The low husky rumble of the cherry-red Corvette, his father's generous birthday present, became the best music to his ears. Zipping along the almost empty highway in the new sports car, better than sex with his girlfriend. But being a smart man, Peter kept that little tidbit to himself. He envisioned Julie naked in his mind. Beautiful, intelligent, classy. And a real tigress in bed.

Instantly, he became painfully aroused. Damn. To err on the side of caution, he slowed his car. Wincing, he tried to adjust his body to a more comfortable position, but with his long legs, it was a serious challenge. Thinking about his girlfriend made him uncomfortable. And not only physically.

A year older than him, a straight 'A' student, Julie Osborn never socialized much. She kept her distance from her fellow students, and earned the reputation of a snob. Or a lesbian. Depended on who you asked. To Peter, Julie was an enigma. Her features—long black hair, slanted golden eyes, dark olive skin— made her look like a pagan goddess, untouchable and exotic as hell. More than one guy tried to get close to the aloof beauty, but only Peter succeeded. They met at the library, hit it off from the get-go, and ended up in bed on the second date. He had no clue why she chose him over everybody else, but he preferred not to question his good luck.

Peter expected Julie to be as reserved in bed as she was in life, but she surprised him. Yesterday, she surprised him even more, by confessing being in love with him. For the first time since they started dating, she made Peter uncomfortable.

And sad. He knew nothing about real love. Or what his feelings for Julie were. Lust? Sure. But love? Peter shook his head. He never fell in love before, but somehow, he knew that whatever emotion filled him for Julie failed as love.

So, he refused to repeat the three little words that Julie expected from him. He couldn't. It would not be honest, or fair. To either of them.

He disappointed her. Upset, she jumped from his still warm lovemaking bed, then walked out.

When he left campus earlier today, she was still royally pissed. Julie refused to talk to him when he sought her out. Peter shrugged. He decided to let her steam for a while, then send her flowers. From his experience with the opposite sex, every female was a sucker for roses. Especially a huge bouquet accompanied by chocolates and a goofy card.

Shaking off his pensive mood, he figured to worry about Julie later. A lot later.

Nothing and no one could spoil his perfect mood on this beautiful autumn day. Not even his girlfriend. Tomorrow was his birthday; his father arrives later today; he was driving his new dream car. What more could a guy wish for?

Joy and happiness filled Peter to the brim, until he all but bursting. Grinning from ear to ear, he fiddled with the radio until he found his favorite jazz station. He turned the volume up, and drummed his fingers against the steering wheel in rhythm to the blaring music.

But despite everything, the unwelcomed thoughts about Julie nagged him. He frowned. What if she decides to break up with him? After a long moment of self-searching, Peter realized that he'd survive. Oh, he'd be mad as hell, pissed off for a long time, and maybe even sad for a while. But he'd survive.

No matter what, Peter refused to break his principles. A long time ago he vowed to never tell anything but the truth. Not even the half-truth, because to him it was the same as flat-out lie.

Lying, the one thing Peter truly hated. He firmly believed that even the most innocent altering of the truth, even the tiny white lie led to danger. It could start an avalanche of the events that hurt people, changed their lives, and sometimes destroyed it. His parent's marriage was the most painful example of it.

Peter frowned. He never liked to think of the past.

He tried very hard to forget it, and almost succeeded. But sometimes, when he less expected it, the past snuck up on him. Like right now.

Gritting his teeth, he reached deep inside himself for anger. Being angry was much better than sad or helpless. Or devastated.

But the past, as much as he hated it, taught him a lesson he would never forget. Life did go on, despite the cruelty and horrors and lies.

Evil did exist, hidden under the most beautiful exteriors.

But love and hope out balanced it all. Because of that, good always won in the end, and the truth always come out. As simple as that.

That lesson made him into the person he was today. And it gave him the gift of Katie and Natasha. Thinking of them, his surrogate mother, and his half-sister, made his heart swell. They made his life bearable when everything around him seemed to have dissolved and fell apart. Five years ago nothing made any sense. Since then they filled his life with purpose, and healed him, and saved his heart and soul.

Natasha never lied to him, not even when a small lie seemed to be a blessing for his confused mind and bleeding heart. And Katie loved him unconditionally. He remembered being thirteen, alone with his joys and fears. Tomorrow, he turns eighteen. Five years ago, he vowed to never lie. Under any circumstances. Even if his life depended on it. With passing years, his absolute aversion to dishonesty and deceit remained the same, if not stronger.

Driving almost on autopilot, Peter barely paid attention to the beautiful scenery.

Since he entered Berkeley two years ago, he navigated this road a gazillion times. But because he missed Natasha and Katie, he tried to be home every weekend as well as holidays.

Thankfully, the drive took only a short time. The close distance from the university to *Zolotoe Selo* was the main reason he chose Berkeley over Harvard despite his grandmother's wishes. Since he came to live with Elizabeth, Peter complied, or tried to, with all her demands. When she suggested that he'd be more useful for the company as a lawyer, Peter agreed and chose law over marine biology. But he firmly refused her choice of school. Harvard was far away from home, from Katie and Natasha, and because of that, simply unacceptable.

Peter found it easier to abandon his childhood dream of being a marine biologist than to be away from two people he loved.

He might have put his foot down and insisted on his chosen major, but he understood a law degree was more important. Not for the company or because his grandmother expected it of him, but for himself. If he ever wanted to make a difference, he had a better shot at it well equipped with the knowledge of law. Not to bend them, but to abide and adhere to them. Always a realist, and coming from the long line of entrepreneurs, Peter understood the complexity of the business environment.

He knew he could never change the world, but he must give his best to make it a better place.

First, he must finish university, and then law school. And of course pass the bar exam. He shook his head in frustration. Another five years before he accomplished it, dammit. An eternity! But if he pushed himself hard, and finished Berkeley next year, that might cut off a year. He intended to give it his best.

Logic told him there were enough battles for him in a few years, but his impatient heart urged him to hurry. He had done that with high school, finished in three years instead of four. Why not university, or law school?

Peter held a deep trust in the justice system, even though it wasn't perfect. But justice always prevailed. And there lay the beauty and wonder of it.

He never regretted his choice of law over biology. Besides, he chose marine biology as his minor, so he hadn't abandoned his dream completely.

Yes, Harvard Law School was one of the best, and yes, it has a nice ring to it, but who cared what school name will be on his diploma?

If he became a good lawyer, and Peter compelled himself to be the very best, nobody should give a damn from what school he received his *Juris Doctor* degree.

Making the last turn, he finally glimpsed the massive golden gates to his family estate. His heart started to beat faster with anticipation and joy. He was home.

CHAPTER FIVE

D mitry watched the snazzy Corvette zip through the gate. It came to a stop just inches from the manor house steps. He chuckled. God, the boy drove like a pro. His son was a bright and intelligent young man, and Dmitry's heart swelled with pride. Everything Peter did, he usually excelled at, be it martial arts, languages, or driving. The only thing that he flunked was his infamous scuba diving lessons his late mother preferred over everything. As far as Dmitry knew, the boy never dove again after Polina's death.

Impatient to greet his son after the long months since they separated, he raced down the steps. Peter visited him in Paris often during the last five years. Sometimes, for a long weekend, sometimes for a week. They traveled all around Europe, and Dmitry smiled, happy to have shown his son so much of the world. Thanks to their trips, Peter knew Italy, Switzerland, Germany and, of course, France. Peter adored Paris, and loved everything French, from food to architecture. But he loved his home more. Not once had Peter extended his stay with Dmitry longer than a week, or expressed any regret about his decision to live in *Zolotoe Selo*.

With a pang of sorrow, Dmitry accepted the fact that Peter easily endured the separation between them. Unlike him. Dmitry hated the distance he put between himself and Peter, hoping against all odds that one day his son will change his mind, and decide to stay in Europe for good. But that never happened.

The older his son became, the more determinate he was to live in California, to get his education there, and make his life in the States. Where he belonged.

Dmitry envied him that sense of belonging, and the constant pull of that singular unique place called home. His mother's estate was home to Peter, but not because of the building, despite its grand architecture, or its long history. Two special individuals made *Zolotoe Selo* the sanctuary for Peter: his half-sister and her nanny. He called them a family. *My family*. It grated on Dmitry.

I am your family, dammit. I am the only real family you've got!

But he never voiced that thought out loud. Because of pride? Because he didn't want to show how much he hurt? Probably. But mostly, because Dmitry knew the fault lay with him that his son failed to include him in *his family*.

Five years ago, Dmitry erected an impenetrable barrier between himself and *Zolotoe Selo*, intentionally and deliberately separating his life from everything that belonged to his mother. Peter chose to stay on the other side of that barrier. But the connection between them unwillingly linked Dmitry to the people and the world he intentionally left behind. During the last five years, he and his son managed to build a good, solid relationship based on mutual respect and love. They honored each other's privacy, and differences while they talked about business, art, music, the stock market, women, and politics. But never about the family they shared.

They both recovered after Polina's death, but never forgot or forgave.

They both healed, but still bore the invisible scars.

Dmitry hurried down the steps and wondered how he might manage to stay a few days under his mother's roof, and survive in one piece. But for Peter's sake, he promised to try. He needed to do his damnedest to make his son's birthday a happy celebration. And then escape.

Peter jumped from his Corvette, and glanced at Dmitry's car parked in the driveway. He stopped, clearly wondering about it, then shrugged. Turning away, he started toward the house, then yelped in surprise, "Dad!"

Skipping like an excited child, he further spoiled his adult image by hurling himself into Dmitry's arms. Such an open display of emotions was unusual for Peter. His normal demeanor always remained calm and a bit reserved. Pleasantly surprised, Dmitry decided not to question his good fortune.

Peter finally dropped his control around him. Hallelujah! His throat became tight, as something hot pressed against his eyes. Afraid to embarrass them both, but unwilling to let go of the moment, Dmitry held Peter close in his embrace.

With a great effort, he finally managed to take his emotion under control.

Dmitry gained control of his voice, let go of Peter, and smiled. "It's good to see you, son."

As always, looking at his son, he was taken aback by the boy's arresting features.

No other description fit other than Hollywood handsome, tall and dark and dazzling.

And now he grinned like a little boy at Christmas.

"We expected you later in the evening, Dad. When did you arrive?"

"An hour ago."

"But that's wonderful! Wait 'till I tell the family!" Peter tugged him up the stairs toward the main door. "Did you see everybody? Natasha? Katia? Grandmother?"

"No. Everybody was still upstairs when I got here."

He dreaded the time when he must see and talk to everybody. Dmitry shrugged it off. For now, it was only two of them, and he refused to share Peter with anybody just yet.

"But your grandmother sent a welcoming committee."

"Let me guess, Ivan the Terrible and his trusty minions."

Dmitry chuckled. "Something like that."

"Did he make a 'Welcome home, Your Grace' speech?"

"He did." Dmitry winced in recollection. He never took his title seriously, forgetting most of the time that his veins carried blue blood.

His title, *Knyaz*, stood high in the aristocratic ranking of the former Russian Empire, a dead society that ceased to exist almost eight decades ago. Dmitry considered his title as a useless joke, nonsense and anachronism. He totally ignored it.

But here, in his mother's domain, every servant addressed the members of the Rostoff family by his or her aristocratic title. Such was the rule. *Elizabeth's rule.* One of many he despised. One of many he tried to rebel against growing up in this mausoleum of a house. He lost on every single count. Dammit.

Dmitry reminded himself that was a long time ago, in another lifetime.

He was neither a child nor a disillusioned teenager anymore. He no longer must obey his mother's ridiculous rules. He was a castoff, a renegade. A pariah.

Did Elizabeth still consider him family? As a matter of fact, he knew in his heart that she didn't.

And thank God for that. I don't belong here. I never have.

"Well, how is she running for you?" Eager to change the subject, Dmitry nodded toward the Corvette.

"Like a wind!" The boy exclaimed. "She's like a dream. Thank so much, Dad."

"You always wanted that kind of car, although I personally prefer Germans."

"I know you do, Dad. But... just look at her!" Peter eyed his new car with clear adoration. "Isn't she a beauty? So slick and curvy..."

Dmitry chuckled. "You talk like it's a woman."

"Oh, she's better. Never nags, argues, or complains. And doesn't demand constant attention. Although Natasha would nail my behind if she ever heard me talk like that," Peter murmured, lowering his voice.

Hearing the name, Dmitry's heart gave one quick thud.

"How is she?" Quite deliberately, as if inquiring about some mutual acquaintance out of politeness, he schooled his face and voice into neutral mode.

"She's fine." Peter frowned and turned his head toward the house. "Usually, she's up and running by this time. I wonder why she isn't down yet."

"She's probably with your sister."

Or avoiding me.

"Yeah, probably." Peter's shoulders visibly tensed.

Dmitry realized they wandered into the wrong territory – an absolute taboo between them for the last five years. Uneasiness filled him and he thrust his hands in his trouser pockets.

What now?

Dammit, he could not freeze every time the subject of Katia or Natasha came up. He was bound to run into them sooner or later. And sooner or later, Peter and he must talk about it. But not now. No, not right now.

"We should go inside." Peter's cheerful voice dragged him from his thoughts. "I don't know about you, but I'm so hungry I can eat a horse."

Despite himself, Dmitry laughed. "Well, I could use a cup of coffee. A sandwich sounds good, too."

As an escape, this one was temporary. But Dmitry was pathetically grateful.

Coward.

Together, they started up the steps leading to the huge double doors of the mansion. The cook prepared breakfast just for the two of them. Immensely relived, Dmitry ate, but mostly listened to his son, who proved to be a fountain of information. But Dmitry noticed that Peter preferred to talk about neutral subjects.

School, cars, movies. Fine with him.

After breakfast, Dmitry suggested a stroll in the gardens. Peter accepted, but his facial expression maintained a reserved politeness. Dmitry swore under his breath. Maybe, an aimless stroll will draw the boy from his protective shell.

"It's been too long since I saw you last time, son. Almost four months."

"Yeah, and I'm sorry, Dad. I wanted to visit, honestly, but I'm so busy with school. I want to squeeze in as many classes as I can this year. I'm planning on graduating next year, as I told you." Peter shrugged, but avoided looking at him. "So, studies, and lectures, you know."

He pulled the nonchalant act, but Dmitry knew better. *Cherchez la femme.* He was dead sure of it.

They walked casually along the path leading to the rose garden.

As always, the beauty and fragrance of the flowers calmed Dmitry. Even as a boy, he loved this part of the estate. So lovely, and peaceful.

The day was pleasantly warm. Peter's company brought back the long-forgotten felling of joy and delight. Even the silence between them became comfortable.

After a while, Dmitry asked, "So, what's her name?"

"Huh? Whose name?"

"The girl who kept you occupied and busy. Studies and lectures, you know." He shrugged, too, parroting Peter's gesture. They both laughed.

"Julie," Peter answered after a short pause.

"Julie, huh? Beautiful name."

"She is beautiful, Dad. Like a jewel."

"Oh? I'm glad. At least your taste in women has improved since last time."

"Yeah, and considering that my last serious crush was on my high school biology teacher, it does say a lot." Peter grinned. "Ms. Brown was probably forty, and wore thick round black-framed glasses. But they say love is blind, especially when an object of your adoration uses Latin. *Ornithorhynchus. Leotonychotes.*"

"And what happened with that Barbie from your junior year in Berkeley? Or that cute little dancer?"

"Bambie, Dad, her name was Bambie. And cute little Nancy was a mime, not a dancer."

"Oh, well."

"Yeah, well. " Touching his heart with one hand, and bowing his head in a mocked regret, Peter let out a fake exasperated sigh. "What can I say? Mistakes of the youth."

A bark of laughter burst from Dmitry. He realized he enjoyed every moment with his son. Immensely. He failed to remember last time he felt so light and carefree.

"So, what's the story between you and that Jewel?"

"Julie. Simple enough. You know, boy meets girl, girl meets boy." Once again serious, Peter fell silent, as a deep V formed between his eyebrows.

Simple my ass.

Dmitry put a hand on Peter's tensed shoulder. "My dear boy, when there is a woman, especially a beautiful one, nothing is simple."

"Says who?"

"Your old man."

"You're not old, and it is— was—simple, until..."

"Until?" Dmitry prodded quietly, momentarily alert. Peter's eyes grew dark, a true sign that he wasn't willing to talk on that particular subject. Peter and him were so alike, it might be amusing under different circumstances. Right now, it troubled him. Just like himself, when Peter chose not to share his thoughts or feelings, he immediately pulled the shades down.

But you are competing with a master here, boy.

Dimitry promised to get to the bottom of his son's problem in no time. He was positive. And it *was* a problem. He knew Peter too well not to recognize all the signs. Jittery and uneasy and guarded. Dmitry's inner antenna twitched.

After a long-charged pause, Peter finally replied, "Well, let's just say she wants to upgrade our relationship to the next level. And I'm not sure I'm ready for it."

Dimity stopped abruptly and turned to face his son. "Don't let anybody push you into something you are not a hundred percent comfortable with."

Peter stopped too. "Have you ever known me for a pushover?"

His calm, cold response came accompanied by a hard glare. An icy chill charged up Dmitry's spine. He shivered. When irritated or angry, Peter could be tough as titanium and cold as Siberian winter.

Well, look who's talking.

Yes, even in that regard, he was the carbon copy of Dmitry.

Dammit it.

"No. You've never been a pushover, son."

Peter nodded and continued. Dmitry followed.

Uncomfortable with the subject, he asked nevertheless, "Are you careful?"

"What do you mean?"

"You know very well what I mean."

"Dad, I am always careful," Peter said coolly.

"That's what we all think."

Peter stopped again. "Explain, please."

"You need an explanation? Very well. I was dead sure I was careful six years ago. I took every precaution known to man. Result— your half-sister."

"And you still regret it."

"Yes. I still do." That was the honest to God truth.

Peter remained quiet, but looked at him long and hard. And just like that, the time for a confrontation finally arrived. The subject of his daughter was impossible to ignore or avoid any longer. And too tired to walk on eggshells around it.

"I know you don't share my feelings toward her, son. But I can't and won't lie to you. I loved her mother more than I loved anyone, except you. And that girl snatched her away from me by being born. So, yes, I regret it. I still mourn her mother. And I'm still hurting. And that's the truth, Peter."

Not one word left Peter's mouth. He continued to stare at him, his eyes intense and unfathomable. Finally, by silent agreement, they resumed their slow pace.

At length, Peter spoke, "Dad, I have a favor to ask."

"Anything, son."

"When you meet Katie, please promise me not to hurt her. At least, try."

Instead of a reply, Dmitry nodded.

"And please, try not to hurt Natasha."

Anger flooded through him. He stopped and swiveled to face Peter. "And how on earth can I hurt Natasha?"

Peter stopped, too. His dark and intense eyes were impossible to read. For at hushed moment, the only sound between them came from the chirping of birds.

Like a statue, Peter remained absolutely still. His voice, when he finally spoke, turned to ice. "You will, if you hurt Katie. And, besides, you managed that already."

"Managed what, for goodness' sake?"

"Hurt Natasha."

"How? I didn't even see her yet."

The more agitated Dmitry become, the calmer his son's reaction. Dmitry bristled, absurdly hurt by Peter's cold demeanor. But the boy wasn't finished yet.

"You hurt her five years ago, Dad, by leaving and not saying goodbye," Peter answered quietly. "She was in love with you. Did you know that? Your abrupt departure hurt her. Do you know she waited for months, jumping at every phone call, watching for the mailman every day? And that look on her face when another day passed and no news came from you. It was heartbreaking. Then she stopped waiting. And stopped loving you. And you didn't even know you lost the best woman in the world any man could only dream of."

Guilt squeezed Dmitry like a boa constrictor toying with a rat. In fact, slime ranked higher on the scale of life.

"Why are you telling me this?" Raw and scratchy, his throat made speaking difficult. "Why? Why now?"

"I think it's time you know the truth. And maybe, because I still can't forgive you for that empty look in her eyes. And for Katie, because you still think of her as a mistake, when you should thank God for such an amazing daughter. Maybe because you're my father, and I love you, but I'm sick and tired of playing this cat and mouse game with you for years and—"

Abruptly, Peter stopped talking, and pivoted sideways. A mix of tenderness and pleasure flooded into his face, as a huge smile lifted the corners of his mouth.

"Ah, here is my own true love."

CHAPTER SIX

Dmitry braced himself, preparing to face his daughter at last. But when he looked over his shoulder, there stood not a child, but a petite woman with huge green eyes and a long braid. She stared at him with wide wary eyes.

For a moment, Dmitry failed to recognize her. But when it finally dawned on him, he sucked in a sharp breath, and stumbled back. He was more than shocked. Poleaxed. Thunderstruck.

Astonishing!

Five years ago, Natasha appeared charmingly cute, now she was beautiful. The first word that came to his mind – exquisite. Dmitry swallowed around the fist in his throat.

My God, how she's changed.

Her curly mane of hair now tamed into a braid, gleamed with myriad shades of red and gold, it lay over her shoulder like a long silken rope. Her milky white skin, make-up free, glowed under the sun cascading over her while her pointy chin, with its hint of a cleft, had remained stubborn. But her eyes. God, her eyes! Huge, almond-shaped, impossibly green with thick fringes of dark russet lashes, they shone like two priceless gems, dominating her face. She wore a silky dress that shimmered in the gentle autumn breeze. Paralyzed, he couldn't take his eyes off her.

Slowly, he dragged his gaze down from her hair to her generous breasts to the gently rounded hips. Petite and sensual, her body reminded him of a Japanese netsuke. Yes, the small, carved ivory piece was as delicate as Natashia appeared to be. Five years ago, he compared Natasha to an elf, funny, and a bit peculiar.

The woman that stood in front of him now clearly elegant, classy, and sexy as hell. No, not just sexy, but exotic. And intriguing. And riveting.

Looking at her stole his breath.

Natasha stumbled on the father and son, her mind quickstepping as she took in Dimitry.

He hasn't changed.

Sneaking out of the back door earlier, she was dead sure that Dmitry and Peter remained in the house, eating breakfast. Katia should be in the middle of her art lesson, so Natasha luxuriated in a precious half-hour to herself. To calm down, and regain her self-control.

Dmitry has arrived.

Did she imagination it, or did the atmosphere of the house change?

Restless and fidgety, Natasha slept poorly. She woke hours before dawn, jumpy, sweaty, and uneasy.

Dmitry was here.

She needed to face him. But not yet.

Of course, she must, sooner or later. No feasible way to avoid Dmitry forever since they lived under the same roof, at least for a few days. But she preferred it to be later, much later. And that's why, panicky and shaky, Natasha sneaked out of the mansion, and ran to her sanctuary— the little white gazebo in the middle of the estate grounds.

Halfway to her destination, two intense and angry male voices stopped her. One voice belonged to Petya. The other?

She hesitated, torn between the impulse to back away and her maternal instinct to protect her child. After a heartbeat, she sprinted toward those voices. Whoever dared to argue with her child needed to deal with Natasha first. The idea that Petya wouldn't appreciate being called a child, and especially being rescued, flashed in her mind.

Too bad. He'll have to deal with it.

She stopped at the path that lead to the rose garden and sucked in a few short breaths.

There she found two men faced off like a pair of duelist.

The man Petya addressed in a heated tensed voice stood tall and broad shouldered, with a familiar shock of black hair. He raised his eyes and stared at her.

Silver eyes. Dmitry's eyes.

Natasha's heart did one hard flip-flop inside of her chest. Air stuck in her throat and her legs became liquid. Before father and son fell into silence, Natasha overheard their conversation.

Even though shocked to see Dmitry, she was plain poleaxed to learn that Petya knew the truth about her feelings. All these years, he knew Natasha loved his father.

Oh, my God!

And there she thought she managed to hide her secret so well. More fool she. If she was so pitifully transparent, did someone else besides Petya notice it? Probably. Possibly. Dammit.

Embarrassed, shocked, Natasha wanted to flee, but too late. Both men turned in her direction.

Time to face the music.

Gathering all her courage, Natasha snapped her spine back, squared her shoulders, and lifted her chin up. Inside, she stood there shaking like a leaf in a strong breeze.

"Natasha." Peter grinned, and raced toward her.

"Petya." Despite trembling from head to toe, Natasha's lips curved. She always found it impossible to ignore Petya's sunny smile. She walked into his arms.

"Natasha," he whispered softly, burrowing his nose in the crown of her hair.

Ever since she first met him they shared a private way of greeting. Petya was always taller than her, even as a teenager. Now, at eighteen, he topped her by almost a foot.

When he enveloped her in his arms, like now, Natasha felt small and fragile.

But with Petya, the sensation comforted. Natasha hugged him even harder, grateful for his strength and warmth. In the state she found herself, she needed his familiar presence more than she needed air in her lungs.

After a moment, Peter stepped back, but held Natasha in a lose embrace.

Natasha smiled at the boy who she considered her son. "I missed you, darling."

"I missed you, too, Gorgeous." He dropped his voice. "Ready?"

"No," she replied honestly.

"I'm here. I won't let him hurt you again, I swear." Somber, earnest, Petya's expression made him look older than his years.

With a deep sigh, Natasha nodded. "I know."

"Let's go meet the prodigal father." And flashing a dazzling grin, he tugged her gently forward.

Flabbergasted, Dmitry stood frozen to the spot.

Move, idiot. Don't just stay here like a bloody statue.

But he still found himself glued to the spot, watching the warm greeting between Peter and Natasha. Stabbed with sudden jealousy, he cursed to himself. Ridiculous. Downright stupid.

You're acting like a moron, pal. Get a grip.

With an effort, Dmitry forced himself to unclench his fisted hands. Briefly, he wondered if his facial expression betrayed him, and all his confusing feelings became visible for Natasha to see. Then he fixed his gaze on her pale face, and noticed her uneven breathing, and her helpless wide eyes. A realization that she was affected as much as him, gave Dmitry a jolt of satisfaction. It grounded him. It bolstered him.

Once again, calm and composed, he looked straight at Natasha. And found himself lost into her huge emerald eyes.

"Natasha." Just that, just her name, because his vocal cords refused to function.

"Good morning, Your Grace," she replied, coolly and regally. Somehow, it sounded insulting.

"Please, not that stupid title." Dmitry forced his lips curve into a tense smile.

"After all, we were on the first name basis before."

CHAPTER SEVEN

He hasn't changed at all.
Natasha trembled from the force of emotions that she buried long ago.

God, I'm such a fool! How could I think I forgot him, and everything he made me feel?

One glance of those silver eyes, and she was thrown five years back in time, dazed and shaky, aching with the sweet pain of recognition.

"Let's try that again. Good morning, Natasha." Like a caress, his deep voice reached her ears, and sent a shiver down her spine. Cursing herself, she tried to clear her suddenly dry throat.

"Good morning, Dmitry." Her own voice came out husky and uneven.

Unable to tear her eyes from the face that haunted her for years, Natasha concentrated on keeping herself as still as possible. Inside, her emotions churned, threatening to shatter her composure.

Can he hear my thundering heart?
Or see the tremors raking my body?
She bit her lip painfully, and forced herself to hold his gaze.
He is more gorgeous than I remember.
Tall, dark, charismatic. Time was kind to him. His temples now touched with a hint of silver, gave him a distinguished look. Shorter than he used to wear it five years ago, his hair remained still thick and ink-black. The short sleeves of his white polo shirt accented the golden tan over his arms that were roped with muscles. For the first

time he wore blue jeans rather than tailored slacks. Absolutely illegal what those Levi's did to his body. But his most dramatic feature was still his eyes. Pale gray, almost silver, they held Natasha captive with their mesmerizing gaze.

God have mercy.

Her treacherous body turned warm and cold at the same time, sporting goosebumps the size of Texas along her skin. At almost thirty, far from the naïve girl of once before, she recognized the first signs of arousal churning inside her. An unwelcome sign, to say the least. The betrayal of her own body angered her. In pure defense Natasha firmly thrust her chin forward, setting her teeth, and seething inwardly. The anger was much preferable. Concentrating all her senses on that blazing rage aimed at herself, Natasha held Dmitry's gaze.

"You look well," he finally said. "Actually, more than well. You... you look fantastic."

Open and honest admiration in his voice made her shiver. Her legs grew wobbly and almost folded in. Thankfully Petya chose that moment to slid his arm around her waist.

"Thank you," she mumbled to Dmitry and Petya at the same time. God, she turned into an idiot.

"You've changed," Dmitry stated after a short pause.

"I believe, we all have. Long time, five years."

"Yes, yes, it is." He watched her closely and intently.

She felt exposed. Vulnerable. Lost.

Then she realized he held her hand in his. She tried to tug it free. Dmitry resisted for a moment, then opened his fingers. Her palm slid against his, and that simple caress made Natasha lightheaded.

Dammit.

His sheer impact on all her senses terrified. It shook her to the core.

Get a grip, you featherbrained idiot.

CHAPTER EIGHT

Peter grinned as he watched the pair of them. But his amusement was short-lived. Natasha trembled, even though she worked hard to hold herself still. Her voice, not its usual warm and welcoming, sounded neutral. She kept her head high, replying to Dmitry with mild politeness. For anyone else but him, she looked the picture of a calm and aloof woman, totally in control of herself. Peter bet his new car Dmitry hadn't a clue that Natasha barely stood on her own, fighting her emotions with all her might. But he knew it. And hated it.

Damn, why had he thought Natasha's feelings for his dad were long gone?

Now he realized that foolish mistake. She loved him still.

As much as Peter loved his father, he knew Dmitry was wrong for Natasha. His short-lived stay meant breaking her tender heart all over again. Peter cursed silently.

Maybe shouldn't have invited Dad after all.

Definitely not a brilliant idea. He frowned, watching them closely, fretting about it. A strong undercurrent between them seemed intense. Even the air sizzled with electricity.

Damn it all to hell and back.

Natasha will suffer, and he hated it. He remembered her the last time his dad took off. She was lost, hurt, and sad. And she will be again. Peter needed to act. Immediately. He must keep them apart. As much as possible. His fault that Dmitry came, so it was his duty to protect Natasha. But how?

And then, it dawned on him. He will always be with her and Katia, keeping Natasha occupied as much as possible, and preventing the unintentional meetings between her and his father. Feeling a little better, Peter switched his attention back to the moment. Dmitry said something, Natasha quietly replied, and then she tried to step away from the protective circle of Peter's arms. Still unsettled, he tightened his hold. He finally realized Natasha was talking to him, and she wore a worried expression.

"Petya?"

"What, Gorgeous?"

"I said, let me go, please. I'm needed at home. Art lesson will be over by now."

She added nothing more. No need to. Peter understood her loud and clear. Katia was finished with her studies and probably searching for Natasha. She seemed reluctant to let the little girl meet her father for the first time in five years unprepared, stumbling on him like she herself did.

"Yes, you're right. I must make a call, so I'll walk with you."

On the spur of the moment, he decided to call Julie.

"Dad?" Peter turned and eyed his father. "Coming?"

But Dmitry stepped back, and shook his head. "No, I'll stay here for a little while. You go ahead. I'll be in shortly."

Then he faced Natasha. "I'll see you later."

"Yes, later." She replied quietly.

Together they started toward the house.

CHAPTER NINE

Dmitry needed time alone after being shaken when he met Natasha. To think, to sort through his emotions. To recover from the shock of discovery that he still was crazy about her. Now even more than before. Five years ago, he took just one look at Natasha, and wanted her. He still did. Painfully, savagely. But this time around, he meant it to be different. Five years ago, he resented the fact that he lusted after her, punishing her for it, trying to hate her for it, but all for naught.

Back then, Svetlana's ghost stood between them, and the trauma of her death clouded his mind and emotions. Whenever he looked at Natasha, guilt swept over him, and he punished himself for betraying Svetlana. Recognizing Natasha's innocence, Dmitry knew he could destroy her easily because he had nothing to offer her except sex.

Five years ago, he struck a deal with his mother to stay away from each other's family. And he left, protecting her from himself. He wondered if she knew what it cost him then.

Of course not.

But now he failed the strength to leave her alone.

The best decision for both of them – he needed to turn around and leave. Right now.

Not gonna happen. Not yet.

No, he wasn't ready to leave before he explored his own feelings. Before he understood what might happen between them.

He won't stay away from Natasha this time around. Peter said she loved him. Dear God, was that possible? Does she still feel something for him? Or did she forget him completely?

When Dmitry looked into her eyes, her emerald gaze unwavering, yet guarded, and unreadable, made his insides twist into a brutal painful knot. Dammit, he was losing his heart faster than his mind. Strangely, he felt no fear or guilt, only elation. He became energized, and determined. Dmitry stuck his hands into the pocket of his jeans, stared at the towering structure of the mansion ahead, and inhaled deep. No, he won't leave. He'll stay as long as needed to find out the truth about his own feelings. And hers. And nothing and no one—not even his mother—can stop him this time.

CHAPTER TEN

Katia knew where she to find Natasha. She needed her mommy badly right now. Her father came back. He might send for her any moment. Scared, Katia ran from the house in search of Natasha.

She was glad her father came home, but a trickle of fear gnawed at her. What if he still didn't like her? What if he thinks her a stupid little girl, and then leave again? Katia knew he didn't love her, not like he loved Peter. And that was all right with her. Peter was the best person in the world. She thought it natural that their father loved him. Katia loved Peter more than she loved anyone or anything, more even that her paintings. Sometimes, she believed she loved him even more than Natasha. At those moments her cheeks burned, and she became ashamed of herself for thinking such things. Children are supposed to love their mommies and daddies best, right? But her real mommy died. As for her father...

Katia didn't even remember him. She saw him only in pictures. And she hid them, those images of the big, dark man who was her father. Even from Natasha. She sensed that every time someone mentioned her father's name Natasha became sad. Even her eyes seemed different.

Katia couldn't say *how* different. Some things were hard to put in words. She could probably paint it, but she didn't want to. She hated to see Natasha sad and quiet, because when that happened Katia's tummy began to ache, and her eyes grew itchy and hot. And then Natasha became really scared that Katia caught a fever. She wanted Natasha happy, not worried or scared. Especially because of her.

Where is Natasha?

She bit her lower lip. She wanted her mommy. She needed her hug, and her promise that everything will be okay. Natasha always kept her promises.

Katia hurried through the gardens toward her destination, moving faster and faster. And then running. Finally, she burst into the clearing where the little white gazebo sat in the middle, and stumbled to an abrupt stop. Someone sat in Natasha's favorite chair, but not her mommy. He was a man, big, dark, and beautiful. The man from her pictures.

Her father.

He didn't see her, but she recognized his face, and it had a funny look. Like he was angry and scared and sad at the same time. Her little heart ached. Katia wished to go to him, to touch him, to comfort him. But she couldn't.

She wanted to cry and laugh, she wanted to run back to the house and hide. But most of all, she wished to stay and watch him, this big man, a beautiful stranger with black hair and a sad face.

He turned, and looked at her. His eyes were so light, almost silver. Mesmerized, Katia froze.

CHAPTER ELEVEN

Dmitry failed to name what prompted him to look over his shoulder. He was lost in his thoughts, still shaken, and confused, when something jolted him, and brought all his senses on instant alert. He carefully moved his head right. And jerked upright as his heart gave a mighty thud, then thundered painfully against his ribcage.

Two huge German shepherds, one black, the other gray, watched him a few feet ahead. They both were in full alert mode, growling menacingly, poised to strike. And between them, stood a tiny slip of a girl with ash-blond curls. Her eyes grew wide and held a frightened expression under long bangs almost covering her delicate eyebrows.

Katia. Svetlana's baby.

Guilt prickled his consciousness, as Dmitry realized that he still didn't think of her as *his* baby, his daughter. The little girl vaguely reminded him of someone, but in his hazy state, he couldn't figure out who. Not Svetlana. No, she looked nothing like her. Somehow, he experienced disappointment, and relief at the same time. It would be unbearable to see Svetlana's beloved features on the face of the child.

Motionless, flanked by two furry beasts, she struck him as a tiny doll. Unblinking, her huge eyes stared at him like she just saw a ghost. With a start, he realized he was scared, staring at his daughter, the child he refused to see in years.

What on earth can I say to her? Does one have a real conversation with a child?

He vaguely remembered her as an infant. Now, at six, she was skinny and small for her age, but not a baby anymore. She also seemed scared.

Guilt swept through him as he realized the child must be terrified.

Even from a distance her eyes sparkled suspiciously. Damn, the last thing he wanted was to make her run away in tears, like he was some kind of monster. Peter's urgent request echoed in his ears,

"When you meet Katie, please, try not to hurt her."

He also remembered his son's warning that if Dmitry hurt Katia, he'd hurt Natasha. He didn't want to hurt either of them, but, dammit, what could he do now?

She still didn't move. Neither did she run away, which he considered a good sign. But that doe in the headlight's expression tore at his heart. He must reassure her he meant no harm.

Okay, that's what I'll do.

Dmitry started to rise from the chair, but stopped when he heard an unmistakable growl. The two dogs immediately bared their teeth in warning, poised and ready to attack to protect their young charge.

Now what?

If someone needed reassurance now, it was him. Annoyed, he plopped back into the chair. Both dogs quieted, but eyed him with open distrust.

Where the hell had Peter and Natasha gone? He needed all the help he could get right about now.

"Don't be afraid. They won't hurt you."

Her tiny voice sounded clear as a silver bell.

"If you say so," he replied, disgusted with himself.

If you say so? Really? Nice words to say to your daughter for the first time, moron.

Dmitry frowned when he realized he thought of her as *his daughter.*

"They are very good dogs, kind and soft," the bell-like voice chimed in. "Here is Misha," her tiny hand landed on the huge head of the black beast, "and this is Pasha." Another arm went around the gray shepherd's neck. Both dogs uttered a sound somewhere between a whine and a moan, but they seemed pacified. For how long was anybody's guess.

At least their teeth are hidden behind those black lips.

Pathetically relived, Dmitry studied the furry pair. "Hello, there, Misha and Pasha."

Am I really talking to dogs? How much more ridiculous can I get? Polite conversation with two huge animals, for goodness' sake.

"Strange names for dogs," he said since nothing better came to mind.

"They are Russian names, but I didn't name them. They were already named when they arrived." She tilted her head then, aimed a quizzical gaze at him. "Don't you remember?"

"No, I... Oh, yes, I did buy the pair of trained dogs, but I didn't see them arrive."

"No, you already left by then." She lowered her eyes and glanced at the dogs.

"Boys, say hello to... Mr. Rostoff."

That small pause gave Dmitry an unpleasant jolt. Is that how she saw him? Both dogs pricked their ears and stared straight at him.

"If you let them smell you, then they will know you, and won't do anything bad to you, even when I'm not here." The mixed expression of hope and fear on her thin pixy face stole the breath from his lungs.

Dmitry held back for a moment, reluctant to let the two huge beasts sniff at him like a prime meat bone, but, then again, an idea that he might encounter that duo alone wasn't pleasant, either.

And you don't want to look like a damn coward in front of your child.

Startled that the second time in minutes he thought of her as *his* daughter, Dmitry frowned. And when did he start to care about her opinion?

He turned to Katia and asked, "Okay. How do we do that?"

She started toward him, a bit hesitant at first. Unfortunately, the two dogs followed closely with a stride nowhere near hesitant. When Katia finally stepped inside the gazebo, she stopped short and studied him while tilting her head upward.

Probably still afraid.

Dmitry gave her a nod of reassurance.

Apparently, that was what she waited for. She stepped closer, then lifted her tiny arm as if asking his permission. Dmitry offered his hand, palm up and waited for the dogs to amble over and sniff at it. Instead, Katia put her own hand over his and smiled. "Don't worry, Mr. Rostoff, I won't let them hurt you."

And just like that, his heart jumped into his throat, then settled heavily in its proper place. That tiny slip of a girl was protecting him! It touched some deep chord in him, and filled him with mixed feelings of admiration and guilt. She called him Mr. Rostoff. Twice. For some reason, it failed to sit well with him.

Katia turned to the dogs, then murmured to them in Russian. The two beasts approached her, then began to sniff their joined hands. The contrast between her tiny palm on top of his much bigger one startled him, and his throat burned from the emotion he had to hide.

"See? Now they know your smell, know who you are."

"And you? Do you know who am I?" Surprising himself, Dmitry asked the question, and realized that he held his breath.

"Yes." She let go of his hand. Reluctantly, she lifted her huge eyes at him and answered, "You are Peter's dad."

Dmitry's brows shot to his hairline.

"I'm also your dad," he added gruffly, upset by her choice of words.

She lowered her head again. "No," she said quietly then after a small pause, "you're my father."

"And there is a difference?"

"Yes." Her eyes peered at him from under her long bangs, her expression that of sad acceptance.

A sharp and painful ping of guilt shot through him.

As gently as possible, he asked, "Explain it to me. Please."

"It's really simple. You love Peter, so you're his dad. You don't love me, but I am your daughter, so..." her bony shoulders lifted in a helpless shrug, "you're my father."

So simple. And heartbreaking.

The logic of a six-year-old child rejected even before born.

She knew it, and accepted it, and somehow that made it more devastating.

Hurting, humiliated, Dmitry wanted to run, fast and far, away from this strange little girl who looked at him with eloquent sad eyes.

"I... I'm sorry," he managed through the lump in his throat.

"That's okay," she said with a smile even sadder than her eyes, "You can't help it."

Dear God, who is this tender-hearted creature?

"But you gave me Misha and Pasha, so they can watch over me instead of you."

A good substitute for a parent, two German shepherds.

Self-disgust ate at him like acid.

Son of a bitch.

If only she knew he insisted on acquiring these dogs for Peter's safety, not hers. He didn't even think of her then, although this little girl was the target of his late wife's hatred. The infant who almost died that terrible night five years ago.

You are a bastard, Rostoff.

Squirming under her gaze, Dmitry cursed himself. It was unbearable to look at her.

These eyes. Oh, my God!

Despite being in the open gazebo, with fresh air all around him, Dmitry was suffocating. His lungs burned, his throat tight and dry as Sahara.

In a flash he realized who Katia reminded him of. Dmitry closed his eyes, and shook his head in denial.

No, the fate can't be that cruel.

His little girl was the exact replica of Elizabeth.

Same pewter eyes, same ash-blod hair, same oval of a face. And that perfectly sculpted mouth with its fuller upper lip.

Shocked, he stepped back, gawking at Katia in pure horror. In his mind's eye, she momentarily transformed from a little doll-face pixy to the devil reincarnate.

Katia flinched. She was scared. Really scared. She couldn't name the expression on her father's face, but it looked huge and bad. Like love, only upside-down. What had she done to displease him so much?

Close to tears now, she desperately wished for Natasha. Because at that moment, she understood her father would never ever become her dad.

CHAPTER TWELVE

Natasha frantically searched the manor. Katia had disappeared, and nobody knew where. Together with Petya they examined every inch of the house, looking for her, checking all Katia's favorite hiding places to no avail.

"She has to be hiding somewhere and drawing in her sketchbook as usual." He shrugged. "Undoubtedly she forgot about the time."

"I'm not so sure." Some sixth sense told Natasha that Katia's disappearance had something to do with Dmitry.

Dammit.

He showed up just mere hours ago, and already managed to wreak havoc in her life, not to mention her peace of mind. Mr. Angelini, Katia's art teacher, assured Natasha that the lesson finished at its usual time, and Katia went looking for her. Both dogs disappeared, too, and that meant they were with Katia. Thank God for that. At least her little girl was protected. But still, Katia never went off by herself, without telling Natasha or Petya.

God, where is she?

Natasha tried to calm herself, but to no avail. How could she stay calm with her baby missing? Shaking, she paced Katia's room. Her dread made her nauseated and lightheaded. Where was Katia? Did something terrible happened to her?

The memories of the horrible night five years ago reared their ugly head, tormenting her with the vivid pictures. But this time, she wasn't there to protect her baby. Petya went to search outside, convincing Natasha to stay in the house, just in case Katia was somewhere inside, and about to emerge from her hiding place.

Just when Natasha was ready to jump out of her skin, she happened to turn to the window, and stopped dead in her tracks.

Dmitry and Katia walked toward the house. Two people she loved, her precious little baby and her father. Together. Well, not exactly together. The dogs flanked Katia while Dmitry stayed nearby. Even from the distance Natasha saw his scowl. Was he mad? Or scared?

And what did it matter? Her main concern was Katia.

Looking straight ahead, her little girl marched, tensed and pale, as if approaching a firing squad. Not once did she glance in Dmitry's direction. After they walked a few steps closer, Natasha glimpsed the expression on the girl's face. So forlorn, so devastated. It broke her heart, and fueled her anger.

Damn you, Dmitry, what have you done to her?

Natasha ran out of the room and down the stairs, skipping two steps at a time.

Her legs barely touched the ground, as she hurried to Katia. Her lungs burned yet she continued to run until they stood face-to-face. The dogs thumped their tails in greeting, but Natasha paid no attention to them.

"Katia." Dizzy and weak with relief, she almost swayed, but managed to stay on her feet. Her smile was wobbly, as she waited for her little girl to run to her in their usual greeting, but Katia stood where she stopped. Her eyes huge and sad.

"Mama," she whispered softly.

Natasha's heart squeezed painfully. Looking at that somber, reserved expression on her baby's face made her want to cry, and rage, and rave.

With an effort, Natasha composed herself. "Where have you been, kitten? I was crazy with worry."

"I'm sorry. I was looking for you in the gazebo and..." she paused, then sighed, "I met my father." She still avoided to glance at Dmitry.

"So I see." Natasha kneeled in front of Katia, and enveloped her in her arms.

She needed that physical contact, that reassurance that her baby was well and unharmed. At first, Katia seemed almost rigid, but after a while, she slowly relaxed against Natasha, her body now pliant and soft like that of her favorite rag doll. Poor brave little solder, she fought to be strong in front of her father, but the fight depleted her. Natasha gathered her precious child even closer, holding her protectively. She squeezed her eyes shut, fighting for her own control. Whatever Dmitry had done to upset her girl, she'd do that later. Without witnesses.

Oh, will I ever!

Dmitry's discreet cough brought her back to reality. She glared at him over Katia's shoulder. No doubt her expression said everything, especially that thebastard hurt this gentle child.

"I'll go inside." Obviously uncomfortable, he nodded to no one in particular, then continued toward the house. Natasha watched his progress, cursing inwardly. Later. She'd deal with him later.

Now, her full attention belonged to Katia.

Smiling at the child, she tweaked her nose. Still tense and somber, no smile came in return. Natasha stood then lifted Katia. The fact that she failed to utter a peep of protest said everything. The little girl burrowed her face into the crook of Natasha's shoulder and breathed deeper. Katia sniffed as she held onto Natasha with all her strength.

"He didn't like me, mama. He didn't like me at all."

Her tiny voice broke. Close to tears, Natasha rubbed Katia's back in soothing circles and nuzzled her silky hair.

"Shhh, baby, shhh, kitty. Of course, he liked you. He just... he felt a little shy, that's all. Men sometimes don't know how to show their true feelings, especially to the little kids."

"Petya does," Katia contradicted stubbornly. "He loves me, and he doesn't feel shy with me."

"Of course he doesn't. He knows you, kitten. But your father doesn't know you well. You were just a little baby when he went to France. He needs some time, Poppet. And when he really and truly gets to know you, then he'll fall in love with you."

She desperately hoped her prediction came true. Who could not love such a bright and wonderful child? She sent a silent prayer to the Almighty.

Dear God, please open his eyes and heart.

Natasha whispered into Katia's ear, "And besides, he's your father."

"Yes," Katia lifted her grief-stricken face, "but not my dad."

Natasha wanted to weep. She also wanted to break something, preferably against Dmitry's hard and stubborn head.

Later, she promised herself again. Later she will indulge, and let Mr. Rostoff know her true opinion of him. The bastard.

But now, her priority was Katia. Plastering a fake smile on her face, Natasha deliberately switched the subject.

"And how did your art lesson go today, Kitten?" Art, the one thing that mattered the most to Katia. "Is my portrait ready yet?"

"Almost." She brightened immediately, as Natasha predicted. "But you can't see it, not until it's finished."

She flashed an adorable mischievous little grin. God bless the resilience of children. The little girl's mood switched from forlorn to openly delightful. Pure joy lit up her face. Natasha gulped in a relived breath. Art had always been the main source of Katia's happiness. To draw for her was as natural as living. Her paints were her best and most cherished toys, her brushes the extensions of her arms.

A unique little girl and truly special. They called her a prodigy.

But to Natasha, Katia was her little girl, her kitten, her darling daughter.

Natasha picked up their usual familiar game and pouted. "Oh, please! Pretty-pretty please with a cherry on top?" Wiggling her eyebrows in an exaggerated manner, Natasha made a funny face. Katia giggled.

"No, no, no!" She shook her head vigorously. "Not until I finish. You promised, mama!"

"Okay, all right," Natasha slumped her shoulders in mock defeat. "So I did promise. And a promise is a promise." Then she tickled Katia's tummy with one hand, all the while bouncing her as much as her strength allowed. They both burst into giggles. The dogs, completely ignored up to this point, started to whine, asking permission to join in the game. Natasha obliged. Soon it was one big whirlpool of two humans and two canines, carousing and enjoying themselves. Katia wasn't in a hurry to leave Natasha's arms, laughing and tickling her in return, her incident with Dmitry clearly forgotten.

When they both were weak from laughter and their silly game, Natasha put Katia down, scratched both dogs between their ears, and finally managed to steer her little group toward the house. Dogs complied eagerly, thirsty from exercise. She realized Katia didn't want to leave yet. Either that, or she was reluctant to go inside, and see her father again.

"You better hurry, Kitten, and finish my portrait. Remember, I might get too curious, and try to steal a peek." Her maneuver worked.

"Oh, no, you won't, Mama." Momentarily distracted, Katia started to skip merrily toward the house.

"I will, too!"

"You will not!"

Laughing and mocking each other, Natasha and her little girl accompanied by the dogs finally reached the entrance of the house. Movement in the window above them caught Natasha's eye.

CHAPTER THIRTEEN

Dmitry let go of the curtain when the little group entered the house and cursed. What was he doing? Hiding inside his room, looking out the window, and spying on his daughter and Natasha? Pathetic. And in his own house, no less.

No, this is not your house, you fool. This is your mother's house. Her mausoleum.

And speaking of the devil, where was she? Undoubtedly, Her Grace knew of his arrival. One of her snitches surely reported it. Apparently, she chose to ignore him. Fine with him. More than fine. If he avoided seeing her altogether, even better, but his luck never ran that well. The big party in honor of Peter's eighteenth birthday was tomorrow. Elizabeth will attend. And so will he. After all, why else should he have returned to California.

Obviously, his mother wasn't excited about his presence if she went to all the trouble to avoid him. Well, too bad. He should have booked into a hotel. He only knew he needed to be here, in this mausoleum, but couldn't explain it to himself. Elizabeth's betrayal five years ago left a mark more painful than he wanted to admit.

My own mother, a traitor.

Dmitry still had a bad taste in his mouth about that incident. Even after all this time.

So, why was he pacing the room like a caged animal and swearing like a sailor?

Good question, Rostoff.

He ran away from this very house five years ago like all the demons of hell chased him. He vowed to never to come back. But fate intervened.

He returned. And it proved more difficult than he expected.

Only this morning he was sitting in the car, arguing with himself, itching to turn around and drive away. He should have done that. Should have gone immediately, driven to the airport, and boarded his plane. And fly the hell away from San Francisco.

Dmitry swore again, and massaged his throbbing temples.

Peter. What might he feel if I ran off like that?

What would Natasha think?

Dammit, what does he care what *she* thinks? She may well be happy and relieved if he took off for good. If the glances she sent him this afternoon were any indication, she loathed him now even more than she did five years ago. Fine, perfect. Let her hate him. For herself, for Katia. It didn't matter. Easier for them when he leaves, because sure as hell it must be the last time. He'd never come back again, never. Dmitry paced the room. If he had any smarts, he'd leave immediately, without any explanation.

"You hurt her five years ago, Dad, by leaving and not saying goodbye."

Peter's quiet words zipped through his memory, and made him sick with guilt.

If he left now, it was a repeat of his last disappearing act.

Would his sudden disappearance hurt her, just like it did all those years ago?

The selfish part of him hoped yes, that he still had the ability and power to do so. But his decent part cringed in shame and self-disgust, and prayed to God that it dare not be the case this time.

"Lord, let her hate me."

At least this time his heart suffered, not hers. That realization stopped him dead in midstride.

His heart.

He finally succumbed to the truth. He sank onto the edge of his bed, closing his eyes in defeat. God help him, he was falling for her. Again. Because even before he knew his infatuation went deeper than mere lust.

Much deeper. The reason why he spent a long time fighting it, forgetting it, and her. He thought for sure he succeeded. He put a wall of deliberate silence between them, and then relocated out of the country. He engrossed himself in re-building *Rostoff & Co.* with eagerness and abandon. He met other women, became intimate with some of them. He had everything under control, and a life perfect as it could get. Or so he tried to convince himself. Fool himself.

What an idiot. One glance, one second in her presence, and boom! Totally lost. Memories he tried to erase from his mind and his heart all those years ago resurfaced with the speed of a tornado, mocking him, tormenting him. He'd laugh at his own stupidity if he weren't so disturbed.

He quickly realized he was dead wrong. He already fell for her, laid on the very bottom after hitting it with a pathetic thump.

Before the wide-eyed naïve girl watched him with the wonder of just awakened passion in her impossibly green, gem-like eyes.

Now Natasha was all woman, composed and reserved, and watched him with cool eyes clouded with distrust.

God, her eyes.

Dmitry shuddered. Dark-green, long and eloquent... They'd have burned her for those bewitching eyes of hers hundreds of years ago, somewhere in Salem. Remembering her last glare, he swore again. Damn it. He should be relieved. He should feel elated. Why, dammit all to hell and back, did he want to scream from frustration and disappointment? God, he was losing his mind.

He plodded back to the window like a man going to his execution. He opened the curtains, and took in the beauty spread out before him. His mother's gardens were the only thing he loved here, even as a child. That, and the gazebo where he ran too often, hiding from his mother's wrath or his father's docile acceptance of it. Did Natasha know that the very place she picked as her favorite was his sanctuary as a child? Did she feel the same emotions as he did, while hiding inside of that island from broken dreams and false hopes? He learned later that his father often used the gazebo as a place for his clandestine affairs. Since then, Dmitry stopped visiting it, feeling violated and disgusted as if the very walls of that fragile wooden structure were smeared with slime.

Strange, but while he visited that gazebo today, he felt nothing.

Unpleasant memories of his childhood switched to pictures of Natasha and Peter bent over the cradle, smiling at the baby. The baby he didn't want, had no desire love and gave to his monster of a mother to raise. Guilt charged through him as he looked away from the window.

For giving up his daughter, Svetlana's daughter, to Elizabeth and severing all ties and bonds between them. Intentionally, voluntarily.

Meeting Katia today shook him more than he expected, in many ways. True, he still couldn't feel anything remotely close to love toward the little girl, but neither did he feel that burning and all-consuming hatred as before. He wondered if his mother loved his daughter, but quickly dismissed the thought. Elizabeth loved no one. She simply couldn't. Katia was Elizabeth's obsession with a female heiress. Love had absolutely nothing to do with it.

Six years ago, Dmitry made Elizabeth's dream come true by giving her the granddaughter she so longed for. But not because he wanted to please her.

His motivations were anything but noble. Quite the opposite, in fact. He simply wanted nothing to do with his daughter except to punish her for taking Svetlana's life.

But now... What did he want now? Did he want his daughter in his life? Did he honestly wish to claim her as his, and take all the responsibility for the little girl? Was he ready for such a drastic step?

Dmitry didn't know the answers. But after all these years, he started to question his own decisions. Whether a bad sign or a good one, the jury was still out.

He turned from the window. Time for him to make a few calls, check with Vlad on several unfinished business matters. But, God help him, his heart wasn't on business right now.

So, where does that leave you, champ?

He was sick and tired of hiding inside of the walls of his room. But at the same time, reluctant to leave the sanctuary it provided. Even a false one.

Dmitry finally realized what he must do. A wry smile curved his lips as he glanced at his watch. His good luck held. He just hoped Elizabeth's schedule hadn't changed with time. Well, he'd find out soon. He paused in front of his unpacked suitcase and picked up a fresh shirt, then went to the bathroom for a quick shower. He had plenty of time. Thirty-three minutes to be precise. And then— show time.

CHAPTER FOURTEEN

D mitry strode briskly toward the pool tucked away in a secluded area of the estate, where neither guests nor servants dared go. The intricate iron fence proved to be a masterpiece by itself. It circled around the pool, ensuring total and complete privacy. Dmitry knew Elizabeth was inside, enjoying her daily one-hour swim, a habit that became her religion. Sounds of soft splashes and the familiar smell of chlorine assaulted him with unwelcomed memories. They were bittersweet, these memories of his lonely childhood. Some of them he cherished, but many of them he longed to erase from his brain forever.

Truthfully, he had his share of joy and happiness here as a child, but limited. He wasn't abused, mistreated, or deprived. Simply unloved and ignored. An abuse much uglier than a physical one, at least to him.

Oh, he survived, all right. He discovered plenty of things that kept him happy and content: his books, sports, and a vivid imagination. That, and the amazing resilience of a young mind and soul. Yes, he survived. How sad to think of one's childhood as the time of survival.

On the other hand, those years shaped him into the man of today: strong, controlled, independent. Powerful.

Dmitry inhaled deeply that familiar odor of chlorinated water.

How he loved to swim and dive as a child. He was good at it, too, much better than his older cousin Alexei, to his mother's dismay and his own private joy.

It wasn't a secret to anybody that Elizabeth preferred her nephew, her husband's nephew, to be accurate, to her only son. She never made a secret of that fact.

Quite the opposite, Elizabeth openly and vocally compared the two boys, praising one and humiliating the other, constantly and relentlessly, challenging her son to be more like his cousin. To his defense, Alexei never paid attention to Elizabeth's opinion, and the relationship between two cousins existed normally, if not overly friendly. Kind, content, and blissfully happy, that was how Dmitry always remembered his older cousin, a wonder boy his mother preferred over her own flesh and blood. Alexei – the only male Rostoff she considered worthy of her love and attention. While Dimitry enjoyed poetry and music, often cooped inside his room for hours, he preferred physical outdoor activities. The seclusion of the pool provided not only the exercise he loved but the privacy he craved even as a boy. The time he spent here was the happiest hours of his childhood.

Now he stood near the pool gates, observing with the detached eye of an outsider all the changes. Mercifully, they were minimal, leaving almost everything as he remembered.

He was about to make a drastic change by entering the gates at the forbidden hour, while Elizabeth stayed inside. Something he never did before.

Her Grace herself established the taboo hours from one to two o'clock in the afternoon, and eight to nine in the evening. She demanded that the pool area be completely deserted, clean and clear. And if anyone disobeyed, consequences were harsh and immediate.

Dmitry stood there, listening to the splashes inside, imagining his mother's shock. Especially when she'd realize the identity of the intruder. The decision to confront his mother came to him on the spur of the moment. And dictated by one reason only: to deny Elizabeth the pleasure of staging their first meeting and be prepared for it emotionally and mentally. He wanted to catch her off guard, to rob her the satisfaction of a grand public scene she undoubtedly planned for their reunion. And yes, to simply rile her. Invading her territory during the sacred hour was in a way a protest, even if a belated one, against her domineering tyranny he endured as a child. Dmitry's lips curved into a wry half-smile. Resolutely moving forward, he pushed the iron gates. They swung open without a sound, and then he stepped inside.

Elizabeth lay in the deep end of the pool, floating on her back with her eyes closed. Her arms and legs were outstretched; her fingers lazily caressed the water. From a distance Dmitry couldn't tell if she wore a bathing suit. He hoped not. Another memory stormed through his mind, this one humiliating as well as painful.

As a teenager, he overheard a conversation between two servants. Elizabeth just recently changed her royal rule, and allowed his cousin to visit the pool during the sacred hours. Oh, how envious Dmitry grew. How mad. Not at Alexei, because nobody could be mad at him. But his mother. Yes, anger swelled in the young boy until he thought he might burst.

Two unfortunate servants, thinking they were alone, heatedly shared the latest gossip about his mother and her favorite nephew, who was almost sixteen at the time. At first, Dmitry didn't understand what they were so ecstatic about, then he froze in horror. According to gossipers, their mistress enjoyed much more than a swim during hours she spent in the pool with Alexei. Why, the boy himself confessed that his aunt practiced skinny-dipping in front of him, and suggested that he try it, too.

Enraged, Dmitry ran up to Alexei's room, demanding his cousin take back the ugly lies, and set the servants straight. But his cousin just shrugged, smiled, and flashed his famous Rostoff dimples. He added that his aunt, Dmitry's mother, was a very beautiful woman who simply had no shame of her body. And what's wrong with that?

What's wrong indeed, Dmitry thought with resentment and disgust, looking at Elizabeth now. She floated silently in a middle of the pool, completely unaware of any intrusion. Dmitry fisted his hands, shoved them into the pockets of his trousers. She did manage to steal his great joy, and his piece of heaven then, because after Alexei's admittance, the pool became something dirty and twisted for Dmitry. At thirteen, he didn't understand the concept of depravity. Now, he preferred not to dwell on it.

Thrown back in time, Dmitry realized that both his parents stole from him something tender and beautiful, his innocence. He felt still mad and hurt, still refused to let go because it was impossible to forgive. Impotent rage at both his parents still left him shaken. Dammit, he was just a kid. And he hated them for what they did. His father even more than his mother. Lord knew how many times little Dmitry made his vows to be nothing like his papa when he grew up; to be different, strong, proud, and fearless. To be bold enough to stand up to Elizabeth even if just once.

He succeeded five years ago. He did stand up to his mother, thwarting her plans to ruin his career, and his life. He won that battle, forcing Elizabeth to retire and give all the power over the *Rostoff & Co.* to him, to the very person she tried to ruin. She will never forget nor forgive that ultimate humiliation she suffered because of him. Because he exposed her scheme and openly defeated her. Finally.

Strange it didn't make him happy afterward, nor proud of himself.

If anything, that victory hurt him. Satisfaction wasn't sweet, rather bitter like her parting words to him:

"It's not finished, son, it'll never be until only one of us alive."

No, the battle between them continued, and promised to become more brutal.

Looking at her now, completely relaxed and probably naked under the water, made Dmitry uneasy. No longer a child, he didn't have to obey his mother's ridiculous rules.

With that, Dmitry stepped forward, and planted his feet in front of the marble steps. He deliberately blocked the exit from the water. Crossing his arms over his chest, he continued to look at the lonely figure splashing in the pool.

Elizabeth eyes snapped open, as if she sensed his presence. With a start she twisted to an upright position. Before she went under the water, Dmitry noticed two black straps on her shoulders. So, she wore a suit after all. Pity. He'd have enjoyed the situation immensely. He chuckled without any merriment. She probably gave up on skinny-dipping after Alexei's death.

When Elizabeth finally broke the surface, Dmitry was elated to catch her wild and shocked expression. In a heartbeat, she managed to hide it under her usual blank mask.

"Good afternoon, Mother," he drawled, leaning on the steel arm railing.

"Dmitry. What are you doing here?"

"Isn't it obvious? I came to say hello. You were so overwhelmed by my visit, you went to all kinds of a trouble to avoid me. So, I took it upon myself to take the first step."

"After five years you finally decide to show up, and expect me to greet you with open arms?" Her retort came out in an indifferent, insolent voice.

"Oh, God forbid, Mother!" Dmitry exclaimed in mocking shock. "It never crossed my mind. But hiding inside your own house, er, pool, only to escape me? Isn't it a bit extreme even for you?" His fake smile almost hurt his face.

"Your arrogance is unbelievable, Dmitry. Did you honestly think your presence in *my* home would be so important to me?" Elizabeth let out a sharp bark, shaking her head in disbelief.

Damn her. Her barb found its target. He grew angry with himself for letting her words matter still.

Dammit, will I ever be free of her?

On the surface, he made sure his face never changed.

The hard gaze he aimed at her, never wavered. Again, he realized Elisabeth, who gave birth to him, lacked the ability to be a parent in a real sense of the word.

Just like you to Katia.

No, God, no.

He wasn't like his mother. Or was he?

Something dark and cold unfurled from the depth of his soul. Shaken, Dmitry cursed under his breath. Dear Lord, yes, just like Elizabeth!

The only difference between them, his understanding of the gross mistake he made, and his willingness to fix it. He will become a father to Katia. He will make any effort to breach the chasm between them. He will get to know her better, and hopefully, one day she will call him dad.

I swear on Svetlana's memory.

After his sudden decision Dmitry immediately felt lighter, like a huge weight lifted from his heart. His mood restored, he once again became calm and in control.

CHAPTER FIFTEEN

E lizabeth noticed every single nuance of emotion on her son's face.

Hurt, confusion, anger. But his unexpected calmness and contentment bothered her. Why? One thing for sure, Dmitry learned to mask and control his emotions much better over their lost years. And he remained an enigma to her. Shaken more than she wanted to admit, Elizabeth demanded in a deliberately cold voice, "Will you step aside? I'd like to get out."

Dmitry eloquently lifted one brow, not moving a muscle.

"Please," It grated on her. Damn him.

"But of course." With a mock gallantry, he nodded, and lifted the towel from the railing, then handed it out to her with a small bow.

She accepted both his gesture and towel with a regal nod, but refused to say thank you. She dried herself with quick sure movements, then turned and strolled to the nearby chair. Unhurried, she picked up her robe, slid into, then tied the sash.

Sitting down, Elizabeth aimed her gaze at her son, once again in total control of her emotions. Did he really think he managed to rattle her? Foolish man. Majestically, as if she was holding court, she tilted her head, and narrowed her eyes at him. If he expected her to talk first, to ask him questions, he'd be sorely disappointed. Long ago, Elizabeth learned the value of silence. So, she settled into the chair, stared at him, and waited.

CHAPTER SIXTEEN

Dmitry winced as he watched her. Elizabeth well knew her wet one-piece bathing suit hid nothing from his view. Her body was still trim, lean, and firm for her age. Her breasts remained high, her stomach still flat, her hips narrow.

In a hushed uncomfortable silence, Dmitry surveyed her body. What did he see? She knew that at seventy, she could be easily mistaken for a much younger woman. Did he wonder how she used to look a couple of decades ago? Again she smiled. Let him.

Dmitry crossed over to the little table with refreshments and, without waiting for her invitation, poured himself a glass of cold orange juice.

"By all means, son, help yourself," she drawled with cool amusement in her voice.

"Thank you," he nodded curtly and drank the entire glass of juice in several quick gulps.

She scrutinized her only child. She admitted Dmitry's unexpected arrival threw her off balance. Just for a moment, though. She recovered quickly, but not quick enough to suit her.

The bastard. He did it on purpose.

Now he was here, and as much as Elizabeth regretted to be caught by surprise, she knew their confrontation inevitable. Why prolong it?

Oh, how she hated him at that moment. Bold, arrogant, as if he controlled the universe.

We'll see about that, son. *We'll see how long and how well you manage to keep your balance or your cool.*

On the inside, she bubbled with rage. But on the outside, she appeared as calm and composed as ever. All her seventy years on this earth, she had honed that one skill to perfection. Her son wasn't even remotely close to her level, no matter how badly he wanted to think otherwise. He figured he'd embarrass her by barging in like that? Foolish boy.

Elizabeth maintained the fake smile on her lips, all the while watching Dmitry.

By all the saints, he's blushing!

Clearly embarrassed and uneasy, he averted his eyes, and cleared his throat.

Overjoyed with his obvious discomfort, Elizabeth decided to ante up the stakes.

With false nonchalance, she shrugged her robe from her shoulders, then reached for a bottle of lotion. Unhurriedly, with an exaggerated thoroughness, she rubbed the cream onto her forearms. Then she bent forward, and repeated the process on her legs, deliberately exposing her cleavage.

"Would you help me with the task, Dmitry?"

That threw him off. Taking an involuntary step back, he lifted both brows.

"Excuse me, w-what?"

"Can you rub lotion on my back?"

His eyes shot open, then he swallowed spasmodically, his Adam apple bobbling up and down and almost comical. Enormously pleased, Elizabeth bit her cheek to hide her grin.

"Then again, better not." She shrugged. The gesture caused one strap of her bathing suit to slid down, exposing her shoulder and part of her breast. She decided not to tug it back. Chuckling silently, soaking up his obvious discomfort, she added after a deliberate pause, "My skin is too sensitive for your rough hands."

Check mate.

CHAPTER SEVENTEEN

D ammit, Dmitry was embarrassed. And blushing Hell. Her pebbled nipples poked against the thin fabric of the damp bathing suit. He lowered his eyes to avoid looking at his mother's body.

Mortified, he mumbled a curse. He shook his head. All too much. Humiliating. Indecent.

The woman was his mother, for crying out loud.

Elizabeth obviously felt no embarrassment at all. Calmly, she shrugged off her robe, and proceeded to lather her arms and legs with lotion, generously applying and massaging it vigorously. She seemed to ignore him completely. Then she pivoted around, deliberately presenting Dmitry with a view of her backside. Half bared by the cut of the bathing suit, it gave him a full view of her buttocks. He choked on his drink. Appalled, Dmitry hastily averted his eyes, but not quick enough.

Swearing crudely in his mind, Dmitry snatched the juice jug and poured himself another glass. Her body disgusted him, like something unnatural, and artificial. She deliberately taunted him by parading in front of him half-naked. If she wanted to embarrass him, she succeeded.

But not for long, Mother. Two can play this game.

Dmitry, always a quick study, purposely cast his feelings aside and concentrated on cooling his temper. It wasn't the time to let his emotions cloud his mind. He couldn't afford any foolish mistakes right now. Nearly time for battle, so Dmitry emptied his mind, took a firm grip on his control, and brought all his senses to full alert.

"You're looking well, Dmitry." Finished with the task of lathering her body, Elizabeth joined him at the table. Thankfully, she tugged her robe on.

"Paris agrees with you." Her eyes were cold, assessing, calculating.

Like two fencing partners, they circled each other, looking for any weak point to exploit and pounce. To draw blood.

Dmitry nodded, sipped his juice, and gauged her mood. Elizabeth's eyes fastened on his face. He held her gaze, all the while remaining silent. She flinched but maintained her stoic expression. Clearly his coolness started to grate on her nerves. Elizabeth shrugged, adjusted a collar of her robe, then wrapped her fingers around her own glass of juice, and tilted her head.

"You've seen Peter, I presume?"

"You presume correctly."

"Hmm-mm. And how did you find him?"

"Grown."

"Well, he's turning eighteen tomorrow."

"I remember."

"I wonder what else you remember," she snapped, obviously annoyed by his non-committal answers and insolent pose. Dmitry smiled, just to rile her more.

"Oh, Mother, I remember a great deal," he drawled sarcastically.

"Indeed?" Sharp lift of her eyebrows.

"You'd be amazed." He kept that enigmatic half-smile on his face.

"And do you happen to remember that you also have a daughter?" Toying with her ring, Elizabeth lifted the corners of her lips. Only a blind man could have mistaken it for a smile.

"Yes, I do."

"She's very unusual child." Elizabeth murmured after a long pause.

"Unusual? How?"

"Well, for starters she is a prodigy. She paints."

"Does she?"

"Yes. Then, she happened to have a very impressive IQ for her age. She's fluent in three languages, and can read and write."

"You don't have to showcase her to me, Mother. After all, the girl isn't a piece of merchandise you're advertising."

"Touchy, touchy." Elizabeth shook her head and presented him with another fake smile. "And why do you, care, Dmitry? If my memory serves, you shipped her to me exactly like a piece of a merchandise you didn't want. Or am I wrong?"

"No, Mother. You are not. But times change, and so do we."

"Is that right?"

"Absolutely. As a matter of fact, my feelings toward my daughter have changed drastically, especially in the past hour."

Elizabeth dropped all pretenses of calmness and gaiety. Tense, she slinked forward, like a snake poised to strike.

"What do you mean? What happened in the past hour?" Her voice became clipped.

"I met my daughter," Dmitry replied neutrally, ignoring his mother's visible agitation. "By the way, she is the image of you, a fact that doesn't please me at all."

"Well, that's too bad, because she does look exactly like me." Relaxing a little, Elizabeth arrogantly lifted her chin.

"Oh, well." Dmitry shrugged then sipped the juice that tasted like acid.

"So, tell me, son, what do you think of *my granddaughter*?" Elizabeth stressed the last words.

"I think the child is very thin. Do you feed her well?"

As he predicted, Elizabeth bristled. "Stop that rubbish, Dmitry. The girl is just skinny by nature, and it has nothing to do with her meals. She eats well balanced nutritious food. She's absolutely healthy, normal six-year-old."

"If you say so." Dmitry frowned and glanced down to the frosty glass in his hand.

"I *do* say so. The girl is well fed, clothed, and educated. And don't you dare to imply otherwise."

"What about love?" He asked quietly.

"What?"

"Love, Mother. Is she well loved?"

"You saw her. You tell me. Does Katia looks like she's unhappy? Mistreated? Abused?"

"No, she doesn't look unhappy. As for an abuse... it comes in many different varieties, some of them hard to notice with the naked eye."

"What is that supposed to mean?"

"Only that some scars are invisible. But that doesn't make them any less painful."

"You talk in riddles now." Calmly, Elizabeth sipped her juice, but her eyes became a deeper shade of gray. Oh, she was shaken, all right.

Hold on, Mother, I've just begun.

"Am I? Well, you won't understand, anyway." He lifted his eyes, and glared at her. "But enough of that. I've met my daughter today. And that made me aware of many things. For example, mistakes."

"And she happened to be one of those." Her words held all the bitterness she held in her heart.

"I thought so. For a long time. But I'm not so sure about it anymore."

"What do you mean?" Her sudden movement almost toppled her drink. Out of courtesy, Dmitry leaned forward, and steadied her glass.

"I mean that I feel guilty for abandoning her."

"Don't be an idiot. You didn't abandon Katia—you gave her to me, her grandmother." Elizabeth fisted her hands in her lap until her knuckles went white.

That involuntary action didn't escape Dmitry.

Good, very good.

All indifferent, he shrugged. "Gave, left, abandon—call it what you please. The fact remains: I simply washed my hands of her six years ago, and thought that it better for everyone."

"It was. It still is."

"I disagree."

"What are you saying, Dmitry?"

"I want my daughter, Mother."

CHAPTER EIGHTEEN

Elizabeth never expected this. Anything but this. He managed to catch her by surprise again, damn him. Trembling with rage, she carefully unclenched her fingers, and carefully leaned back.

"And you think you can just show up, snap your fingers, and easily take my granddaughter from me? Do you honestly think I will let you take Katia?"

"No. I don't think so."

"At least you're a realist."

"That I am. I don't think I can easily take my daughter, but not because of you, Mother."

"Oh? May I ask what else is stopping you, besides me, of course?"

"Of course. Not what, but who. And the simple answer is Katia."

"Katia? I don't understand what Katia has to do with it?"

"No, you wouldn't." Dmitry shook his head. "You know what, Mother? I actually feel sorry for you."

"Take your sorry and shove it," she hissed, insulted to the tips of her toes.

Dmitry smiled, but his smile failed to reach his eyes.

"I do feel sorry for you, but if it's any consolation, I feel sorrier for myself right now."

"Your sentiments are no concern of mine, Dmitry."

He seemed to ignored her remark.

"You know why I feel sorry for myself? Because I suddenly realized I am more like you than I thought. And I realized that because Katia, my daughter, that tiny slip of a girl, said something today that stopped me cold."

"What did she say?"

"She said that I am her father, but not her dad. Sad, isn't it? I'm forty, and my six-year-old daughter already understands something that I only now begin to comprehend: the difference between being a parent and being a biological one, or a sperm donor, if you wish."

"Well, no surprise here. She is a very smart child, I told you."

"Yes, you have. Funny, she also made me think that you, Mother dear, always were a mother to me, but not once in my whole godforsaken life I thought of you, or called you, Mama. Why is that?"

At last, he managed to rattle her chain. Even though she sat still, one leg negligently crossed over another, Elizabeth's posture reminded him of a tightly coiled spring. Or a predator waiting to pounce. Her French manicured fingers dug into the armrest of the chair like claws, as she glared at him long and hard. Scorching hatred pulsed in her pewter eyes like lava about to erupt. He barely suppressed an urge to wince.

"Strange, that Katia calls Natasha *mama*, although she knows that she isn't her mother, but you... I always knew I was your son, your flesh and blood, but it never crossed my mind, not even as a child, to say a simple Mama to you."

CHAPTER NINETEEN

Elizabeth kept silent, avoiding his eyes. Dmitry couldn't tell what she thought or felt behind that perfect infifferent mask. But he couldn't stop now. Like he was pushed by some unknown force, he persisted, "Did you ever notice that, Mother? Did it ever bother you?"

She remained silent. But when she stared at him, her dark grey eyes sent a shiver along his spine.

"No."

"No what?"

"No, it never bothered me."

"Why?"

Do I really want to know?

Yes, he needed to know. To understand.

"Because you never mattered enough." Her voice never wavered, her face remained expressionless. Only her eyes betrayed her true feelings. Grey-black, hard, and clear, they sparkled like two gems. With intense, raw hatred.

Cringing inwardly, Dmitry managed to keep a steel fist on his emotions.

A slap in the face would have been more merciful than her reply, but he expected nothing less from his *mother*. Nodding, as if they continued to discuss nothing more than the weather, he leisurely rose to his feet.

"Well, Mother, I'd say our first meeting in five years went very well, indeed. We even managed to agree on something, and that is a small miracle."

"And what is it you think we agreed on?"

"The sad truth. Both of us are rotten parents. But the difference is, I realized it , and I'm willing to correct my mistake. So, I'm telling you up front, Your Grace, I want my daughter. I want to try to be a parent to her as I am to Peter. And I will stop at nothing, if only she'll agree to give me a chance."

"Never! You hear me? *Never.*" Her face turned purple as she stood shaking her fist at him. "You will never take her from me, not while I'm alive and breathing!"

"Fair enough, Mother. Now we both know where we stand."

With that Dmitry wheeled around and left her to wallow in her anger.

CHAPTER TWENTY

"Never, Dmitry. You will never have her, not if you're willing to sacrifice one child for the sake of another." Elizabeth hissed to his retreating back.

You want a war, son? Well, you've got it.

She had a weapon in her arsenal sure to make Dmitry regret he ever crossed her. Gleefully, Elizabeth rubbed her hands. Finally. She waited a long eighteen years for this day to arrive. Time to open her Pandora box, and let the secret out. Then, she intended to sit back and enjoy the destruction. Oh, she planned to enjoy it, enormously. Gloating, Elizabeth imagined Dmitry's shattered expression. She chuckled, then burst into a full laughter. She readjusted the strap of her bathing suit, then leaned back into the chair, and closed her eyes. Tormenting Polina, God rest her pitiful soul, was satisfactory, but still not enough. Now, tormenting Dmitry? Oh, priceless. A pure delight. A rapture.

She so deserved the pleasure.

That secret almost consumed her, but Elizabeth knew well the virtue of patience.

It burned inside her like acid. How many times had she guessed she might go out of her mind, looking at Peter, the *essence* of that secret, the fruit of deception and betrayal? One word, just one small word from her, and his whole world would smash to pieces. But the ultimate goal was not her grandson, but Dmitry.

She swore to destroy him after the fiasco five years ago.

The time has finally arrived. Sooner than she anticipated, but what the hell. She couldn't risk him taking Katia away. Elizabeth doubted Dmitry had the ability to make his threat a reality, but she refused to find out.

A better defense is always an offense, especially such a sudden and unexpected one as she was about to deliver. She'd strike, all right, and from the one and only side Dmitry never expected—his dead wife's past.

"You're in for a big surprise, my son." Her malicious delight dripped from every syllable. "I'll tell you all about the difference between the real and biological parents. Better yet, I'll show you. Tomorrow."

Elizabeth laughed, long and hard and loud, until tears began to stream down her face. Tears were a weakness she never tolerated, but giddy with anticipation, she allowed herself the moment. She wiped her face with both hands. After several deep calming breaths her heartrate returned to normal. Once again in full control she rose from the chair. Small tremors still wracked her body, but she chose to ignored them. She clenched both hands into white-knuckled fists, lifted them, and turned in the direction her son disappeared through a few minutes ago.

"You won't have a son or daughter after tomorrow, Dmitry. As God is my witness, you will have no children at all!"

CHAPTER TWENTY-ONE

If Dmitry thought his confrontations for the day were over, he was badly mistaken.

A soft knock tapped on his door. He rose from the armchair, then walked to the door, and opened it. And froze.

Natasha stood on the threshold, glaring at him. The shepherd at her side did not reassure him.

He realized the most difficult of battles was about to begin.

Definitely not a peaceful one by the green fire in her eyes and determinate set of her jaw. Natasha was primed for a fight.

She wore blue jeans and a yellow sweater, and left nothing to his imagination. Unable to help himself, Dmitry skimmed his eyes down her long slim legs, curvy hips, and tiny waist. Her breasts weren't as visible as before, hidden under the bulky oversized sweater, but he remembered the gentle sway of two pointy mounds. To his utter embarrassment, he realized that one part of his anatomy began to swell, straining against his pants.

Wonderful, just what I need.

Dmitry scowled, looking past her shoulder at the dog.

"Where is the second beast?"

"Guarding Katia. She's asleep."

"And this one, I presume, is your guard?"

"You presume correctly." Her voice, husky and deep, washed over him like an erotic caress, although her tone and her words meant to bite his head off.

"May I come in?" She asked curtly.

Sarcasm was his only weapon now, so he rushed along to employ it.

"What, into the lion's den? Alone? Aren't you afraid, Natasha?"

If he intended to scare her, and send her running, he failed miserably.

"I'm not alone, as you can see," she nodded sideways at the shepherd, "and you're as much a lion as I'm the Queen of England."

"Yeah? And why is that?" Mildly amused, he curved his mouth into a half smile. Obviously, Natasha wasn't amused. If anything, she seemed irritated.

"Because lions are famous for fiercely protecting their cubs, sometimes with their lives."

No need for her to elaborate further. The meaning of her comparison came out loud and clear. His smile vanished. He looked straight into her eyes. A fierceness shone back at him. Natasha would go to hell and back, give her own life to protect little Katia. She did that five years ago. If not for Natasha, his daughter would be dead. Strange, but he never realized that until now.

"Thank you."

"W-what are you talking about?"

"For saving Katia's life five years ago."

Clearly taken aback, Natasha stared at him with confusion. She probably failed to notice she took a step forward, closing the distance between them.

Dmitry lifted his arm. Natasha flinched, and sharply drew back. Did she think he might touch her? Hit her? Was she afraid?

Instead, he reached above her shoulder, and with a curt command "stay" to the dog, shut the door. Then Dmitry faced, and studied the woman who stole him from the moment he lay his eyes on her. Did she know that she held his heart in the palms of her delicate hands?

CHAPTER TWENTY-TWO

Dumbfounded, completely at a loss, Natasha stared back at Dmitry. His breath whispered along her cheek. She swiped at her skin to rid herself of the sensation. Her anger quickly faded, and left her shaky and vulnerable and uncertain.

And it's all his fault, dammit.

She came here to yell and rave, and give him a piece of her mind. For upsetting Katia today. For making her child miserable.

She came to request—no, to demand—he leave her baby alone, or else.

How on earth can she yell at him now that he looked at her with such kindness? He thanked her for saving Katia, and completely disarmed her. He gave every indication he didn't care about the girl, even hated her. Was she mistaken?

Natasha's head spun. Mesmerized, she stood glued to the spot, staring at Dmitry. Absently she noticed the reflection of moonlight in his eyes. Wide open, the Palladian windows let the air in, saturating the room with the flavors and sounds of the night. Her mind immediately conjured the scene from the last time they were together all those years ago.

Another night, perfumed with roses...The stars high above...The faint music coming from the ballroom...And Dmitry, holding her close.

She remembered his heartbeat against her chest, his warmth encircling.

And his mouth hovering above hers...

Those images played havoc with her peace of mind. Defenseless, she shut her eyes and shook her head. Straggling to keep herself from falling apart, she offered up a silent prayer.

Dear God, help me forget.

But the memories bombarded her, leaving her suspended between reality and the dream she desperately tried to erase from her memory.

Dmitry's unexpected kindness undid her. The thin barrier of her defense crumbled rapidly, like a poorly built sandcastle under the breeze.

Terrified, off balance, she forced herself to open her eyes. She sucked in a calming lungful of air and managed to bring herself under control. Barely.

"You... you don't have to thank me. She is my baby, too. Every mother would do the same."

"No, not every mother. Believe me, Natasha, I should know..." His voice trailed into silence, as his face became hard and drawn. A faraway expression clouded his eyes. She was sure his thoughts were of his own mother. Elizabeth. Natasha gritted her teeth. God knew, over the years, she had enough of the woman's interference in her life. Her shadow lurked everywhere, daunting, chilling, cruel.

"And I do have to thank you." Dmitry continued, "I should've done that five years ago. But I didn't, and for that, I am very sorry. I'd like to tell you how grateful I am for your presence in my daughter's life. She doesn't even know how lucky she is to have you. I do hope she will realize it with years to come, and will never give you the reason to regret giving up so much for her."

"But I didn't give up anything."

"You did, even if you don't think that." He raked a hand through his hair, making the thick strands jump to attention. "My God, Natasha, I literally dragged you away from your home, playing on your feelings for Svetlana. Using it. And using you to get what I wanted."

She cringed, but Dmitry wasn't finished yet.

"I brought you here, from a totally different world, and then without an ounce of a remorse, shipped you off to my mother. I acted like a bastard, Natasha, and there is no excuse for my behavior."

She shook her head opened her mouth to object, but he laid his right index finger across her lips, stopping her protest. "I'm sorry, Natasha. I'm very, very sorry. For everything."

CHAPTER TWENTY-THREE

S he glanced up at him, wide eyed, and confused. Her lips tremble where he laid his fingertip. On its own volition, his finger slid lower, caressing her lower lip. The tiny mole on the corner of her mouth drove him crazy. He dreamed of that generous, lush mouth almost every night. As he trailed his fingertip across her lips, his blood started to churn. And just like that, his legendary control began to evaporate like smoke, leaving him wild, raw, and hungry. The need to taste, to touch overwhelmed him. Dmitry couldn't stop himself even if he wanted to.

"But most of all I'm sorry for something I failed to do then." Dark and husky, his voice a mere whisper. His eyes traveled to her mouth. "Something I was dying to do."

She licked her lips, brushing his finger with her tongue. Even though not a deliberate gesture, it set him on fire. A deep sound rumbled in his throat.

The wild panic in her eyes was unmistakable. She jolted, scooted back, only to be stopped by the solid barrier of the wooden door behind her. Dmitry stepped forward, caging her between the door and his body.

"Natasha..."

"Don't."

"Why?"

"Because... I didn't come here for this..."

"I know."

"I ... Dmitry, please..."

"Say you don't want it, and I let you go."

"I...I..."

"Say it, Natasha."

"I... can't..."

The helpless surrender in her eyes undid him. Something stirred inside him, something strong and hot and right. His heart melted, sighed, stuttered.

Then she murmured his name, and Dmitry was lost.

With a half moan, half sob trembling in his throat, Dmitry lowered his mouth, and gently touched her lips. A jolt of electricity went through him like a bolt of lightning. Shocked from the force of it, he drew back, and stared at her.

Paralyzed.

Mesmerized.

Lost.

And then pure madness ensued.

CHAPTER TWENTY-FOUR

Moving in unison, they fused their lips into the ravenous kiss that spun out of control. He claimed her mouth almost brutally, bruising her soft lips under an onslaught of his teeth and tongue. She opened to him, giving him the entrance he sought and craved. Her taste, something sweet and potent, went through Dmitry's gut like a gulp of strong liqueur. It stopped his breath. A huge tidal wave sent his system into a spin of sensations. He couldn't think, he just felt. And felt and felt...

With her arms around his neck, Natasha held onto him like he was her one and only lifesaver, the single tangible link to reality.

Not enough. Not nearly enough.

Shaking, straining, she molded her body to his. But he needed more. Kissing her stopped to be enough.

Angling her head, Natasha began her own explorations. Tentatively at first, she thrust her tongue into his mouth. A deep growl of approval burst from his throat.

Dear God, how much longer of this torture he could endure? He was but a man.

Cursing in his mind, praying for patience, Dmitry deepened the kiss even more.

Dammit, it's not enough.

He wanted to touch her skin.

Desired.

Craved.

He needed to feel her bare skin. Wrestling with her sweater, he slid both hands inside, trailed them along her naked torso, until he encountered the barrier of her bra. Impatiently, he cupped both generous mounds. Her swollen nipples pressed into his palms. He circled them with his thumbs. A low helpless moan— his? hers? —was erotic and wild. Mad with desire, he continued to devour her mouth, then moved his hands lower to knead her bottom.

When she pressed her softness against his aching hardness, Dmitry groaned in pure agony. Hungry for more, desperate, he rubbed his middle against hers in the rhythm as old as the world itself. Tearing his mouth from hers, he covered greedy kisses along her jaw and throat, slowly inching lower. When his teeth closed around her nipple, Natasha cried out.

CHAPTER TWENTY-FIVE

The unbearable heat of his mouth and sharp edges of his teeth worked their way through the fabric of her bra. Strong tugs and pulls at the tip of her left breast generated a vortex of feelings. And the heat!

All-consuming.

Scorching.

Unbearable.

Dear God, what's happening to me? I'm burning alive!

Her feet lost purchase as he lifted her off the floor. A brief sensation of weightlessness made her dizzy. Disoriented, guided by pure instinct, she hooked her legs around Dmitry's waist, and circled his neck with both arms. His mouth trailed up her collarbone, back to her mouth. Their lips fused.

Through the blaze of passion, a sudden thought knifed her foggy mind, it was happening too fast, too soon. Too much.

Natasha shivered violently, but how much of it sprung from desire and how much from fear she didn't know. Despite the warning bells in her mind, she let him take her farther, far beyond common sense, but reality intruded in the form of a loud, angry noise. What on earth...?

Obviously, hearing her scream Misha got agitated behind the closed door. Trying to get to her, he jumped, bumping the door with his paws and chest. Thundering sounds of barking reverberated, and were sure to fetch an unwelcomed audience. Dmitry failed to hear, or give a damn about the commotion, but Natasha did. In a desperate attempt to stop him, she began to struggle.

"Stop, Dmitry, stop it!" she yelled before he lifted his face.

He panted hard like he just finished a marathon. His eyes turned dark, glazed with desire and hunger.

"Stop. We have to stop."

"What? Why?"

"Misha."

"Who the hell is Misha?"

"My dog, Misha. He's trying to bring this door down, can't you hear?"

"Oh, Misha... right. Why?"

He was still beyond simple comprehension, and although it pleased her very much, Natasha had a more pressing matter at that moment.

"He's afraid you're hurting me," she explained urgently. "Put me down. I must calm him before he alerts the entire household."

"God damn it." Dmitry dropped her to her feet, and together awkwardly they wrestled with a doorknob. Not an easy task since her hands shook so hard. On the third or fourth attempt they both managed to open the door, and a hundred pounds of enraged canine rammed into Dmitry, throwing him off balance, and plunging him on the floor.

CHAPTER TWENTY-SIX

The impact of the punch knocked him off his feet. For a second, Dmitry saw stars. Sprawled helplessly, stunned, and shocked, he never thought to cover his face. Misha put his front paws on Dmitry's chest, pinning him to the spot. He heard Natasha's voice, crooning to the dog, and soon that huge weight lifted from his ribcage. Taking a first tentative breath, Dmitry tried to assess the damage to his body. Nothing seemed out of order, thank God for small favors. Bruised pride, yes, but his flesh was intact.

"Dmitry? Oh, my God, are you all right?"

"I'll survive," he muttered, trying to bring his body to an upright position. When he finally managed that, he found himself nose to nose with the dog. Misha immediately bared his teeth in warning.

"Impressive. Who's your dentist, pal?" But the huge shepherd was not in a mood for jokes. He growled deep in his throat as he eyed Dmitry like a prime steak.

"Oh, God, you're hurt." Natasha grabbed the dog by the collar, and tried to drag him away. The beast refused to move. "How badly? What did you break?"

"Nothing, I'm fine."

"I'm sorry, Dmitry, I should have realized—"

"Stop fussing. I said I'm okay. The only thing that got hurt is my ego."

Squinting at him, Natasha frowned. "Are you sure?"

"I'm positive."

"Thank God, oh, dear..." She bit her lip. "I was so afraid..."

"Did you worry about me, Natasha?" Her concern sent a ripple of pleasure through him. Different from sexual, but no less gratifying.

"Of course! It was all my fault. Dmitry, I am so very sorry."

"Woman, one more time you say 'sorry,' and I'll be pissed."

"But—"

"But nothing." Ungracefully, because his legs remained unsteady, he lifted himself from the floor. "You didn't attack me, your dog did."

"Dmitry, he didn't know what was happening here, he heard my... scream, and just reacted."

"Yeah, it's a real champion you have here. Thank God he ran solo tonight."

"I hope you won't do anything rash. Katia will be heartbroken if you..." Her voice trailed off, as she watched him, obviously uneasy.

"What are you talking about?"

"Well, Misha attacked you. I just hope you won't insist on getting rid of him."

"Getting rid of him? Why? For defending you? He didn't do anything wrong. He did what he's trained to do." A jolt of anger rocked him.

"I'm so glad you understand." Her sigh of relief rubbed him the wrong way.

"What do you take me for, an idiot? Do you honestly think I could order anyone to throw the dog out of the house for performing his duty?"

"Well, you said your ego was hurt."

"Yeah, so what?"

"Well, I assumed..."She shrugged, her fingertips drumming against her thigh.

"You assumed wrong. And you obviously don't know me if you believed that even for a second." His angrily retort earned another menacing growl from Misha.

How stupid of him to scowl back at the dog. He probably looked like an idiot.

He didn't give a damn. Natasha's quiet voice put a stop to his folly.

"That's true. I don't know you. I don't know you at all."

That statement infuriated him even more.

Damn you woman and your dog!

He had enough. But when Dmitry attempted to stand, a low rumble of warning stopped him midway.

"Steady, boy, steady," he murmured to the dog.

But Misha edged a little closer, and bared his teeth again.

"Save it, pal. I'm not impressed anymore. And I'm not a bad guy, understand?" Dmitry crouched lower so his eyes maintained a line with the dog's.

"I won't hurt her." He stated quietly, but firmly.

Misha stared into his eyes for the longest moment before he whimpered and lowered himself to the floor. Tentatively, he patted the dog's head. Misha glanced up with sad eyes.

"He trusts you," Natasha whispered with quiet wonder.

"And that surprises you?"

"Yes, it does. He never trusted any stranger before."

That didn't sit well with Dmitry.

"Well, maybe he figured out that I'm not a stranger." Belatedly, Dmitry dusted his behind. His tailbone smarted, which aggravated him further.

"You're not a member of the family, either." Natasha retorted.

"Then who the hell am I?" He stepped closer to her. Sidestepping him, she went to the open window. Damn. She knew how to withdraw from him, emotionally as well as physically. That annoyed him. How could she just shut him out after that kiss? His whole foundation crumbled, as she built a wall around herself. Like nothing out of the ordinary just happened. He'd be damned if he let her do that.

"Natasha."

"Hmm-mm?"

"Look at me." She stood perfectly still, so he walked closer, grasped her by the shoulders, then turned her around. Her face, white as milk. In sharp contrast two angry scarlet patches that bloomed on her cheeks. Stubbornly, Natasha kept her gaze averted, not meeting his eyes.

By God, she's embarrassed.

A moment ago, she burst into flames in his arms, kissing the hell out of him, and now she blushed like a schoolgirl. A woman full of contradictions and a complete mystery to him. By God, he intended to be the only one to solve this mystery.

Even as he made that vow, he noticed that Natasha's color deepened even more. Dmitry smiled. Her blushing was very sweet and endearing.

"Look at me, little one," he repeated more gently this time.

She tensed, then, after a pause, lifted her eyes. Her red and swollen lips glistened. Her curls broke loose from his impatient hands, and tumbled around her face in a charming disarray. She never seemed more beautiful to him.

But her shining emerald eyes were wary and guarded. Desire no longer shone on her face. Determination and strength, as if she had made up her mind. It annoyed him to no end. His annoyance gave way to anger, then panic. He felt her slipping like dry sand through his fingers, and he was powerless to do anything about it.

"Natasha," Dmitry repeated in a harsh whisper. To his utter dismay, he heard desperation in his own voice. Fear charged through him, and damn if he liked it. He clutched her shoulders with much more strength than required.

Undoubtedly her tender flesh now had bruises, but Natasha never flinched, or blinked an eye. She continued to stare at him.

"Don't, damn you."

"Don't what?"

"Don't shut me out like that."

"You're hurting me." The tremor in her voice betrayed her inner turmoil.

Dmitry released her immediately, then stepped back. "I'm sorry, I didn't mean to hurt you."

"I know."

"Natasha, what happened—"

"A mistake," she rushed to interrupt him. "And my fault entirely."

Anger crashed into him. "Yeah? And how did you figure that out?"

"I could stop you, but I haven't."

"Why?"

"Why what?"

"Why haven't you stopped me?"

"I..." she paused, lowering her eyes. Then she added in a whisper, "I didn't want to."

Pure joy flooded his heart, but her next words crushed his euphoria to smithereens.

"Now I apologize, and want you to forget all about it."

"The hell you say!" His loud roar bounced around the walls. Once again Dmitry clasped her arms in a tight grip. "What happened between us was not a mistake, and you know it. And don't you dare take this insulting servant to the master tone of voice with me. Apologized, didn't you? Well, if you are waiting for *my* apology, you have a long time coming, lady, because I won't apologize for kissing you. Forget about it? Oh, how convenient! But guess what? I have no intention of forgetting it, and make it easy for you. Moreover, I will do my damnedest to remind you about it every moment I can. If I have to suffer, so, by God, will you!" He shouted out the words in a ragged voice.

"Suffer?" Natasha repeated, narrowing her eyes. Then louder, "Suffer!" She wrenched from his grip. "How dare you! What do you know about suffering, *Your Grace*?"

Trembling from head to toe, Natasha exploded. With blazing eyes, she rounded on him, shoving both hands at his chest. His jaw dropped with the transformation. She was so mad, he expected her to slap him. Natasha gave another mighty shove at his chest, and muttered a very colorful Russian expletive. Despite himself, Dmitry grinned.

She glared at him. "Suffer, you say? Oh, that's rich. That's just so rich it's not even funny." She poked his chest with her finger, all the while shaking with outrage.

"Well, let me tell you something about suffering, *Your Grace*. Did you ever wonder where you came from? Or about the people who conceived you, and then deserted you at a dumpster to die? Did anyone ever laugh at, or pick on you because you were so ugly and puny and sick, you could not defend yourself? Have you ever been hungry? Really hungry? Did you ever have to work to the last drop of your endurance because you simply needed to eat and clothe yourself? Have you ever been at the mercy of a monster that decided to brutalize you just because he could, and you were unfortunate enough to be in the wrong place at the wrong time?" Her breathing became choppy. "Have you ever tried to pick yourself up, piece by piece, from filth and mud, and build up your life anew, all the while wondering if it was your own fault after all, and you deserved the punishment? Have you ever lost someone you loved so much your heart simply refused to beat from the loss?"

Natasha failed to notice tears trickling down her cheeks. She trembled so hard her teeth clicked. In her agitated state, she revealed more than she probably intended. He cringed inwardly. Every word from her punched in his gut.

"Have you ever found yourself falling in love for the first time in your life with the wrong person? Who didn't give a damn about you? Who found it so easy to walk away without a glance or a word, flicking you aside like you were no more than a pesky fly?"

"Natasha—"

"Have you ever looked into the eyes of a child whose hopes and dreams were shattered by a careless word?"

Damn, she was killing him. "Natasha—"

"So don't you dare to tell me about suffering." Her broken whisper rang with finality.

CHAPTER TWENTY-SEVEN

D mitry's smile faded at the beginning of her speech. He was shocked, appalled, and angry.

My God, she went through hell.

This tiny slip of a woman endured so much pain and rejection, it was horrifying.

His heart wept for the lonely sick girl tossed out like a piece of garbage by a dumpster, then raised in the orphanage, starved for love and compassion.

At that moment, he wanted to commit murder. He shook from the burning desire to kill the monsters, who robbed Natasha of a normal childhood, with his bare hands.

The mention of an accident, sketchy at best, left him trembling with rage. Dmitry remembered that night, five years ago, when he stumbled upon Natasha in the gardens after dark. She literally became paralyzed with fear.

Now he understood why.

Dear God in heaven, how could you allow it? Why didn't you spare her? Hasn't she suffered enough?

And what about you? His inner voice supplied with vengeance. *Haven't you selfishly used her, and then rejected her when she became an inconvenience?*

Sick with self-disgust and remorse, Dmitry cursed himself. He wanted to break something. He wanted to yell and rage and rave. But most of all he wanted—needed—to take her into his arms, to soothe and comfort, to give her even the smallest measure of love and warmth refused to her as a child.

His gut told him she wouldn't accept it. Not from him.

"I... I'm sorry, Dmitry." Natasha's soft words interrupted his inner battle with God and himself. She closed her eyes and shook her head. "I came here to talk, and... I'm sorry."

"We do need to talk, Natasha," he added quietly, getting a firm grip on his own emotions. "About many things, and we will. But not now."

She seemed dead on her feet. His last drop of control began to slip away.

No, not now. Bad timing.

"Yes, not now," she echoed faintly. "I... I have to go. It's late."

"Yes."

"I say good night, then."

"Good night."

She casually glided to the door, calling gently to the dog to follow, but Dmitry didn't want to let her go, not like that.

"Natasha?"

"Yes?" She froze with her shoulders straight. The muscles so tight he thought they might tear.

"Thank you again."

"What for?"

"Katia...she told me today..." Dmitry heaved a deep sigh. "She believes I bought these dogs for her, because I couldn't be here to take care of her myself. I presume I have to thank you for that merciful lie."

"Actually, Petya told her that. But I didn't correct him. I couldn't."

"Thank you, nevertheless."

"You're welcome." Natasha glanced at him over her shoulder. Her green eyes incredibly sad.

"She loves you, Dmitry. God knows why, but she does. She keeps your pictures, hides them. She thinks I don't know." She inhaled deeply, her voice small and quiet. "And she waits for you. Constantly. She's been waiting for you all these years..." Her voice trailed, but not before Dmitry recognized a wistful note of hope in it.

"We'll talk about Katia, I promise. She's turned out to be quite a surprise for me, I admit."

"I'm glad." Natasha opened the door. Misha flew out like a rocket, impatiently waiting for her to follow.

"Natasha?"

She stood on the threshold, her back to him. "What?"

"Did you wait for me?"

God knew he didn't want to ask, but the question popped out of his mouth before he realized it.

Her shoulders tensed, then she calmly turned around, and faced him.

"I did. For a long time. I was in love with you, and foolishly believed in a dream. But not anymore."

And then she left.

As if glued in place, Dmitry stared at the closed door.

Not anymore.

He wondered if she meant that she wasn't in love with him anymore, or that she no longer believed in dreams.

Or both.

CHAPTER TWENTY-EIGHT

Dmitry's foul mood continued into the next day. He replayed the events of the previous evening in his mind. He glanced at the bedside clock. Barely six. He swung his legs off the mattress and prowl his room like a caged animal. Restless and edgy, he decided to go for a run to spend his excess energy. He pulled on jogging shorts, then old Nikes, before exiting the room to race out the front door. He ran until he ran out of air, but his troubles refused to be pacified even after the vigorous exercise. Continuously his mind returned to Natasha's parting words, pondering the true meaning behind them.

They needed to talk. That became imperative. They needed to sort out everything, and find a solution. He clearly realized it was impossible for him to live far away from Natasha and the children. Yet simply unbearable for him to visit his mother's estate. Period. So, he must do something, and do it quick.

The best option, relocate them all to France, but it wasn't completely up to him. Peter liked Paris, and loved with everything French. He is a brilliant student who speaks French like a Parisian, so the transfer from Berkeley to any other university was not a problem.

Katia? Just a little kid and no problem as well.

But Natasha...

What would she say? What if she refused to relocate?

Why object? After all, both Peter and Katia would be with her. Hell, he'd adopt Pasha and Misha to make this all happened, although where he'd find space for the dogs in his flat he had no idea. Dmitry shrugged it off.

A small problem, but he'd find a solution to that, too. Buy a house. Yes, that's the answer. He needed to call Vlad immediately and ask him to contact a realtor.

The idea Natasha might object for more personal reasons flashed in his mind. He stopped, cursed, then resumed jogging at a faster pace.

Was she seeing someone? Did she have a man in her life? Dammit, how could she kiss him like that and be involved with someone? Ridiculous.

Of course, she wasn't involved with anyone. Or...

His mood plummeted. Dmitry decided to postpone his call to Vlad until he spoke with Natasha again.

He refused to think she might be in love with someone else. No, impossible.

She loved him once upon a time, and knowing her, Dmitry had confidence she still felt something for him. After all, she couldn't have been so uninhibited, so passionate with him yesterday. My God, she burst into a blazing inferno in his arms.

He shuddered just thinking of her response to him. So open, so honest, so hot.

The first unmistakable sign of arousal made him wince.

Cut it out.

Too late. He was already hard as a rock.

Dmitry entered the house, then ran up the staircase with the speed of a man on fire. He hoped everyone was still asleep. He shuddered at the thought of some unsuspected servant might see him in his indecent state. He scanned the family portraits displayed along the walls as he jogged up the stairs. Then he did a double take, and slowly turned around. Handsome as sin, the face of his late cousin met his gaze. A new addition to his mother's collection. Dmitry never noticed that portrait of Alexei before. He didn't know that it even existed.

The old witch.

She did it on purpose. Just to spite him. Something subtle but painfully familiar caught his eye. Dmitry frowned, uneasy, because he saw that expression just recently. On his son's face.

Unmistakable Rostoff's grin, slashed cheekbones, bold wings of eyebrows. And those wide dark eyes... A cold foreboding settled heavily in his gut. After a short moment, Dmitry shrugged it off. The heck with the old meddling witch.

Thank God it could be chalked up to the family resemblance.

You think I don't know? You think you can manipulate me with this? Think again, Your Grace.

All the fine hair on his neck raised up. Without turning, he knew someone watched him.

Dmitry glanced over his shoulder, and tensed.

Two beasts looked at him with something close to insulting indifference. He guessed it was all for show, since both dogs were now on duty, flanking the tiny figure of his daughter. Almost hidden between their muscular fury bodies, Katia wore frilly pink pajamas and clutched something square shaped in her hands. Still sleepy, with her ash blond curls tousled, and her heart-shaped face wrinkled from a pillow, she watched him with somber grey eyes.

Why is she sneaking out of her room?

And then it downed at him. Of course, Peter's birthday.

Obviously, the little tyke wanted to be the first one to wish her older brother happy birthday. God, what a picture, so tiny, so fragile.

He still hadn't settled on his true feelings toward her, but it sure as hell wasn't the hatred he held dear when they first met. But it didn't feel like love either. He frowned at the little girl and felt guilty. Damn, he stood just three steps from her, and words failed him. According to his mother, Katia had a higher intelligence than other children her age. What did Elizabeth say? Oh, yes, the girl liked to paint. No wonder. His own father fancied himself to be a Great Russian artist.

He fell well short of the mark, but Nicolay Rostoff had a talent for small watercolors. Must be genes, Dmitry mused, pondering once again the wonders of nature.

It played such a cruel trick on him by giving his daughter his mother's face and his father's artistic talent. Talk about the irony of fate. What other surprises did the little girl have hidden under the sleeves of her silly pink pajamas?

"He's looking just like Petya," the little girl whispered then, interrupting his silent musings.

"Hmm-mm? Who?"

"Him." She pointed to the portrait with her eyes.

Dmitry studied the picture of late Alexei Rostoff. The resemblance between his son and his late cousin was unquestionable. An older, more mature version of his son's face looked back at him from the picture on the wall.

Talk about the irony of fate. Did somebody else notice it? Did Peter? He sincerely hoped not. And what about Katia? He tore his gaze from the portrait to look at her.

She hunched her shoulders and cast her eyes downward. Did that picture scare her? Seemed like it.

"Nothing to be scared of. Just a family resemblance. That man was related to Peter, so..."

But Katia inched closer to him, shivering visibly.

"I don't like him," she whispered to Dmitry.

"What? Why?"

He noticed Katia refused to look at the portrait. Instead, her eyes were glued to the floor, and she all but plastered herself to the body of one of the dogs.

"His eyes," she explained in a tiny voice. "They are... pretty as Petya's, but not... alive." She shrugged her tiny shoulders.

"Of course, his eyes are not alive. It's a portrait."

For a reason he couldn't comprehend, he derived pleasure with his daughter's negative reaction to Alexei's portrait.

"No," she stubbornly shook her head, frowning at him. "No, it's not that. It just..." she stole a quick glance at the wall, and averted her gaze again. "I don't know. His eyes are empty. He looks like Petya, but he is... not kind. And empty."

She stressed again almost vehemently. Dmitry smiled. Why, Katia was his son's champion. Her brother's champion, he corrected himself.

After a moment, he nodded. "Yes, I think you're right."

"For real?" She looked up quickly, staring at him in wonder.

"For real."

"Grandmother said he was Petya's uncle."

"Twice removed, but still an uncle, yes."

"That makes him your... cousin?"

"Right again."

"I'm sorry," she murmured.

"Whatever for?"

"He's dead. You probably miss him."

"He's dead, yes, but I don't miss him."

Katia nodded jerkily, sending her hair flying. "You didn't love him."

Trust the child to get to the crux of it.

"I guess not."

No, Dmitry realized. Liked him, definitely, but never loved his cousin as family members should love each other. It took many years for him to get it. Katia grasped it in a moment. She was smart.

What did Elizabeth say about her IQ? Something on a genius level? Dmitry wasn't sure about that, but her intuition proved uncanny.

"I love Petya," she supplied in a soft whisper.

"You do, huh?"

"Yes, very, very much. Sometimes I think..." She slid her gaze down again, then lifted her head and focused on him. "Promise you won't tell?"

"I won't tell," he assured her solemnly. "Now what is it you think sometimes?"

"That I love him more than anybody, even more than Mama."

She seemed so miserable, so forlorn, confessing her horrible sin to him. Dmitry's heart squeezed. Something moved inside him, something warm and almost painful. Her huge somber eyes held his gaze, as she finished in a whisper, "Even more than you."

And just like that, she broke his heart.

Unintentionally, in her own special way, little Katia just confessed her love for him. Her little heart shone in her eyes. And it staggered him. His knees wobbled. Unsteady, Dmitry knelt in front of Katia, and looked at her. He swallowed around the lump in his throat.

He didn't want to hurt her, to harm her unintentionally with careless words.

Who if not him should know that the verbal blow is more devastating than a physical one?

God, she's so tiny. So heartbreakingly fragile.

Katia tensed, but didn't avert her eyes. Those somber pewter eyes of hers held him spellbound.

Something in her gaze pierced his heart. Not fear, or pain, but trust. Strong and absolute trust. She confessed her secret, shared it with him, and asked him a favor: not to tell anyone, because she didn't want to hurt Natasha's feelings.

She put her trust in his hands. And that shook him to the soul.

Silently, Dmitry vowed that he'd be dead before he betrayed her.

Deep inside, he knew her trust mattered more to him than anything else.

"I won't tell, Katia." He meant every word. He realized that he called her by her given name for the first time. "I promise."

"Thank you," she murmured, staring at him as if mesmerized.

"You are welcome."

The moment stretched. The silence became absolute.

Unable to look away from those eloquent eyes, Dmitry held his breath. The little girl, who stared at him with open adoration in her huge eyes, bewitched him. Drowning. He felt himself drowning in those grey pools and relished the moment. One of the dogs gave a whimper, and the spell broke.

Awkwardly, Dmitry rose to his feet. "You'd better go if you want to catch Peter first, and wish him a happy birthday. He'll be awake in no time."

Dear God, he stammered.

But Katia didn't seem to notice. She tilted her head and eyed him curiously.

"How did you know?"

"Know what?"

"That I wanted to wish him happy birthday?"

"I kind of figured it out." Lightly, he touched the wrapped package she held in a death grip. "It's a present, right?"

"Yes. But how... how did you know that I wanted to be the very *first*?"

"Simple. You love him."

"I do. Petya told me when he was a little boy you were always the very first to wish him happy birthday. While you were away, I thought I would do that, to make him happy. But since you're here now, if you want to be the very first, I don't mind. Really." Her miserable expression said quite the opposite.

Dmitry smiled.

God, she is something, all right, this little daughter of mine.

"No, kiddo, you go ahead. I wouldn't want to break the tradition. And, anyway, I don't have a present with me, I need to fetch it from my room."

His grin seemed less awkward this time, because now he felt much easier in her company. With a mocking salute to her furry guards, Dmitry briskly started up the stairs.

"Father?" Her tentative voice stopped him midstride.

"Yeah?"

"You better put a shirt on or you might catch a cold. That's what Mama always says."

With that remark, she bounced away, toward Peter's room.

Only then Dmitry remembered of his state of dress, or rather undress, and glad Katia couldn't see the rising color of embarrassment on his face. Darn, he completely forgot about his bare chest. Probably scared her out of her PJs.

Looking down at himself, he cursed out loud. Geez, what must she think about him? But she hadn't looked scared or repulsed, just shy.

And she lived with his adult son, so she must have seen a bare-chested male now and again. Especially, during pool season. But, dammit, Peter wasn't her father. Dmitry hurried to his room, and wished never to go through that again. Only when he showered and shaved and about to put on a shirt, did he remember Katia's last words: " ... *you might catch a cold.*"

He smiled as he realized she worried about him. Damn, but she was sweet. And smart, too. If only she didn't resemble her grandmother so much...

He sobered immediately. What to do about her? About this situation? He shook his head, and decided first things first. Today was Peter's big day, and he still hadn't wished his son happy birthday.

Dmitry pushed open his bedroom door and headed for the closet. He grabbed his suitcase, opened it, and lifted out a small velvet box with the *Rostoff & Co.* logo. Should he wrap it?

He deliberated on it for a few moments, and decided against that silly idea.

He shoved the box into his pants pocket, and went in search of his son.

CHAPTER TWENTY-NINE

A soft knock on his door made Peter smile. Heck, he loved his birthdays. It probably wasn't very grownup of him, to love so much having his family come one after another into his room with presents and birthdays wishes, but he just couldn't help it. Grinning from ear to ear, Peter loudly called out, "Come in!"

His father walked in. "Happy birthday, Champ," Dmitry smiled, pulling Peter in a bear hug, and thumping him on the back several times.

"Thanks, Dad."

Peter knew he grinned like a fool, but he didn't care. Something on his father's face gave him a pause. "Dad? What's the matter?"

"Hmm-mm? Nothing. Why?"

"For a second you looked at me kind of funny like you saw a ghost or something."

"No, Peter, nothing so illustrious." Dmitry shrugged, then smiled. "Just thinking that you're a grown man now. I can't spank you anymore."

"And when did you ever spank me, Dad?"

"Yeah, that's true, too."

Rubbing his earlobe in his usual absentminded gesture, Dmitry did a slow survey of the room. Peter knew he was never tidy, something his grandmother reminded him of constantly. Piles of clothes and papers and whats-not occupied most of the space on his desk and chairs. He glanced down at the floor.

Dad's going to break his neck falling over my stuff.

Bookshelves covered an entire wall, packed to the extent of their capacity. Yes, he loved his books, and made a painstaking effort to keep them just so, every volume in its special place. And he kept his photo gallery on the other wall free of every speck of dust. Peter made sure of that. Almost all the pictures were of Katia.

Peter watched his father, following his gaze.

What did he think? What did he feel looking at the image of his unwanted illegitimate daughter? What happened to his heart? He couldn't read his father's face. Dmitry held the championship when it came to hiding his true emotions under that cool unreadable mask. But his eyes appeared too intent. It gave Peter hope. After a while, Dmitry switched his gaze to the sketches and drawings lining up on all available spaces.

Does he know? Did he recognize a signature on the bottom right corner of every drawing? And if he did, what did he think of his daughter now?

When silence became too uncomfortable, Peter asked, "You still blame her?"

"For what?" His father continued to stare at Katia's face in the pictures.

"For the death of her mother."

"No."

The answer came out curt, but Peter believed him.

"Do you still hate her?"

"I don't."

"Good. So, I know you two met already. What do you think of her?"

Dmitry seemed to ponder that for a moment. "She is a bright, and sweet little girl."

"But?"

"But nothing."

That answer irritated Peter. "For goodness' sake, Dad, she's your daughter. How can you feel nothing toward your own child?"

"I didn't say I feel nothing, Peter. I just..." Dmitry shrugged. "It's too complicated to explain. I've met her, yes. Do you want to know the truth? She spooked me. Her uncanny resemblance to my dear mother horrifies me. And I rarely had to deal with children her age. Well, except you, but that was a long time ago. So, yes, I feel ill at ease with her. That's the truth. But I don't hate her. I feel guilty."

"But you don't care about her." Peter concluded grimly.

"I don't know."

"Bullshit, Dad."

He clenched his hand into tight fists then exploded, "I don't know, Peter!" He paced back and forth then turned to Peter. "Give me a break, son. I just met her for the first time after five years. The circumstances of her birth are difficult, to say the least. I need time to get used to the idea that I have a daughter, okay?"

He viewed Peter straight on, and the torment in his dad's eyes was unmistakable. Peter's heart squeezed painfully in his chest. For his father, for his little sister, for them all.

"Sorry, Dad," he murmured, ashamed of himself.

"Yeah, me, too," Dmitry replied quietly.

An awkward silence filled the room. His father frowned.

"Damn, I completely forgot." He removed the small box from his pocket.

"Happy Birthday, son."

Peter immediately recognized the trademark blue color of the logoed box.

"Dad! You already gave me Corvette. Honestly, it's too much." But as he said that, he reached for the box and opened it. On the bottom lay the most beautiful ring Peter ever saw. It was exquisite but utterly masculine with its heavy platinum base, and square cut blue diamond, and the exact copy of the one Dmitry always wore on his right ring finger.

"Oh, wow. I don't know what to say."

"Say you like it," Dmitry chuckled.

"Like it? Dad, it's a masterpiece. It's just like yours. I love it!"

"Good. I'm glad."

"But it's still too much."

"Nothing's too much for my only... son."

Did he almost say my only child?

Probably. But he stopped himself. A progress of sorts. And because of that, Peter let it slide.

"This one belonged to my father." Dmitry continued, looking at his fisted hand. "It came to me after his death. I was barely thirteen when he died, so...we didn't have a chance. But you and I...I well, we could start a fine tradition." He squinted at Peter. "When you'll have a son, I'll give him my ring, and you'll give yours to your grandson, and so on." Obviously uneasy, Dmitry shrugged, avoiding his gaze.

Peter was more than surprised. He knew his father well, or so he thought. The idea of traditions and family never ranked high on Dmitry's list. Clearly, Peter was mistaken.

"It is a terrific idea, Dad. Let's go for it."

"Really? You approve?"

"Yeah, I do."

"Well, then..."

His relief seemed almost palpable. Dmitry smiled. Then his face darkened. Watching his father's facial expression, Peter noticed his joy, then a cloud of confusion, which in turn changed to deep sadness.

"What is it, Dad?"

"Hmm-mm?"

"Is something troubling you?"

"You mean, except being in your grandmother's house who hates my guts and can't wait to be read of me?" The corners of Dmitry's mouth curved into a small smile that didn't reach his eyes. "Or tonight's party, where I am obliged to rub shoulders with young people of the next generation and try with all my might not to embarrass you in front of your friends?"

"You never could embarrass me, Dad. My friends will like you and find you fascinating."

CHAPTER THIRTY

"Fascinating, huh?" The fact that Peter chose to avoid the subject of his grandmother and her feelings toward Dmitry didn't escape his attention. It spoke volumes to him. The boy was too honest. Even to placate his father. His chest swelled with deep respect and admiration for his son. Yes, he grew up into a fine young man, indeed.

"Yes, fascinating, and don't change the subject," Peter replied.

"I'm not. Changing the subject, that is."

"But you don't want to talk about it."

"No, I don't. Not now, anyway."

"Okay. But if you decide you need someone to talk to, I'm always here."

The relationship between males worked on much simpler and easier levels.

"Thank you, son."

"You're quite welcome, but I still wish you'd trust me with your problems."

"It's not the matter of trust, Peter, honestly. It's just...too complicated and too new to me. I have to waddle on my own for a while, to sort everything through, so to speak."

"All right."

"Thanks."

"Anytime, Dad, anytime."

By silent mutual agreement, they dropped the subject.

Dmitry absently walked to the shelves, touching books and knickknacks. He reeled around to look at Peter and raised his eyebrows. "Russian fairy tales?"

"Yes. This is Katia's." Peter took the big ancient volume from his hand. "This," he pointed to the corner between two walls, one of which was lined with shelves, another with photos, "is her favorite spot. She prefers to curl up in here, on the floor, and read her books while I'm studying."

Did he hear that correctly? No, impossible. "Read? But she's five. How can she read books? And in Russian."

"Dad, she's six, and she can read and write in Russian, English, and French. She's started at two-and-a-half."

Poleaxed, Dmitry blinked. Really? Damn, was Peter joking? But no. He seemed serious. Something shifted in his heart almost painfully. Astonishment? Wonder? Pride?

He probably had no right to feel like a proud parent. He barely knew his daughter, spent less than two days with her. Even according to Katia, he only rated as her *Father*, not her *Dad*. But dammit all to hell and back, he did feel proud of her.

Ridiculous.

Dmitry frowned, at odds with himself. Mistaking his frown for a doubt of Katia's talents, Peter immediately jumped to her defensive.

"She's very bright for a child her age. And she's enormously talented. She's an artist."

"You know, son, you don't have to sell your sister to me. Many children of her age are very clever with crayons and coloring books."

"You still don't get it, do you, Dad?"

"Get what?"

"That your daughter is an extraordinary child. She's called a prodigy."

With this comment, he pointed at the drawings displayed on the walls.

Those paintings were the first things Dmitry noticed when he entered Peter's room. Every drawing more beautiful than the other. Simply breathtaking. They changed this spacious, but ordinary place, into something sunny and cheerful. He almost asked Peter where on earth did he get these magical pictures, but the photos of Katia distracted him. Now, as he faced the drawings—some black and white, some in color—Dmitry frowned.

What do these objects of art have to do with Katia?

Then he focused his eyes on a male portrait, and stopped cold.

It was a portrait of him.

He turned to his son and glimpsed at his desk. There, propped by the paperweight, sat a charcoal drawing of Peter. A new addition to the collection? He did a double-take, when he noticed the ripped wrapping on the floor. He recognized it immediately. Only a short time ago, Katia held it in her hands.

Dear God in heaven.

Approximately twelve by ten inches in size, this charcoal portrait was one of the best sketches Dmitry ever saw, and in his line of work he met a lot of talented artists and designers. Barely penciled in, the surroundings were in deep contrast with the precise execution of the subject of the portrait. The sensuality of the pose was unmistakable. She sketched Peter half-sprawled in the lounge, with his right leg bent at the knee, and his arm draped carelessly over it. His expression both intense and dreamy, as he looked at the horizon only he saw in his mind.

Dmitry could almost feel that inner concentration. His fingers tingled from the sudden urge to touch the drawing and feel the texture of Peter's hair, silky yet heavy, with a small wave to it. It seemed so real, almost unbelivable.

Shocked, mesmerized, he studied the portrait of his son. For a second, he forgot that it was done in black and white, so masterfully were the shades and lights put together. The drawing breathed with life and love.

He dragged his eyes to the lower right corner. Two small letters: ER.

Dmitry exhaled slowly. Of course not. Her name begins with a K for Katia, or Katie as Peter christened her a long time ago.

Relieved and vaguely disappointed, Dmitry almost looked away, when the finality of truth hit him full force. His daughter's real name was Ekaterina.

Ekaterina Rostoff – ER.

Dear God in heaven...

Dmitry studied the other sketches and drawings.

Watercolor of the garden in full bloom... the image of a gazebo in pastel chalks... charcoal portraits of German Shepherds, Pasha and Misha... small oil of scarlet rose with its dewy petals... and the portrait of himself, standing on the balcony with subtle outlines of the Eiffel tower in the background...

And every single sketch or canvas was signed E.R.

"Mother of God," he managed in a low rough whisper.

"Yeah, my point exactly."

Dmitry was in shock. Poleaxed. Dumbfounded. Stunned.

His eyes took it in, but his brain refused to process the truth.

The girl barely six years old created this magical world of art all around him.

Katia's technique was mature beyond belief, and absolutely fabulous.

Expression, execution, mood, light, shades, strokes...

Sweet baby Jesus, her sketches are more talented, more exquisite than Marie's.

And considering the international recognition of Marie's name in the art world, it said a helluva lot.

"She is... she is..." In a helpless gesture, Dmitry lifted his arms, and let them fall.

"She is brilliant, Dad," Peter answered in a somber, quiet voice. "It is so big, this talent of hers, it's almost spooky. Can you imagine what she'll be like in a decade or so?"

"God, it's unbelievable." Dmitry still couldn't tear his eyes from his daughter's art.

"Yes, it is. It's also very demanding and nerve-wracking. Sometimes we need to drag her out of her room, and physically take the brush and palette out of her hands. When she paints, Katia tends to forget everything, including time. Her talent *is* huge, but it lives in the small body of a child. Her physical strength is limited compared to it."

"What do you mean?"

"I mean, she's concentrating so much and so deep, that it sometimes swallows her whole, draining her strength. Once she passed out."

Dmitry swiftly turned his head to Peter.

"She what!"

"Fainted. Thank God, Grandmother didn't know about it, or she'd definitely forbid Katie's art lessons. And without it, she would whither. It's in her blood, her DNA. It's part of who she is."

"But if it dangerous for her health—"

"No, it's not."

"But—"

"But nothing."

That harsh outburst was so unlike Peter, Dmitry stepped back.

"Sorry, Dad. I overreacted. I know that you're concerned. Believe me, so are we. Natasha is doing a fine job raising Katie. It is a very delicate and demanding process, but she's up to the challenge. The art is as necessary for Katie as breathing. She simply won't survive without it. We just need to be very careful, and love her. That's all."

"How does Mother react?"

"You mean, if she approves of Katie's talent?"

Dmitry nodded.

"No, she's doesn't. She planned a grand future for our girl, but she's smart enough to know where and when to bend. So, she gave her permission for the art lessons, and treats it like a harmless hobby that will eventually pass."

"Elizabeth is not that smart." He didn't even try to mask his disgust.

Clearly Katia's paintings were anything *but* a hobby. Only the blind, or ignorant, could mistake it as such.

Her talent was huge and deep and permanent as the color of her eyes, or the birthmark on her thigh. Humbled, he looked at his portrait.

Where did that talent come from? What on earth grew inside of that small, scrawny kid that allowed her to create such a powerful and amazing world of shades and colors?

A mystery. *She* was a mystery to him. But still, she was his flesh and blood, a child he conceived in love... and shame. A daughter he never wanted. A kid whose very existence was a constant reminder of pain and loss and tragedy.

Or so he thought.

"Why didn't you tell me?" Dmitry finally asked not looking at Peter.

"About what?"

"About her talent."

"I just did."

"Why didn't you tell me about it before?"

"Why? Would it really matter that the bastard daughter you never lay eyes on was a child prodigy? Would it change something? Anything?"

Dmitry flinched, then turned to face his son, his accuser.

"No." He couldn't lie to Peter, to himself. He repeated quietly, "No."

"Then why bother?" Peter asked him coolly. "You made a silent taboo of the subject of Katie, and I went along with it. And for that, I am deeply ashamed."

"It wasn't your fault, son. Nor your choice to make."

"Fault? Maybe not. Choice? We all have choices, Dad. And I made mine by locking my feelings and my thoughts inside myself; by keeping my mouth shut and playing your game of silence."

"It was not your choice."

Only now Dmitry realized how deeply he hurt his son by avoiding the subject of Katia all these years. Dear God, Peter somehow convinced himself that it was his fault and his mistake. And he silently endured his shame.

Mad at himself, at his own stupidity, Dmitry repeated more forcefully, "It *never* was your choice, Peter."

"At least I could try to change your mind—"

Peter began, but Dmitry interrupted him, "You were just a boy, a mere boy of thirteen, Peter."

Peter ignored his father and continued, "But I preferred to avoid the subject of Katie because I am a coward. I went along, pretending she didn't exist like it's the normal way of things to have two homes, and two families—one in California, the other half the world away."

"You could have stayed with me. You knew that."

"Yes, I did. But how could I? I love you, Dad, but I love Katie, too. And Natasha. Both of them never had a place in your life. You made that crystal clear. But they are part of mine, a very big and important part." Peter lifted his dark tormented eyes. "I'm all the family she has left, Dad. Natasha and I, that is. To abandon her would be like repeating the history of her short life. First her mother, then you."

"Her mother didn't abandon her. She died giving birth to her."

"Try to explain that to a three-year-old asking where's her mommy."

Dmitry closed his eyes, shutting off the image of Peter.

Even though the fear of his voice betraying him took hold, he forced himself to quietly replied, "I don't know how to say it, but I'm sorry, son. For everything. I'm so damn sorry."

"Yeah, and so am I."

Tired to the bone, Dmitry cursed under his breath. Damn it, how did they end up shouting at each other?

"Did she ever ask... for me?" Dmitry managed around the lump in his throat.

"Yes, she did."

"What did you tell her?"

"That you were working overseas, and very busy."

"Did she buy it?"

"What do you think? A smart and bright child like her?"

"She didn't."

"No, although she never told us otherwise." Peter plowed his fingers through his hair, the gesture like the one Dmitry often did. After a long pause, Peter added, "The dogs' presence helped a lot, for she thinks you left them to watch after her."

Dmitry gave out a humorless chuckle. "Sorry excuse for a sorry father."

"Well, we needed all the help we could get."

"So you lied for me," Dmitry concluded with the weight of an anchor pulling at his heart.

"Yes."

"Sorry, son."

"Don't. I did it for Katie, not for you. And after my mother...what she had done..." Peter voice hitched, but he quickly controlled it. "I just couldn't look her in the eyes. I couldn't see her hurting. She didn't deserve that."

"Does she know about Polina?"

Peter visibly paled although his face wore a detached and hard expression when he starred back at Dmitry. "No. And she never will as long as I live."

The cold finality in his voice sent a ripple of goosebumps along Dmitry's spine.

He realized that Peter bore not only the weight of *his* sins, but also that of his mother's. He completely forgot about the circumstances of his late wife's death. But not Peter. The boy still remembers everything, and still hurts.

And blaming himself.

"God, what a mess." Dmitry muttered.

Peter remained quiet. He walked to the far corner of the room and looked out the window, his hands balled into tight fists. Overwhelmed with guilt and helplessness. There he stood, a man of incredible power and strength, and now as weak and vulnerable as a child as he watched his son. He didn't know if it was a result of the various shocks he received this morning, or maybe the leftovers from yesterday, or a combination of both. His mind spun with confusion and bewilderment. His brain and insides were torn apart. His content existence of the last five years burned to cinders in a matter of two days, and he had no ability to do anything about it. He knew this visit was going to be difficult. He failed to imagine to what extent. Now he did, and damned if he liked it. He felt like he opened Pandora's Box, but the poor Greeks with their mythical horrors had nothing on him in that department. Damn, he wished he had stayed in Paris. He made a huge mistake coming here. Then again, maybe not...

Maybe he needed that explosive jolt to put everything in perspective once and for all, to realize just what he missed in life, to face himself, and his sins, and finally face the reality he avoided for so long, hiding under the comfortable protection of self-delusion.

"I made a terrible mess," Dmitry finally acknowledged more to himself than to his son.

"What do you mean?" Peter asked, still focused on the gardens.

"I will explain it after I talk to Natasha," he answered, already moving toward the door.

"Wait, wait just one damn minute!" In two strides Peter stood beside him, grabbing his forearm. His fingers pressed into Dmitry's flesh with surprising strength. "What are you going to talk to Natasha about?"

Something in his son's voice stopped him and made him take a good look. Peter stood with his legs braced apart and his face set in a hard, cold way that meant one thing only: full battle mode.

What is that all about?

More curious than insulted, Dmitry lifted his brow.

"Peter, what's got into you?" He glared at the fingers that bruised his forearm. Peter held tight.

"I want to know what Natasha has to do with it."

"Why?"

"Dad, I asked you to leave Natasha alone." He ignored Dmitry's questioning stare. His dark eyes burned with determination.

"Peter, what's your problem?"

"My problem? I tell you what my problem is—"

A loud knock interrupted whatever he was going to say.

"Petya? May I come in?" Natasha's voice sounded muffled behind the closed doors.

Peter lifted his vicelike grip from Dmitry's arm.

"Leave her alone, Dad," he said in a low voice meant for Dmitry's ears only.

"What if I can't?"

"Petya? Are you there, *miliy*?"

Peter studied Dmitry hard and long.

"Leave her alone," he muttered again, but this time Dmitry heard a plea rather than an order.

With a last look at him, Peter opened the door.

CHAPTER THIRTY-ONE

From her secluded spot Natasha watched the crowd of partygoers. Everything seemed to run fine and smoothly, thank God. Food rapidly disappeared as the guests enthusiastically devoured the mix of Russian, Italian, and Mediterranean cuisine she helped to choose. Loud music played from the various speakers inside and outside the house, the subject of endless battles between herself and Elizabeth who insisted on a live classical quartet.

And what a disaster that would've been if Natasha hadn't won the battle of wills.

Laughter drifted from everywhere saturating the night with the carefree atmosphere of youth. The older guests preferred to gather inside in a quieter room, with the noise level reduced, and where long tables were set with a traditional Russian feast of caviar, boiled and grilled beluga, young potatoes sprinkled with fresh greens, meat, and mushroom *pierogies* for starters.

Yes, everything was going fine. Why then couldn't she get rid of the dread gathered in the pit of her stomach? Why did she sense something was terribly wrong? Premonition of looming disaster haunted Natasha since the moment she entered Petya's room that morning. Dmitry stood there, and if father and son's intense faces gave any indication, she had interrupted a quarrel.

Quarrel – that's putting it mildly.

They looked mad enough to go a round or two with each other. For the hundredth time, Natasha wondered what could have triggered that near-explosion of tempers she managed to interrupt.

When she asked, Petya refused to answer. She hadn't the courage to question Dmitry. Her bravery raced right out the window, and after yesterday she had no desire to approach him on her own.

God, what was I thinking? Why did I let him kiss me?

More important, what got into her and made her kiss him back?

Dear heaven, she behaved like a shameless hussy, melting all around him in a fashion she could only describe as wanton. And even that was a mild term for her insane state of mind and body. Squirming, Natasha called herself every bad name she knew.

Brainless idiot, dumb fool, silly pea brained imbecile.

But cursing didn't help, and nothing could erase her memories that seemed to be branded into her brain. So, Natasha hid, employing every possible and impossible way to avoid Dmitry after that brief meeting inside Petya's room.

To escape barging into him, she must know his exact location. As much as it galled her, she watched his every movement from the cover of a palm tree, praying that the party might finally wind down, ending her torment. Currently, Dmitry stood outside, mingling with Peter's friends. Tomorrow he'd leave.

All she had to do was live through tonight. And then...

Her heart squeezed painfully. Dear Lord, he planned to leave tomorrow, and she may never see him again.

That's fine, that's just terrific.

She stubbornly chided herself, trying to gain control of her senses. After he departed tomorrow her life must go on as before. Everything fine as usual.

Everything will be terrible.

She couldn't prevent a small sound of despair from escaping. With a start Natasha realized her eyes filled with hot tears. She sucked in several deep calming breaths. So, what if it became terrible after tomorrow? She still needed to live, to function, to do her job. She must remember her main goal in life: Katia and Petya. Her children. They both needed her. It didn't matter if her heart shattered. Even if she refused to open her eyes in the morning or couldn't swallow a bite of food, her children needed her. For their sake, she must be strong. But God, how she wished she didn't have to.

Squeezing her eyes tight and refusing to shed the tears that choked her, Natasha stayed in her dark hidden corner, fighting her inner battle in solitude and misery.

CHAPTER THIRTY-TWO

As Peter danced with Julie, he desperately tried to play the role of a happy host. Natasha spent so much time preparing his big party, he couldn't disappoint her. Utterly miserable, he continued to smile until his face hurt from the effort. To his great surprise, Julie showed up, beautiful, polished, and dazzling like the excellent diamonds on her earlobes.

Son and grandson of jewelers, Peter managed to appraise the carats and clarity of her gems before he noticed her new hairdo or the sinful way her dress hugged her body. Instead of lust, a mild annoyance crept into him. It surprised him, puzzled him. But what irritated the heck out of him, the fact that Julie monopolized him all evening. Like poison ivy, her arms clung to his neck. He barely contained the urge to remove them.

"Why are you frowning? Aren't you happy to see me?" The velvety timbre of her voice dropped several degrees. Instead of enticing, like she undoubtedly intended, it irked him.

"What? Sorry, Jules." Peter frowned, then managed to plaster a fake smile on his face. "You were saying...?"

"Exactly. You're not paying any attention to me or what I'm saying." Her eyes sparked with annoyance.

"Sorry, baby, just thinking of something else." To placate and pacify Julie, he drew her closer, as they swayed to the rhythm of the slow melody.

But she bristled. "Oh? And what was that *something* you were thinking about, dancing with me? Or should I ask *who*?" The accent on the last word sounded deliberate and almost malicious. Her face became taught with anger.

Dammit, there's no winning with her.

"What's gotten into you?" More wary than annoyed, he squinted at her.

"What are you talking about?"

Instead of answering, she glanced over her right shoulder. He followed her gaze. A tiny figure sitting on the grassy lawn nearby warmed his heart. Totally engrossed in her sketching, Katia didn't pay any attention to anything or anyone.

She sat alone, because for the guests' sake, the dogs remained locked inside. Katia seemed absolutely absorbed, drawing on her ever-present pad perched in her lap. She seemed so fragile and so frighteningly detached from the events around her. His concern for her washed over him like a tidal wave. As a result, he accidentally tightened his grip on Julie's arm.

CHAPTER THIRTY-THREE

"**O**uch! You're hurting me." Seething with anger, she wrenched from his arms. Oh, that look in Peter's eyes when he glanced at that little brat! It created a tornado in Julie's abdomen. Peter introduced her to the little monster earlier in the evening.

Julie hated her on the spot. And she looked like a horror, tiny and scrawny, with unusual dark-grey eyes, and almost white hair. And when she lifted those spooky eyes at her, icy chills raced along Julie's body. She still wasn't sure if her imagination played tricks or if the little girl's eyes were really so... *intense* for the lack of a better word. The brat was just jealous. Considering how Peter doted on his sister, she expected no less. All sisters were usually jealous of their brother's girlfriends. But the power of that look, that otherworldly knowing stare, like the girl saw inside Julie's mind and read all her secrets simply threw her off balance, and made her feel insecure.

And for that alone, Julie refused to forgive the spooky brat, no matter her age. She immediately became Julie's rival.

The way Peter looked at his little sister, actually half-sister, she snorted inwardly, as if she was something special, something unique and totally awesome irritated Julie the most.

He never looked at me that way.

That unpleasant discovery gave her even more reason to loathe the kid.

Peter gazed at the girl *that way* again, and a sharp pang of jealousy pierced Julie's heart. How dare he! He still held her in his arms, but she sensed Peter forgot about her while keeping his eyes on his sister.

"I've had enough of this." She wrenched herself from Peter's embrace, then stomped her foot.

"What's the matter, babe?"

"*What's the matter?* Don't you dare ask me what's the matter, Rostoff. You know very well what the matter is." Several heads turned in their direction, but she didn't care that her voice became shrill and loud.

"Calm down, Jules." His voice barely above a whisper. "You're making a spectacle."

"A spectacle? Me? Ha! Look who's talking. It's *you* making a cheap spectacle of yourself."

"Care to explain?"

His cool response irritated her even more. She narrowed her eyes.

"You wish me to explain? Okay. I will." She jerked her hand back before Peter grasped it. "The way you look at your little sister while dancing with me is simply maddening. The way you ogle that child like she's something... something special."

"She is special, Julie," Peter's voice became deceptively soft.

His eyes grew dark and cold like two gemstones ready to be cut. If Julie were less agitated, she might have been a little scared, so dangerously still and intense was his face, so alert and poised his stance. But her anger at him won, especially at that spooky little kid, to truly fathom what he might do. Seething, she plowed ahead, "She's also a child, for God's sake. And your *sister*. Yeah, only half-sister, but still. What kind of man are you, Rostoff?"

At the loud sounds of a brewing argument, a small army of older guests stepped from the house outside, to see what was going on. Soon any attempt to ignore the quarrel between the guest of honor and his girlfriend became impossible. All conversations around Peter and Julie ceased to exist. Everyone stopped and openly stared at the young couple.

The music still blared, but even the sounds of a popular hit failed to muffle Julie's voice. The fight festered, but no one tried to stop it.

CHAPTER THIRTY-FOUR

D mitry left the drink he was nursing all evening and hurried toward the noise, then stepped between the young people. He sensed a tiny figure following him. Stopping just a few feet from Peter and his date, he didn't bother to hide his growing annoyance.

Damn that Julie.

Somehow Dmitry knew trouble followed that girl from the moment Peter introduced them. For some reason, he disliked Julie on the spot, tensing at the sight of a cold beauty clinging to Peter's arm like a strangling vine.

He missed the beginning of her tirade, but what he did overhear locked his jaw, and boiled his blood.

"What do you mean by that, Julie?" Peter's voice came out mild and soft, but Dmitry knew his son too well. The boy was strung tight, and mad as hell.

An indifferent, almost bored look on Peter's face combined with a full battle stance, and his quiet voice made an extremely dangerous combination. His son teetered on the brink. And that girl was either too enraged or too stupid to recognize it. Dmitry opted for the second. Peter stood poised, and ready to strike. Murder blazed in his son's eyes. Time to squelch the situation.

Dmitry was about to interfere, when Natasha's voice knifed the charged silence.

"I think that's enough excitement for tonight, Peter." Her accented English added a note of coolness and firm finality. Just for a second Dmitry marveled at her melodic pronunciation before Julie's next remark broke his spell.

"And who the hell are you, barging in here and interrupting our argument? Servants are supposed to stay invisible, or did you forget your place?"

Dmitry saw red. But before he could reply, Katia's clear voice erupted with barely controlled anger, "She's our mother, you stupid cow! And don't you dare talk to her that way!" Katia's small body trembled, her tiny fists balled. Her face was awash with barely controlled indignation.

The complete and total silence that followed Katia's outburst grew deafening.

"Oh, how touching." Dripping with sarcasm, Julie's voice became harsh and cruel. Her face twisted into a horror mask. "The family is presenting a united front. The prodigal father, the loyal son, the surrogate mommy, and the little bastard."

"Shut up!" Peter exploded. He fisted his hands as he stepped forward.

The deep guttural growl Dmitry barely recognized as his own scared the gaping crowd. Natasha sucked in air while Katia uttered a small sound of distress. Peter jerked his head, blinked several times like coming out of a stupor or a deep shock. Dmitry figured it was a combination of both. His son relaxed his hands, then tucked them into the pockets of his slacks. His breathing, however, remained labored and uneven.

"I think your girlfriend overstayed her welcome, Peter. Show her out."

Frostbite in Dmitry's voice didn't mask his anger. Peter nodded, then turned toward Julie.

CHAPTER THIRTY-FIVE

Confronted by both Rostoffs glaring at her in silence, a real fear swept over Julie. The father's eyes, pale grey, almost silver, scorched her to the bone with their chilling intensity. Not a threat, Julie thought in panic, but a promise of retribution. Uneasy under his stare, she failed to suppress a shudder. Julie wished he'd stop looking at her like that. She switched her glance to Peter, and lost her breath. Hard and drawn, his face that she knew so well became the face of a stranger. She recognized resentment in his stare, and something else that she failed to put a name to. Hatred? Disgust?

Oh, God, what have I done?

Who knew that Peter was so sensitive when it came to the little brat's nanny? Protectiveness toward his half-sister she understood. To a point. But such a strong reaction toward a servant? Unthinkable. Something wasn't right with this family.

Aren't they supposed to be of noble blood?

Julie scanned the room, desperately searching for one sympathetic face. Surely, the female part of the guests weren't so judgmental. Jumping from face to face, her eyes finally landed on the short redhead. The nanny.

The woman kept her hand on the little girl's shoulder, as her glowering green eyes sent daggers at Julie. Cold panic zipped through her body. If both Rostoffs emotions were tucked under rigid masks, the woman didn't try to hide her temper. She all but vibrated from it.

And that brat... Julie shivered, looking at the girl. If the grownup's gazes frightened her, then those eerie spooky dark-grey eyes petrified her.

She wished she had never come to this damn party tonight. She wished she had never meet Peter's family. Especially, his little sister.

Desperate to escape, she sprinted away, almost tripping in her haste.

In total silence, the crowd parted before her like the Red Sea in front of Moses, creating a corridor.

CHAPTER THIRTY-SIX

P eter stood in the middle of the empty dance floor, and glanced around the room now that the guests all fled. Caterers managed to clear away the remaining food and drinks, and clean up the area, except for the decorations and flowers Natasha so painstakingly chose for his imfamouse birthday party. Hundreds of balloons, now half deflated and pitiful, floated drunkenly around. A few jerked spasmodically on their ribbons, trying to escape. Long tables stood naked now, stripped of their cheerful covers. The maintenance men were ordered to take them away tomorrow. Everything around him looked exactly as he felt: lost and miserable.

Happy fucking birthday.

Peter never imagined that inviting Julie might hurt Katie or Natasha. It never crossed his mind that Katie, his sweet little princess, might be caught in a crossfire. As usual, he went to kiss her goodnight. Her question "What is a bastard?" simply destroyed him. So, Peter ran away without answering her question. Because he didn't know what to say. With some sixth sense, Katie knew it was a bad word, but she failed to understand its meaning. Thank God for small favors. He frowned, fighting down the anger that built inside him. Knowing Katie's curiosity and her tenacity, she will ask that same question again and again. Eventually, she'll find out what a *bastard* means. Should he tell her, explain? It must be kinder to find out from someone she knew and loved, like him or Natasha. Probably. The perfect moment presented itself tonight, but God help him, Peter hadn't the heart to do it. He just couldn't. He was still raw and vulnerable after the grand finale of his party to deal with this.

A disaster of major proportions. And what did you expect?

Peter cursed again, raked all ten fingers through his hair. Hell. On some basic level, he knew—sensed—that something unpleasant might happen. But he sensed the seed of his uneasiness sprouted from his father's visit. No question, it was difficult for everybody. But Julie? Dammit, he never expected trouble from that direction.

Hands down, tonight's fiasco was no one's fault but his.

Julie's nasty behavior disgusted him. But what shook him to the core, the discovery of his own weakness: his volatile nature. For the first time in his life,

Peter lost his control in the snap of a finger. After Julie delivered her last remark, he wanted nothing less than to put his bare hands around her throat, and break it in two. He imagined it so clearly and vividly in his mind, he almost felt that silky skin under his fingers. Almost see the look of wonder and shock swimming into her deep blue eyes as his hands squeezed.

The sheer force of his rage made him deaf and blind and mean as hell. For some terrifying moments, his vision dimmed, narrowed to a tunnel. His ears rang, his heart thundered. Julie dared to touch something pure and clean, something he considered sacred, and sullied it. She deserved to be punished.

Thank God for his father. Like a splash of icy water in the face, Dmitry's voice shattered Peter's rage, and managed to pull him away from pure madness. Gradually, Peter's senses and the reality of the moment came back, but it cost him a great deal. For the first time, he understood the exact extent of his temper. Savage. Wild. Ferocious.

And only an enormous self-discipline, and his father's timely interference saved Peter from stepping over the line. It scared him, terrified him like nothing else.

Which of his ancestors was responsible for this killer instinct of a warrior?

Does it matter? Clearly Peter flat out inherited that instinct.

What now?

He could either tuck it in the farthest corner of his conscious mind, and hide it, or simply accept it, and learn to control that explosive murderous rage. Otherwise, it might take control over him. And maybe even take him under. What did Nietzsche say? When you are looking long into an abyss, it will look back into you? Well, that abyss Peter stared into tonight shook him to the core.

CHAPTER THIRTY-SEVEN

Natasha's heart broke as she watched the boy, she considered her own from across the room. His current mood was written all over him from his stiff posture to the expression on his face. Bewildered, hurt, vulnerable.

Damn it, his birthday, it should have been the happiest day of the year!

Instead, it became a disaster.

She wanted to go to him, to hug him, to comfort, but feared he might reject her kindness. Petya had grown into a man.

Then again, Petya wasn't a boy since he came to live with them. Five years ago, Natasha took him under her wing. He allowed her take him under her wing because he trusted her. And she never betrayed his trust. She tried to be his friend, not his mother, no matter how hard she wanted it. Because then, the boy needed a friend and confidant first and foremost. He lost his mother under the most tragic circumstances. Shocked and bewildered, Petya turned to her in his moment of grief. Her instinct to protect him and offer comfort came as no surprise. But now, she hated seeing Peter so lost, so tormented. Natasha approached him with great care, then wrapped her arms around his rigid body. After the initial tensing, he relaxed. He laid his hands over hers, then held her tight. Natasha rested her head against his chest, inhaling his dear, familiar scent. Like Petya, it too changed with years, becoming more dark, strong, and masculine. She smiled, burrowing her nose in the fabric of his shirt. Her boy had grown into a man in every essence of the word.

Ridiculous, but an odd uneasiness crept through Natasha. The first time she noticed those differences in Peter, she almost panicked. She wasn't ready to let go of the darling boy she loved with all her heart. What did she know about men? Nothing. Absolutely nothing. Should she talk with him about sex and girls? God forbid. Natasha left that subject to Dmitry, thank you very much.

She felt awkward and ill at ease, and unwilling to broach that issue.

Dammit, she was still a virgin. What could she possibly share with the young man on the topic of sex? How might she guide him, or lecture him, while she herself was totally ignorant on the subject?

Natasha sighed. The role of a mother proved extremely difficult at times. Never mind that she only had surrogate status. But she also was his best friend, and knew him well. Maybe even better than he knew himself. And that knowledge gave her the insight about what bothered him the most now.

She finally broke the silence. "It's not a crime, you know."

"What's that, Gorgeous?"

"To lose your temper, to want to hurt someone so badly that your guts churn with it."

Petya stilled, but didn't pull away from her.

"How did you know?"

The note of shame and wariness in his voice touched her soul.

"I know you."

Peter chuckled without any merriment. "My God, Natasha, sometimes it's scary, you know."

"What is, *miliy?*"

"Your ability to read my mind."

"I just saw your face... you're not very good at controlling your emotions."

"Wrong. I am very good at it, just ask anyone. But you," he added circling her small waist with both hands, "you are a dangerous woman, Natalia." The mocking scowl on his face was endearing and familiar. Natasha fainted a surprise.

"Me?"

"Yes, you."

CHAPTER THIRTY-EIGHT

P eter dropped a quick kiss on Natasha's nose, then tucked her head under his chin. She was so tiny, this little adorable woman he began to feel awkward around. Ridiculous, really. But he was so much taller, and larger than her, he was afraid to damage her.

"Petya, there is not a dangerous bone in my body." Natasha's peep of protest came out serious. She leaned backward, and squinted at him. "I just love you."

"That's the whole point, Gorgeous. Love." He smiled at her. "You are the first woman I fell in love with, you know."

She offered him a radiant smile, one that lit up the darkest night.

"I still do, although my teenage crush on you changed in time, mind you." He tapped her perky little nose. "But you're still the one and the only woman I truly and deeply love. And I'm not afraid to say it."

"*Dorogoy moy,*" Natasha's smile turned wistful, and a little sad. "One day you'll meet the right woman, the one and the only. You will fall in love with her, and then you'll never be afraid to say it. Ever."

He disagreed, but preferred to keep his thoughts to himself.

"If and when I meet this woman, she'll be second best, because I will never ever in a million years be able to find a woman like you, Natasha."

"Never say never, Petya," she scolded him with humor.

He laughed and let the tension of the evening finally slip away. "You are amazing, Gorgeous."

"No, I'm not."

"Yes, you are. You became a mother to me when I lost my own; you became the best friend when I needed one badly. You healed me when I hurt, and gave me the strength to believe in a family when my own crumbled apart. You showed me kindness and gave me your love, and for that, I will be entirely grateful to you. You saved me from a disaster, from self-destruction, when I was at my most vulnerable. You became my anchor in life."

Natasha's eyes misted. Smiling tremulously, she touched his hair. Catching her hand in his, he brought her fingers to his mouth. He kissed her hand as he did thousands of times before, but something felt different now, and knew she did too.

"You, small and tiny creature, pack such strength and power, Natasha. You are the most amazing woman I've ever met. And I'm honored to have you as a mother and friend."

"Petya..." Her whisper was barely audible. For a long moment, they just stood there, looking at each other in comfortable silence.

"Can I ask you something?" Peter cleared his throat.

"Anything, *miliy*."

"Don't you ever wish to have a family and kids of your own?"

"No." Her answer rang with absolute sincerely. "You and Katia are my family, my children. I always thought of you as mine. In my heart, you both are mine."

"But what about love?"

"What about it?" Did Natasha tense?

"No, don't you freeze up on me, Gorgeous." When she tried to pull from his embrace, he tightened his hold. "I know you loved once. Deeply. Am I wrong?"

"You know the truth, Petya." She lowered her gaze.

"He hurt you."

"Yes. He didn't mean to. He just... didn't love me back. It happens, you know. More often than not."

"Yeah, I know. What I wonder is, was it worth it?"

Natasha slowly lifted her eyes. He really couldn't say why her answer meant so much to him, but he held his breath waiting for her answer.

"Yes, dear, it was worth everything. And then some."

He nodded, while he held her eyes with his. "You're still in love with him."

"Yes, Petya. I am. Are you upset?"

Peter mulled that for a moment. "No, not upset, no. It just... It makes me sad."

"Why?"

"Because he'll leave, and you'll be hurt again. I hate to see you hurt."

"Thank you, *miliy moy*." She gently disengaged herself from his arms, then stepped backward. "Let's not talk about it, okay?"

"Okay." Once again, misery flooded Peter. He couldn't change anything, couldn't shield the woman he loved from pain and hurt that will come. And that impotence ate him alive.

"I was so mad, you know," she said, changing the subject. "Your party was such a smashing success until that vile girl... I wanted it to be perfect for you. I'm sorry, Petya."

"Don't be. You gave me a wonderful party. As for Julie... you know, I'm even glad now. Relieved. We dated exclusively for some time, and she began to hint for something more permanent."

"Dear Lord!" Natasha whirled around, looking at him with an expression of pure horror on her face.

"No, not *that* permanent," he chuckled, amused despite everything.

"Thank God," she muttered.

"Yeah, well..." All humor slipped away, leaving him unsure and depressed. "She said she loved me."

"And you...?" Natasha prodded gently.

"I don't know. I felt... uncomfortable, even panicky. It's not supposed to be like that when you're really and truly in love, is it? I mean, that panic and everything..."

"No, it is not."

"I thought if I really loved her, I wouldn't be so uneasy. Or so afraid."

"No, I don't think so."

"It bothered me, but deep down I knew I wasn't ready for it, you know. And after tonight..." He raked his hair one handed. "Needless to say, it's over. And I'm glad I discovered her true nature now."

"Well, there's always something good even in a bad situation, isn't there?"

"Always an optimist," Peter chuckled but sobered quickly. "She hurt Katie. She insulted you, and I didn't do anything to prevent it."

"Petya, who put you in charge of the world?" Natasha asked softly.

"I still had to stop her before... before, you know."

"No, I don't know, and you can't control other people, darling. She was angry and wanted to hurt you, so she chose the dearest to your heart— your sister. Although I understand her psyche, I still wanted to kill her myself."

"And so did I." He glanced down, frowning. "Katie asked me what bastard means."

Natasha sucked in sharply. "What did you answer?"

"Nothing. I said nothing, Natasha. I'm sorry. I just couldn't."

"It's all right. I... I will try to explain it to her tomorrow. Better me than anybody else, don't you think?" But she shivered.

"Yeah, she'll find out, anyway. Dammit!" He kicked at the loose stones, helplessly raging inside. "I'm sorry, Natasha. I put you in a hot spot with this. It's all my fault."

"Stop it, Petya. It's not your fault, and you know it."

Peter shook his head. "Natasha, I love Katie, she's my baby sister. And Julie... she hinted at something so dirty and... unthinkable..."

CHAPTER THIRTY-NINE

U*h-oh.*
  Natasha was almost afraid of what might come next. The conversation promised to be difficult, and she desperately needed a few moments to compose herself. Taking Petya by the hand, she gently tugged him toward the small settee nearby.

After a second of resistance, he obliged. She sat, and drew in a calming breath.

"That Julie is one mean and a nasty girl, Petya. Whatever she hinted at is very sick and unworthy of repeating. No one would ever take it seriously. Especially, the people who know you. Forget it, darling. Forget that vicious girl."

"She made it sound so... dirty. She made *me* dirty."

"I know, *miliy,* I know." She went to him then, framing his face with her hands. Fire burned in her when the tormented look in Peter's eyes registered.

That malicious ugly creature camouflaged in the body of a beautiful young woman managed to hurt both her children. But Petya especially.

Damn you, Julie. Damn you, and your sharp poisonous tongue. How could you do this to him if you claim to love him?

Natasha stressed, with all the motherly firmness she was able to muster, "Listen to me, Petya. What she said was a lie. A deliberate, hateful revenge. She lashed out to hurt you, and she did. Don't let it matter, *miliy*, or she will win. And I hate to let that bitch win. Please, Petya, let it go."

"Natasha, this... happens sometimes. I'm familiar with the works of Freud."

"There *are* sick weirdoes in this world, so what?"

"You don't understand. My mother...she told me a long time ago that Grandmother loved her own nephew, and not in a good way, who was just a few years older than Dad. God, it's so sick..." Peter shook his head, awerted his gaze. His voice dropped to a mere whisper. "Grandmother seduced him when he was barely fifteen years old."

God almighty.

Natasha's guts knotted into a tight fist. Sour bile rose up, burning her throat.

For Petya's sake, she controlled her reaction. But inside, she raged.

Whatever possessed a mother to revealed such an ugly secret to her son?

What was Polina thinking, dragging these skeletons from the family closet, and poisoning a young boy's mind?

"Petya, I'm sure it is not true."

"Unfortunately, it is true. My mother knew the nephew, and he told her himself."

"God, that's disgusting!" A cold and violent shudder charged through her.

For a split second, Natasha heard a noise coming from the bushes behind her.

Who is outside at this hour?

Everybody should be tucked in for the night, safe and sound. She had more pressing matters now than wondering about strange noises.

CHAPTER FORTY

"Yes, it is disgusting," Petya replied quietly. "His name was Alexei. That's his portrait on the second floor. "

One that looks like me. Or is it I who looks like him?

A ripple of fear swirled through his body, chilling his heart. Peter did his best to fight it off.

"So, I can't help but wonder: maybe it is also in my genes? Like the color of hair or eyes. Maybe—"

"Stop, please." Natasha's harsh voice interrupted him mid-sentence. "Whatever happened, or not happened, between your grandmother and that Alexei, has nothing to do with you. We can't be sure he told the truth, can we?"

"I don't know. He died a long time ago. I never met him."

"Exactly." She nodded. "So you don't know what kind of person he was. Maybe, he just lied to your mother. Maybe it as a joke."

Peter snorted. "Rather a stupid joke, don't you think?"

"Stupid?" Natasha shook her head. "I'd call it ridiculous. And distasteful. And obnoxious." She was so cute when angry, Peter almost laughed. Then he sobered and frowned.

"But that infamous portrait. Grandmother hung it in a most visible spot. Why?"

"Along with a dozen other portraits of your ancestors." She reminded him.

But Peter knew Natasha hated that portrait as much as him.

Why had Elizabeth ordered to display it just a few weeks ago? It hung in her bedroom for ages. Why she chose to change its place was a real mystery. Whenever Peter saw it, it gave him the creeps.

Strange, but Katia too, appeared uncomfortable around that portrait. She claimed the man reminded her of him. The resemblance was easily explained, taking into consideration the blood relation between him and the man in the picture.

But still, it made Katia uneasy, and a little frightened.

I wonder why.

"But did you notice..." Peter swallowed around the lump in his throat.

"What, *miliy*?"

He hesitated, then shrugged. "Nothing, really. But sometimes I can't help but wonder about the tricky way of genetics." He thrust his hands in the pockets of his slacks, and softened his voice. "Here is my baby sister who looks exactly like her grandmother, and here I am, looking like my late uncle. You noticed, don't you?"

Natasha hesitated. The loud sound of running footsteps startled them both. They jumped from their seats and turned toward the noise. Dmitry burst into the clearing, then halted to a stop. After one look at his father's dark, drawn face, Peter knew something was terribly wrong. He tensed.

"Dad, what is it?"

Gasping for air, Dmitry stared at him, his silver eyes wide and full of desperation. Peter never saw that expression on his father's face before. His gut squeezed.

He repeated louder, "Dad? What's the matter?"

"I have to leave." Dmitry answered in a harsh voice. He stared at Peter, then at Natasha and back again. "I have to go back to Paris."

Natasha's soft gasp echoed in his ears. More alarmed than disappointed, Peter frowned. Something was wrong. Very wrong.

"But...now?"

"Right now. Immediately."

CHAPTER FORTY-ONE

"What happened?" Natasha asked softly. Whatever happened, must be horrid.

Dmitry's blood-shot eyes landed on her. He blinked, like he only now realized she was here.

"Natasha, I have to go, but I'll be back. I promise. I need to... No, not now." Shaking his head, he interrupted himself. "When I come back, we need to decide. We will talk, and decide, and..."

The words tumbled from his mouth, desperate and urgent, as his eyes implored with her. Silently, she nodded.

Peter grabbed Dmitry's arm. "Dad, tell me what's this all about."

"There was an accident. Vlad."

Vladimir Albrecht. Natasha remembered Dmitry's friend and second in command. No wonder his hands trembled.

"Oh, my God! Is he okay?"

"I don't know, son. I just got a call from Marie. She's hysterical. I couldn't reach the hospital. Dammit, how many times I warned him..." Dmitry plowed his hands into his already disheveled hair, and swore. "He's driving too fast, too reckless. Christ!" He reeled around, swore, then fixed his eyes on Peter.

"I need a ride to the airport. I hate to wake up my driver, and besides, he is in San Francisco, so it'll take him at least an hour-and-a-half to get here. And I cannot drive myself because I had a few drinks at the party. I would risk it, but..." Dmitry outstretched his shaky hands. "As ashamed as I am to confess it, I am in no shape to drive."

"Of course I'll drive you, Dad," Peter added quickly.

"I'll drive you." Natasha didn't know who was more surprised by her offer, she or both Rostoffs. The father and son stared at her in mute shock. "Natasha—"

"Gorgeous—"

Rolling over them, Natasha added firmly, "I'll give you a lift to the airport, Dmitry." Then faced Peter. " I need to talk to your father. It's urgent and can't wait until his return."

"But..."

"Don't worry, Petya. I'll be fine." Her decision was made. "I'll be fine, I promise."

Peter seemed unsure and hesitant, but Natasha's mind was set. "Please, *miliy*, don't fight me on that one," she added softly.

Finally, with a great reluctance, he relented. "Be careful, Natasha. Be very, very careful. Promise me."

"I promise."

Natasha ran to fetch her purse, after arranging to meet Dmitry by his rental car in ten minutes. She checked in on Katia one more time, and pacified both dogs, then hurried downstairs. She hugged Peter, and promised she'd be back safe and sound. She slid into the driver's seat. Peter scowled. Natasha noted his pale, grim face in her rearview mirror as she pulled out of the winding long driveway.

For some time, they drove in total silence.

"Why did you do it?" Dmitry asked at last.

"Do what?"

"Insist on driving instead of Peter?"

"It's very late, and he's had quite an emotional day. I also know how much he likes to drive fast, so..." She shrugged. "I worry about him."

"And that's why you volunteered to drive me to the airport," he stated coolly.

What's wrong with him? You'd think the father might appreciate her concern for the boy's safety. Dammit.

"Yes, that's why." Her response came out dry and sharp. After a long-charged silence, she decided the heck with it. She needed to concentrate on the road. Natasha wasn't used to driving in the dark. Petya knew that. After all, despite Elizabeth's disapproval, he taught her how to drive. She avoided looking at her passenger, and with great determination concentrated on the road.

After what seemed like forever, Dmitry broke the silence.

"You don't really need to talk to me, do you?"

"No." She replied curtly while maneuvering a narrow part of the road that led to the intersection.

"So, it was only a pretense for Peter's sake."

"Basically, yes."

"You lied."

That cool accusatory tone of voice gritted on her nerves.

Annoyed by his interrogation, Natasha snapped. "Yes, I did. So sue me."

"Peter was reluctant to let you drive."

"No kidding." Finally reaching the freeway, Natasha muttered a prayer. In truth, she hated driving.

"He seemed even more reluctant to leave you in my company."

"What are you talking about?" With her attention divided between the freeway and Dmitry, the last thing she needed right now was this stupid conversation.

"He warned me to leave you alone."

"He did what!" Taken aback, she tore her gaze from the road long enough to look at him.

"Watch the road, Natasha."

She immediately tore her eyes from Dmitry.

Quietly, he added, "He warned me to stay away from you."

"Good Lord! I can't believe it!"

"Several times, actually."

"But why?"

"You don't know?" Raising one eyebrow in mocked surprise, he challenged her.

"Well, he didn't have to. That's ridiculous. I'm a grown woman, for goodness' sake. I can manage perfectly well to look out for myself, thank you very much."

She didn't know if she should be insulted or ashamed. As if she was a pea-brained idiot. As if she couldn't avoid trouble, and stay away from the likes of Dmitry Rostoff.

Did you? Did you manage to stay away from him, Natasha? What about yesterday?

Oh, shut up!

Natasha silently snapped at her nemesis, her inner voice. Oh, how she hated it sometimes. Like right now.

As if reading her mind, Dmitry asked in a soft voice, "Then what were you doing in my room yesterday, Natasha?"

She opened her mouth, shut it again, all the while seething.

Damn him.

"I came to your room to talk, nothing more. What happened next..." she hesitated.

"Yes? What happened next?" He prodded.

"Was as much my fault as yours." She shot back, losing her control. "Only a kiss, for goodness' sake. Nothing more."

"Just a kiss?" Dmitry twisted in his seat to look at her, then he repeated, "*Just* a kiss? Well, let me tell you, lady. If not for that blasted dog of yours, you'd be out of your clothes in the nick of time, and flat on your back, under me."

"Oh, yeah?" Natasha grew angrier because he was absolutely right.

"Yeah. And you know what else? You'd be liking every moment of it."

Too humiliated for a retort, Natasha bit her lip.

Dmitry swore out loud.

"I'm sorry."

She'd rather die than acknowledge his apology.

"I'm really sorry, Natasha," he repeated in a weary voice. "God, what a day."

He rubbed his eyes, then laid his head back, propping it against the headrest.

Natasha cleared her throat but remained quiet.

After several minutes, he turned and looked at her.

"Still mad at me?"

"I don't know."

"At yourself?"

"Yes." This time she didn't hesitate. His soft chuckle caressed her ears.

"It was bound to happen, you know."

"What?"

"You, me, us. That kiss. Perhaps it is for the best that your dog interrupted us. It was too soon, too much. You weren't ready. And honesty, me neither."

"You could've fooled me," she muttered before she thought better of it.

Dmitry twisted toward her, his eyes flashing in the dim interior like lightning. Natasha wished she bit her tongue instead of her lip. Or better yet, found a deep dark hole and hid in it. A typical knowing, masculine smile spread on his face. That smug smile said he knew exactly what went through her mind.

"Dammit, why is it every time I am in your company, I behave like a brainless fool?" She muttered more to herself than to him.

Dmitry grinned, then grew serious. "Natasha, look at me." Stubbornly, she refused to oblige. When she braked at the red light, he reached out with one hand, and angled her face toward him.

"I want you." He said it simply, sincerely. Her insides began to melt. "I've wanted you from the moment I saw you." Answering her surprised look, he nodded. "Yes, I wanted you even then, in Moscow. You looked like a street urchin, and I just lost a woman I loved. But it didn't matter. My blood boiled every time I spotted you. I'd become so hard so quickly, pure torture, not to mention embarrassing."

Frozen in mute shock, Natasha couldn't believe what she heard. She searched his eyes. Was he telling the truth? My God, yes.

After a moment, Dmitry continued, "I was angry at myself. Mad. My only wish was to get away as soon as possible, and never see you again. But the problem with the adoption interfered. I couldn't do it without your help. Was I relived? Yes. Angry? Absolutely. But mostly, scared, because that made me stuck with you forever. I told myself I was just horny, or insane from grief and pain. I've found thousands of excuses for myself, but still I wanted you. More and more every day. And Katia... and all that mess..." He let go of her face and leaned back again. Furious sounding horns jerked her to reality. She put her foot on the gas pedal and propelled the car forward. She stared at the road with such intensity her eyes hurt.

"Why do you think I behaved like a bastard? Why did I send you and the baby to my mother's the very next day?"

"To get rid of us," she managed through the lump in her throat.

"To a point, yes. But mostly to rid myself of temptation. Of you. I couldn't touch you. You were so innocent, so vulnerable. Bewildered. And you were grieving. It killed me to see you under my roof, and not be able to touch you."

"Did it ever occur to you that maybe I wanted to be touched?"

"Yes, it did. I knew you wanted me, too."

"Why, then...?"

"Because I couldn't give you more than sex, and you deserved better. Much better."

The simple truth of his statement devastated her. Like a fist in the solar plexus, it robbed her of breath.

"So, you tried to save me from yourself." Why didn't she see that five years ago?

"Yes."

"Even knowing how I felt."

"Yes."

The silence fell, uncomfortable, deafening. She wanted to cry.

After a long pause, Dmitry inhaled deeply.

"It didn't work. You spoiled me for any other woman. You bewitched my dreams, got under my skin, into my blood."

She briefly closed her eyes. Her hands became so sweaty she had trouble holding the steering wheel. Clutching it with both hands like a life-saver, fighting her tears, Natasha drove ahead.

Again he cursed. This time softly, helplessly.

"Elizabeth saw it immediately. I guess, I'm more transparent than I wish to believe. So, she sent me to France."

"And you obeyed." It was not a question, but a statement. An accusation.

"Yes, I obeyed. I told myself I have no business messing up your life. I left because I knew how close I came to seducing you. Even despite my best intentions. You remember that evening in the gardens?"

"Yes. I remember everything."

"Someone watched us, and reported to Elizabeth."

Horrified, Natasha gasped. "You mean, someone spied on me?"

"You or me. She confronted me the next day, and threatened to make your life a living hell. Then she mentioned Peter."

"Petya? What had Petya to do with it?"

"Nothing, but it didn't matter to her. Elizabeth knew he was the only thing I truly loved, so she decided to play her ace card. Gave me the ultimatum: to leave you and Katia alone, and get the hell away from your lives forever, or she'd make Peter suffer. Because of me. "

"How?"

"I don't know exactly. But I never doubted for a moment she could and would do just that. My mother has a devious mind and ruthlessness of a tigress. I couldn't let that happened, Natasha. I couldn't jeopardize the welfare of my son. Or your well-being. I felt responsible for you. I dragged you from your country under false documents. I knew you burned all bridges coming to my aid. You also didn't have any legal papers. You understand?"

Bewildered, she shook her head. Calmly, Dmitry explained, "One call to the immigration, and you'd be deported back to Russia in twenty-four hours."

The full implication of his words hit her like a sledgehammer. Yes, five years ago Elizabeth could make her life a living hell by simply reporting her to the authorities. Her visa was false, her papers regarding Katia's adoption meant nothing to Naturalization offices. And going back to communist Russia in 1990 after her departure with false documents, and under the dubious pretense of having relatives in America, meant one thing only: KGB, an ultimate arrest.

Probably for the rest of her life. Shocked to the core, and unable to shake off the fear that shot through her, Natasha sucked in a deep breath.

"Now you understand."

"Yes, now I do." Instantly she remembered. "So, that's why you warned me to hide Katia's adoption papers?"

"Yes. I wanted you to have some kind of leverage if things got nasty. It is an official document of sorts. I doubted it could help very much, but still."

God, all this time she was blind. He protected her all those years ago, placing her well-being before his own. Because he felt responsible. Because he *cared*.

He bought her freedom in exchange of his own, shielding her from his mother's wrath, and his own desire. Dmitry traded his pride for her peace of mind.

God, how could she not love him?

She loved him from the first, but her feelings were that of a naive girl blinded by confusion and newly discovered passion. He simply dazzled her. To her, Dmitry Rostoff was Prince Charming, handsome, aloof, magnificent. Perfect.

Now, a mature woman, who experienced pain and loss, she loved him deeply.

Truly.

Unquestionably.

Her love, tested by time and heartache, miraculously survived. And transformed into something bigger and stronger.

As she looked at him now, Natasha realized he wasn't Prince Charming, but a man, complex and imperfect, a human being with his faults and shortcomings.

Now she looked beyond the magnificent exterior and see the soul, kind and pure, sad, and troubled. God, how she loved him.

"So I made a deal with the she-devil, and left," Dmitry continued, completely unaware of Natasha's inner turmoil. "Then Polina attempted to kill Katia, and all hell broke loose."

Once again, he fell silent. Desperately trying not to cry, Natasha concentrated on the road and prayed to get them safely to their destination.

But she needed to know the whole truth. "Why did you leave like that? After the funeral. Why did you just disappear without a word?"

"You still don't know what happened five years ago, do you?"

"No."

"Elizabeth didn't explain? About my departure, and her retirement?"

"She said she decided to dedicate all her time to her granddaughter, that she was too old and tired, and chose to retire and turn the company over to you."

"And you believed her?"

"I didn't know what or who to believe. After the attack..." She swallowed, then cleared her dry throat. "Everything happened so fast. The police, interrogations, and then the funeral. I was afraid to lose my mind. Katia was just a baby and Petya... God, he was so tormented, hurting. And then you left."

CHAPTER FORTY-TWO

"And then I left." Dmitry's quiet reply sent a ripple of goosebumps along her spine.

She braked at the red light, and turned to look at him. He stared at her, his silver eyes full of sorrow and sadness.

Then he turned away, and looked straight ahead. When he began to talk, his voice came out cool and detached.

"My mother wanted to destroy me, Natasha. I still don't know why. I don't know when or how she came to that decision. I only know that five years ago she jeopardized the company to the point of almost no return. She made sure that everything pointed back at me. Because I never expected it, I didn't understand it. Never paid attention, but thankfully, Vlad did. You met him."

"Yes, I remember him."

The light changed. She pulled away, driving slower than the limit, listening to Dmitry.

"So, he gathered the evidence on his own, and confronted Elizabeth. He presented her with the ultimatum: go to jail or retire and turn over the reins of power to me.

"She made her choice. After that, I couldn't live under her roof. I couldn't stomach to even hear about her, not to mention see her. She ceased to exist for me. And when I realized how much damage was done to the company, I became mad. Mostly at myself. For my stupidity, for letting my personal feelings blind me to the degree where I almost lost the business. It took me a long time to fix things, to put everything back together. I don't know if I would have succeeded without Vlad."

Thick and raw, his voice trailed off. She hazarded a quick glance at him. Pain and sorrow crept into his eyes, darkening his face. Natasha understood. His best friend, the one who saved Dmitry's reputation, and his company, was now in danger. Silently, she reached out her hand, and covered his white-knuckled fist.

"I hope he'll pull through."

"Yeah, so do I."

After a long time, Dmitry shifted his body.

"You understand why I have to leave now, don't you, Natasha?"

"My God, of course, I understand. You must be with your friend. You are needed there. I would do the same."

"Will you explain it to Katia? Please? I don't want her to think that I... that I abandoned her again."

"I'll explain to her, Dmitry. She'll understand, I promise."

Seemingly relived, he slumped into his seat. "Tell her I'll be back as soon as possible."

"I will."

"I'll be back, Natasha," he murmured. "Do you believe me?"

"Yes."

"I wanted to talk to you about Katia and ... everything, but, damn it all to hell, timing is all wrong now."

"I understand."

"I want to change it, Natasha."

"What?"

"Everything: the children, me, you. I want to make up for my mistakes. I want to take Katia from my mother."

"Absolutely not!"

CHAPTER FORTY-THREE

Natasha's sharp reply threw him off. More surprised than insulted, Dmitry stared at her. Did she really say '*absolutely not*'? He never expected that from her.

Unbelievable.

After a lengthy pause, he finally found his voice. "Why?"

"Dmitry, she's a living, breathing person." Agitated, she dragged her eyes from the road, shook her head. "She has feelings."

"I'm well aware of that. And?"

Natasha glared at him and demanded, "Tell me, why you want her."

"She's my daughter."

"She was your daughter five years ago, too. Why now, Dmitry?"

"I met her."

"You met her, okay. So what?"

"Damn it, Natasha! She's a kid with an extraordinary talent. She lives with a monster of a grandmother who will destroy her given half the chance."

Natasha ripped her gaze from Dmitry, and concentrated on driving.

"I agree, but again, you should've considered that five years ago. And by the way, I live with her, too. Do you think I will let anybody harm her, even Elizabeth?"

"Natasha, you don't know my mother. Christ, weren't you listening to me? She is a dangerous, cold and ruthless and cunning. She's obsessed with an idea of an heiress that has nothing to do with love for a child. Katia is nothing to her, nothing! She's just the obsession of a sick person. She'll destroy her, and you too, if you stand in her way."

"That's my problem, isn't it?"

"God, woman, are you deliberately trying to annoy me? Because if you are, you're succeeding!"

After a few calming breaths, Natasha faced him. Somber, her green eyes watched him.

"Tell me something, Dmitry. Do you love your daughter?"

Dammit.

He couldn't lie. Not to her, not to himself.

"I don't know."

She held his gaze for a heartbeat longer, then nodded. Dmitry had a sinking feeling he didn't pass the test.

"Well, then it's better just to leave things as they are."

"I don't understand. I just told you I want my daughter back. I thought you of all the people will be elated."

"Really? To sweep Katia away from everything familiar, from the only place she calls home, from the people she loves? And for what? For the sole purpose of soothing your conscience? And you assumed I would be elated?"

"That's not why I want to take her, and you know it!"

"No, I don't. And what's more important, neither do you. When you know for sure *why* you want your daughter back, when you feel you need it—not just wish it, but really truly need it— then we will talk again."

"Dammit, I hoped you might understand, that you'd be on my side with this."

"I am only on Katia's side, Dmitry, and no one else's. Not even yours."

Calm and quiet, her response grated on his nerves. Hurt down to his soul, he looked away.

"Well, you made that clear enough."

Seething, he exited the car, then slammed the door. He knew, pissed as she was, the tires had to screech as she spun drove away. But she surprised him. Hearing the click of the car door behind him, he turned and glanced over his shoulder. Shoulders squared, back ramrod straight, she glared at him for a moment, then marched ahead.

In total silence, he trailed behind her to the International Terminal of San Francisco airport.

CHAPTER FORTY-FOUR

Time was of the essence for Dmitry. Because his private plane sat in a hangar at a different airport, he booked a commercial flight to France. But his name and status clearly commanded a lot of attention from the airport personnel, including private security. For the first time in her life Natasha witnessed the treatment of a VIP passenger. A uniformed man ushered them to the opulent lounge equipped with all sorts of gadgets, food, drinks, and plush furniture.

Natasha tried not to gawk, even though the large room was like something out of a fairytale, but failed.

My God, the luxury. Mindboggling.

Since Dmitry was the only departing VIP guest, they were alone. The entire area eerily quiet except for the low murmur of the huge TV mounted on the wall. Dmitry sat at the leather couch, frowning.

"My flight is in an hour."

Natasha nodded. Uncomfortable, she scanned the room, and avoided looking at him. Finally, he pushed from the couch, and came to his feet.

"Let's go. I'll walk you to the car."

Obviously, he no longer needed her presence. Or he didn't wish to be in her company any longer.

And what did you expect?

Natasha threw her untouched coffee into the nearby trashcan, then followed Dmitry outside. She was unwilling to continue their conversation, and clearly, he too. Natasha tried to convince herself that he needed to calm down, to see his friend first, to make sure everything went well.

Please, God, let him be okay, let him survive.

Natasha uttered a silent prayer for the man she saw only twice in her life. He was a good and loyal friend to Dmitry. Petya talked about Vlad Albrecht constantly and liked him immensely. In Natasha's opinion, he was a member of the family. Of course, Dmitry acted half out of his mind with worry. But as soon as he came back to his senses, he'd realize the truth, and that he wanted Katia for all the wrong reasons. The unwelcomed idea that he may be motivated by revenge against Elizabeth flashed in her mind. If true, his motive was understandable. But she still couldn't approve it.

Until Dmitry truly loved Katia, taking her away from San Francisco was a huge mistake.

She trotted after him, trying to match her stride to his much longer one. By the time they reached his rental car parked where she parked it, her breaths came out in pants.

Dmitry opened the driver's door, and motioned Natasha to get inside. She was almost ready to duck in, when he yanked her back. Natasha had a split second to react before he clasped his arms tight around her.

Her soft gasp broke free, quickly muffled by his mouth. The kiss was hungry, intense, and almost brutal. Thrusting his tongue past her lips, Dmitry swiped it against hers, demanding a response. She was powerless under the onslaught.

Before her brain had a chance to realize it, she kissed him back.

Too soon, it was finished. Dmitry ripped his mouth from hers.

"I'll be back. And then we'll finish what we started, Natasha. Count on it."

She didn't know if it was a promise or a threat. Probably both. He'd come back, and that's what mattered the most. On an impulse,

Natasha stood on her tiptoes, then planted a hard quick kiss on his scowling mouth.

"I'll hold you to that, Dmitry. Count on it."

Almost lightheaded, she jumped into the car. Closing her eyes for a moment, Natasha took a couple of deep breaths. Then she pulled off, but kept her eyes on the rearview mirror. Standing where she left him Dmitry watched her retreating car with something close to astonishment. His expression was almost comical, but instead of laughing, she started to cry.

He'll be back, he'll be back, Natasha repeated silently, looking at him through a mist of tears. *He'll be back.*

She only hoped that this time his return came sooner than five years.

CHAPTER FORTY-FIVE

At almost two in the morning, Natasha opened the back door, then quietly crept inside. Her bones ached from being so tired and were worn out by the turbulence of the events. Peter's fiasco of a birthday, Dmitry's urgent departure, their troubling conversation...

Layer after layer, the stress accumulated, weighting her down. As if the weight of a huge boulder laid on her shoulders.

Dragging her feet up the stairs proved more difficult than she imagined. She looked at the long curving wing of the main staircase, and almost whimpered in dismay. God, she just wanted to curl up right then and there, on the floor, and go to sleep. Impossible. She needed to climb to the third floor, and check on Katia first. Poor baby had such a trying day.

Damn that Julie.

Natasha winced in recollection. And poor Petya. Everybody tried so hard to give him *the* best birthday party ever, and that vile girl ruined everything.

Well, not everything, but still Julie managed to dim the atmosphere of the evening. Then again, don't most things work out for the best? She remembered Petya's admission of being relieved to discover Julie's true character. Better sooner than later before he got more emotionally involved with her. Of course, it might have been nice if he made that discovery some other way. Nothing could be done about it now. Suddenly the staircase seemed to sway before her eyes. She grabbed the banister, and silently ordered her legs to shuffle forward.

Just a tiny little bit, just a few dozen steps.

And then, she will collapse, and rest for a while. But first, she must check on Katia. Nothing could happen to her little girl, since both dogs stood guard, but still. She'd feel better after she checked, and made sure Katia was safe and soundly asleep. Just in case. Promising herself at least six hours of undisturbed oblivion, Natasha maneuvered the stairs, then jerked to a stop.

What had she heard? A muffled noise. A sob?

Now on high alert, Natasha drew still and listened. Nothing. She almost convinced herself that she was mistaken, when she heard that odd sound again. Coming from above? Who could be hiding in the dark at this hour of the night? A prowler? Her mind screamed to get to the phone, and dial 911. But what if someone from the household roamed the halls? If the person on the second-floor planned harm, she'd discover it quickly, and then call the police. Otherwise, if it was some poor soul wandering harmlessly in the dark—for a cup of milk, or returning to his or her room after some intimate nightly activity—Natasha didn't want to make a great deal out of it, and put whomever in an embarrassing hot spot. Not to mention it made her look like a fool. She stood quietly, straining her ears for any sound.

For several heartbeats everything remained silent and she sighed with relief. Then she heard it again, that strange little sound. Half-moan, half-sob. And a whisper. The words came as gibberish, quiet, desperate, gaining in volume. The timbre of the voice undistinguishable. Male? Female?

To be able to see and hear more clearly, Natasha needed to be closer to that person.

Spooked, trembling from fear, she started to climb the staircase as silently as possible. With every step, that strange feverish whisper sounded louder, more audible. The chills she failed to suppress ran along her spine. All the fine hair on her nape stood at alert. It seemed like the person was confronting someone. How many people were up there? Maybe, should call the police after all. Natasha hesitated for a moment, straining her ears, then crept forward. As she stepped onto the second-floor landing, she almost collided with the dark figure.

The figure faced one of the portraits.

Ducking back, Natasha plastered herself to the wall.

She sagged with relief to see only one person.

That's okay, one is not bad.

She could tackle one person if necessary. If nothing else, she planned to create a lot of noise, and hope that somebody woke up and came to her aid. She shivered. God, she hated violence. But if she sensed danger for her children, she'd use what nature gave her—legs, hands, teeth—in order to defend them. That strange murmur went on and on, sometimes pitching to an exclamation. The dark figure grew more and more agitated. Damn.

You should turn around, and go away. You should call the police immediately.

But despite her brain's urging, she stood still and watched the strange person.

With a start, she realized it was a woman. The slender form, the long light hair, the glimmer of jewels at the earlobes. The woman stood in front of a portrait, shaking her fisted hands at it.

What on earth...?

More curious than afraid now, Natasha lifted her eyes and stole a quick look at the painting. She barely caught herself from gasping out loud as the portrait of Alexei Rostoff caught her gaze. His smiling face appeared waxen from the flickering candle held in the woman's hand. Her voice rose in volume, desperate, imploring. Russian? Yes, she spoke Russian. Frowning, Natasha strained her ears.

"Damn you!... never should... touch... that bitch. How could... all we had and shared... Fool... What could she...... I could not give...?"

And finally, Natasha recognized the voice.

Dear God in heaven, it is true!

Shocked, she clamped her eyelids tight.

Please, God, let it be a figment of my imagination, an apparition, a nightmare— anything but the truth.

Because the truth seemed incomprehensible.

She opened her eyes and stared at the formidable matriarch of the Rostoff clan dressed in black, shaking her fisted hands and hurling accusations toward the portrait of her late nephew. Nauseated, scared, Natasha trembled from head to toe.

Something in the cadence of Elizabeth's voice, in her speech and posture was off. For the lack of a better word, it was not *normal.*

During her years in the Rostoff household, Natasha never heard Elizabeth talk like that. Guttural, raw, feverish, her voice almost unrecognizable. Never had she witnessed the Ice Queen Rostoff in such a rage. Elizabeth continued talking non-stop, her words tumbling out, faster and faster, as if she didn't possess the ability to control her vocal cords. Or herself.

Frightened in earnest, Natasha started to slide backward, pressing her body against the wall. Elizabeth didn't sound her usual self. She did not look like herself. She wasn't herself, period.

She's insane.

She behaved and looked like a crazy person. A sporadic flickering of the candle in Elizabeth's hands added to the overall macabre scene.

Even though Natasha stopped listening to the words, the timbre of that voice sent waves of goosebumps along her exposed skin.

Abruptly, Elizabeth stopped talking, and attacked the painting with her fists, beating her flesh against the canvas. In the total silence of a sleeping house, those hollow angry sounds reverberated, echoing off the walls. Undoubtedly, it could be heard everywhere. Somebody might wake and venture out to investigate. Soon.

Dammit.

Natasha didn't want anyone to see Elizabeth like that. True, there was no love lost between them, but to cause an embarrassment to the older woman went against her nature. And Natasha certainly didn't want to be found spying on her employer.

What to do?

Torn in a million different directions, Natasha finally chose the only one that seemed less painful for both of them.

Muttering a silent curse, she slid away from her hiding place, and stumbled toward the enraged figure.

"Elizabeth," she whispered.

The older woman spun around. Holding the candle high like a weapon, eyes blazing, mouth scowling, she was poised to strike.

Natasha froze. One look at that distorted face, and Natasha's fear intensified.

My God, she truly is insane.

Her heart skipped a bit as her breath hitched. Pure madness stared back at her. Chilled to the bone, Natasha lifted her hands palms up, a gesture of non-threatening intention.

What's next?

Shivering, Natasha stared at the older woman.

What should I do?

Should she try to talk to Elizabeth, and try to calm her down?

Without recognition, Elizabeth looked straight at her. Her oddly disfigured features made her beautiful patrician face frighteningly ugly. Lips pulled back, teeth bared, glazed eyes unfocused.

Immobilized by shock, Natasha froze like a rabbit in front of a snake. Her mind screamed at her to run, but her body froze. She found herself in a stupor, mesmerized. Horrified.

A low growl from behind broke the spell.

The dog. Thank you, Lord.

Natasha jumped back. Never before was she so happy for a German Shepherd's presence in the house. As soon as possible, she vowed to kiss her savior, Pasha or Misha. Heck, she'd kiss both of them, and make sure to give them special treats for the rest of their doggie lives.

Thank you, Dmitry.

Ridiculously weepy and light-headed, Natasha touched the comforting warmth of the shepherd's fur. An answering lick on her hand was followed by a soft whimper.

Feeling stronger, Natasha straightened her shoulders, and looked Elizabeth straight in the eye.

The appearance of the dog obviously confused the woman. She blinked several times, frowning. Slowly, degree by degree, the veil of madness slipped from her face.

Finally, her eyes focused. An expression of total bewilderment mixed with something close to pain crossed her features. Lifting her hand, Elizabeth rubbed her forehead and glanced around. Her gaze switched from Natasha to her hand with the candle, then to the portrait of Alexei Rostoff.

The low moan that burst from her throat sounded inhuman. Raw and wild and savage.

She snapped a hand over her mouth as if to physically stop the sound. She turned to Natasha, her face blank and calm as usual.

In the weak flickering candlelight, she reminded Natasha of a ghost.

For a split second, she wondered if it was just a play of her imagination. Just an illusion. After her stressful day, Natasha wouldn't be surprised.

But Elizabeth stood in front of her, and the dog panted behind her. If she was hallucinating, then Elizabeth and the dog were along for the ride.

A mass hallucination? Highly unlikely.

"Natalia, what are you doing up at this ungodly hour?" Clear and calm, with just a hint of a slight tremor, Elizabeth's voice came out almost normal.

Natasha knew her too well. Her eyes looked huge and almost black, and her hands shook. No, not even remotely calm.

Elizabeth Rostoff seemed scared, badly shaken, and barely holding it together.

A mix of emotions brewed behind her mask of false serenity.

Quietly, Natasha replied, "I just came home, Your Grace, from driving your son to the airport."

"Did he leave? Already?"

"Yes. An emergency arose, and he was needed back." Deliberately, Natasha evaded the real motive for Dmitry's hasty departure. For some unknown reason, she felt reluctant to let Elizabeth know about Vlad's accident. Especially after Dmitry's revelation of the true cause for her "retirement" and Vlad's role in it.

The Ice Queen was sure not to be sympathetic. If Natasha knew her employer at all— and she did know her very well— Elizabeth would undoubtedly be elated. Natasha refused to give her that satisfaction.

"It doesn't matter. He left..." For a split second something flicked in the depth of her eyes. Disappointment? Relief? Quickly, Elizabeth managed to shake it off. "Did he tell when he's going to return? Or *if* he's going to be back at all?"

Her voice rang with a heavy dose of sarcasm.

"I... don't know." Natasha spoke the truth, even if not all of it.

She really didn't know when. She only knew he'd be back. But again, for a reason she was unable to explain to herself, and reluctant to admit it to Elizabeth.

"It doesn't matter."

Elizabeth, worn and frazzled, looked her age.

"It's late, Your Grace," Natasha said after a moment, "It's time I call it a night, if you don't mind."

"What? No, no, of course. Go, Natalia, go to bed."

Only Elizabeth called her *Natalia*, the full version of her given name. Even though it always irritated Natasha, she never broke the older woman's habit. The heck with it.

"Good night, then." Still, Natasha hesitated. "Do you wish me to accompany you to your room?"

"I am capable of doing it on my own, Natalia, thank you." Cutting her off, Elizabeth straightening to her full impressive height. Tall for a woman, she towered over Natasha.

"All right. Good night."

"Good night."

With that Elizabeth strolled forward, not sparing Natasha a second glance.

For a long time, Natasha watched Elizabeth's retreating figure.

Then, as if someone pulled the plug, she folded and slid to her knees beside the dog. Pasha. She hugged him, kissed his cold, wet nose, and buried her face against the dog's thick furry neck.

"Thank you, boy. Thank you very, very much." Pasha made low whimper deep in his throat, and licked her face while Natasha still shook from the eerie confrontation.

"Yes, definitely scary. What was it, anyway?"

Her question proved rhetorical. She still failed to understand what had happened here, or why Elizabeth acted so strange. Arguing with the portrait? Then attacking it with her fists? Weird. Mindboggling. Unbelievable.

But one thing appeared clear as day: Elizabeth Rostoff was not well.

CHAPTER FORTY-SIX

The next day Natasha rose earlier than usual, barely six o'clock, but sleep eluded her after she finally dragged herself to bed the previous night.

What a day! After a quick shower that refused to revive her, Natasha went to wake Petya. Being Monday, he must return to Berkeley.

She was sad he must leave, but at the same time, glad that the boy will be out of the depressing atmosphere of the house. She met Petya as he walked out of the bathroom, his hair still damp from his shower, his shirt hung unbuttoned.

"Good morning, Gorgeous." He opened his arms, and Natasha willingly stepped into his welcoming embrace. "When did you come back? I tried to wait up for you but fell asleep."

"That's all right. I returned quite late. But everything went fine."

"Did Dad say when he's going to be back? Or is he?"

"He'll be back, Petya. As soon as he is able." Once again, Natasha wondered why she was so reluctant to admit to Elizabeth yesterday that Dmitry planned to come back.

"Well, that's good, isn't?" Peter let go of her and began to button his shirt.

"Yes, that is good, indeed. Now, hurry up if you want breakfast. It's almost time for you to be on your way."

They entered the kitchen together. Natasha went to the refrigerator, pulled out a carton of eggs, butter, and a jug of milk.

Definitely not a cook, but a simple breakfast of scrambled eggs and toast was something even she could master.

She had the option to wait for Vera to do it, but she preferred to make meals for the kids herself. Especially breakfast. Instead of the formal breakfast room, they usually ate it in the kitchen. The atmosphere was much cozier and intimate despite the size of the room. Painted a pale yellow, with its distressed furniture and the copper skillets hanging above the butcher block, the kitchen gave a pleasant homey vibe. The oversized stove intimidated her at first, but she quickly learned how to use it. Expertly, she cracked four eggs into a glass bowl, added milk, then whisked the mixture. Pouring it into a heated pan, she gently swirled the spatula until the eggs set. Satisfied with the result, she nodded to herself.

Natasha cherished the pleasant chore of feeding her family, even if it only occasionally.

Elizabeth disapproved of it, but often, Natasha deliberately disobeyed her employer's wishes. Like now.

"Here, eat while it's still hot." She plopped scrambled eggs onto Petya's plate, then returned to the counter, grabbed three pieces of crispy bread that jumped from the toaster, and generously buttered them. Petya's appetite never ceased to amaze her. He shoveled food into his mouth like person starved half to death. She smiled as she watched him eat. No matter how tall and big her boy he was still growing.

Natasha poured a tall glass of orange juice for him, and a cup of strong black tea for herself, then brought it to the table, and sat across from Petya.

CHAPTER FORTY-SEVEN

Peter watched Natasha out of the corner of his eye. Distracted and preoccupied, and sad if the downward curve of her lips meant anything. Probably, shouldn't have let her drive his father to the airport. Did Dmitry manage to upset her? What did he tell her? What did Natasha need to talk to him about?

But he didn't ask. She was a grown woman, and it wasn't his place to question her decisions or to pry into her personal business. But, damn it, he cared about her wellbeing and happiness because she was more a mother to him than his real one.

"Natasha," he began, frowning into his plate. "Did you... Did Dad..."

"We talked, Petya." Natasha smiled, then ruffled his hair. "Don't pout. It doesn't look good on you."

"Who's pouting? I'm just concerned, that's all."

"Well, don't. Everything's fine." But her smile didn't reach her eyes.

"No, it is not," Peter stubbornly repeated. "Natasha, it's not my business..."

"You're right, *miliy*; it's not. So, let's leave it at that." To make the point, Natasha lifted one brow at him, then sipped her tea.

"One more question, and I promise to shut up."

"Okay, shoot."

"Do you plan to have an affair with him?"

"What!" She almost choked on her tea.

"I'm sorry, damn, that was a stupid question."

"Stupid is a mild word for it." Natasha coughed, then blotted her lips with a napkin.

"But you *are* going to get involved with him."

"Petya, my boy, I'm already involved up to my ears, in case you didn't notice." Chuckling, Natasha watched him with amused eyes.

"No, I meant..." He cursed softly.

"You meant am I going to sleep with him?"

Heat charged up his neck. Damn.

I'm too old to blush!

"Natasha, it's... that's... not what I... Okay, okay! That's exactly what I meant. Well?"

"Well, what?"

"Are you?"

"I don't know." After a heartbeat of silence, she lowered her eyes. "I love him, Petya. Always have. You know that."

"Yes, I do. But what about him?"

"He... he's attracted to me." Natasha cleared her throat, looking into her cup.

"He said that?"

"Yes."

"Well." Peter frowned. Attracted? Really? Dammit.

"You're disappointed." Natasha's soft words were accompanied by a sad little smile.

Am I that transparent?

"No. Yes. I don't know," he admitted. "I'm worried about you."

"You don't have to. I'm a grown woman. I know what I'm doing."

"Do you? Sometimes I wonder."

"Of course, I do." Disappointment and anger sparkled in her bewitching green eyes.

In a gesture of comfort and apology, he gently placed his hand on her much smaller one. "No offense, Natasha, but in some areas you're as innocent as Katie."

"I'm not an idiot, Petya." The first notes of annoyance crept into her voice.

"No, you're not. But you're naïve, and too open for your own good. You just can't do anything half measure. And sometimes, it's dangerous."

"Petya..." She began, but he interrupted her by putting his finger against her lips.

"He's my father, and I love him. And you. I hate to see one of you hurt. Or choose sides." He finished quietly.

"Well, I cannot guarantee that nobody will be hurt, but I can promise you one thing, Petya: whatever happens between your father and me, you won't ever have to choose sides. Not you, not Katia." She reached out and clasped his hand tightly. Stressing her words, she vowed, "I promise you, *miliy*."

Unconvinced, Peter decided to let it go. For now.

Natasha shivered violently. She froze, as the color drained from her face, leaving it whiter than snow. Alarmed, Peter grabbed her hand. A hand cold as an icicle. Something was very wrong.

"Natasha?" She didn't move a muscle. "Hey, what is it?"

After a brief pause, she blinked at him, "Umm? Oh, just something I remembered. It's nothing, really. Well," suddenly Natasha was all action," it's time for you to leave. Please, be very careful driving, and don't speed."

She pulled him from the chair, then propelled him toward the back door.

"Call me as soon as you're there, all right? And call me during the week. And—"

"Natasha, slow down, for goodness's sake." Despite his grim mood, he laughed. "I swear to God, sometimes you're like a steamroller."

"Thank you, it's always nice to be appreciated," she replied with a fake grin.

"Okay, all right, I'm gone." He bent down then kissed her on the cheek. "I'll see you and Katie this weekend."

CHAPTER FORTY-EIGHT

He sprinted toward his car, lean and tall and heartbreakingly handsome. As usual, Natasha's heart broke a little. She always hated to say goodbye to her boy, if even for a few days. As if feeling her eyes on him, Peter shifted and looked at her hard and long.

"I love you, Natasha. Remember that. Always." After a pause, he slid behind the wheel and with the reckless speed he loved, took off.

"He'll be lucky to live 'till his next birthday," said the familiar cold voice somewhere behind her. Natasha gathered all her will and strength turned to face Elizabeth. Oh-uh. She cringed inwardly. The older woman was poised for battle.

"Good morning, Your Grace. What are you doing here?"

"You didn't expect to find me in the kitchen, did you, Natalia?"

Elizabeth ignored the polite niceties of morning greetings, and cut straight to the matter. Fine. Natasha had her own question she wanted to ask. The sooner the better.

"No, I did not." Natasha thrust out her chin, an action she knew Elizabeth detested.

Good.

"Well, it is my house, after all." Sarcasm dripped from her words like honey from a spoon.

"Of course, it is."

"How nice of you to remember. " Elizabeth curved her lips in a parody of a smile. "Where is my Granddaughter?"

"She's still sleeping."

Elizabeth scowled, then sighed. "Was she very upset?"

Natasha understood the question. "Yes. But knowing Katia, she cared more about ruining Petya's party than anything else."

Wait a minute. Elizabeth wasn't present when that unfortunate event happened yesterday. Wasn't she inside? Yes, Natasha clearly remembered Elizabeth entertaining the older guests.

"How did you find out?" More curious than surprised, Natasha gazed at the older woman. As Elizabeth pointed out, it was her house, and her staff kept her well informed about anything and everything happening on its premises.

"Why, did you think I wouldn't be aware of a scandal in my own home? You know me better than that, Natalia."

"Yes, of course, silly of me, I suppose."

"I hope Peter made it clear to that person she's not welcomed here anymore?"

"He did, Your Grace."

"I'm disappointed in my grandson. His taste in women is simply deplorable. To be attracted to such a flashy piece of trash." She shrugged as her face flooded with disgust. "Then again, he's just a man. A *Rostoff*. Every skirt will do," she muttered wryly.

"He's just a boy." Natasha bristled, immediately on the defensive. "How could you—"

Coolly, Elizabeth cut her off.

"I know what I'm talking about, Natalia. All Rostoff men are lusty, hungry beasts. You'll be smart to remember that."

"What do you mean by that?" She knew exactly what Elizabeth meant, damn her.

"Why, nothing, my dear. Only that Rostoff men are selfish, self-indulgent, a self-centered lot, all of them. My son and my grandson included. Someone who's stupid enough to get close to them could get hurt. Badly." She lifted one brow, and somehow it made her perfect porcelain face even more beautiful.

And chilling.

Her hidden message between the lines came out clear and loud. And a great insult, to the father and son, and to her. Natasha took it personally. Her anger simmered as she retaliated.

"And was your late nephew one of those self-indulgent, selfish, self-centered lot, Your Grace?" She deliberately kept her voice soft, and impersonally mild, as she answered with her own insult.

Elizabeth reacted as if she struck. She jerked and failed to suppress her gasp. She narrowed her eyes to burning slits, then hissed between her teeth, "You leave my nephew alone. Do you hear me?"

"I hear."

Hit the nerve, didn't I, Your Grace?

The subject of Alexei Rostoff was definitely a sore spot. Good. Finally, a leverage.

Pleased, Natasha stared at the older woman, her lips curved in a half-smile.

"I just can't help but wonder." Natasha tilted her head and squinted. "He was a Rostoff, too. What excludes him from the others? What was so special about that particular man that you still carry a torch, even after so many years?"

Briefly, she wondered if her recklessness pushed Elizabeth too far. She shrugged it off. Enough of Elizabeth's games. The name Alexei Rostoff continued to pop up. Somehow, he was tied to Elizabeth and Petya's mother. But how? Both women seemed close to him. Polina revealed his dark secrets to her son. Elizabeth talked to his portrait, accusing him of... what? Natasha tried to remember what Elizabeth told her last night. Something about the other woman, what she could give Alexei that she, Elizabeth, could not... something about love and age and betrayal. And her voice, that feverish frantic whisper, angry to the point of madness... She behaved like a woman scorn by her... lover.

Lover! Sweet Lord...

So, Petya's mother revealed the truth when she accused Elizabeth of seducing her own nephew? Her husband's cousin but still... Nauseating. Disgusting.

"You're talking utter rubbish, Natalia." Elizabeth's cold, calm voice sliced into the havoc in her mind. "My nephew was the most decent human being, and we shared a very special friendship for we both had many things in common. He may have been different, yes, and I liked him immensely. The feelings were mutual. When he died, I mourned him. I still do. If I would be the one to pass first, I'm sure he'd mourn me, too. But I do not carry a *torch* as you so indelicately inferred. It is silly of you to think that, and plain rude. I'm disappointed in you, Natalia."

What else is new?

She looked at Elizabeth. Not a trace of agitation marred her smooth face. Erased of every emotion, her features were blank and vacant. Totally impassive. The woman was hands down scary.

Yesterday, Natasha unwillingly witnessed Elizabeth's astonishing transformation from raving lunatic to normal person. From sheer madness to serene tranquility in a matter of seconds. Natasha shivered in recollection.

She was more afraid now than last night. Elizabeth was truly unbalanced, teetering on the thin edge. And Katia... She might be in danger. Not because her grandmother wished her harm, but because she was mentally ill, and therefore a threat to everybody. Even to herself.

Natasha's rising panic grabbed her by the throat.

She must do something. But what? How soon until something switches inside the older woman's brain, snapping her control, and plunging her into an abyss of madness? And how long it might take her to recover the next time?

What if it weren't Natasha, but, God forbid, Katia, who stumbled onto Elizabeth in her dark, violent mood? And what if she failed to recognize the child, and physically hurt her, like yesterday when she tried to assault Natasha with a candlestick?

CHAPTER FORTY-NINE

The swirl of emotions on Natalia's face shone so clear that Elizabeth smiled.

Oh, she noticed everything: confusion, then fear, and finally, panic.

But underneath it all, dead set determination.

It dispelled her doubts whether Natalia witnessed one of her spells yesterday. Yes, most unfortunate that it happened to be this stubborn creature. To her utter dismay and annoyance, Natalia never appeared afraid of her. And she was the only one.

Unlike the other servants, she couldn't be browbeaten or persuaded to keep silent. No, Natalia refused to be silenced easily.

That little hellcat was not manageable. But still. Nothing was impossible.

If she couldn't be scared, then it meant blackmail, a familiar and dependable way that always worked. Elizabeth plotted as she watched every nuance of Natasha's expressive face. And worried. No one knew her little secret. Except for Ivan. Had she made a mistake to confide in him? But Elizabeth did it out of pure necessity. Because sometimes, when her spells became too violent for her to master them alone, she needed his physical strength. She hated him for this. Hated needing him and being indebted to him. But most of all, she hated to see that pitiful and disgusted look on his face after she came back to her senses.

But she always came back, and that was most important. When she conquers this weakness of hers, those unfortunate spells, then she'll dispose of Ivan. Forever.

Elizabeth never doubted that she will eventually find the cure.

But Natalia... another problem entirely.

Finally settling on a course, she decided to talk with her. Today. Immediately. Yes, probably risky, and sooner than suited her, but time was running out. And the consequences might be unfortunate. If not catastrophic.

"I need to talk to you."

"Talk? About what?"

A worried frown spread along her mouth. Good.

"About secrets. And lies. And people." She answered at length, taking gratification from the younger woman's acute discomfort. "But later."

"Why wait?"

"Because I want to show you something in my office that I'm sure will be of great interest to you. But not now. Katia will be up and about, and I'd rather have our conversation in private."

After waving her dismissal with one hand, Elizabeth sashayed to the door.

"Elizabeth. Your Grace!"

Natasha's loud outcry made her smile. Oh, yes, the girl was unsettled, and confused, and definitely off balance.

Must keep her that way for a bit longer. Just to build up the tension.

The anticipation of the future confrontation bubbled inside of her, but Elizabeth squelched it. Timing was everything. Pleased, she threw over her shoulder, "Later, Natalia, later."

CHAPTER FIFTY

aris, France
P Dmitry shifted on his plastic chair in the hospital waiting room, wondering about the similarities between all the medical facilities in the world. The universal smell of them, the hard uncomfortable chairs, the sterile atmosphere. Everything added to the torture of waiting. He arrived straight from the airport two hours ago, and still was not allowed to see Vlad, or talk to his doctor. Dmitry drew his comfort from the news that his friend was alive, even if in critical condition. He had a skull fracture, smashed ribs, one lung punctured, but he was alive. Thank God.

A teenager who crashed his brand-new sports car into Vlad's Mercedes wasn't that lucky. God Almighty, the boy was just sixteen. Reckless, stupid. And now dead.

Unwillingly, his thoughts turned to Peter, and the brand new Corvette he bought him for his birthday. It scared the hell out of him.

I won't think about it.

Driving himself crazy with fear was not an option. Not for his son, or for his friend. He must stay strong, and level-headed. Otherwise, what help will he be?

Impatient, Dmitry requested several times to speak to Vlad's doctor, but told he was currently in surgery. Frustrated and cursing quietly, he remained in that damn hard chair, and waited.

Dammit, they refused to let him see Vlad. He only wanted—needed—one brief glimpse, just one short moment to convince himself that his friend was still alive, still breathing, but the medical personnel refused to allow him even that small luxury. Tyrants. Morons. Fucking robots in white uniforms. Not humans. How else could they bear coming here day after day, and make a living out of other people's pain?

His anger helped. Dmitry welcomed it, deliberately stroked it to ignite the burning fire in his blood. Better be angry, than helpless. And vulnerable. And so impotent.

He hated hospitals with their antiseptic smells, impersonal waiting rooms, hurried and harried personnel, and, yes, those bloody chairs from Gestapo.

And those walls, white, pristine, cold...

Behind those walls, pain and blood and struggles reigned supreme.

Behind those walls lurked death, watching like a hungry predator, waiting.

Always waiting.

Dmitry swore again. The very air thick and cold like London fog. Every breath he took abraded his throat. He remembered another hospital, in another country, where he too sat waiting, utterly helpless and scared.

Svetlana...

He shut his eyes, pressed both thumbs against his sockets until he stars flashed.

Six years ago. God, it seemed like yesterday.

Ever since that horrible day in Moscow, Dmitry avoided the hospitals.

Today, as he stepped inside the AP-HP - *Hôpital Universitaire Pitié Salpêtrière*, all the feelings rushed back, ambushing him.

Did he really think he might have forgotten?

Arrogant fool.

Every tiny detail was etched into his memory like a hot rod stabbed into his brain.

He swore again, then checked his watch. Hell, how much longer?

"Dmitry!"

The breathless exclamation pulled him out of his reverie. He jumped from his chair, opened his arms, then caught Marie in a bear hug. He held her trembling body, swaying with her. For the life of him, he failed to utter a single encouragement.

"You made it, *mon cher*. You're here." Her words tumbled from English to French, and back. Then she sobbed, sagging against him, clutching his shirt in a desperate grip. "I was so scared, Dmitry, so scared! I've never been so scared in my life. I don't know what I will do if..." her voice hitched, then simply broke. After a moment, she lifted her face. Her imploring eyes broke his heart. "Please, tell me that he'll make it, Dmitry. Tell me."

"Shh-hh, sweetheart, he'll make it. Of course, he will. Vlad is strong and young and too stubborn to let go without a good fight. He'll make it."

I hope. I pray.

"Now, wipe your tears, calm down, and tell me everything."

Marie let go of his shirt, scrubbed her face with both hands. "*Mon Dieu*, I'm a mess. I have to be strong for him and the girls, but when I'm here... I just can't. These walls and smells—everything makes me so small and helpless."

"I know, sweetheart." He knew exactly how she felt since he did too.

"Did you see him?"

"No. They won't let me in. Said I'm not a member of the family."

Marie swore out loud. "They let me in yesterday for a moment, but he..." Her eyes overflowed again. "He was asleep. He didn't even know I was there"

"Honey, he's still sleeping, it's good for him."

Damn, and how do you know?

He tried desperately to come up with something positive for her sake.

For both their sakes. Vlad was his best friend and Marie's husband and father of her children. More than that, they shared a very special relationship based on true love and deep respect for each other. Hell, they were positively crazy about one another, even after five years of marriage. Dmitry was genuinely happy for them, and a little jealous. Whenever he caught them together and watched those long meaningful gazes, he felt so... alone. And cold. And old.

Sometimes he wondered if he might ever share the same kind of relationship with Svetlana if she lived. He shrugged. He honestly hoped so. And he supposed, it was silly of him, not to mention totally pointless to think about it, or speculate about what ifs. But sometimes Dmitry couldn't help it. Like right now...

He shook it off and concentrated on reality. Marie continued talking, her eyes shiny and red-rimmed from tears, her generous full mouth bare and vulnerable. Dmitry didn't think, he just reacted. Reaching forward, he caressed her lips with his finger. His touch held nothing intimate, just a gesture of comfort. Marie gave him a small tremulous smile, then lifted his hand, and pressed her cheek against it.

"Thank you, Dmitry."

"For what, Marie?"

"For being here. For being such a good friend."

"You don't have to thank me for that. Vlad is very important to me, you know that. He is more than a friend."

"I know. Still, I want to thank you. For everything. Everything, *mon ami*. I've never... we've never..."

"Don't. Please just...don't." Uncomfortable, Dmitry stepped back.

He knew what Marie meant. That bleak autumn day five years ago, when he almost lost his company thanks to his mother's scheme. Unwillingly, Marie has played an essential role in that fiasco. But even under pressure of blackmail, she never berated him. The information she gave Vlad helped to expose Elizabeth, and eventually stop her.

Dmitry never brought that subject up with her or Vlad. By their mutual silent agreement, they never talked about that autumn. Now Marie broached that taboo intentionally. He still felt ill at ease and reluctant to talk about it.

Both Vlad and Marie knew about his profound gratitude. He made sure of that, although he never acknowledged it verbally. His actions spoke louder than words.

"Please, Marie." He winced under the scrutiny of her amber eyes.

She nodded her understanding. After a heartbeat of uncomfortable silence, she took his hand. "I just wanted you to know I will always be grateful for what you've done. I know you did it for Vlad, but—"

"No, Marie. I did it for you too."

"But Dmitry, I betrayed you!"

"You didn't."

"Okay, all right, you stubborn Russian. I *almost* betrayed you."

"The key word is *almost*, Marie."

"Still, how could you not hate me, letting me resign instead of firing me and pressing charges?"

"You were innocent, *mon ami*. Vulnerable. Elizabeth used you. For that alone, I would do everything for you."

"But why? I mean, I was nothing to you, I tried to seduce you, I complicated matters, I almost destroyed your reputation..."

"Again, the keyword is *almost*. And you also helped me tremendously. You saved me from myself."

"Oh, Dmitry." Christ, her eyes filled up again. Women's tears always made him helpless. And panicky.

"Stop it, Marie. This is not the time, nor the place." It came out harsher than he intended.

Good job, Rostoff, you moron.

He swore, and wanted to apologize, but Marie beat him to it.

"All right."

She dropped her gaze.

He swore again, more richly this time. "It's not... it's just... Oh, hell, Marie, I can't talk about it. Still can't," he admitted quietly. "It hurts too much."

"I understand."

He wondered if she really did.

"Vlad will be okay. He will be fine. I feel it. I know it."

"Yes, me too." Her beamed one of her famous smiles at him, gathered both his hands in hers, then gave them a squeeze. "Me too, *mon ami.*"

"God, where is that damn doctor?"

At that moment, a man in surgical scrubs entered the waiting area, and walked toward them.

"That's him," Marie whispered, scrambling awkwardly to her feet. "Doctor Tullard."

"Him?"

Dmitry didn't know what he expected, but definitely not a short, scrawny boy who seemed not old enough to shave. In his pale green scrubs, and surgical mask dangling from his neck, he looked like a kid in a Halloween costume. What the hell! Why did the hospital let people's lives depend on someone that young! He jumped from his chair, ready to give that joker a piece of his mind, but the moment Dmitry caught the young man's eyes, all the words stuck in his throat. Ruthlessly intelligent, laser beam sharp and ancient, those eyes held him immobile. Dark blue, almost indigo, tired, and bloodshot, they were in such contrast with a youthful face and skinny body, it was almost shocking.

"Hello, I'm Doctor Tullard." His deep baritone only added to Dmitry befuddlement. Silently, he shook an outstretched hand.

"Hi, doctor. This is *Monsieur* Rostoff, my husband's closest friend and colleague." Marie, bless her, smoothly performed the necessary introductions.

"Nice to meet you," the younger man replied, watching Dmitry.

The impression of being scanned with a laser beam disconcerted. Uncomfortable, off balance, Dmitry nodded. "Likewise, doctor."

"I just saw your husband, Madame." He nodded to Marie. "He's still in a coma, but his vital signs have much improved since yesterday. His color, too. I'm sure he is out of the woods, so to speak." The small smile that curved his lips was warm, and reassuring. At the word coma, Marie drew a sharp intake of air, then made a low moan, leaning on Dmitry.

"God, oh my God, oh my..." Shaking, she mumbled in an endless chant, as tears rolled down her face.

Dmitry finally found his voice. "Thank you, Doctor. Thank you very much."

He squeezed the younger man's hand harder than he intended. Wincing a little, Doctor Tullard pulled his hand free.

"That's my job, but you are very welcome."

"Any idea when he may wake up?"

"I'm afraid, not. Your friend underwent major surgery, and had a tremendous shock to his system. He lost a lot of blood. We pumped in transfusions, but his body needs some time to adjust, to regain its own balance and strength. He'll wake up when his body is ready."

"But he *will* wake up, right?"

"Oh, most definitely." The young doctor flashed an arrogant smile. "I didn't spend six hours sewing him up for nothing."

Startled by that blatant bluster, Dmitry gaped, then chuckled. "Well, I suppose not."

"I'm good, *Monsieur* Rostoff." The doctor smiled again, then winked. "Looking at me, many people make a mistake. But, as you Americans say, appearances are deceiving, *non?*"

"Damn," Dmitry mumbled with a mix of amusement and annoyance. "Was I that obvious?"

"Let just say...*oui*," Doctor Tullard finished a crooked grin.

Arrogant son of a bitch.

And just like that, his fear dissipated. He liked the young doctor, scrawny body, enormous arrogance, and all.

Relived, Dmitry let out a rumble of laughter. What do you know, the rumors about overinflated egos of surgeons were true after all.

But looking at it now from a totally different perspective, he realized it was only natural. After all, if you play God on a daily basis, it ought to make you feel superior. An admiration for the people in scrubs filled Dmitry to the brim.

"Thank you, Doctor." Marie took the young man's hand and shook it vigorously. "When can we see him?"

"He is in an ICU, but you can go inside for five minutes."

"I want to see him, too." In his best CEO voice, Dmitry butted in.

Lifting one brow, Doctor Tullard surveyed him with barely suppressed amusement. "Well, if Madam Albrecht doesn't mind sharing her time, then it's fine with me."

"No, I don't mind at all." Hurriedly, Marie nodded, and grabbed Dmitry's hand. "We'll see him together."

"Fine." The doctor shrugged and added, "You can go together, but no more than five minutes. I'll check on him later, and we'll see if you can have another five minutes tonight."

They said their goodbyes, and Dmitry soon found himself ushered into ICU. Horrified, he stared at the unrecognizable prone figure on the bed. Vlad? His friend's head was swathed in white bandages; a thousand tubes attached to every imaginable and unimaginable spot-on Vlad's body.

Monitors of every size and shape... And beeping, my God, that beeping!

Dmitry's eyes became itchy and hot; his throat and lungs constricted. Unable to swallow, or draw a breath, he watched the still figure on the bed.

My God, if these are good signs and color, what do they call bad?

The room around him tilted, then slowly righted itself.

Marie, whose control seemed better than his, approached the bed, then touched Vlad's hand. She murmured words of love and reassurance in French, her deep velvety voice raspy from tears. Feeling like an intruder, Dmitry stood glued to the spot. That one-sided conversation between a husband and wife was intimate, and special, and poignant. Finally, Marie turned in his direction, then held out her hand. Dmitry managed to step forward, then took her offered hand.

With his other, he tentatively touched Vlad's palm. "You scared the shit out of me, you son of a bitch." His voice trembled, but he couldn't help it. Vlad lay unmoving as a corpse, but his skin warm to the touch.

Thank God.

His face was pale, but not grayish, his eyelids half-closed, but not still. Like a butterfly's wings, they flapped a bit. Dmitry took it as a good sign.

"I'll break your neck myself for driving so recklessly, you asshole. You just wait and see if I don't."

Laughing through tears, Marie asked her husband, "You hear that, *mon ami*? You better wake up soon, promise? We miss you terribly. The girls miss you. And I... I love you so much, darling, that it really hurts. Don't you dare to give up, understand?"

Vlad's eyebrows were the only spot on his body free of any bandages or tubes. Gingerly, Marie caressed them with one fingertip.

Dmitry cleared his throat. Damn, he was so uncomfortable, and out of place here. And so bloody scared.

On top of that, hot tears pressed against his eyes. He fought them like a man possessed. When the sturdy nurse came to usher them out, Dmitry felt giddy with relief. And ashamed of himself.

Marie didn't want to leave Vlad, but the doctor's order was strict: five minutes. All the way out, she wept quietly. Feeling envious of women's prerogative to cry openly, Dmitry held her trembling body, cursing silently.

God, he'd give his right arm right now for a good hard cry. But men didn't do that. They were supposed to be strong.

Strong, my ass.

Bitterly, he swallowed his despair. He shook his head to erase the picture of Vlad, a big robust man, reduced to the status of a helpless invalid. He was suffocating. Taut and feverish, his skin seemed a size too small for his body, stretched to the point of breaking. His heart drummed a crazy staccato inside of his ribcage, bruising his bones.

The moment the elevator stopped on the first floor, Dmitry almost ran out of the hospital.

"Will you come over?" Marie asked, hurrying after him. "The girls always love to see you."

"No, not now. I need to..." God, what *did* he need? "I need to take a shower and change my clothes. Then I must go to the office. Later I'd like to swing by the hospital and check on Vlad."

"I'll be here, too. So, see you later?"

"Yes."

Marie kissed his cheek. "Thank you, *mon ami*. It is so good to have you back."

CHAPTER FIFTY-ONE

L ater that evening Dmitry found himself in Marie and Vlad's house with a tumbler of *Armagnac* in hand.

What am I doing here? To comfort Marie? Or to draw comfort from her?

He asked himself that question for the umpteenth time, but still failed to come up with the answer. A huge amount of work accumulated over the several days he was gone. Plus, he wanted to call Peter, to tell him about Vlad's progress. But most of all he wished to talk to Natasha, just to hear her voice, just to make sure that the last three days weren't a dream.

God, I'm acting like a lovestruck boy.

He brooded while staring into his drink.

He consumed two glasses of the flavorful, rich cognac, but his mind refused to go numb. Instead, he was painfully sober, and more miserable than before.

As soon as Marie comes back from seeing the girls, I'm out of here.

"Well, thank God they're in bed," Marie announced as she plopped onto the sofa beside him. "The girls are so upset and frightened," she murmured, referring to the four-years-old Nicole and Michelle, the identical twins, or double trouble, as Vlad lovingly called his daughters, "and mad at me for refusing to take them to the hospital."

Absentmindedly, she rubbed her forehead. "But I think your presence diverted their minds from the accident. You're good for them, *mon ami*. They adore you."

Despite his current mood, Dmitry smiled. Nicky and Micky, as he christened them, never failed to show their true feelings toward him. He felt humbled by the love and attention they bestowed upon him. Sometimes, Vlad joked that the twins simply worshipped him. Even though he always shrugged it off, Dmitry was secretly pleased. The feelings were mutual. Whenever two pairs of identical golden eyes looked at him with an utter and open adoration, his heart melted.

They called him Uncle Dim, and accepted him as part of the family.

God, they are just a year or so younger than Katia.

Why can he love these two little girls, but not love his own child? He didn't even know Katia's favorite toy or color, or her preferences in food. He didn't know her, period.

Never wanted to know. And now I sorely regret it.

And she... Dear Lord, she collected his photos, hiding them from everyone, and sketched his portraits. Guilt and shame flooded his heart.

Nicky and Micky always wore the tiny diamond studs that he gave them for their third birthday, while he never bothered to send his own child a simple birthday card. Not even once.

Damn it all to hell and back. Dmitry shook his head, then tossed back his drink in one gulp.

The curious gaze Marie sent in his direction caught his attention. Curiosity quickly gave way to concern, then Marie frowned.

Without a word she stood up and refilled his glass again. Fourth drink.

"As a matter of fact," she began in calm voice, "you managed to take my mind off the accident, too, *mon ami.*"

"Hard to believe. If I hadn't dragged you out of the hospital, you'd live and sleep there."

"True. But he needs me, Dmitry."

"Girls need you, too. Even more so."

"You are right, of course, *cher*." After a lengthy pause, she asked, "Are you okay, Dmitry?"

"What? Oh, yeah, yeah... thanks, Marie."

He plastered a lopsided grin on his face. By the disgusted look on her face, he obviously failed to fool her.

Damn, forgot how perceptive she was.

Marie returned to the sofa, then tucked her legs under her, and glued her eyes onto his face. A sure sign that she settled in for a long talk. Dmitry groaned inwardly.

Why do some women feel the need to talk?

"How was your visit home, Dmitry? With all this," she made a noncommittal gesture with her hands, "I forgot to ask you about it."

He failed to swallow his helpless oath. To allow himself a moment to think, he investigated the glass in his hand while swirling the golden liquid. "It was... eventful."

"How is Peter?"

"He's well, very well. He sends his love. I'm pretty sure you'll have a call from him tomorrow or so. He was very upset about the accident. I already phoned him to let him know about Vlad's condition." He avoided looking at Marie, trying to escape that knowing gaze of her golden eyes.

"He is such a wonderful boy," she continued in a soothing, gentle voice, "You should be very proud of him. *Mon Dieu*, just eighteen, and he's already into his second year in college."

She didn't fool him for a second. Marie inched toward the main subject, trying her best to keep him unaware and at ease. More amused than irritated, he decided to humor her.

"Yeah. He's anxious to finish as soon as possible. I bet he'll manage to squeeze a four-year course into three. The boy is restless."

"He will be fine. He is eager to spread his wings and fly, that's all. Remember how it was when you were so young?"

Oh, I remember. Too well.

"Yes. Restless and eager to fly, too, until my mother clipped my wings, and successfully grounded me." Damn, he failed to realize the bitterness he still held close.

"Oh, but you flew, Dmitry. Very high. Despite everything," Marie contradicted him in a gentle voice. He frowned, neither agreeing or disagreeing.

"And how is your daughter?"

Finally.

Uncomfortable, Dmitry tensed. He never talked about Katia with anyone, even Vlad and Marie. Obstinately, he refused to acknowledge the fact that he had another child. Even to himself. For many years.

You stubborn fool.

He scowled. How is your daughter? she asked. His daughter that he didn't know, and didn't love, and never talked about with anybody.

You are such a bastard.

His choice of word made him angry. Even though aimed at himself, and not his daughter. Still, it reminded him of Peter's birthday, and Julie's outburst. She called Katia a bastard, referring to her illegitimacy.

At the time, it made him mad as hell and ready to strangle the hateful bitch with his bare hands. That swift anger and his surge of protectiveness toward the little girl stunned him. Was it just a normal, natural reaction to defend an innocent child, any child, or something more? He still didn't know. Dammit, he was afraid to know.

"Dmitry?" Marie's voice broke into his troubled thoughts.

"Hmm-mm?"

"Are you all right?"

"Yes. No. I don't know."

"Is that because I asked about the baby?"

"She's not a baby anymore."

"Yes, I know. She's five now, isn't she?"

"Six. Going on fifty," he muttered helplessly.

"Well? Are you going to tell me about her, or should I shut up, and mind my own business?"

Despite everything he laughed and it felt good. "And when was the last time you did that?"

"Mind my own business?"

"Shut up."

"Never," she replied and grinned at him.

"Yeah, that's what I figured." Dmitry smiled, then sobered. For a long time, they sat in comfortable silence. He didn't want to talk. He *needed* to talk.

And who if not with Marie?

When he finally opened his mouth, a floodgate broke free. He knew his words tumbled, like they were in a hurry to get past one another. He told her about his first meeting with Katia, and about his shock when he realized that she was a carbon copy of his mother; and his amazement when he found out about her talent. He told Marie about his shame and remorse for abandoning an innocent child, and blaming her for death of his lover.

He talked for a long time, until spent and empty. But he needed that. Needed to take that heavy burden from his soul. This painful and draining confession left him shaky, but miraculously, at peace. Yes, he needed that.

FORTY-NINE

Marie never interrupted him, not even once. But her expression relayed everything in her heart. She smiled and nodded, obviously pleased.

Had he taken the first step toward his healing? The first and the hardest one of all. His road to self-forgiveness lay ahead, long, and bumpy and unpaved.

I have the strength to overcome any obstacles, and get to the end of the road as a victor.

When Dmitry fell silent, Marie gently touched his hand.

"You should bring her here to visit, *mon ami.* I'll see that she makes good friends with the girls. And I am very anxious to meet her."

"I plan to bring her here. And not just for a visit. Permanently." He surprised himself with his confession.

"Dmitry," she hesitated for a few seconds before continuing, "Do you think it wise?"

"What do you mean?"

"I mean, think about it. You left her at Elizabeth's, didn't visit her, didn't write or call. For years."

He winced, then glared at her. "God, Marie, you don't have to rub it in, you know."

"That's not what I'm trying to do, *mon cher.* I'm just reminding you that *Zolotoe Selo* is the only home this child knew from the very beginning. She took her first steps there, spoke her first word... I mean, she feels secure and protected. She feels at home."

"So, I'll make another one for her here."

Marie heaved an exasperating sigh.

"That's not so simple, Dmitry."

"It doesn't have to be that difficult, either."

"What, to uproot a six-year-old child? No, it is not. But the question is, is it wise? Is it good for the child?"

"Marie, she's my daughter, damn it. I want her to know she has a father. I want her here, with me."

I want her to think of me as a dad.

"Why?"

"Why?" His eyebrows rose in amazement. " You, a mother of two, are asking me *why*?"

"Yes, because I am a mother, and because I know that you, *mon ami*, are thinking *not* of the girl, but only of yourself."

That stung. "Care to explain?"

"Dmitry, I don't want to offend you, or anger you so I will go with my heart. Just think about it: you went back, you met a wonderful little child. You felt wonder, and yes, pride, but mostly remorse. So many years you resented the very fact of her existence, but here she is, innocent, amazing, bright. Of course, your heart broke a little, and of course, you want to make changes. But *mon ami*, this is your own guilt talking; your sense of debt, if you will. Not the real concern and love for the child."

Insulted, Dmitry fought to keep his voice neutral. And failed. "Gosh, thanks a bunch, Marie. You painted me like a real monster."

The heavy sarcasm of his words didn't sway her. If anything, she seemed more anxious to explain.

"Not a monster, *non*. Never a monster. You are the most decent, honest, most honorable human being I've the privilege to meet, Dmitry. You are noble to the tips of your toes. You are kind and generous to the fault." She scooted closer, then laid her right hand on his forearm and held his gaze. "But... don't you see, *mon ami*, you're still confused. Hurt and angry, but mostly confused. And your emotions are getting mixed up."

The truth of her words burst the bubble of his anger. Resigned, ashamed of himself, Dmitry exhaled with a loud *whoosh*. "I'm sorry, Marie."

"*Pas besoin*. I just want you to be sure. I want you to understand that no matter what path you decide to choose, you must first consider your daughter's well-being, and *her* feelings. Don't hurt her more than you already have. The child should come first. Always."

"You are right. Of course, you're right." He leaned back, tired to the marrow.

"So, look into your heart, Dmitry, and think. Are you sure that you really and truly love your daughter? Think about it."

"God, Marie, you make it sound so simple."

"Because it is."

He shook his head. "When I think that she lives with Elizabeth, in that oppressive cold mausoleum of a house... Dammit, she's so bright, so warm and alive, and so... tiny. Fragile. Christ, it would be so easy to break her spirit, her talent, to kill her dreams. I should know. I was a child once, growing up in that house."

"She didn't break you, *mon ami*. Your mother, I mean. She tried, but failed. And you should have more faith in your little girl. She is your daughter, after all."

"Thank you." He sent her a sad little smile. "I mean, really thank you."

"Anytime, Dmitry." Marie patted his hand.

"There is another matter you must consider. You are forgetting that both Peter and the little one has a nanny, that Russian woman. What was her name again?" Her innocent smile as fake as a cubic zirconia masquerading for a diamond.

Brava, Marie. An academy award performance.

Of course, she knew Natasha's name.

Probably knew the color of her eyes, and the exact shade of her hair as well.

He shrugged mentally. "Her name is Natasha as I'm sure you know." He sent her a pointed look. She has a decency to blush. "And she is more mother than a nanny. Actually, she's more of a parent to both Peter and Katia than I've ever been. You know, some women are just born to be mothers. I guess Natasha is that kind of woman."

"Only a *mother*? What about the *wife*?"

"She's not married." He answered quickly. Maybe, too quickly.

"I understand that, but do you think she'll make a good wife?"

Am I so obvious?

"She'll be loving and warm and faithful," he said, as if talking to himself, "and loyal to a fault."

"Hmm-mm." Marie cocked her head. "And where did you find that paragon of womanhood?"

"In Russia. Actually, she found me. She and Katia's mother were from the same orphanage and best friends."

In a gruff voice, Dmitry continued, "When Katia's mother died, Natasha broke the news to me." Lost in his memories, he kept quiet for a moment, then continued, "When I flew to Moscow for the funeral, I met her. Natasha, I mean. I... I needed to bring the baby back with me to the States. In her final letter, her mother asked me to take care of her. Elizabeth wanted a granddaughter almost to the point of obsession. So," his voice trailed off for a few moments, "and I thought, why not? I'd kill two birds with one stone. Fulfill my promise to the woman I loved, and get my mother off my back by giving her my daughter to raise." He took a deep swallow of cognac, then cleared his throat. "But Russian authorities refused to let me adopt the baby. I tried to prove I was her father. DNA tests weren't available then, so my word meant nothing. They refused. The fact that I am a rich businessman from the United States didn't help to earn me the brownie's points in the communist country. Quite the contrary, in fact. The Russian government was adamant. I almost lost my mind when some of my contacts in the American Embassy suggested a solution. I had to find a local woman willing to adopt my baby officially, and then take them both as distant relatives to a visit overseas. That woman wouldn't be able to return, of course, but I made sure to reimburse her financially, and for her to have the opportunity to stay in the States permanently."

"So, you choose Natasha to play that role?"

"Yes. At least, that was my initial intention. But thinking about it, I'm not sure it was such a simple matter."

Marie frowned. "What do you mean?"

Dmitry swirled the remains of his drink, as if searching for answers on the bottom of the glass. After a while, he replied, "Fate. Definitely fate. Natasha didn't have any family, she loved Svetlana, and seemed the perfect candidate for the role. I approached her, asked for her help. She agreed but firmly refused my money. Several weeks later, I brought them both, the baby and Natasha, to the United States. The rest is history."

"So, she's been living with Elizabeth, and carrying for your daughter ever since?"

"Yes. Later, after my wife's death, Peter decided to stay in California. And Natasha became a mother to him too. She's raising both of my children and doing an admirable job." He stared off into the distance, picturing his children in his mind. "Katia calls her mama." Then, shutting his eyes, he swore softly, "Damn it."

"What is it, *mon ami*? What's bothering you so?"

With an oath, he set his glass on a coffee table. "I am the bastard, Marie. And idiot. Stupid, brainless idiot."

In what seemed like an off-handed manner, Marie muttered, "So, what else is new?"

He chuckled, then laughed out loud. "Oh, Marie, you're priceless. I should've snatched you while I could, before Vlad had any opportunity."

"No, you should not, *mon ami*. We were all wrong for each other."

Bracing his elbows on his knees, he propped his face on his right hand, and glanced at her. "Why?"

"Because we're so much alike, Dmitry. Don't you think?"

He pondered that for a moment, then nodded. "You're right, of course."

"*Mais bien sur.* I'm always right. After all, I am a woman."

Amused, he squinted at her. "Meaning?"

"Meaning, I—and every other female on earth—have something you men don't."

"And what's that? Breasts?" He asked jokingly. Marie grinned.

"*Non, mon ami,* an intuition."

"And that's what makes you always right?"

"*Absolument.*" Then, shrugging, she relented. "Well, almost always."

He rolled his eyes. "And she is modest, too."

"When I can afford it." She countered primly, then looked at him and began to giggle.

His own answering chuckle grew into full-blown laughter.

Christ, that felt good.

Almost carefree, like all the weight had lifted from his shoulders. Abruptly, he sobered.

"I'm in love with her. Probably from the start, but I didn't realize it then. Or I didn't want to." He wasn't sure who was more surprised by his confession, him or Marie. "Now I know for sure, and it hurts like hell," he finished quietly.

"Oh, Dmitry," commiserating, Marie draped her arm around his shoulders.

For a just a heartbeat, he resisted her embrace, then he relaxed, and leaned into her arms.

After a long moment, she asked, "Did you tell her?"

"No. I couldn't."

"Why?"

"I..." he swallowed around the huge boulder in his throat, "I hurt her, Marie. Five years ago."

"How?"

"I wanted her, lusted after her. And she... she was attracted to me, genuinely. She was so young, and so naïve, she failed to hide it. I knew—guessed—she was innocent. I was sure she wouldn't refuse me and give me everything I asked for, and then some. But I chose not to. My God, it would've been so easy, and so wrong. So, I tried to protect her from myself. I fought my desire like a man possessed."

With a helpless oath, Dmitry drew back from her embrace, and leaned against the sofa. "But either I was too transparent, or Elizabeth too damn perceptive, who knows? She saw right through me. And soon enough realized the truth. Then, she proposed a bargain: I stay away from Katia and Natasha, and she'll stay away from Peter and Polina. And me. God, what a fool! How could I have believed her? How could I agree to that bargain with the devil? Because that's what Elizabeth is: devil reincarnate." Dmitry swore and closed his eyes in defeat. "So, I left, telling myself it was for the best, that I was doing a great favor to Natasha, even though it almost killed me. But staying away didn't help. Nothing helped. Not the time, or distance. Finally, I became so mad at myself..." his voice hitched, then broke.

"Because you wanted her?"

"Because I never wanted any woman like that. Not even Katia's mother. I blamed it on celibacy, on my personal trauma of losing the woman I loved, even on Natasha, although deep down I knew she was completely innocent, the fault all mine. So, I ran. From her, from myself. But you can't outrun fate." Dmitry turned his head and studied Marie with a sad smile.

"But you did get back. I mean, five years ago, after..." She didn't finish her thought, but he understood.

"Yes, I went back to *Zolotoe Selo* after my wife attempted to murder my baby daughter and got killed instead."

Marie winced.

He glared at the floor. Clipped and harsh, his voice scraped his throat like a broken shard. "It was like jumping right into a nightmare. One shock after another, and every next one more terrifying than the first."

CHAPTER FIFTY-TWO

Dmitry found it impossible to forget those hellish few days. Police interrogations, the discovery of Polina's alcohol and drug abuse, funeral, his mother's betrayal...

But most of all, he remembered Peter's grief, his anger, his shame.

And his own fear. Cold, brutal, all-consuming fear for his son.

Dear God, I was so afraid for the boy.

"In the midst of it all I completely forgot about my daughter."

It shamed him greatly now, but he found no way to redeem himself.

"I even didn't care that she almost died, didn't ask myself why? Why my wife was so hell-bent on killing an innocent child? I just didn't care. Then Peter refused to live with me, and decided to stay in San Francisco. A final blow for me. I came apart, literally. I was hurt, and angry, and mean as hell. I seemed to have been betrayed by everybody: my late wife, my mother, my son. So, I figured, the hell with everything, and left without a single glance back. Or a word."

"*Mon ami*, it is understandable, after all, you've been through—"

"Understandable? Maybe. But forgivable? I don't know, Marie. I don't know."

He still didn't, and it tore him apart. "I aimed my anger at the most innocent: my daughter and Natasha. I could have contacted her later and tried to explain. But I didn't. I know we both have our lives. Mine here, hers in America. Part of the time, Peter visited. I had my business, my friends, and a few semi-satisfying relationships. In short, my life was back on track. I became content. I knew from Peter that she was, too."

"Really?"

"My God, I thought so. I hoped she was happy and got over her crush, or whatever she felt."

That chemistry, that crazy unbearable longing, that intense savage need.

"I never realized she waited. For a long, long time. And then..."

"And then...?"

"And then she stopped waiting. Stopped believing in dreams. That's what she told me: *I stopped believing in dreams*. I hurt her even worse than I could by touching her, and taking her virginity. I stole her innocence, her illusions, her dreams... dreams that she stopped believing in."

"But did she stop loving you?"

Dmitry drew in a deep breath. "I don't know."

"Well, why don't you ask her?"

"Because I'm afraid to hear the answer."

"Oh, Dmitry."

"Pathetic, isn't?"

Tired and sad, he sagged against the cushions.

After a moment, Marie squinted at him, her face set. "I tell you what, *mon ami*. As I see it, you did that woman a tremendous favor. Instead of blaming yourself for killing her dreams, why don't you consider the fact that you dragged her back to reality? Dreams, my ass! What *dreams*? She wasn't a little girl when she met you. But mature enough to want a man, then she should've been realistic enough to bear the consequences, and brave enough to fight for her feelings."

As a kick in the ass went, Marie performed a doozy. Dmitry blinked hard, then stared at Marie, and exploded, "You don't know what you're talking about. She was innocent!"

"So what? We are all born that way. We all lose that innocence one way or another. And in my opinion, the sooner the better."

"Is that how it was for you?" He asked harshly.

"No, *mon ami*. For me, it was too soon and too brutal."

Too late Dmitry remembered about Marie's past, sexually abused as a child, repeatedly, by her own father. He cringed, deeply ashamed of his own stupidity.

Dammit all to hell and back, you're a real bastard, Rostoff.

Tentatively, he touched her hand. An apology trembled on his lips, but he was afraid to voice it aloud. He expected her to pull away from him, but she didn't. Relieved, he gave her hand a gentle tug. Without a word, Marie willingly went into his embrace.

"I'm sorry, sweetheart. I am so damn sorry."

She sniffed, and the sound broke his heart. "It's okay."

"No, it's not."

"It doesn't matter. Not anymore," she murmured quietly. After a long moment, she disengaged herself, and sat back. "You should ask her, Dmitry. Second chances are too rare and too precious to ignore. We both were given our second chances. I almost made a mistake and let my hurt and my past stay in the way of my happiness. Thank God Vlad was too stubborn for both of us. *Mon Dieu*, Vlad..." Her voice hitched, then trailed into silence.

He leaned closer, then put his arm around her trembling shoulders. "He's going to make it, Marie. You've got to believe it."

"I know, I know. It's just..." she shook her head. "I'm so scared, Dmitry. So scared."

"Hey, it's okay to be scared."

"Are you?"

"You bet I am. But I'm also sure Vlad will pull through. He's got so much to live for. And you said it yourself: he's too stubborn to give up."

She lifted her eyes, looking straight at him, into him. "And so are you, *mon ami*. So are you."

"No, not me," he shook his head in denial, "I am a coward."

"Dmitry, look at me." Not waiting for him to comply, Marie framed his face with both hands. "If you love her, if Natasha is the one and the only, don't let her go. Don't make another mistake. Fight her, if that what it takes, but don't let her go."

"I don't deserve her. Or my daughter."

"You deserve everything, *mon ami*. And then some."

"They won't want me. And why should they? After I had abandoned them both."

"Well, you'll never know until you ask, *non*?"

CHAPTER FIFTY-THREE

For the next two days, Dmitry constantly replayed Marie's words in his mind.

You'll never know until you ask...

Ask what? Are you still in love with me?

Absurd! How on earth are you supposed to ask the woman you hurt and deserted if she still has feelings for you? What if she said no? It'd kill him. On the other hand, there's a slight hope that her answer might be "yes." And that killed him even more. Torn between the memories of the kiss they shared and her absolute refusal to take his side regarding Katia, Dmitry stalled, avoiding the moment of truth, and stopping himself at the last second whenever he reached for the phone. Instead, he spent his days in the office, burying himself in work, and his evenings at the hospital, pacing endless corridors and waiting helplessly for his best friend to win his fight with the coma.

He promised Natasha he'd return. And he will as soon as Vlad is out of danger. He can't leave Marie all alone right now.

They didn't talk about it anymore, but by the way she watched him, Dmitry knew she silently urged him to take his second chance.

If only it was that simple.

The combination of constant stress and uncertainty soon morphed into insomnia. But instead of pills he hated or alcohol he was indifferent to, Dmitry found his own type of cure. He began staring up at the night sky and comparing all his problems to the universe. His world seemed so small, his problems so insignificant in the mysterious light cast by the Moon. The span of human life

on earth seemed so ridiculously short compared to the eternity of
the cosmos. Instead of dread, however, it filled him with the deepest
respect for time, for each and every moment of being.

He never felt so thirsty for life. It just hit him recently how really
empty his life was despite his success and wealth. What did it matter
after all?

His stores all over the world didn't warm his heart; his name in
Forbes' magazine didn't make him less miserable. The king of the
Rostoff Empire, a true pauper in the matters of heart and happiness.

But most of all, he craved the feeling of belonging, that certainty
that somewhere, someplace, a spot by the fire waited just for him, a
place where he'd be missed and wanted, where he was an inseparable
part of the whole, a small piece of the puzzle that needed him to be
complete.

He never did belong, not in his mother's world, not in Polina's.
Nor did he fit completely into Svetlana's world, he realized, sadder
than upset by that revelation.

But, God, how he wanted to. How desperately he wished to
belong, to find that place by the fire at last, too warm his soul and
forget about all those empty, cold, lonely days and nights.

At those moments the image of a fiery-haired woman with
emerald eyes usually swam into his mind, beckoning, promising,
soothing... When Dmitry thought of home, family, and happiness,
Natasha always belonged in the picture.

Lord, he missed her. He wanted to call if only to hear her soft
voice, to drive himself crazy just to listen to her breathing. He had it
bad, he realized with wry amusement. He needed to talk to her. But
not over the phone.

As soon as Vlad wakes up, as soon he's out of the woods, Dmitry
planned to return to the States.

And then they will talk.

As it happened, they did have a talk much sooner than he anticipated, but the dire circumstances didn't leave any room for what he really wished to discuss. Once again capricious fate has intervened and placed them both in a middle of the crisis, altering their lives drastically.

CHAPTER FIFTY-FOUR

That morning Dmitry received two pieces of news.

The first one came from the hospital. Vlad has finally come out of his coma. Relieved and elated, Dmitry gave out a boisterous shout of victory, forgetting his whereabouts, and not giving a damn who might witness his strange behavior. Darn, he was so happy for Vlad, for Marie, for the girls. And for himself. Vlad held one of the most important parts in his life. A vital part. For the last few days, Dmitry experienced a terrible void while Vlad hovered on the thin edge between life and death, it was almost painful. He knew that if, God forbid, his friend lost his battle, a part of Dmitry would die too. Maybe his best part. Thank all the saints Vlad awoke. Dmitry burst with hope and joy. And a darn good feeling, too. Terrific feeling.

Whistling a happy tune, he almost waltzed out of his office, but his admin's voice over the intercom stopped him in mid-stride. Dmitry received another call. Impatient to be on his way to the hospital, he snatched the phone.

"It's better be important," he barked in lieu of hello.

"It is," answered a familiar voice he recognized immediately over the static of long-distance connection. *Honey over milk* was his first impression of Natasha's sultry alto all these years ago. Golden honey over warm milk, sweet, sinful, seductive...

"Natasha..." Air and words escaped him. "Natasha," he murmured again, ridiculously happy and immediately off balance.

She called first, was the only thing his mind processed at that moment. *She* called him first. He waged a battle with himself for several days, stopping at the last moment whenever the urge to call her to overcame his better intentions, but not any longer. She called him first, ruining his plan to wait until he was back in States, then talk to her face to face. Happiness filled him, enormously so.

Natasha said something, but he was totally lost in the simple pleasure of hearing her velvety voice. Absolute heaven. He never bothered to hide the silly smile that bloomed on his face.

"Dmitry, did you hear me? Are you there?"

Natasha's worried cry plucked him out of his euphoria, returning him to reality.

"Yes, I'm here."

"Thank God. For a moment here I thought I had lost you."

Never, he wanted to yell.

You'll never lose me again. We'll never lose each other again.

"What were you saying, Natasha? I'm afraid I didn't grasp your last words."

"Dmitry, I'm sorry to be a bearer of bad news. Again."

Her anxiety penetrated his foggy brain, and an alarm went off. Natasha called to deliver bad news. Again. The last time she called...

Christ.

He'll never forget that phone call.

"Svetlana died..."

He shook off the long-ago memories, swallowed hard. "What is it? Peter? Katia? What, Natasha?"

"No, it is not about children, Dmitry. They are fine, thank God. But your mother—"

"Mother? What about her?" Relief washed over him. Thank God his children were fine. He leaned against his desk and exhaled, ignoring the sound of breaking plastic behind him.

"Elizabeth had a stroke, Dmitry. It's very bad. Her doctor is not sure she'll pull through. As a matter of fact, he is pretty sure that she... God, Dmitry I'm so very sorry."

He heard the words; understood the meaning of her message, but still, one part of his mind stubbornly refused to accept it. Elizabeth... Stroke... Doctor... to farfetched, to alien. The image of his formidable, powerful mother ill, broken, helpless... God, so confusing. It couldn't be true.

"Elizabeth?" He repeated dully, still rebelling against the news that the woman he loved and hated all his life now gravely ill and possibly dying. He did a doubletake. Did he love Elizabeth? He shook his head to clear his mind. No. Maybe he was so shaken because in his mind, she was bigger than life, stronger than a mere human being could be. Had a right to be. She made his childhood a total misery, his grown life a bitter challenge; she betrayed him, never loved him, and regretted his very existence. And still... his mother.

As simple as that.

The realization shattered him. His hands shook uncontrollably. He hated himself for the weakness. But he needed to step up and do the right thing. "I'll be there as soon as I can."

"Dmitry? Are you alright? God, silly question. Of course you aren't. I am sorry again," she repeated somberly.

"How is... everybody?" He chose to ignore her question about himself. Truth be told, he didn't know how he really felt at the moment. The realization that he might love his mother rattled him to the core.

I don't love her. I can't. Or can I?

"Petya is okay, although he's pretty shaken. He'll be home tomorrow. Katia... she still doesn't understand the full meaning of what's happening, but she's upset that her grandmother is fallen sick and needed to be taken to the hospital."

"Mother is in the hospital?"

Idiot. Of course, she's taken to the hospital after suffering a massive stroke.

"Yes. The doctor insisted on hospitalization. It was... *is* very serious, Dmitry. I could not overrule doctor's order. We have to think only about Elizabeth's wellbeing now, not about her comfort."

"Yes, of course," he answered ashamed of his earlier outburst. "I didn't mean to snap at you, Natasha. I'm sorry."

"Never mind. How is your friend? Petya told me he was in a coma."

"He's just awakened. I got a call from the hospital not long ago. He'll be all right."

"I'm glad."

"Yeah, me, too."

"Dmitry?"

"Hmm-mm?"

"Come home. Please. We need you." Natasha gulped in a broken breath, then finished softly, "I need you."

Her quiet admission thawed the layer of ice around his heart.

He wasn't alone this time.

That realization revived and humbled him at the same time. He no longer must bear the load alone, not anymore. Natasha was there with him. For him. The fact that she confessed her need for him, admitted and accepted it, trusting him with that much, did a wondrous thing for Dmitry. His chest constricted with near pain, but he welcomed it, holding onto it like an anchor. His throat became so tight that he swallowed several times before he could speak.

"I need you, too," he heard himself to say. Shaken, he realized he came as close to declaring his true feelings.

"Take care of yourself."

Did her voice really tremble, or did he imagine it?

"You, too," he replied and disconnected the call before he said something silly and stupid in his present state. Like how glad she was in his life or how good to realize that finally, he was not alone anymore.

Or that he loved her. Helplessly. Ridiculously. Deeply. That he fell in love with her from the very beginning. And that he always will love her. Only her.

Wrong time, wrong place, he reminded himself. Ruthlessly reining his turbulent emotions, Dmitry forced himself to relax.

Discreet coughing behind him caught him off guard, and he almost jumped from the desktop. The shrewd gaze from Cindy Margolis, his longtime admin, met his startled eyes. Oh, no, he gave an inward groan as realization hit him. Cindy overheard his phone conversation with Natasha from the very beginning. Although he spoke Russian, he suspected Cindy grasped the gist of it. Reading his facial expression and hearing the tone of his voice, it was easy to fill in the gaps, especially for someone as sharp and intelligent as Cindy.

"Didn't your mother teach you that eavesdropping is an unladylike thing to do?" he asked curtly, still a little off balance.

"I'm sure she did mention something along the lines, but then again I've never claimed to be a lady, boss," she answered deadpan. Then, sobering immediately, Cindy added, "I knocked, but you were on the phone, almost yelling. So I took a liberty to enter. Is Elizabeth okay?"

"No. She suffered a stroke, a bad one," he said, still uneasy and uncomfortable, but whether from the aftermath of the shocking news or Cindy's eavesdropping, he didn't know. Both, probably.

"I'm sorry, Dmitry," Cindy laid her hand on his.

He glanced downward. She worked for him for more than fifteen years, and their relationship was based on efficient, calm, detached professionalism that of a boss and a secretary. They respected each other, even liked each other, but from a distance. From the very beginning, they both established firm boundaries they were comfortable with. They shared no open camaraderie, no friendly lunches or silly postcards, and no birthday cakes. They exchanged a little dry banter now and then, but nothing more.

And never had Cindy addressed him by any name or title except The Boss, to his face or behind his back. Even when he barged into her small Brooklyn apartment in the middle of the night five years ago and announced that he decided to relocate *Rostoff's* offices to Paris and take her with him, whether she wanted to go or not. She called him a 'son of a bitch' then, but not because his arrogant assumption that she'd agree to move to the end of the earth with him, but because in his haste he stepped on the tail of her favorite Siamese cat and scared the hell out of the highly temperamental exotic creature. As a result, they both spent a half an hour coaxing the cat from the top of her kitchen cabinet. After that, Cindy packed with an astonishing speed, and both she and the Siamese flew to Paris in a matter of days. She claimed to not have any regretts ever since.

Cindy glanced at her hand then his face. Her eyes widened, but she didn't offer an apology for overstepping. Instead, she went for dry humor, "Hey, don't go all mushy on me now, Boss. It's bad for the image, you know."

"What image?" Dmitry managed to ask, touched and amused at the same time when high color rose on her cheeks.

"Sharp as a blade, cold as ice, hard-as-nails SOB, pardon, CEO with a macho twist. That image," she replied, her gaze not wavering for a second.

"Is that how you see me?" He asked, bemused more than insulted. "Hard as nails, a cold as ice SOB a. k. a. CEO?"

"You forgot "sharp as a blade" with a "macho twist." No, I don't, but that's how the rest of the world does."

"I'll be damn." He shook his head. "And here I thought they like me for my sunny disposition and charm."

"Nope, sorry," she answered absently, already busying herself with her cell phone. He held back a laugh.

Still amused, Dmitry politely asked, "Who are you calling? Or shouldn't I ask?"

"You should, for it is *your* flight to the States I'm about to book. Company plane?"

"Why not." Damn the woman, constantly throwing him off balance. But, then again, she also kept him on his toes most of the time. So he had nothing to complain about.

"Why, indeed? Hello? *Mademoiselle?*" Cindy efficiently switched to French her accent almost non-existent.

There was nothing on this earth impossible for Cindy Margolis, he believed with a mix of grudging respect and annoyance. If he decided to relocate to the Far East instead of Europe, she'd have probably mastered Japanese, too. She did everything with lethal efficiency, ruthless determination, and minimum fuss, traits that were priceless even if a little scary. In less than five minutes she had his plane ready, his chauffeur notified, his part-time housekeeper called to pack his bags, leaving him nothing to do except to meet his limo at the appointed time.

"I'll be damn," he muttered in helpless resignation as Cindy ushered him out of the office with a quick firm order to call as soon as he arrived in San Francisco.

"And don't worry about the Heffner's deal, boss. Jacques will handle it. God knows you're paying him enough to act like a mature adult once in a blue moon," she called as the elevator doors started to close.

Christ, he completely forgot about Franz Heffner! Cindy, bless her heart, once again saved the day. Heffner's deal, a multi-million-dollar project, and very important for *Rostoff's*. Moreover, it was Vlad's baby. He had neither the right nor inclination to let his friend down. It's not that Dmitry didn't trust his executive assistant Jacques Molinari, but this deal was special. Because of Vlad. Dmitry owed his friend to oversee this project personally until Vlad took back command.

So, as soon as he got into his car, Dmitry placed a direct call to the President of Heffner Global Ltd., Franz Heffner himself.

Fifteen minutes later they finished their conversation to his satisfaction. Eager to report the good news to Vlad.

The uniformed man deftly maneuvered the car between the vehicles on the road, and soon Dmitry found himself on the parking lot of *Hôpital Universitaire Pitié Salpêtrière*.

Leaving orders to his chauffeur, he went to the entrance. For a moment, he let himself dwell about his phone conversation with Natasha and his mother's illness. He hadn't forgotten about it, just pushed it out of his mind while dealing with Heffner. But now he had no immediate business to occupy his thoughts or demand his full concentration. So now he let his personal hell out of its hiding place and face his demons. Or, more accurately, *the* demon, his mother.

His steps halted in midstride, his shoulders hunched under the heavy burden of sorrow and pain. Dammit, he hated her; hated the fact they were related. Ridiculous that he considered, even for a moment, that he might love her.

But no matter his confusing feeling toward Elizabeth, he still planned to take away her lifelong obsession, her granddaughter.

All her life she was as healthy as the proverbial ox. She exercised regularly, swam, ate only organic healthy food and spent a few months each year in Switzerland's best clinic, doing God only knew what. But the main kicker — she was seventy years old. The last time he confronted her— God, really just days ago? —she was truly upset. Her familiar insolent mask slipped away, uncovering the real anger. Explosive, her agitation seemed almost shocking. Did that cause her to collapse? The thought chilled him to the bone. He didn't want to be responsible and bear the guilt for being the culprit of his mother's deadly stroke. He already carried the heavy load of remorse and shame for Svetlana's death. One was enough.

God knew, the relationship between them was always strained at best. Lately, it became downright hostile, especially on Elizabeth's side. But still, he never wished her ill. Elizabeth was his mother even though she preferred to forget it, and did not acknowledge the fact.

CHAPTER FIFTY-FIVE

San Francisco, California

S Natasha listened to the annoying "beep- beep" sound in her ear for a long time after the call ended. Those high-pitched little noises reverberated through her head, piercing it with tiny sharp pricks. The mother of all headaches brewed. And still, Natasha held on to the phone unable to accept the fact that the brief moments of connection between them were broken. He told her he needed her. Was it true? Did Dmitry really need her? Not just want, but also need...

She wanted to believe that more than she wanted to live.

Yet she was afraid. Afraid to open her heart. Afraid to let herself trust again.

Was she overcautious? Maybe. But better safe than sorry.

Bull. She was safer than yolk in an egg for the past five years. And sorrier than she ever imagined. Lord, she missed him so much. Never in her life did Natasha miss another human being to the point of feeling actual physical pain. Not even Svetlana. Tears of guilt and shame sprang into her eyes and a hollow, dull pain filled the pit of her stomach. As always at these moments, when she remembered her dear friend, Natasha touched the little gold cross just below her throat, Svetlana's cross, a little token her dying friend asked Natasha to keep for her baby daughter.

The daughter Natasha raised and considered her own. The daughter of the man Svetlana loved until her last breath.

The same man Natasha couldn't imagine her life without.

Maybe the time had come for her to take some risks. Maybe she needed to trust her emotions, her heart. Well pastime. But what about Katia? Even if Natasha took risks with her own life, she absolutely refused to do it with her baby's wellbeing.

Katia needs a home, roots, and family. She needs to feel love and secure. She needs her parents. Dear God, she needs both parents, not only her surrogate mother.

A headache pounded at her temples with a vengeance, turning the tiny beeping sounds in her ear into unbearable loud drumbeats. Natasha placed the receiver in its cradle with the precise accuracy of a bomb rescuer. She scanned her surroundings with unfocused eyes.

Totally and thoroughly spent, she was tired to the point of collapsing. The last two days seemed hard on everyone, but especially her. Somehow, every single member of the household assumed Natasha was the one and only to step into their mistress' shoes while Elizabeth stayed in the hospital. Everybody turned to her in silent agreement, waiting, watching, and trusting her to put everything in order. To take control. Dammit, what did she know about running a house, especially the size of this one? Technically there were several houses with the main one they lived in, numerous outbuildings, two gardens, flower and an organic green, an Olympic size pool with its own small pool house, a barn with horses, and God only knew what else. Natasha didn't want that responsibility. Fear of mistakes rattled her, but somehow it must not show or else she was more in control of her fears and emotions than she knew.

Of course, she had a lifetime practice of it.

In a time of major crisis, the household and all its members moved their anxious gazes at her.

Even Elizabeth's lawyer called Natasha to inquire about the latest updates on his client's health rather than to ask her doctor. Unwillingly, she assumed the role of the head of the household, even if just temporarily. She didn't know why or how it happened. And she was so damn tired of being the one in control.

Thank God, Dmitry is coming.

Natasha felt almost sick with strain. And chilled to the bone. These days she always felt cold. Come to think about it, she became cold the moment she said goodbye to Dmitry at the airport, as if all the warmth flew away with him, along with her heart.

Don't go there, don't even think about it, she warned herself sternly.

The house was dark and quiet like a tomb. She rubbed her forearms covered with goosebumps.

God, so cold.

Wincing, shaking, Natasha made her way slowly because with each step searing pain shot into her skull, and made her dizzy.

She longed for a nap, just to lie down, to relax her aching muscles, to ease the tension in her whole body. An unbearable headache began brewing, her body's usual reaction to extreme stress. But knowing it didn't help, dammit.

Natasha moaned as she eased her way up the stairs. Halfway up, on the landing of the second floor, she stopped. Her gaze collided with the infamous painting of Alexei Rostoff and brought back the disturbing memories in a rush.

Who are you? What role did you play in the lives of Rostoff women? What were you to Elizabeth, except her beloved nephew?

The man in the picture who bore the uncanny and eerie resemblance to Petya, smiled back, arrogantly flashing those Rostoff dimples, mocking her, taunting. Or so it seemed to Natasha. Almost afraid now, she scurried away from the portrait and made her way up to the third floor. But she couldn't forget. In her mind's eyes, she saw it clearly: dark chocolate eyes, high forehead, chiseled cheekbones, and that insolent smile. And Elizabeth, in a long nightgown in front of the painting, heavy candlestick like a weapon in her hand... And her voice... Dear God, her voice.

Was it just a coincidence that a few days after that strange incident Elizabeth collapsed?

Somehow Natasha didn't think so. Something prompted that reaction, that massive stroke which, as a doctor explained to Natasha, usually came as a result of an enormous jolt to the nervous system.

Who could've guessed that Elizabeth had nerves, Natasha thought grudgingly, then she stopped herself, immediately ashamed. Elizabeth Rostoff was a human being.

"Even if it didn't show most of the time," she added under her breath.

Resigned, Natasha let her mind continue on that path. No, she didn't like the woman. And yes, the feelings were mutual. Truth be told, Elizabeth disliked Natasha with a vengeance. She plainly hated her even though she covered it well under her ever-present blank mask. Maybe Natasha was a sinner and a bad Christian. Maybe. But she never, ever, wished Elizabeth harm, all personal feelings aside.

She dragged her feet the remaining distance. Elizabeth's collapse shook Natasha more than she realized. Maybe because it was so unexpected: one moment Elizabeth stood in her office, regal as a queen, after summoning Natasha for their private talk, and next sprawled in a lifeless heap on the floor, convulsing.

Dear God, only two days ago? It seemed like years passed since the morning after Petya's birthday when she awakened with a heavy heart and chilly premonition in her stomach.

She was frightened after the macabre scene she witnessed on the landing, torn between the urge to call Dmitry and doubts about the wisdom of making that call. What if she acted rashly, alarming him without cause? And what could he do being thousands of miles away? Natasha hadn't any idea of what to tell him.

"Hi, how are the things in Paris? Oh, by the way, your mother was talking to the portrait of your late cousin yesterday, and I think she's insane."

She didn't know what happened to Elizabeth, couldn't explain what exactly she witnessed the night before. But Natasha knew Elizabeth behaved like a person out of her mind. When she hinted to the older woman about that strange encounter the night before, Elizabeth acted surprised as if Natasha told a made-up story. As if it was a perfectly normal thing for her to do every evening: stand barefooted before the portrait and shout at it.

Could Natasha prove it? Of course not. She was alone with Elizabeth that night, except Pasha, but Natasha doubted the dog made a reliable witness in this case.

Shuddering from cold and the recollection of that horrible night, she made her way to the nursery door. Katia's soft laughter beckoned her like a breath of fresh air. Her little girl, her dear princess. Thank God for the blissful oblivion of children.

Patience, Natasha, patience.

Just a little longer, then you can fall apart. You won't be in charge anymore, nor will you be alone in a huge, oppressive, dark and empty house, frightening like an Egyptian pyramid.

And once Dmitry gets home, you'll be warm again. Think of this... think only of this... and of him...

Clinging to these thoughts, she gathered the last scraps of her self-control that happened to be the only armor available to her. That and her headache. She'd do nicely without the later.

Already pasting a false smile on her face for Katia's sake, Natasha wondered for the umpteenth time what Elizabeth wanted to show or tell her that terrible morning.

If the menacing, triumphant curve of her lips that made Natasha's skin crawl was any indication, it had to be something more than unpleasant.

Something about... what? Or whom?

She went to Elizabeth's office that memorable day with a heavy heart. Bile rolled up her throat. She choked down the premonition of impending disaster. Panicky, she knew she was going to throw up. Then Elizabeth collapsed without uttering a single word.

Even now, two days later, Natasha still couldn't shake off the feeling that Elizabeth's sudden illness spared her. From what, she had no idea, but immense relief flowed over her.

What did she plan to show me?

Her mind screamed at her to leave it alone. Even without her super sensitive intuition, Natasha knew she was better off not knowing the truth.

Maybe it was her cowardly part or a healthy dose of fear.

Or maybe just old fashion common sense.

But the other bold and daring part of her knew that she would always wonder and dig into it until she found the truth.

But will you able to live with it?

"I don't know," she whispered. "I don't know..."

CHAPTER FIFTY-SIX

F ate was unpredictable. Sometimes cruel, sometimes shocking, but always mercurial. If someone told Dmitry that only a few days after his mad rush to France he would be back on California soil, he'd have laughed it off. But not now.

Because three days ago, Elizabeth suffered a massive stroke, then an ambulance rushed her to UCSF Medical Center.

Another hospital in another country, but the same feelings of sadness and despair. The same smell. Sterile, bitter, with unmistakable undertones of artificial fragrance. It nauseated him. The pounding headache refused to abate, even after the three strong painkillers he swallowed earlier. Dmitry marched toward the nurse's station doing his best to ignore it all.

During the long hours on the plane thoughts of his mother constantly raced through his mind.

Disturbing and sad, his memories played before his eyes, from early childhood to the most recent events. By the time his plane finally landed in San Francisco Dmitry was keyed up and agitated to a dangerous degree. Not fit for any human interactions, he decided to skip the stop at the *Zolotoe Selo*, and instructed his chauffer to take him straight to the hospital. A thousand thoughts crowded his mind. But front and center was the single one: decision. He must make a decision regarding his kids, and their living arrangements. And Natasha. But first, he needed to deal with Elizabeth.

From the short call he made from the car to her doctor, he learned that his mother lived, but remained critical. Her prognosis daunting. The doctor told him straight on that a full recovery was out of the question. If she survived at all, Elizabeth will be confined to a wheelchair for the rest of her life. More than likely, her speech will be affected, and the right part of her face will be deformed because of the atrophy of the facial nerves. In short, Elizabeth Rostoff will be transformed from the goddess of her little universe to an ugly, helpless cripple for the rest of her days. If she recovers. A very big *if.*

Dmitry was sure his mother preferred death to the prospect of a life in a wheelchair. And, damn it, him too. He just hoped that somehow her doctor made a mistake, and maybe a slim chance remained for her to regain full control over her mind as well as her body. A strong-willed, healthy, and stubborn woman with enough ruthlessness and power in her to fight to the end.

At least he hoped so, because to accept her pathetic existence as an invalid seemed unthinkable. Unbearable. For him as well as for her.

If she recovers.

He refused to think about *if.* Elizabeth must pull through.

But what will happen next? What kind of life will it be for her?

Death would be a mercy, but as a Christian and son, Dmitry refused to wish it for Elizabeth, even as an act of mercy. She was his mother, after all.

What about living in purgatory?

He swore out loud, drawing a startled gaze from the nurse. Dmitry apologized, then swore again, only this time in Russian. Of course, he wished her a speedy recovery. But when Elizabeth finally wakes and realizes she's been doomed to the life of a handicap, the situation will quickly become dire.

For her, and everybody around, because Elizabeth will drag into her same purgatory everyone she could manage. Just out of pure spite. And that included his son and daughter.

Dmitry's mind knew that her death would be a mercy, but his conscience screamed that she was his mother and still alive, even if in a coma.

Hell if she lives, hell if she dies. Trust Elizabeth to complicate everything.

Torn between his rational mind and his emotions, Dmitry was helpless, and angry.

The one thing clear to him: if Elizabeth pulled through, she won't be able to take care of herself. Never mind two grandchildren.

And that gave him the opportunity to assume the role of caregiver for Peter and Katia, and take his children away. Dmitry cringed. What kind of a bastard considered the opportunity at the time like that? Then he shrugged it off. If people chose to call him a bastard, then so be it. Elizabeth left him no choice.

By her illness or fate, the major obstacle that stood between Dmitry and his children slid away. Now, no one had the ability to challenge his decision to remove both kids from *Zolotoe Selo*. Not under the current circumstances. Even Natasha won't be able to object. And not a single judge in the country if Elizabeth decided to fight him. But she won't. As a smart woman, she'd realize her limitations. She'd never win a custody battle now.

Her stroke presented Dmitry with the perfect opportunity, but deep down, appalled him. What kind of person takes advantage of the illness of his own mother?

Disgusted, he realized that he was Elizabeth's son, after all.

Ruthless, heartless son of a bitch.

The urge to turn around and run away overwhelmed him. Dammit, he needed to see Natasha, to hear her voice, to hold her. And later he'd return, and face Elizabeth.

Halting in the mid stride, Dmitry stopped. Was it his imagination, or had the walls started to press in on him from all sides? The air appeared to be so thick it hurt to draw a single breath.

Such a miserable place. Must leave. Must get fresh air.

"Mr. Rostoff?" The nurse's voice knifed through the turbulence of his thoughts. "Dr. Litowski is on his way to see you. He'll take you to your mother's room."

Damn. Trapped.

A cold panic surged up and made him shaky. Sticky and pungent, a layer of sweat covered his body. He must run. Just turn around, and run.

And how childish. Stupid and irresponsible and undignified.

Fighting the impulse to bolt, Dmitry curtly nodded to the nurse, and braced himself. He felt like a prisoner waiting for an execution.

And in a manner of speaking, he was.

CHAPTER FIFTY-SEVEN

Natasha was reading to Katia her favorite Pushkin's *Tzar Saltan* when a discreet knock at the door interrupted her midsentence. The low menacing growl of both dogs told her the person behind the closed door. Ivan. She tensed, then called out, "Come in."

Elizabeth's old butler was the one person Natasha couldn't stomach. From the first moment she laid eyes on the tall skeleton of a man with his tiny colorless eyes and crooked hawk like nose, she despised him. With the years her feelings never changed. If anything, they become stronger, and more difficult to disguise. But Ivan was Elizabeth's trusted servant for eons, so they all—she, kids, and the dogs—endured his presence like a necessary evil. Although how the *evil* could be *a necessity*, Natasha didn't understand.

He entered the room, eyeing the dogs. Pasha and Misha bared their teeth and flanked both Katia and Natasha.

"Pardon the interruption, but you have a call." Ivan's gasping falsetto always reminded Natasha of a badly tuned fiddle.

"Thank you, Ivan."

"It's His Grace. He is at the hospital." Frowning, Ivan didn't try to hide his disapproval.

Why on earth does he care who calls me?

Maybe because Dmitry called her? Or that Natasha called him, and let him know about his mother's illness? Probably, all the above. And what did she care? The heck with Ivan. The most important thing was Dmitry arrived in San Francisco, and soon he'll be home. Excited, she allowed her smile to break free.

Thank God, Dmitry's back!

Scowling, Ivan quietly slipped out of the room.

"Father is here." Katia's clear voice broke through the haze of Natasha's joy.

"Yes, Kitten, he's here." Laughing, she swept Katia into her arms for an impulsive fierce hug. "I told you he promised to come back soon. You father always keeps his promises."

"Like he promised my mother to take care of me?"

Natasha's heart did a double take, her joy faded like a morning shadow.

"Who told you that?" She asked carefully.

Katia shrugged her tiny shoulders, pretending indifference, but her eyes were solemn, and unusually guarded.

"Grandmother," she finally replied.

Oh, that horrible woman.

Natasha's heart beat in unison with her surging anger. For Katia's sake, she bore down, trying to stay calm.

"What exactly did your grandmother tell you, Kitten?"

"That Father didn't want me. That my mother disobeyed, and had me anyway, and that he was mad at her. For having me. Then she wrote a letter to him, asking to take care of me." Katia's voice became vacant and neutral, a true sign of her distress. She avoided Natasha's eyes, and stared at her lap. Her small hands clutched into tiny white-knuckled fists.

Damn you, Elizabeth.

Her elation forgotten, Natasha kneeled before Katia, and laid a hand on her shoulder. Eyes still downcast, Katia remained quiet, stiff as a statue like always in Elizabeth's presence. Even though her grandmother was not in the room, her shadow lurked between them. Desperate to shake off that invisible shadow, Natasha searched her mind for words of comfort. The need to reach her little girl became paramount. She must get to Katia's heart, and make her listen.

Natasha remembered her dream that tormented her after Elizabeth's stroke. In her dream, she stood in a large spacious room full of light and flowers and laughter, in a middle of a celebration. Petya was there, and Dmitry too. And her little girl, all dressed up and pretty, smiled in open adoration at her father and brother.

In that dream, Natasha's heart melted from love and joy. Look at her, her little kitten! So happy, so beautiful. Wishing to join the little group, she stepped forward, only to realize that an invisible wall stood between her and the people she loved. Confused, she looked at them, called their names, as her fear slammed heavily against her heart. No one saw her or heard her desperate cries. In her dream, almost insane with grief and pain, Natasha pounded on that invisible wall to no avail. She smashed her fists into bloody pulps, but still unable to break through the barrier. Clawing at it, pressing her face and her body into its cold blockade, Natasha greedily drank with her eyes the scene of a happy family reunion.

What about me? How could you all forget about me?

She screamed and sobbed, but nobody heard her. She sensed a presence behind her. Something dark and powerful, that made her hair stand on end, chilling the blood in her veins. Terrified to look, but unable to resist, she slowly turned her head. Shrouded in dense fog, a long lean figure all in black met her gaze. Hidden under the hood, the face was invisible. But even before the figure lifted their arms and removed the hood, Natasha identified the evil creature.

"I told you, Natalia, all Rostoffs are users. Look at them." Elizabeth lifted a bony finger and pointed. "They don't need you anymore. And neither do I." she raised her hand high above her head. A heavy silver candlestick gleamed like a weapon, poised to strike.

Natasha always woke up at that moment. Not knowing the outcome was a blessing. It gave her some sliver of hope that she managed to turn away just in time to escape the vicious blow, or break through that invisible wall, and reach the people she loved.

Now, as she kneeled before Katia, her dream swam in her memory, turning into reality. Like there, she saw her little girl, but couldn't penetrate the invisible wall around Katia's heart. Panic dripped its poison into her blood, but Natasha ruthlessly pushed it away.

It is not a dream, but real life. I'll be damned to allow Elizabeth to separate me from the people I love.

Shrugging away her fear, Natasha concentrated on Katia. Gently, she asked, "Look at me, Kitten. Please."

When Katia finally lifted her eyes, Natasha shivered. Bottomless, haunted, those dark ancient eyes didn't belong on the face of a child.

Damn you Elizabeth. Damn you to hell and back.

"Kitten," she began when she finally found her voice, "your father wasn't mad at your mama. Not at all. They just had a disagreement."

"Because of the baby he didn't want."

Not a question, but a quiet resignation. It shredded Natasha's heart to a million tiny pieces.

"No, baby, not because of you." Desperate to protect her child, Natasha lied without a qualm. "Never because of you."

"Grandmother said it *was*. Father didn't want a baby because he already had Petya."

"Sunshine, it wasn't like that at all. Believe me. Sometimes grownups quarrel, even if they love each other very much."

"He *did* love her, didn't he, Mama?" Her pleading eyes begged. Weeping inside, Natasha pulled a fake smile onto her face.

"Yes, Kitten. He did. He loved her very, very much." Deliberately, Natasha stressed each word. "And your mother loved him. Very, very much."

"Why then... why did she ask him to take care of me? Didn't she want me?"

Sweet Lord, is that what Katia thinks? Has Elizabeth deliberately convinced her of it? Oh, that cold-blooded, vicious bitch!

"Oh, baby. She wanted you more than anything." Natasha gathered both Katia's ice-cold hands, and implored the little girl with her eyes. "More than she wanted to live."

How she wished to break Elizabeth's black heart into gazillion pieces.

Violence is not the answer.

Natasha drew in a deep calming breath. "Svetlana, your mama, wrote to your father from the hospital, after you were born, and when she knew for sure that she... that she couldn't be there for you. Couldn't protect you. Do you understand?"

Katia's unblinking hard stare stayed glued to Natasha's face. The disturbing intensity of that gaze so unnatural for a six-year-old child.

"She knew she was dying." Katia nodded.

"Yes."

"If she wouldn't have died, she wouldn't have given me away?"

"Never, Kitten. Your mama would never give you to anyone."

"Not even to you?"

"No, not even to me."

"Truly?"

"Really, truly. Cross my heart." Natasha looked Katia straight in the eyes. Inside she was a jumble of nerves and fear and anger. That potent violent mix tore her apart.

Damn that heartless bitch Elizabeth. To lie to a child about her parents? Despicable.

How could she, a mother herself, be so cruel? At that moment, in her heart of hearts, Natasha sincerely wished all the harm in the world to befall Elizabeth. Seething inside, she tried to control her emotions, and keep her facial expression as calm as possible for Katia's sake. Not an easy task.

For a long moment, Katia peered into her eyes, and then the tension began to ebb from her face, her fisted hands, her entire body. Her thin shoulders slumped a little. Natasha's heart broke all over again. How much can a human heart take before it literally shatters from pain and sorrow?

Katia glanced up, and flashed Natasha a sunny smile. And became a six-year-old once again.

Until that moment, Natasha failed to realize she held her breath. She felt a huge weight lifted off her chest. Misty eyed, still shaky, she smiled back at Katia. Then unable to keep still any longer, she hugged her little girl, holding her close and tight. Enormous relief filled Natasha to the brim.

She managed to reached her baby and smash the invisible barrier between them, and chased away Elizabeth's shadow. For now, it was more than enough.

"You better go, Mama," Katia whispered against her shoulder, "Father is waiting on the phone."

"Oh, my God, I forgot!" Natasha jumped. For Katia's benefit, she slapped herself playfully on the forehead, and made the little girl giggle.

"I'll be right back, Kitten. Okay?"

"'Kay," Katia agreed readily. Then, as Natasha walked closer to the door, she stopped her with her question, "Mama, why did Grandmother lie to me?"

She held no doubt that Elizabeth lied to her. Hallelujah. Natasha paused, clutching the doorknob in one hand. Then turned to Katia.

How to answer? The truth is always the better choice, but how do you explain evil? Especially, to a young child.

But Katia saved Natasha from her dilemma. Softly, she answered her own question, "She doesn't love my father very much. Or my mama. And she doesn't love me." Her expression sobered. "She doesn't love anyone, does she, Mama? Not even Petya."

Natasha knew that for Katia, her brother was absolute perfection, the only human being that could do no wrong. By her simple logic, If Elizabeth didn't love Petya, how was it possible for her to love anybody else?

Somehow at the tender age of six, her little girl managed to figure out the complex mysteries of human nature. With burning eyes and heavy heart, Natasha slipped past the doorway.

CHAPTER FIFTY-EIGHT

Dmitry burst through the front door, almost mowing down Ivan in his haste to get to Natasha. Strange, but he couldn't shake the feeling that something terrible might happen if he didn't see her soon. Ridiculous, but still.

After he apologized to the butler, he inquired about Natasha's whereabouts. He deliberately ignored Ivan's shrewd, speculative gaze, and stared at the old man long and hard, until he relented.

"Natalia is currently with Katia."

Without sparing Ivan another word, he ran to the staircase, and took two steps at a time toward the third floor. Something spooked him but he had no idea what. Probably their earlier phone conversation. He called her from the hospital, eager to hear her voice. But she kept him on hold for so long, he wondered if she'd asnwer at all. Maybe, she took off. Or, maybe she didn't want to talk to him. Or maybe...

A thousand different scenarios raced through his mind while he waited, one more daunting than the next. By the time Natasha finally responded, he worked himself up to a boiling point. Because of that, Dmitry was unwarrantedly harsh with her, barking his questions, demanding answers. Truth be told, he was desperate and panicky, but Natasha either failed to notice, or no longer care. She kept her voice calm, but the unmistakable tension in it came through loud and clear.

And something else he failed to put his finger on. Fear? Fatigue? Anger?

Disturbed, Dmitry forced himself to softened his voice. "Natasha, what's wrong?"

"Come home, Dmitry. Please, come home."

A short time later Dmitry sat in the car and realized that Natasha never asked about Elizabeth. Tucking it into the back of his mind, he concentrated on the road, and constantly urging his driver to "floor it."

At last, he arrived at the estate, but instead of ebbing away, his fear increased.

With every step he took to climb the staircase, with every breath his lungs managed to squeeze in and out, Dmitry panicked more. Dear God, why? Why was he so afraid to be late?

Late for what?

He reached the closed nursery door and heard Natasha's muted voice. He forced himself to stop and inhale slowly.

His little daughter was inside. She and Natasha were unharmed and safe. Bad idea to barge in like a maniac, scaring the life out of them.

They are all right. They are together. They are okay.

He mumbled that mantra until his heartbeat slowed and his legs stopped shaking. Combing his disheveled hair with both hands, Dmitry righted his shoulders and knocked on the door. Not waiting for permission, he entered the room.

Both Natasha and Katia sat on the floor, looking at the pictures in a book. They both froze the moment he entered the room. Natasha's mouth turned into a tight thin line. She appeared tired and tense, her skin pale, almost translucent, her eyes dark and huge with smoky shadows underneath. She had wound her hair into a knot at her nape. A few wild wisps of flaming curls bounced around her ears.

Has she lost weight?

Always slender, she seemed almost gaunt. Dammit.

With her face set, she pressed her mouth in a thin hard line. But to him, she was even more beautiful than ever. Dmitry barely held himself from snatching her into his arms. She kept silent. Finally, Natasha nodded to him, and turned her eyes toward the tiny figure of the girl staring at him with wide pewter eyes.

With his mother's eyes.

He wondered how much time must pass to eliminate that shock every time he faced his daughter. He cursed fate for etching his mother's features on the face of this tender child.

"Hello." The impulse to say '*I'm home*' caught him by surprise.

What if they were a real family? Would they greet him with smiles and hugs every time he came home from a workday? A flash of that vision suddenly became vivid and clear, Dmitry shook his head. But the picture refused to fade from his mind.

That's what I'm missing. That's why I always feel incomplete and empty.

It punched him like a fist in a solar plexus, making him breathless.

Shocked, he stared at them. Finally, he found his voice.

"I came back. I'm so happy to see you. Both of you."

Katia's lips began to curve, hesitantly at first. When her sunny innocent smile fully bloomed, his heart stopped, then thudded heavily under his left breastbone. She came to her feet in a single liquid movement, with a natural inborn grace that reminded Dmitry of Svetlana.

Ah, love, our little girl has something of you, after all,

But instead of a bitter regret, a wave of tenderness rose from the pit of his stomach.

Looking into his daughter's luminous face, Dmitry let go of his anger, and the past.

Who moved first? Him? Katia? Did it matter? They took their first steps toward each other. Unexpectedly, Katia jumped up and held her arms out to him, trusting him to catch her. He did. And it seemed so natural. So right.

Dmitry inhaled greedily as he burrowed his face into her silky hair. Her fragrance, of something sweet and clean and heartbreaking, staggered him.

Innocence.

His little daughter smelled of innocence and hope and love. She smelled of flowers and crayons, dolls and adventures, and sweet dreams of childhood.

The dreams he almost destroyed.

Never. I'll never do to Katia what my own parents have done to me.

He vowed to die protecting her dreams, and her. She was his, his second chance, his forgiveness. His salvation. His little miracle. His daughter.

CHAPTER FIFTY-NINE

Natasha noticed the tears that escaped Dmitry's thightly squeezd eyelids and trickled down his cheeks. Unsteady, trembling, she pushed herself off the floor. Her cheeks flamed and she desperately wanted to leave, to give the father and daughter their privacy. And enormously hurt. Because she knew there was not a tiny place for her in that tight embrace. As quiet as possible, she slipped out of the room. Hurrying now, she began to run, and didn't stop until she found herself in front of her sanctuary, the gazebo. Breathless, she stumbled inside. She felt alone and isolated as she gazed at the lacy white walls that surrounded her. Hurt, tired, and confused, she paid no attention to anything, including the biting chill in the air. In her desperate haste to leave she forgot to grab a jacket. Shivers charged up her spine and down her arms as her teeth began to chatter.

But were they from the cold weather or her emotions? Probably, both. Silly, but Natasha sensed like her little girl slipping away, becoming more and more enamored with her father. And what would happen if Katia was taken from her? What if they no longer needed her? She was not her mother, just a nanny.

Natasha shook her head to push away those thoughts, and afraid to think about it.

Her exposed skin sprouted goosebumps the size of small pebbles. In a futile attempt to keep warm, she hugged herself tight. She plunked down on the wicker settee then brought her legs up, and curled into a protective fetal position. She pressed her forehead to her knees, and wept.

CHAPTER SIXTY

Dmitry found her inside the gazebo, huddled on a couch that saw better days. Curved into a ball of misery, her body shook from sobbing. So tiny, so fragile, he feared her bones might shatter from the force of her weeping. He quietly stepped inside, then covered her with the coat he brought from the house. He plucked her from the settee and into his arms. After one startled jerk, Natasha burrowed her face deeper into the folds of the coat, and leaned against him.

He remained silent, and held her. Hard and tight. When he knew she was finally spent, he sat them down, still holding her. She stopped shivering, thank God. An occasional shudder arrowed through her body, but those uncontrollable tremors finally ceased.

She stiffened and tried to push herself out of his arms.

He tightened his embrace, caging her.

"Let me go," she demanded in a raw voice.

"Never."

"Dmitry, let me go, this is... silly."

"You may well stop your struggles. I'm stronger than you, and I'm not letting you up."

After a moment she relented. "How... how did you find me?"

"Pasha, or Misha. I still can't tell these dogs apart."

Natasha glanced over his shoulder.

"Misha," she said, clarifying the identity of the dog guarding the gazebo entrance. "It's okay, boy. I'm all right. Good boy."

Misha gave one short bark, then wined pitifully.

"Go home, boy," he said softly to the dog. "Go find Katia."

Without further prodding, Misha turned and disappeared into the heavy foliage of the trees.

"He obeyed you!" Surprised, Natasha stopped her struggles. "He didn't even look at me for approval. He just obeyed you."

He chuckled. "And you are surprised and a little jealous, right?"

Natasha gazed up at him with furrowed brows.

"Maybe. Probably. It just ... it never happened before. Even when Petya tells them to do something, they both are waiting for me to approve it."

"Sorry, I didn't mean to usurp your role."

"It's not that, it's just... oh, I don't know." Her weary sigh tugged at his heart.

"Natasha, are you okay?"

"No. I'm tired. I'm so damn tired."

To his acute discomfort, her eyes filled again.

"Hush, sweetheart, I'm here, you're going to be all right." He crooned to her as if she were a small child, and rubbed her back in a soothing motion.

But Natasha refused to be pacified. Tears began to roll freely from her red-rimmed puffy eyes.

"Stop it." Her desperate shout accompanied by the jab of her small fist to his chest. "Stop being kind. Don't you see what you're doing to me?"

"I can't." Despite his current mood, Dmitry smiled.

"Can't or won't?" She requested between sobs.

"Either. Both."

"You are... you are... impossible!"

"But you love me, anyway." He meant it like a joke, then realized how it sounded. Natasha stilled. The hell with it. He lifted her face with his fingertips, then examined her tear-streaked face. "You do, don't you, Natasha?"

Scared and desperate, her vulnerability tore at his soul, but he chose to ignore it. Desperate himself and fighting for his life, he decided all was fair in love and war.

"Say it," he urged her in a harsh voice, pushing beyond fair, and not giving a damn. "Say it, Natasha."

"I... can't."

"Yes, you can. Say it!" He tensed and held her chin immobile. For the life of him, he didn't know why it was so imperative for him to hear the words when all the love in the world shined openly at him from her mesmerizing eyes.

After a heartbeat, she whispered, "I love you, Dmitry. Always have, always will."

Tenderly, almost reverently he touched his forehead to her brow, exhaling a breath he had held for the longest moment of his life.

"Natasha..." Just that. Just her name. Wonder and joy, apology, and plea.

She smiled tremulously through her tears.

He raised his head and took his time to look at her. He wanted to sit there like that, with Natasha in his lap, and look at her forever. And even that wasn't long enough.

"Sometimes forever isn't long enough." He suddenly realized he said it out loud.

"Yes, sometimes it isn't," Natasha agreed in a quiet voice.

They looked at each other for a long time, completely unaware of time. Huddled together, they sat, with their arms around each other, and their bodies pressed close together. He relished the intimacy, deep and profound, warm and kind. Whole at last.

Finally, he became aware of their physical closeness. His blood began to heat, his heart started to thunder. Anticipation churned in his gut.

Desire grew to unprecedented heights. He closed the last few inches of distance then claimed her mouth. Fused together, their lips and tongues battled for dominance, as the savage need to taste exploded. In unison, they fought for control, desperate to quench the thirst for one another, to get closer, to become whole.

Drunk on her taste, Dmitry shifted impatiently, as a deep growl rumbled in his throat. Natasha's desperate whimpers drove him mad. She clutched at his shoulders almost painfully, all but plastering her chest into his. One handed, he tugged at her hair, changed the angle of the kiss, and delved his tongue deeper.

Guided by passion and instinct, she pushed her own tongue into the cave of his mouth. The heat became unbearable. Too much. Not enough.

Soon the heat became an inferno. Scorching. Searing. All-consuming.

He should be afraid with everything happening so fast. Too much. Not enough.

But he wasn't. With the first sweep of her tongue inside of his mouth, he stopped thinking, and began to feel. More, and more, and more.

His soul burned, and didn't give a damn. As long as her nails raked his shoulders and her tongue made fast forays into his mouth, as long as her soft, generous lips trembled beneath his, he was able to endure this sweet torture bordering on pain. Natasha rubbed her middle against him in a dance as primitive and old as this world. Not enough. His hunger clawed inside him, a beast desperate to be free. Ripping his mouth from her, he trailed his lips over her face and throat. Impatient now, he tried to strip off her clothes. She didn't make it easy. Moving, undulating, whimpering, while her hands tugged at his shirt. He was losing it fast.

Get a grip, Rostoff.

With a herculean effort, he grabbed her busy hands in both of his, putting a stop to their progress.

CHAPTER SIXTY-ONE

Frustrated, Natasha struggled to free her hands from his vice-like grip and failed.

Several seconds later, it registered that Dmitry went completely still. The only sound she heard was his heavy breathing. She blinked a few times to clear the blurry vision. His face finally came into focus. Eyes closed, mouth pressed in a hard line, jaw set. Did something hurt him? The desire to touch his face, to erase that deep frown between his brows became irresistible. But he still held her hands in a firm grip. A thought slashed through her hazy brain. What if she offended him somehow? What if he found her appalling, or repulsive? Or inadequate? She was inexperienced, totally clueless when it came to the matter of sex. Oh, Lord! Mortified, she moaned, and her shame gave her the strength to finally pull her hands free. The sudden movement sent her backward. Thankfully, Dmitry broke her fall before she landed on the floor. Snatching her in midair, he brought her back into his lap.

"Let me go." She began to fight him in earnest.

"Natasha, stop it. Stop, damn it. What's wrong?"

"What's wrong? I tell you what's wrong, everything."

"What's gotten into you?"

She slapped his shoulder. "Let me go, I said."

"Okay, all right. I'll let you go, but only after you explain what happened. Did I hurt you? Offend you in any way?"

"No, no. But obviously, I did."

"You did what?" He gazed at her in obvious confusion. "What are you talking about?"

"You. Me. My inexperience. Idiot. How could I even have thought...?"

Distressed, she covered her face with both hands, embarrassed beyond belief. She needed to muster every ounce of her control not to bolt. On top of it, her face burned.

Firmly, Dmitry pulled away her hands covering her face.

"Natasha, listen to me: you have nothing to be embarrassed about, you were—"

"Inept and inadequate and shameless and... and wanton." Her voice rose several octaves, but she couldn't stop herself. "And you just feel sorry for me. For goodness' sake, stop! Stop trying to soothe me. Stop being so bloody kind."

"Kind? Soothe? Woman, I could describe what just happened between us in many words, but *kind* and *soothing* have nothing to do with it. And never tell me what I feel. Never assume what I feel." He lifted her chin in one hand, then forced her to look at him. "Listen to me. You are passionate, responsive, open and honest. Wanton? Hell, yes. Shameless? I hope so. I hope with me you'll forget any shame and inhibitions. But not inept or inadequate, Natasha. Never that. And if you'd be a little more experienced, you'd kill me."

"Then why did you stop? If you weren't repulsed or upset, why did you stop?"

CHAPTER SIXTY-TWO

Because I'm an idiot. Or a masochist.

But Dmitry knew exactly why he stopped. With any other woman he'd allow the clawing beast that raged inside of him to go free. With any other woman he'd go farther, push harder. But not with her. Not with Natasha.

He recognized her innocence under a layer of passion. And her vulnerability.

She surrendered to him fully, but her eager abandon spoke volumes by itself.

Yes, her kisses were hot and erotic and wild, and set him on fire.

But he sensed she had more enthusiasm than finesse, and knew that her experience with sex was limited, if not nonexistent. Natasha was way out of his league.

He gathered every ounce of self-control he possessed to stop. Because she deserved better. And because he needed time to tame that roaring animal inside of him that demanded to plunge, to take, to ravish.

He couldn't do that to her. To them.

When he finally made love to Natasha, he planed to take his sweet time. He wanted to build her passion slowly, to bring her to the burning point. Gently, irrevocably. He'd make her tremble and writhe and scream. And then do it all over again.

He will make love to her so many times, and make her realize that she belonged to him. His woman. Only his.

"Because when we make love the first time it should be in bed," he answered at last, and wondered at how even and calm his voice sounded while inside his guts churned from frustration. "Because you deserve better than being taken upright in an open gazebo, with a good chance of an unwelcomed audience. Including the kids."

"Kids..." Still glazed and unfocused, her eyes bore into him. "*Kids*?"

"Yes, kids. Peter has just arrived. I left Katia with him before I went to look for you."

"Oh, my God! What if they decide to search for us? They could be here any moment, and they could..." She became all action. In her desperate attempt to disengage their bodies, she almost fell backward.

"Natasha, relax. They won't come looking for us. I specifically told Peter, not to; that I needed some privacy to talk to you."

"Talk?" The helpless sound she made came out somewhere between a laugh and a sob. "Sweet Lord, look at me. Look at you. We're a mess. How will we face Petya? He'll know immediately what we were *talking* about."

"Natasha, he won't say anything."

" And what difference does that make? He'll know. Don't you understand? He'll know, and he will think that I... that we..."

"Yes, he probably will guess, so what? We didn't do anything wrong. We never hurt anybody. We are both adults, Natasha. And his parents to boot."

"You are his parent, not me."

"You have more rights to be called his parent than I do," he said and meant it.

Natasha, still off balance, frantically fixed her hair curling wildly every which way. Moaning in resignation, she decided to leave it alone.

"What were you thinking about?" She rounded on him, indignant and agitated. Dmitry grinned. Natasha clearly forgot that just a moment ago she complained about the abrupt stop he put on their passionate interlude.

Then he sobered. "You," he answered honestly. "Only you."

Magnified by tears, her eyes sparkled like two star-kissed pools. His heart did one quick somersault. Peace as he never knew before settled around his soul.

Love, sweet, huge, and all-consuming, swelled in his heart, making him tremble with the force and beauty of it. He still didn't tell Natasha that he loved her. Not because he was unsure of his feelings, but because he wanted to hug them close, to marvel and rejoice and wonder. Just for a little while longer.

He smiled and he offered his hand. "Let's go home."

She took it with a quick nod. "Let's go see the children."

And together, holding their hands, they walked toward the house.

CHAPTER SIXTY-THREE

Night finally settled down over the Rostoff's household like a soft curtain.

Dark and quiet.

Dmitry walked to his bedroom window then opened it wide. The arrogant manor house seemed suspended between a starless dome of a sky and the ground, with wisps of white mist blurring the edges.

Such an eerie and surreal picture.

The darkness was absolute but not frightening. Somehow, it seemed kind and peaceful. The hour grew quite late, but sleep eluded him. Wrung out emotionally and physically, after the long and troublesome day, he was restless and on edge.

The turbulent day with its emotional upheavals left him unbalanced.

Same time yesterday he sat on his veranda in France, out of his mind thinking about Natasha. Wondering, brooding, regretting.

Today he faced her, touched her, kissed her. Hell, he all but made love to her in the gazebo.

So much for my prized self-control.

He scowled as disgust wove through him.

Granted, he did stop. In the nick of a time, but still. But God, it cost him.

He still hurt. A pounding headache wanted to split his skull open. His heart drummed a heavy beat, bruising his ribcage. Not to mention the one part of his anatomy that still pulsed and strained against his pants. Dammit, he wasn't a green youth at the mercy of his glands! He should be able to control his lust. And that was the crux of the problem. Dmitry cursed. *Lust* he could control. But his feelings for Natasha went much deeper, and were more complex. Need. Tenderness. Protectiveness.

Love.

The word humbled him, and unnerved him, and staggered him. It made him feel larger than life. Invincible. Happy. Free.

She made him feel whole and complete.

She made him feel good about himself. And she gave him his family.

Family.

Finally, Dmitry had a family, the kids and Natasha. And he vowed to never let them go. Exhilarated, he promised to take them away from *Zolotoe Selo* as soon as possible. Away from the cold and forbidding place. Away from his mother.

He intended to relocate his family in Paris, where they will live together, and become a true family.

He'll stay here as long as needed for Elizabeth's recovery. But as soon as she felt stronger, the kids, Natasha and him were gone.

Elizabeth was a smart woman. She must understand that she couldn't take care of the children anymore. But if she won't, Dmitry had an ace up his sleeve: her obsession with the Rostoff heiress. If Elizabeth wanted to see her granddaughter at all, she must agree with his decision, and never interfere.

Using Katia as a bargaining chip burned a hole in his gut, but if it helped him to reach his ultimate goal, God help him, he had no choice. Once they settled, he intended to pray for Katia's forgiveness.

Of course, he'd take his daughter from California no matter what, but Dmitry still didn't want to do it the hard way. But if Elizabeth made any effort to stop him, then he swore to fight her tooth and nail to the very end. She had to know she must lose.

He cursed, and wondered why he the restlessness, frustration, excitement.

Maybe something in the air. He closed his eyes, and drew in the fragrance of the night. Alive. So right. And then a powerful shiver shot through him. An eerie premonition of something dark and chilling sent goosebumps rioting along his exposed arms. Spooked, Dmitry scanned the room.

Plunged into the shadows, the familiar scene seemed oddly disconcerting. The furniture, the rugs, the clock on the wall—everything appeared the same, but at the same time, a bit blurry. He blinked, and brought the picture into focus.

Ridiculous. And when did you become such a fanciful fool, Rostoff?

But still, he failed to erase the sudden sensation of fear. With an effort, he shook it off. Just a remnant of his turbulent day, nothing more. He turned to the open window again. Listening to the silence of the night, Dmitry realized that he waited. But for what? He supposed it probably silly, but he knew something was about to happen. Good or bad?

CHAPTER SIXTY-FOUR

Natasha rolled over in her bed, wide-awake and restless. She pummeled her pillow a few times, plopped on her back, then turned again. Exhaustion ravaged her mind and soul. Why, then, was sleep her enemy? Why spend the night tossing and turning for hours on end?

God, who was she kidding? She knew exactly why and who to blame for it. Burrowing her face in the pillow, Natasha uttered a helpless moan.

Damn you, Dmitry, what have you done to me?

Her body pulsed like an exposed nerve. She wanted to go to him, put her hands around him, feel him. All of him. She craved to taste his mouth again, to tear away all the clothes from his body and then...

And then her imagination deserted her. Natasha didn't know what she to do *then*. And how could she, if she's never done that before?

"Idiot." She hissed through her clenched teeth, and covered her burning face with a bent elbow. "Stupid idiot."

Almost thirty years old, a grown woman, for goodness' sake! And totally clueless about the matters of sex. She had a general knowledge of the act itself, at least the physical aspect of it. But she never really considered it in terms of personal participation. Or wondered about it. Why would she? Her one and only close encounter with the act was her near rape thirteen years ago. That horrific episode left her traumatized, and scared of men, and intimacy.

Until Dmitry.

He burst into her life, spun it upside down, and made her fall in love with him. He hurt her, then walked out. Then he came back and kissed her. Twice. And touched her. And set her on fire. And then...

Shivering, Natasha pulled the covers up to her chin as she scooted higher in the bed. She refused to think about him. She intended to sit for a while and think of something else. But instead, she kept remembering the moment when they walked back to the house together. Her nerves were stretched too far, making her afraid to meet the kids, especially Petya. Terrified, a more accurate word, said it all. What if he guessed what they were doing earlier in the gazebo? Her disheveled hair and wrinkled clothes. And her mouth all puffy and tender. Would Petya know?

But everything went well, all things considering. Both children met them downstairs, waiting impatiently.

After a brief glance at her, Petya suggested a late supper. Katia squealed with excitement, then ran around, hugging Natasha and Dmitry in turn. The entire time she prattled on a mile a minute.

She seemed unusually cheerful and chatty all evening, smiling and laughing, asking Dmitry all kinds of questions. By nature, Katia was shy and a little aloof. Or so Natasha thought. Maybe the atmosphere of the oppressive house, her home, or maybe the lack of the children her own age to play with.

Her little girl spent all her time with adults, the youngest of whom eighteen years old. Natasha brought this problem to Elizabeth a hundred times, asking her to enroll Katia in preschool, or at least allow her to communicate with other kids, but to no avail. Elizabeth was adamant in her decision to keep Katia inside *Zolotoe Selo*, away from other children and the influence of the modern culture. Natasha strongly disagreed. Vehemently, she voiced her protests, trying to force Elizabeth to reconsider, even begging several times. She desperately tried to convince her that closing Katia from the world, or treating her like a grownup, was wrong and harmful to the child. Unfortunately, Natasha never succeeded. Elizabeth forbade Katia to go to kindergarten last fall, enrolling her in homeschooling program instead.

But Natasha refused to lose hope. Someday Elizabeth must give in. Someday. But until then, her little girl remained raised by the household full of old servants, the ancient art teacher, Petya, and herself.

Today, for the first time Katia acted and behaved like a six-year-old. Because of Dmitry. His presence made a miraculous difference. Like awakened from a deep freeze, her little girl became animated and carefree and happy.

He is good for her. Good to her.

She smiled as she watched them together. Both Katia and Dmitry seemed like different people. The bond between them rooted, and strengthened with every passing moment. Natasha was happy for the father and daughter. And obviously, Petya too who smiled as he continued to watch them throughout the evening.

He shared family stories most of which he invented on the go. The three of them made a spectacular picture. Both men were dark, tall, and handsome. Katia, fair and fragile like a spring flower, pretty in her own quiet way. Her elegant tiny features hinted on the great beauty that still slept inside the child.

Happy for them, Natasha tried to squelch the odd feeling that she was a fifth wheel. An outsider. Sadness crept toward her heart. She didn't belong. Even the dogs ignored her, trailing after Dmitry like two shadows.

She wanted to resent Dmitry for it, but God help her, she couldn't.

Preoccupied with the children, he paid her little to no attention.

She told herself that she was glad, even grateful for it. Still off balance from their earlier encounter in the gazebo, Natasha didn't know how to act as if nothing happened. How to pretend normalcy when her life spun out of its axis. She'd probably make a complete fool of herself if he asked her a single question. Or just smiled at her. To be excluded from his and kids attention was truly a blessing. She should be relived. Dammit, she was miserable!

Even when Natasha reminded Katia of the time, and about to take her upstairs, Dmitry looked away. Then he spoke to his sulking daughter in a soft voice, promising her to come up later to say goodnight.

What about me?

Frustrated and unbelievably hurt, Natasha fought her tears.

First, he kissed me, touched me, and then ignores me all evening.

Now, hours later, Natasha agonized, still agitated, and hurt. Damn him. Who the hell did he think he was? Fuming, she threw her blanket back.

He has no right to treat me like this.

She needed to give the mighty Dmitry Rostoff a piece of her mind.

She snatched her robe from the foot of the bed, then shrugged it on. She raced to the door and flung it open, then flew out of her bedroom.

Ignore her, will he?

Well, we'll see how he ignores me now!

Barefooted, she ran all the way to Dmitry's room. She stopped at his door and inhaled slowly. When she gained full control, she lifted her arm and knocked. Loudly.

Dmitry flung the door open as if he expected her. After a short pause, he grinned at her. Natasha forced herself not to explode.

"If you think you can kiss me, and then ignore me, you have another—"

He tugged her hand and pulled her close, then kissed her. It went on and on, until she forgot her own name.

"You were saying?" He asked at last, his lips hovering above her mouth. His warm silky breath that had a tinge of red wine caressed her.

"Hmm-mm?" Dear God, her head spun in lazy circles. "W-what?"

"My thoughts exactly." And he covered her mouth again.

CHAPTER SIXTY-FIVE

Shaky and loose as two overcooked noodles, Natasha's legs folded. Dmitry caught her just before she hit the floor. Holding her hard and fast, he devoured her mouth, swiping his tongue sensually along the inside. He tasted like coffee and chocolate and whiskey.

Decadent.

Delicious.

Marvelous.

The textures, the flavors, so unfamiliar, so fascinating...Ravenous, she opened her mouth wider, allowing him better access. In one easy swoop, he whisked her into his arms, and carried her deeper into the room. Floating, momentarily confused, she grabbed his shoulders. Airborne and helpless, she held on to him like an anchor, her one and only constant in a world that was spinning away.

She liked being carried. So romantic. No one ever did that before. She tightened her arms around him and smiled against his full lips. Dazed and lightheaded, she wished the moment to go on forever. But her euphoria was short lived. As soon as she felt the mattress beneath her back, the moment of sanity crashed into her like a brutal wave. No longer thrilled, she panicked at the squeaky sound of the bed under their combined weight. Cold fear paralyzed her from inside out. Even her vocal cords seemed frozen, and refused to obey. Momentarily mute, horrified, Natasha gasped for air to no avail. After a brief terrifying moment, she finally found her voice.

"Wait. Dmitry, wait." She pushed against his shoulders to no avail.

Please God don't let him think I'm being modest or coy.

Blissfully unaware of her torment, Dmitry continued to caress her with his hands, as he murmured words of reassurance, "Don't be afraid, baby. I won't hurt you, I swear. We'll go slow, very slow."

"I... I'm not afraid," Natasha lied, torn between the need to melt into his hands, and the desperate urge to get away from the weight of a male body pinning her to the bed. Her fear won. Terrified, trembling, she froze as her teeth began to chatter.

Desperate now, she struggled to control her reaction, but failed. The moment he covered her body, something inside her snapped, and the memory of her attack flashed back. Snippets of images, smells, and noises...and fear, enormous, all-consuming, debilitating. Torn between past and present, trapped in a nightmare.

Helpless.

Hopeless.

Vulnerable.

Drenched in cold sweat, unmindful of her brain's command, her body bucked against him, trying to get free of his weight.

It didn't matter that it was Dmitry, not the brutal mad rapist. Or that she laid on her back, not face down like that night. Nothing mattered.

Her vision began to blur. Her lungs constricted. To draw a single breath became an impossible struggle. Natasha started to suffocate. She recognized her panic attack. Soon, she must fight him with every fiber of her being.

Dear God, no.

She didn't even realize that she screamed. Dmitry stilled.

"Natasha? What's wrong?"

"Get... off... me. Get... off."

The next instant his weight lifted from her Natasha greedily gulped a lungful of air.

CHAPTER SIXTY-SIX

Natasha's body shook liked she suffered an electric shock. Dmitry looked at her in awe, afraid her bones might shatter. Puzzled, he drew back. Whiter than snow, eyes wide, she gazed up at him with a petrified expression.

Dammit, she isn't faking.

Whatever prompted her to stop their lovemaking, was serious. When he looked deeper into her eyes, shock rocked him.

A chilling fear turned her irises into frozen pools of terror. He lifted his body off her. As soon as he did, Natasha jumped off the bed then raced for the door. Her raspy breathing came in a short, desperate staccato.

"Natasha..."

But hearing his voice, she all but folded into herself. Low and tiny, the sound that burst from her throat sent chills along his spine. Horrified, Dmitry somehow managed to keep his voice soft and gentle. "Don't worry, little one, I won't touch you. Just tell me what it is? Did I scare you?"

"No, no, it wasn't you... It's me." Her teeth clinked so badly, she barely uttered the few words. "It's me. I'm s-sorry, s-so... s-sorry."

Tears streamed down her face in rivulets. Torn between the urge to gather her into his arms, and fear to scare her even more, he watched helplessly as she struggled for control. After what seemed an eternity, she seemed to breathe more evenly. She dropped onto the bench at the foot of the bed, then covered her face and hid her eyes.

On, no, you don't.

He'd be damned if he let her to withdraw from him.

He asked in the quietest voice his deep baritone allowed, "Tell me."

"I... It's not you, Dmitry. I didn't realize I couldn't...that I was ..." She calmed herself by inhaling slowly. "When you kissed me today, I thought that everything would be all right, that I forgot, but I guess not."

"Forgot what, Natasha?"

She whispered, "My attack."

"Attack? What attack?"

Then it hit him. Her frozen panic in the gardens, five years ago. What did she say? Something about a monster that abused and dragged you through the mud only because he held that power. Dear God, of course! How could he forget? She had been abused, maybe even raped.

Dammit all to hell and back.

And he charged like a bull, all but ravishing her. Bastard.

Dmitry sat next to her and gently touched her shoulder. But inside he trembled with barely suppressed anger. In an instant he wanted to kill the bastard who did this to her. Natasha didn't pull away, but neither did she look at him.

She kept her eyes focused on the rug, and remained silent. She wasn't going to confide in him. She didn't trust him enough.

And what did you expect?

Resigned, he edged farther away from her. But then she started to talk. He barely recognized her voice. Bleak, lifeless, a void of any emotion. It chilled his blood.

"It was... a long time ago, in my old country. "

"Natasha, you don't have to—"

"But I want to. Need to. I never talked about it. Maybe if I confide in someone, then it will all go away? I don't know. But at the time, I simply couldn't. I was too ashamed."

"Did Svetlana know?"

"No. No one knew except my doctor and the nurses at the hospital, and of course *militia*. And a man who was walking his dog. He saved me. Or his dog did. Maybe that's why I love dogs so much."

She rubbed her forearms, then hugged herself. "It happened during my junior year of college. I moved to Leningrad from Moscow. I always dreamed of *Pushkin* college of Russian Language and Literature. When I was accepted there, my dream came true. I lived in a dorm with four other girls. I had to work because I needed to eat, so I took the job in a small cafe washing dishes. Because I was a fulltime student, I had to go to classes in the morning, and work evenings. Salary was miserly, just barely enough to buy bread and milk, but our manager sometimes would give me leftovers, and besides I was raised in an orphanage, so..." she shrugged, "I was used to it. And I don't eat much, anyway. I even managed to save money for the theater and books."

She droned on like a mechanical device, but Dmitry heard despair and misery under a layer of cool detachment. She ripped him apart. His heart broke for a malnourished lonely girl with her big dreams, and for the beautiful woman who now revealed that girl's biggest nightmare.

"One night, I was returning from a late shift. And walking fast, very fast, because of the cold. In Leningrad, is always cold, especially in winter. So, I hurried as fast as I could. Street lights were dim, and—" Her voice hitched, then became a raw whisper.

Some part of him wanted to stop her, to spare her the horror of recollection. But he knew that she needed to talk, to open up, to purge that nightmare once and for all. And if he wanted to have a future with Natasha— a real normal future that included intimacy—he needed to heart it.

No matter how badly it hurt.

"The street was deserted because of the late hour and cold. Did I tell you how cold it got there? God, I was freezing, didn't feel my toes. I was always afraid to catch frostbite, and then they will have to amputate my toes. Silly, so silly..." She made a little helpless sound that went straight to his wounded heart. "At first, I just heard the steps from somewhere behind me. Somebody almost running. I didn't think much about it. Probably somebody like me, in a hurry to get home, to get warm. Then a hand, a huge hand clamped my mouth. He pressed it so hard that my lip split. And then he lifted me so effortlessly, like I weighed nothing at all. He started to carry me deeper into the trees, away from the main street. I didn't even realize what was happening. He just dropped me on the ground, face down, and fell on top of me." Shutting her eyes, Natasha whimpered.

He couldn't take it any longer. With a silent oath, he enveloped her into his arms and buried his face against her hair. She didn't protest, but neither did she lean into him. Rigid, her body gradually relaxed, and finally she pressed her face into his shoulder.

"Sometimes I forget, or even think it happened to another girl, not me. But time after time, the memories return, when I least expect it. Mostly in my dreams. I thought that was the worst: to wake up covered in sweat, to feel your heart in your throat. What a mistake."

She lifted her face and looked at him. The misery and acceptance in her eyes tore at his soul.

"When I felt the weight of your body on top of me, something just snapped. I forgot it was you. I couldn't think or feel anything. Only fear. I'm afraid I can't do it, Dmitry. The attack...it left me crippled. I didn't realize that until now."

Haltingly, with resignation, she pulled back from his embrace.

"Natasha, did he... rape you?" He needed to know. *Must* know.

"No. He didn't finish what he began. I told you, a man walking his dog stumbled upon us. The dog began barking, and he just ran away."

"Did they catch him?"

"Yes, but later, much later. After he raped and killed five more girls. I was very fortunate. That's what they told me in the hospital. I was very, very fortunate." She sighed. "Ivan Resnik, a notorious serial killer terrorized Leningrad during the late 70s. I was the only one that met with this monster and lived to tell the tale. *Militia* caught him in 1980. He admitted to killing and raping forty-eight girls. All were young students."

"Dear God!" Dmitry groaned, covering his face with both hands. What if the dog's owner happened to walk his dog earlier or in another place? What if that Resnik bastard had more time? Jesus, fear coiled through him like a snake thinking about it. Natasha was fortunate, indeed. Very fortunate.

"Natasha—"

"I'm sorry Dmitry, I'm so very sorry."

She jumped to her feet, and headed to the door.

"Wait. Please, Natasha, just tell me this: how did you manage the intimacy before?"

"You mean sex?"

He nodded.

"I didn't."

For a long moment, Dmitry gazed at her in amazement. "You mean..."

"I've never been with a man before, Dmitry. I never wanted to until... until you. That's why I didn't know that I couldn't go through with it. If only I knew, believe me, I would never..." She lifted her hands, dropped them, and shook her head.

"I'll be damn." He guessed she had limited experience, but not *how* limited.

Gratitude to whatever force made him to stop in the gazebo filled him. But wait, there, in that little gazebo, she wasn't afraid. She became upset and angry when he stopped. She didn't feel threatened, she didn't freeze up.

But why? What was so different there, that she...

Oh, God. Of course. A simple answer. She said it herself: her fear started only when she felt his weight on top of her. In the gazebo they sat so she never felt trapped, caged, or forced down. Relived, he sucked in a deep breath.

I honestly wanted the first time to be in bed, but...

To have a normal physical intimacy with the woman he loved, he was ready to improvise. "Do you trust me?"

Without hesitation, she nodded. "Yes."

"Enough to let me make love to you?"

Natasha drew back, as if he slapped her.

"You saw what happened. Please, don't do this to me again."

"You said you froze when I got on top of you, right?"

"Yes, but—"

"Then, I won't."

She squinted at him. "But...but how—"

"Trust me, Natasha. Please."

She was so transparent. He watched the play of emotions over her face: doubt, misery, reluctance. Then, squaring her shoulders, she stared at him long and hard.

Say something, you idiot. Convince her.

But he kept silent. The decision whether to stay or flee was hers.

After a long moment, he held out his hand, silently inviting her to take it, to trust him. As if mesmerized, Natasha stared at his outstretched hand, then again at his face. Will she take it?

When Natasha's shoulders hunched, Dmitry's hope plummeted. She didn't trust him after all. He bit back an oath.

As if coming to a sudden decision, Natasha lifted her pointed chin, and stepped forward then clasped his hand.

For a moment he froze. Couldn't believe his luck.

Trembling, clad in a robe, with her prim high-necked nightgown peeking through, pale and barefooted, she made a unique mix of vulnerability and determination, innocence, and sensuality. The urge to cuddle her like a child collided with the desperate need to touch her, to make love to her. Her courage astonished him, her trust humbled.

For a moment, he shut his eyes.

Control, Rostoff, first and foremost. Keep your desire under lock and key.

Natasha was scared, yet she trusted him. He'd rather die than betray her trust.

Holding himself in control took enormous strength. His body screamed in frustration. Every nerve ending was fried raw. He opened his eyes.

Like a marble statue, she stood still. Even her breathing became shallow. Pale and drawn, her face resembled an alabaster mask. But her eyes shone like two brilliant gemstones. Her beauty stole his breath away.

For as long as he lived, Dmitry swore to remember this moment in time.

And then fear crept up his spine. She was innocent. Untouched. Pure like newly fallen show. Dmitry never had a virgin in his bed before. His first time and the irony of it wasn't lost on him. He would laugh except for the fear that terrified him.

Finally, Natasha ended the unbearable silence. "You are afraid, too, aren't you?"

He couldn't lie to her. "Yes."

"Want to forget about it?"

"Do you?"

"No, but if you have second thoughts, I'll understand."

Damn, what a woman. No wonder he loved her.

"No, Natasha. And I don't want to stop, but most of all I don't want to hurt you."

"You won't." Her shy, tentative smile was sexy and provocative as sin. Or so it seemed to him. It went through his gut like a bolt of lightning.

He swallowed around the fist in his throat, then found his voice. "I'll try my damnedest not to, I promise."

After a moment of hesitation, she tilted her head. "What... what do you want me to do?"

Loaded question.

If he answers honestly, and tell her what he really wanted her to do, she'd undoubtedly run screaming. No way.

Gritting his teeth, he gave himself a mental shake.

"Come here, sweetheart. " He wondered how normal his voice sounded, while inside his nerves became a jumble. "Sit on my lap. You weren't afraid in the gazebo, remember?"

"Yes, I remember." Barely audible, her hesitant answer reached his ears.

Then she closed the remaining distance between them and sat on his knees.

CHAPTER SIXTY-SEVEN

Natasha sat on his lap and kept still. She frowned, then bit her lip.

Probably trying to assess her feelings. Was she afraid? Degree by degree, her muscles relaxed against him. She leaned forward, then pressed her side to his chest. Dmitry watched her and waited. Still pale, her face grew taut, but not panicky. Her eyes were no longer glassy, thank God. That mindless terror he'd glimpsed earlier was the scariest thing he'd ever witnessed. That image will be in his mind for as long as he lived.

After several more minutes she blew out a small gust of air. She stole a quick glance at him, then averted her face, but not before he managed to take a good look at her expression. She now seemed more curious than nervous. She wiggled her butt, then settled into his lap more comfortably. She glanced up at him. Her eyes sparkled like fresh cut emeralds. Her face appeared calm, composed, with the look of a woman who knew what she wanted. He was surprised she didn't ask him 'what are you waiting for.'

She was killing him. His blood whooshed in his veins so loudly, he thought for sure she heard it. His heart did its best to break his ribcage. As to that one part of his anatomy...he failed to find words to describe its condition.

Natasha blinked, then gave him a tentative smile. "Well? What now?"

What now indeed.

He held still by the tips of his fingernails but just barely.

Dmitry infused as much calm in his voice as possible, "And now, sweetheart, I am going to kiss you, and you will kiss me back."

She blinked again, nodded, then looped her arms around his neck. Gently, soothingly, he rubbed her back with one hand. A small violent shiver went through her body. He sucked in a breath.

God, she was so sensitive, so responsive. If she reacted that strongly to a simple caress, what would it be when he touched her all over?

He grew hard as a rock and prayed she didn't feel him pressing into her bottom.

Stop it. The first time is for her. Only for her. So, down, boy.

But his engorged dick heeded him not. With an enormous effort Dmitry ignored his discomfort.

He dropped an almost chaste kiss onto her soft lips, then asked, "Do you like that?"

"Yes, very much so."

Polite, even a little prim, her voice set his gut on fire.

Damn. He was losing it.

Bearing down on his impatience, he traced her chin with his index finger, then turned her face upward. He lowered his mouth, and rubbed his lips against hers. Gently, softly. Drawing back, he smiled at her. She smiled back, tentatively, shyly.

Her eye color changed, from deep emerald to the color of an evergreen forest at dusk. Natasha licked her puffy lips as she studied his mouth. Intently, hungrily. His blood shot to the boiling point. A point of no return.

The smile slipped from his face. He stared at her full moist mouth. Since the first, the tiny mole on the corner of her upper lip drove him crazy. It tormented his dreams for years. Damn, he was only human. He could take only so much. With a low guttural groan, Dmitry claimed her mouth. Hard. Almost brutal.

CHAPTER SIXTY-EIGHT

Natasha tensed for a moment. She never expected an ambush. When his tongue slipped inside of her mouth, she held herself still, stunned and unprepared.

Dear God. He made her feel so much. Too much...

Not enough.

Helpless under the savage demands of his lips, she held on to him, and let herself feel. The heat, overwhelming, scorching; the flavors, rich and decadent; the textures, unfamiliar, exciting. Bombarded by emotions, steeped in them, she began to sink into the depth of that whirlpool. Dizzy, delirious, she clung to him, afraid to drown.

My God, what's happening to me?

Her skin seemed too tight, her heart too huge, her bones almost liquid. She burned, disintegrating into a million fiery pieces. Another moment, and she'd explode.

But soon that passive role ceased to satisfy her. Angling her head, she met each thrust of his tongue with her own, rubbing, exploring. He complied, opened his mouth wider, giving her free rein. Greedy for more, she tugged at his hair, seeking better access. The desperate moan that rang in the air was her own. She stilled. Her mind screamed at her that a lady ought to be embarrassed at wanton behavior. Her heart overruled. The hell with it! She was done with her goody two-shoes persona. She burned alive.

She was alive.

Feverish, she drank from his mouth, desperate to quench her wild thirst.

Not enough.

With a strangled cry Dmitry ripped his mouth from her.

"Easy, love, easy. Please." A tortured whisper. A desperate plea.

"Don't stop, Dmitry. Not now, not again." A fever burned inside her as she trailed her open mouth along his throat, jaw, face. His groan sent shivers along her exposed skin.

"Natasha, darling, I won't stop, I promise, but... wait, just give me a second—"

"I can't. I won't." She peppered her words with kisses across his face. "I've waited for you so long... all my life... Please, Dmitry."

"Let's get rid of your clothes." He unbelted her robe. She smiled when she noticed his hands were unsteady. He looked deep into her eyes, raised his hands, then parted her robe. Her nightgown was simple and long, made for comfort, not seduction. She bit her lip wishing she wore something lacy and provocative.

Like what, you silly goose?

She owned nothing that might be described as frivolous. Even marginally. That went double for her night garments. The hell with that.

With a mental shrug she grabbed the hem, bunched it in both hands, then afraid to lose her nerve, quickly drew it up and flung it away. With only her panties on, she felt reckless and brazen and oddly unashamed.

A light breeze from the open window was like a gentle caress. Natasha's breasts tingled, her nipples puckered to tight points. Something hot gathered between her thighs. She held still, absorbing all those unfamiliar sensations.

But she wasn't afraid. She went beyond that emotion. Without an ounce of embarrassment, Natasha held his smoldering gaze. Swallowed by the dark irises, his eyes became almost black, like two coals. Intense, fierce, they held her captive for a long breathless moment. The silence became deafening.

And still, he didn't lower his gaze from her face. Why did he wait?

Finally, he dragged his eyes lower. A dark, almost pained expression swam over his face. She tensed.

Was he disappointed? She admitted to not being a great beauty. Her breasts too large, her hips too wide. But her legs were long, her skin smooth and healthy. Maybe too pale? Too fat? Uncertainty slithered through her. She bit her bottom lip, fighting the urge to cover herself with her arms.

Why doesn't he say something? Anything?

She couldn't bear it.

"Dammit, Dmitry! Say something!"

Silence. Finally, after what seemed like an eternity, he raised his gaze.

Her heart stuttered. The molten silver fire in his eyes scorched her soul.

"You are exquisite, Natasha."

CHAPTER SIXTY-NINE

Dear Lord, she was beautiful. Her breasts were surprisingly full and heavy, two perfectly round mounds tipped with dark rose nipples.

Two cones of vanilla ice cream with cherries on top.

His mouth watered in anticipation. Dmitry had to remind himself to breathe.

Did she realize she trembled? He devoured Natasha with his eyes as he studied her expression. She didn't protest when he unbelted her robe. She didn't squirm, or freeze. Instead, she shrugged the cloth away. She didn't appear afraid. Thank God.

Unable to control his rampaging desire any longer, he cupped one generous mound. She shuddered. He smiled.

He wanted her to become accustomed to his touch, so she believed him a gentle man who cared more for her instead of greedily satisfying himself. Not an easy task. Inside, he boiled, a churning volcano of wild urges and screaming demands. Take. Devour. Conquer. Enraged, his shaft pulsed painfully. He wasn't sure how long he'd be able to control the beast clawing inside. With every ounce of his willpower, he ignored the demands of his body.

Patience, Rostoff.

She was a novice, a virgin. She was a victim of a violent crime. He vowed to make her first experience as pleasant as possible. Even if it killed him.

Struggling to keep his inner beast chained, he murmured sweet words to help her relax further, seducing her with his voice. He kissed her collarbone, then trailed his fingertips under her left breast, making lazy circles. Finally, he allowed himself to touch her nipples.

Whimpering, she arched her spine. He swallowed the groan. He'd give anything to take that tight bud into his mouth, and suck hard.

Not yet. Don't scare her.

Natasha sighed, then smiled tremulously. Encouraged and relieved, he lowered his head and dropped small light kisses onto her chest, inching toward the puckered dusky tips he craved. Unable to help himself, he flickered his tongue over one nipple. She grabbed his hair in both hands and cried out. God, yes. Emboldened, he drew that rigid peak into his mouth, and suckled. It tasted like sin and honey. His control slipped a notch. Growling deep in his throat, he devoured her other breast.

She jerked violently, then leaned back, writhing. The beast inside of him roared in triumph. Still, he kept it chained. Barely. Just for a little while. Just another moment...

"Dmitry, please. I can't stand it."

Neither can he. But still, he held on to control. "Soon, baby, soon, I promise."

"Not soon enough. Do something!" The tug on his hair made him wince.

Despite everything, he chuckled. Only Natasha could make him laugh at a moment like that. But she was right. If he didn't do something soon, he'd combust.

Now, Rostoff.

Biting back the helpless oath, he hoisted her across his lap until she sat astride him.

Their torsos bumped against each other, bringing two different cries, hers of delight, his of frustration. His discomfort became pure torture. Did she have any idea what she was doing to him? Not a clue. Guided by instinct, Natasha rubbed her belly against him. A low desperate groan escaped before he stopped it. Damn, she was killing him. He never knew the full meaning of the word agony until now. His manhood rioted against the fabric of his slacks. His blood churned, his heart thundered. He held onto his control by the skin of his teeth, and fought the lost battle.

He glided his hands down her ribcage, then lower, making forays under the edge of cotton panties. Not meeting with any protest, he dipped his hand and covered her belly with his palm. Soft as silk and warm like sunshine. And all woman. Her stomach muscles quivered, but she didn't tense or pull away. After a short pause, he cupped her mound. She gave a short-strangled sound of surprise, but didn't protest. Encouraged by her reaction, he dipped his hand lower. Liquid fire scorched his fingertips. She was wet, hot, and ready. Reeling, half-mad, he captured her mouth in a searing kiss. Natasha moaned deep in her throat as she clutched his shoulders. When his thumb touched her center, she tore her mouth free, gasping from the shock. Her thighs tensed, as if she tried to bring them together. He stayed in place, refusing to let her. One-handed, he spread her legs wider, opening her completely. He looked deep into her eyes and continued to caress between her legs, while he slowly lost his mind.

"That's all right, baby. Don't be afraid. You like that, don't you?" He whispered against her swollen breast.

"Dmitry, I think..."

CHAPTER SEVENTY

"N o, don't think. Relax for me. Relax and feel."

How to relax when his fingers stirred a fire inside her? She was burning alive! Straining against his hand, she moaned.

Oh, sweet Lord, yes. Please.

She forgot her initial embarrassment. She forgot everything. Her body no longer seemed like her own. Blindly, it obeyed every command of Dmitry's voice.

Slowly, irrevocably, Natasha was sucked into a whirlpool. A kaleidoscope of emotions, a riot of feelings. So strong, so confusing! Fear overtook pleasure. Something huge gathered in the pit of her stomach. Another moment, and something must break inside of her. Scared, she clutched his shoulders tighter, gasping. Desperate to end this unbearable torture, she pleaded, "Dmitry, please, no more. Please...I can't..."

He failed to comply. Instead, he increased the pressure while his fingers circled unerringly around her center.

"Oh, God...Dmitry..."

"That's right, Natasha. Let go, let it happen, baby. Don't fight it."

Fight? Is he kidding?

Natasha croaked a short laughter, that quickly faded into a moan. She rushed headlong toward something frightening, and brilliant, and unimaginable...

And still, she was unable to reach it. A sob broke loose from her throat.

I can't bear it anymore!

Mindless, she pressed her lower body into Dmitry's hand and begged silently.

Dear God, please. Please!

So close, so scared, so confused.

A slow wave of heat rose through. The force of it built with each passing moment. She tensed, then froze in shock, as a finger slid inside of her. Massaging, pressing, caressing. Then something broke free, and she was flying, free like a bird, hurtling toward a brilliant light of silver and gold shards.

Her last helpless cry of surrender was his name.

Have I died and go to heaven? Surely, I must be dead. Why else can't I feel my body?

Something warm and smooth tickled her cheek.

Nice. Warm. Fuzzy...

Were clouds fuzzy?

Something pulsed under her left ear... A strong, fast beat.

Natasha stirred and forced her eyes open. She blinked, as a familiar face came into focus.

"Welcome back, baby," the soft deep murmur caressed her ears. "I assumed you'd fallen asleep on me. Not very flattering, if you get my drift."

Drift? What drift?

"Yeah, I guess I was drifting..." She blinked. "Dmitry?"

That earned her a chuckle.

"Did you expect anyone else?"

"I don't know, maybe angels."

"Angels, huh?"

"Yeah, I thought I was in heaven."

"Heaven? That's more like it." He kissed her on the tip of her nose. "So, did you like it?"

"Like it? Dmitry, I don't have words to describe..." She glanced away, too embarrassed to face him. He tipped her chin up with his forefinger, and grinned.

"Try."

"It was...so good and so... right."

"Yes, *milaya*." He smoothed the curls from her face, "It's never been so good and so right before."

Was he humoring her? Surely, he had been with many women, more beautiful, sophisticated, and definitely more experienced. She studied his face. His smoldering silver gaze direct and somber.

She smiled as relief flooded through her. "I'm glad."

"Me too."

He kept touching her. Her shoulder, her collarbone, her earlobe. He grazed a sensitive spot below her throat with his fingertips, then traced a lazy path between her breasts. She shivered with pure delight and stopped herself from purring. His hand stilled. She glanced down, and winced.

The thin gold chain with a tiny cross that she always wore dangled from his hand. Svetlana's cross. She cursed herself for not removing it earlier, and watched him. He lifted it, then stared at it. Of course he recognized it. How could he not?

You are such a fool, Natasha.

Her euphoria plummeted. Were his thoughts on Svetlana, his beautiful swan, his lover? *The mother of his daughter.* Hot tears pressed against Natasha's eyelids. How could she compare to

Svetlana's beauty and her grace? She was a star, bold, bright, sparkling. And Natasha? A grey sparrow, awkward and pitiful.

Dmitry's face was closed, his eyes full of sorrow.

He studied that cross for a long time, rubbing it gently between his fingertips. Was he feeling guilty for betraying Svetlana? Or sad? *Did he regret what happened between us a short time ago?*

She couldn't bear if he did. Anything, but not a regret.

"She was beautiful. Fragile, graceful, and gentle."

Then as if sensing Natasha's discomfort, he cupped her face with both hands. "But even with Svetlana, it wasn't as good and right as with you."

Dizzy with relieve, she smiled through the sheen of tears.

He shifted his gaze from her face to the cross, and then to her eyes again.

"She was my swan, my fairy tale, my dream." With both thumbs, Dmitry wiped the tears from her face. "You are my soul, Natasha, my blood, my life. Never forget that."

Undone, Natasha lifted his hand, then kissed his palm that framed her face. "Do you want me to take it off?"

"What, the cross? No."

"Do you... feel guilty?" She had to know.

"No, *milaya*. I made my peace long before. I let her go. I don't feel guilty anymore." The simple truth of his words rocked Natasha to her soul. "Right now I feel happy. How about you?"

"Oh, I am happy. I've never been so happy in my entire life. Only..."

"Only...?" he prompted gently.

"You didn't... I mean, it was only me. Only for me."

"Yes, *milaya,* for you."

"But what about you?"

"We have time, Natasha. Later we can do it again, and it will be for both of us."

"Later? Why later? Are you tired?"

CHAPTER SEVENTY-ONE

Dmitry laughed.
Tired? Dear God in heaven, he was tired! Tired of keeping a steel fist on his control, tired of gritting his teeth from frustration. Tired of torturing himself.

Still chuckling, he tapped her perky little nose. "I am, *milaya*, but not *that* tired."

"Well, then." Squaring her slender shoulders, Natasha bit her lip, then started to work on his shirt buttons. One button, the second, the third.

He blinked, then stared at her.

"What are you doing?"

"Getting you out of these clothes." Without looking at him, she continued her task.

Unnerved, he watched her busy fingers. She freed another button. "Why?"

"Why? To make love to you, of course," she muttered, all the while tugging at his shirt. "Damn, stubborn little thing!" Natasha cursed quietly, then glared at him. "Well, are you going to help me or sit here all night?"

She made such a picture! Naked, except for her cotton panties. Her hair disheveled with a few auburn wisps flying across her beautiful face. She resembled a nymph. A very determined and irate nymph. He chuckled, then tucked one of the locks behind her ear.

"You are unbelievable, Natasha." Hope chased by anticipation hummed in his blood. But he covered her hands with his, stilling her efforts. "Are you sure?"

"Of course, I'm sure." And once again she attacked his buttons enthusiastically.

He felt like he was being swallowed by quicksand and struggled hard to hold on to the last thread of his control.

"Natasha, you don't have to do this."

And when do you became a masochist, Rostoff?

Damn, she almost got his shirt open. Gritting his teeth, he closed his eyes. Another moment and he'd lose it.

"But I want to."

Her response jerked his eyes open.

Lost. Hallelujah.

Impatient now, Dmitry ripped his shirt away, and sent the remaining buttons flying. The tiny noise reverberated in his ears like a cannon blast.

Natasha gasped, then quickly placed her hands on his belt, trying to unbuckle it. He groaned deep in his throat when her fingers brushed against his engorged shaft.

Torture. Pleasure. Ecstasy.

Just a few seconds of sanity left.

"Last warning, Natasha." He swore he heard his blood roaring in anticipation. But that was nothing compared to his dick's dance of victory.

"I don't need it." With the last successful tug on his belt, she gave a low sound of triumph, and lifted her eyes. Defiant, she threw it over her shoulder, then stared at him.

Daring.

Demanding.

Challenging.

Well, then, God knows I tried.

Quickly, he whisked her off his lap, then set her on her feet. He knelt in front of her, then swiped her panties down her long legs. The fiery curls between her legs begged for his attention. He inhaled greedily its musky smell. Soon. He promised himself to indulge to his heart contents soon. But not now.

He held her gaze as he stood, then tossed her panties out of the way.

She stood gloriously naked, totally unashamed, smiling. For a moment, he allowed himself the pleasure of looking at her. But the beast inside of him demanded satisfaction.

Shedding his trousers. Clad only in briefs, he scooped her up, and in two hurried strides, approached the bed. Plopping onto his back, he carefully positioned Natasha on top of him.

She squirmed and bit her lip. "What do I do?"

CHAPTER SEVENTY-TWO

Mother of God, there was so much of him! Broad shoulders, lean muscular legs, taut stomach. She tried to keep her mind off his thighs, but the heavy bulging between his legs poked her, scorching her tummy. The heat that radiated from him was unbelievable. She rapidly lost her nerve. What did she know about pleasing a man? Absolutely nothing. What if she made a stupid mistake? What if he found her inadequate?

Lifting herself up, she scooted backwards. "What do you want me to do?"

His answer came out a deep low rumble.

"Whatever you want, Natasha. Whatever feels right to you."

"I want to please you, but I don't know how." The words came out in a miserable whisper.

"You pleased me already." He gave her a smile that seemed a bit strained.

"I did?" She desperately wanted to believe him.

As if sensing her doubts, Dmitry rose to a sitting position, looked deep into her eyes.

"Enormously. You're so lovely, so responsive." He ran his hand along her thigh. "God, you don't know what you're doing to me."

Emboldened, she braced both palms against his naked chest. The black tufts of hair fascinated her. Like a magnet, his dark male nipples drew her gaze. So different from hers. Were they as sensitive as her own?

After a moment of hesitation, she gently touched one tiny tip. He shuddered in response. Natasha smiled. Oh, yes.

"Again," he rasped as if he was in pain.

She repeated the action.

Dmitry groaned. "Oh, Lord..."

"Do you like it?"

"Yes."

"I thought you might. I liked it, too. Especially when you did this." Remembering one of his caresses, Natasha lowered her head, and licked each nipple in turn.

He exploded, "Jesus Christ!"

Encouraged, she grew bolder. Pushing with both hands against his torso, she made him lie back. Now he was at her mercy. Vulnerable. She liked that. Grinning, Natasha smacked at his hand when he moved to touch her.

"My turn." Parroting his earlier words she added, "Just relax and feel."

He chuckled, then sucked in air sharply as she began to experiment with her fingers and mouth. A lick, a scrape of teeth, a touch. Heady with new discovered power, she trailed her fingertips along the warm flesh of his ribcage. She chuckled at his helpless swearing, and continued her explorations. The play of muscles beneath her hands fascinated her; the feel of his skin, so unexpectedly soft and smooth, captivating. She didn't want to stop touching him.

But try as she might, she couldn't bring herself to look lower, or touch him there. Gently, he lifted her hand, and brought it to the rigid throbbing wedge. The unbelievable heat almost scorched her skin. She gasped, tensed, and tried to pull her hand away. She may have succeeded, if not for his pleading raw voice.

"Please, baby, I need you."

Unable to refuse him anything, she shut her eyes, and pressed her palm firmly against that pulsing fire.

My God, it's huge.

Involuntarily her fingers flexed. Now his groan sounded of pure torture. Afraid she had hurt him, she opened her eyes.

"Are you in pain?"

"Oh, yes, yes. Yes!" His fists were bunched at his sides, and his body arched. His throat worked as if trying to swallow a huge rock.

Oh, Lord, what have I done?

She let go of his *thing*, almost drew her hand away, but he brought it back, circled her fingers around it. She bit her lip. "Maybe I shouldn't..."

"You definitely should."

Again, she tried to pull her hand away, to no avail. "But you're hurting."

"From wanting you. From needing you. Can't you see what you're doing to me?"

A raw whisper. A desperate plea. His eyes were half-closed, but she read their expression. Intense. Dark. Smoldering.

Confused, she shook her head. "I didn't mean to hurt you."

"I know, little one."

Still unsure, Natasha gazed into his face.

He was so pale, his face so drawn, as if he endured great pain. His breathing came in broken gasps, scraping along her nerve endings.

Dammit it, he *was* suffering, and she had herself to blame. Close to tears, Natasha scooted back. Cursing herself, miserable, she forced past her trembling lips, "What can I do, Dmitry? Please, tell me. I cannot bear to see you like that."

CHAPTER SEVENTY-THREE

Dmitry gritted his teeth. Her shy exploration of his body drove him out of his mind. But when she cupped his shaft, he was a goner. He gritted his teeth and tried to control his savage hunger. She made it impossible.

Gloriously naked, she studied him with her impossibly green, innocent eyes, asking what she could do.

Dear God, the woman is lethal.

"What, Dmitry? Tell me, darling. I'll do anything for you!"

He swore he heard his control snap. Dmitry ripped off his briefs. Her eyes widened. "Oh, my..."

Without letting her have a chance to think, he tumbled her on top of him. She let out a short gasp that faded abruptly as he covered her soft lips with his mouth.

Teetering on the brink of sanity, he murmured, "Natasha, it will hurt, but only for a moment, I swear."

"I know. I don't mind."

He placed his hands on her tiny waist then changed her position so she straddled him. The warm flesh of her inner thighs drove him crazy. He positioned himself at her entrance. With great restraint he tried to slow entering her heat, but it was a lost battle. As he encountered the barrier of her innocence, he gritted his teeth, and gripped her hips with both hands.

"Forgive me, *milaya*." And surging forward, he filled her.

Natasha cried out. The sound of her agony reverberated through his skull. He covered her mouth, swallowing her cries. For a long moment, he kept himself still, letting her grow accustomed to the invasion.

"Relax, baby, don't fight it. Relax those beautiful long legs for me, please."

She whimpered. "It hurts."

"I know."

He opened his eyes to see her glaring at him.

"How the hell do you know?"

"Oh, baby, I'm so sorry. It'll pass in a moment, I promise."

She pressed her cheek against his shoulder. Her skin felt hot and damp from tears. He called himself a thousand bad names, then rocked her while he murmured in a soothing voice. Gradually, the deadly lock of her legs lessened. She sighed as she slid backward, and involuntarily buried his shaft deeper. He winced, waiting for her new cry of pain. But instead, the expression of amazement and wonder lit up her flushed face.

"Natasha, are you still in pain?"

Intently he watched every change of emotion that played across her features.

She glanced down, then lifted her eyes and slowly shook her head.

"Baby, talk to me. Please. What do you feel?"

She bit her lip, then shifted her hips up, and down. "I feel...wonderful." Her dazzling smile shone with awe and surprise. "I feel...whole."

If he were standing, her quiet confession would have brought him to his knees.

Dmitry let go a sigh as relief washed through him.

"Dmitry?"

"What, *milaya*?"

"Is that... all? I mean, is that all there is to it?"

"Oh, Natasha," he groaned, torn between laughter and physical frustration. "You'll be the end of me."

"I didn't mean to." Her pout was sexy as hell. As soon as he saw it, his blood began to churn.

Save me, this woman has no idea what she's doing to me.

After a few moments he found the ability to speak. "You bewitch me, Natasha. You make me lose my head. But most of all, you make me crazy from wanting you."

Hugging her brought their bodies in full contact.

Torso to torso.

Skin to skin.

That impact akin to a flash of lightning. Scorching, unmerciful.

Her puckered nipples brushed his chest. A deep moan he barely recognized as his own, echoed in the room. He swept his palms from her shoulders to her butt, then kneaded her flesh. She shivered, closed her eyes, and let out a soft mew. She was so hot. So wet. He hardened until he thought he might explode. He was turning into a mass of a blind desire and brutal need. The passion pulsed all around, like an inferno, greedy and impatient.

Mesmerized, he watched her face as he flexed his pelvis. That raging beast inside of him urged him to move faster, deeper. Her eyes glazed. Shock? Pleasure?

Relentlessly he drew her higher, his slow and deep and sure.

Sobbing his name, her body taught as an arrow, Natasha started to pump her hips in a feverish rhythm. And finally, he surrendered to the clawing howling savage inside. Free now, his passion flew, soaring high, burning him alive.

Oblivious to anything, helpless and lost, he was caught in that erotic dance older than the world. Faster, higher, deeper.

Natasha froze, then climaxed with a force that almost shattered him. A second later, his own orgasm, explosive and violent, ripped through him like a tornado, leaving him dazed and almost paralyzed.

CHAPTER SEVENTY-FOUR

The aftershocks of his release went on and on. Dmitry seemed numb even though his skin burned, and his blood whooshed madly through his veins. He didn't want to move. He wanted to stay like that forever. They were still joined intimately, with Natasha draped over his body like a rag doll. Shaking, he held on to her like she was his lifesaver. His hips remained in the clamped viselike grip of her legs. The sensation heaven.

Dear God, what just happened?

It had never been like that before. Not for a moment did he expect it to be like that. The heat, the force, the ultimate explosion...

Wrung out physically and emotionally, vulnerable, and defenseless, yet he felt more alive than ever before. Slowly reality intruded. Natasha sprawled over him barely breathing. He remembered pounding into her like a jackhammer in a frenzy. Dammit, he hurt her again. Must be hurting her even now, since he was still sheathed deep inside. He lifted her rump carefully to separate them. She remained still. He nestled her on top of him, then caressed her back in a slow soothing motion.

How soon would she be willing to make love again?

He mentally slapped himself.

Really Rostoff? Really? You are an animal. Definitely a pig.

Still shaken from his explosive orgasm, he desperately wanted her again. And again.

Natasha murmured something inaudible against his chest. A delicate shudder of her body made him aware of the rapidly cooling temperature in the room. Damn, the open window, and the nights were cold this time of year.

Cursing his own stupidity, he wrestled the blanket from under him, and after a few attempts managed to covered them both. She burrowed her nose deeper into his shoulder. Despite his concern, he laughed. Like a tiny kitten, she lay on top of him, curled and content. He listened to her even breathing as he started to drift off. They needed to talk, but...not now.

In the morning, and then I'll make love to her again.

Pacified with that, he closed his eyes and fell into a contented sleep.

When he opened his eyes much later, Natasha was gone.

Groggy, he blinked, then scanned the room. He inhaled deep. The bed still smelled like her. The pillow still carried the indentation from her head, but the woman had disappeared. Dammit all to hell and back. Irritated, he dragged himself to a sitting position. He planned to talk to her this morning. But how?

The stubborn creature crept out so quietly, he failed to notice. And why did she sneak out?

And why didn't you wake up, you stupid oaf?

The simple answer, he was so content and spent and dead to the world.

Idiot.

The door flew open, banging on its back wall. He turned, and froze. Pale and trembling from head to toe, his son glared at him.

"You!" Peter growled deep in his throat. He reached the bed in two strides, then flung the covers off Dmitry's body. "You bastard. How could you?"

Peter grabbed Dmitry's shoulders then shook him hard enough to make his teeth chatter. Even though the boy's height topped him, Dmitry was much stronger. He had the ability to shake him off without any effort. Instead, he reined in his own temper and kept his voice cool and even. "Peter, calm down."

But it seemed to infuriate his son even more.

"Calm down?" Peter voice flew up an octave. "You're telling me to calm down after I saw—"

"Saw what, for crying out loud?" But God help him, he already knew.

"Natasha. She leaving your room, in her robe, barefooted. And crying. Damn you, do you hear me? She was in tears!"

Dmitry controlled his voice, forcing it to sound as calm as possible, "I hear you, along with every bloody soul in this house."

"I don't care!"

"You don't, but I do. And so, undoubtedly, does Natasha."

Shaking with fury, Peter let go of Dmitry, but his blazing eyes held him fast.

"I trusted you! I asked you to leave her alone. How could you? How could you do it to her, Dad?"

"Please kindly explain what exactly do you think I have done?"

"You slept with her. You wanted her, and you slept with her."

"Yes, I did."

"And you are confessing it to me so calmly?"

"I don't have to confess anything to you, son. What happened between Natasha and me, it's our business, and it doesn't concern you."

"The hell it doesn't! She is... was innocent, and you knew that. You exploited it, exploited her."

Dmitry's facial muscles twitched, and still, he managed to control his temper.

"I didn't exploit anything, Peter. For the love of God, son, give me some credit. You know me long enough. Or so I though." He looked Peter hard in the eyes. "Whatever my shortcomings are, I am *not* a user. Or a rapist." Unbelievably hurt, he barely suppressed his own anger. "If any other man stood in your place, Peter, I would personally take him apart, limb by limb, for merely suggesting the thing you're accusing me of."

The first twinges of uneasiness swam across Peter's face. Still pale, he gazed at Dmitry, before averting his eyes.

"But because I know how much Natasha means to you, and yes, because you are my son and I love you, I will tell you this. Natasha came to my room. I would never touch her if she wasn't willing. Whatever happened here was mutual. And that is the truth. Now, if you'd be so kind, please turn around, and allow me some privasy. I feel quite embarrassed arguing with my grown son stark naked."

Peter blinked. He veered right, as two scarlet patches flushed on his face.

"Thank you." Dmitry swung his legs over the bed, then located his pants.

Peter muttered something, then raked his fingers through his hair.

"What's that?"

"I'm sorry, Dad." Even though his words came out gruff, his shame rang clear. In total silence, Dmitry continued to dress.

"Dad, I'm sorry. I mean it."

The mix of misery and guilt tugged at Dmitry. He turned to look at the boy.

"I know, son."

"I had no right..." Peter's voice hitched. Helplessly, he uttered a little oath.

A tender smile touched Dmitry's mouth. A little boy still lurked in his son's grown body. The boy with a quick temper and deep-rooted sense of loyalty, who appeared miserable after his angry outbursts, and tried hard to make amends. Like now.

"It's okay, Peter." He laid a hand on his son's slumped shoulders. "I understand."

"I was going to jog, and saw her. She was sneaking quietly from your room, and crying. What was I supposed to think?"

"God," Dmitry closed his eyes warily. "I am sorry that you witnessed that, Peter. I don't know why she cried. I swear to you she wasn't unhappy before."

Unhappy, hell.

Anything but, burning alive, writhing, screaming. Demanding.

He made a mistake by not talking to her right after their lovemaking. He should have. And why not? Fear, he addmited.

Coward.

Before the day was over, he vowed to speak with her. He intended to make her listen, even if he must beg. But now, his priority was Peter. He looked at his son straight on.

"I didn't abuse or hurt Natasha. I swear."

"But... she..." Visibly struggling with words, Peter swore, as his face flushed with embarrassment.

Dmitry chuckled. "Hell, son, for someone who barged in here with the intention of beating the hell out of his old man, you're acting like a bloody virgin yourself."

Peter blushed even more, and averted his eyes.

Dmitry sobered. "Yes, Natasha was innocent. I am very privileged to be her first, and have every intention to be the only."

Peter squinted at him. "What do you mean?"

"I mean I'm going to marry her."

"Like 'till death do us part' kind of marry?"

"Is there any other?"

"Hell." Peter gaped at him. "I don't know what to say."

"Say you're happy for us. For all of us."

"I am happy, Dad, but... did she agree? To marry you, I mean?"

"Why object?" He shrugged, faking nonchalance. Damn, how could he give a straight answer if he wasn't even thinking about marriage last night? Hell, he wasn't capable of any rational thought then.

Peter frowned. "I don't know, Dad. I know she loves you."

His pointed gaze appeared to be more eloquent than any words.

"Is that a polite way of asking me about my feelings?"

"Yes, I suppose it is. Natasha deserves the best. So, if you don't love her, you'd better leave her alone."

"I can't leave her alone, Peter. I just can't."

"But you don't love her," Peter finished quietly.

After a long moment of charged silence, Dmitry relented. "I do."

"What did you say?"

"I do love her." He swallowed around the fist in his throat. "So much that I'm afraid."

Peter's brows lifted in confusion. "Afraid? But why?"

"Yesterday, I realized something I was blissfully unaware of. When you make love with the woman you love, it takes something out of you. Like losing part of your soul to another human being. It's astonishing. And terrifying."

Peter mulled that for a moment. "But if the woman loves you back, you gain a piece of her soul as well."

In mute fascination, baffled and humbled, Dmitry gazed at his son.

"Dear God, how did you get to be so wise?"

Peter shrugged, but the grin that spread his lips into a smile was pleased, and a little smug. In an instant, the boy became all action, like he desperately wanted to leave the room. With his hand on the door knob, Peter glanced over his shoulder at Dmitry.

" Ah... I'm going to run. I guess, I'll see you later."

"Sure."

"I love you, Dad," Peter blurted, before his hasty retreat.

Dmitry stood still, looking at the closed door. Something hot gathered behind his eyelids. He loved his son. He made it so easy, really. Peter was everything every parent dreamt of. His boy turned out to be a fine man. A very fine man indeed. And Natasha deserves full credit for that.

Natasha.

Where was she? What was she thinking? Did she regret last night?

He walked toward the bed. An image of Natasha, naked and covered in a sheen of sweat, swam before his eyes. Instantly aroused, he gritted his teeth. A small rusty spot on the wrinkled sheets drew his attention. What on earth? And then he realized what it was: blood. Natasha's blood.

His arousal deflated like a punctured balloon. He silently berated himself, and drew his gaze away from the bed. He must talk to her, tell her that he loved her. He must propose, the sooner the better. But first, he needed to calm down.

Easier said than done.

He stripped the bed, then deposited the soiled sheet in the hamper after which he went to the bathroom to shower and shave.

And then, Natasha, I will find you wherever you are, and make you explain why you left my bed. And why were you crying.

CHAPTER SEVENTY-FIVE

A long black shadow crept along the narrow corridor. It trailed after the tall skeletal figure of a man whose laborious steps brought him to the northern wing of the house. The servant's quarters. He reached his room, used his keys to open the door he always kept under a double lock, then entered. Once inside, Ivan pursed his lips.

So, that's how things are, huh? Interesting.

Her Grace will erupt once she learned about it.

Downright shameful! His Grace carrying on with the nanny, that red-haired bitch.

He fisted his gnarled hands in impotent rage and swore out loud.

We'll see how you carry on under this roof when Her Grace Elizabeth returns.

He had no doubt his mistress will indeed come back home. She can't die. She was too ornery, too mean, and stubborn to die like that.

No, sir. She'll outlive us all.

His malicious satisfaction was mixed with a dollop of pure fear. Because when Elizabeth returned, a broken invalid chained to a wheelchair, she will make his life a living hell. Undoubtedly.

Ivan must distract her mind with something new, something juicy and scandalous. He'll turn her hate to someone else. Someone like His Grace, or Natasha. Or, better yet, to both of them.

Ivan despised Dmitry from the time the puny thing wore short pants.

And Natasha? He choked on his hate for her from the first.

That little midget of a girl, that bastard with her spooky eyes, made his skin crawl. He hated both dogs with a vengeance, and decided to poison them long ago, but Her Grace forbid it. Elizabeth made it clear: she wanted the dogs alive and well, period. A pity, really. A mistake on her part, but who was he to contradict?

Busy now, Ivan plucked his eyeglasses and perched them on top of his nose.

He plucked a stubby pencil from the old mug on his desktop, then unlocked the secret drawer of his desk, withdrew his secret journal, then started to scribble. His arthritic fingers made the writing process laborious and quite painful, but it didn't stop him from jotting down all the details in his spidery old-fashioned handwriting.

He fancied himself a self-appointed chronicler of the Rostoff household, a keeper of records, immortalizing a history of this family for future generations. One day his journal will be priceless. One day it might be published for a great price.

But until then, he intended to present its contents to his mistress once she came home. Only then will things get back to normal in the Rostoff household. Only then. Painstakingly, he wrote down every event that happened in Her Grace's absence.

CHAPTER SEVENTY-SIX

D mitry wasn't able to talk to Natasha that morning. A call from the hospital drastically changed his plans. Doctor Litowski informed him that Elizabeth has awakened. Although her condition remained critical, the doctor had every confidence Elizabeth was out of the woods. But he asked Dmitry to come to the hospital right away.

Dmitry ended the call, and reluctantly turned away from the staircase that led to his room. He took time to break the news to Peter, then departed.

Since he didn't have his own car, he was forced to use Elizabeth's Rolls. Damn, he hated that car. Like the name of the estate, that old monstrosity was golden in color, and in his opinion, preposterous. It represented everything Dmitry despised: in your face opulence, an unapologetic display of wealth, and a distasteful grandeur. Snobby, condescending.

He made a mental note to rectify the matter, and buy his own car as soon as possible. If he was stuck here for the duration, he'd rather have his own transportation.

Irritation gnawed at him because he didn't see Natasha before he left. He slid into the seat, then slammed the door hard enough to make the pompous car shimmy. He brooded the entire drive, trying to plan a time to speak with Natasha. As the familiar grey building of the hospital rose ahead, he braced himself, dreading the upcoming conversation with Dr. Litowski. But most of all, he dreaded meeting Elizabeth.

CHAPTER SEVENTY-SEVEN

For the past hour Natasha called herself many names, none of them favorable. Try as she might, she failed to erase from her memory the events of last night.

Shouldn't have happened, shouldn't have let him touch me.

Oh, God, what was she thinking? Shameless, naked, sitting astride on his lap... She behaved like a floozy. No, a slut. She should be ashamed of herself. She should be mortified!

But I love him.

Surely that made it right, losing her inhibitions with the man she loved.

Dmitry.

So gentle, so kind. And then intense and demanding. He made her burn and beg, and then sent her flying. Shuddering in recollection, she closed her eyes. If it was wrong, then so be it. She wouldn't change a single thing about last night, even if possible. But facing him –impossible. So, before he awakened, she ran away, and hid in her room. Coward.

I am not! I just need some time.

For what?

Restless, she shot to her feet, and winced. Still sore, her inner muscles twitched, causing her a mild discomfort. The faint bluish marks on her breasts and thighs that she discovered in the shower made her weep.

That won't do, Natasha. Keep your head high and your emotions in a tight fist.

She covered her misty eyes with both hands, and uttered a helpless little prayer,

Please, God, please, send me strength.

Confused and terrified, she tried to calm down, and think clearly.

Was Dmitry angry? Upset? What would he do next? Come looking for her, or ignore her?

But the predominant worry in her mind was, did he enjoy their time together?

She remembered his feverish praises, his caresses, and then his triumphant shout when he found his release. Yes, she gave him pleasure.

Nothing more? Was it just physical to him?

Better for you if it really was just that. Probably, better for him too.

Who was she kidding? She'd die if the physical gratification was all he wanted from her. Because yesterday Natasha lost something more vital than her virginity: she lost her soul. As for her heart—he owned it from the moment they met six years ago. She loved him with every cell of her body, every drop of her blood, with everything that she was.

But Dmitry never said he loved her.

Clearly, he wanted her. But did he need her? As much as she needed him? No way to know for sure, and that's why decided never to go to him again.

She vowed not to make love with him until he cared for her. Just a little. And if not, then so be it. She'd live her life as before, and remember last night like a wonderful dream. Enchanting, magical, bittersweet.

A knock on her door pulled her from the unhappy thoughts. She pulled the door open to find Peter.

"I came to tell you Grandmother is awake, and Dad left for the hospital."

Natasha let out a sigh of relief. She pasted a fake smile on her face, glad to be granted a short reprieve from the imminent confrontation with Dmitry.

"What do you say we go for ice cream after Katia's art lesson? A trip to the city will be good for all of us."

After a long look at her, Peter shrugged. "Why not? Let's get out of this mausoleum for a while."

Katia's delight at the outing was contagious. Natasha's heart squeezed, even as she gave her little girl a wobbly grin. Such a simple thing as a trip for ice cream should be a normal part of every child's life. But not for Katia.

Natasha sighed. She should talk to Dmitry. High time for some changes in Katia's life. To live such a sheltered secluded life for a bright and talented child was wrong. Natasha must make Dmitry see the danger his mother caused by keeping Katia away from the real world, from interacting with other kids her age.

Elizabeth treated the girl like a prisoner, literally locked up inside the dark walls of the manor, robbed off a normal childhood. Granted, Katia was a very special little girl, a prodigy with a genius IQ. But despite all of that, she was just a little kid.

So, after Katia's lesson, they all piled into Peter's car, happy and carefree, they drove away. As soon as they went through the heavy golden gates, Natasha's troubling thoughts evaporated. Elated, she swept her eyes along the beautiful scenery unfolding before her. San Francisco, the picturesque city she lived in for several years, but had rarely traveled around.

The buildings, the landmarks, Fisherman's Wharf, and the famous Golden Gate bridge, simply magnificent. Like a little kid, she gazed around, soaking up the easygoing atmosphere that seemed to saturate the air.

They stopped for ice cream, overindulging their sweet cravings. Peter bought Katia a huge balloon shaped like Mikey Mouse, and sent the girl squealing with delight. Such simple little things made such a huge difference. For the first time in ages, Katia acted like a typical six-year-old, chatting and giggling, sharing some funny stories. Too soon they needed to head back.

On the way home, both kids laughed and sang to the radio. Peter's tenor endearingly off-key, unlike Katia's clear, bell-like voice. She sang like an angel, joyous and sweet and heartbreaking. But with each mile that brought them closer to *Zolotoe Selo,* their collective exuberance faded, until it dimmed completely. Natasha squirmed as the tall manor house loomed closer. Soon she became agitated. Was Dmitry back from the hospital? Will he seek her out? And if yes, what might she say to him?

Her mood became glum the moment they drove through the golden gate .

Katia too stopped chatting, and sat somberly with her tiny shoulders stooped, and her eyes downcast. A deep frown marred Peter's handsome face.

Dear God, everything here is so depressing.

In a flash, Natasha realized she hated *Zolotoe Selo.*

Vehemently, furiously.

"I hate this house." She didn't mean to say it out loud.

As soon as Katia was out of earshot, Peter turned to her. "Are you unhappy here?"

"No, *miliy,* not unhappy, but..."

"But not terribly happy, either, huh?"

"It's hard to explain. Sometimes I feel like I'm suffocating. And sometimes I feel scared."

"Scared? Why? I won't let anything happened to you, or Katie. You know that, don't you?"

"I know, *miliy.*" She cupped his face in her palms, and managed to put a smile on her face. "It's the house. Look at it, Petya. It is so oppressive, so arrogant, so... mean, somehow." She scanned her surroundings and shuddered.

"Natasha, it's not the house," Peter interrupted gently, "but the people who live inside. Brick and stone cannot be mean. Unlike humans."

CHAPTER SEVENTY-EIGHT

The front doors opened and Dmitry stepped forward.

Katia ran toward her father. He caught her, easily, effortlessly, kissed her upturned nose and laughed at something she said.

Then his eyes zeroed in on Natasha. An odd expression crossed his face.

She froze to the spot, watching Dmitry with hooded eyes. Peter was on her left, shuffling his feet. What should she do? Run or stay?

And then she found her spine.

"Petya, please take Katia, and go inside. And make sure she changes her clothes. I'll be along shortly."

When he hesitated, she gave him a little smile of encouragement. "Go, *miliy*. Please. I'll be alright."

Peter nodded, and took Katia from his father's arms, then carried her through the doors.

She started to tremble. Dmitry's silver eyes kept her immobile. He watched her in silence, his expression drawn. The moment stretched. After what seemed like an eternity, she got irritated. Lifting her chin, she stared at him in defiance.

If he decided to say nothing, so help her God, neither would she.

Resolutely squaring her shoulders, Natasha stepped forward. Silence.

The hell with it. She moved faster, with the single goal in mind to reach the door and get inside. As soon as possible.

She stood on the threshold, when he stopped her with his voice.

"Natasha."

Her name sounded like a caress when whispered by that deep familiar baritone. She shivered, and cursed her strong reaction. Pointless to berate herself. She knew she was lost the moment she first met this dark aloof stranger. Nothing changed since that day. If anything, she was more lost and vulnerable now.

Schooling her voice into a neutral mode, she managed to answer, "Dmitry."

But her vocal cords refused to listen to her brain's command. Instead of impersonal, it sounded breathless and husky. Dammit.

After a pause, he asked quietly, "Are you alright?"

Those few words instantly made her weepy.

"I'm fine." She glanced down to hide her eyes from him. "I'm fine," she repeated more firmly, desperately trying to convince herself.

No, I'm not. I'm miserable, and embarrassed, and afraid.

Holding onto her pride like a drowning person to a lifesaver, she stiffened her spine.

Dmitry frowned. "I need to talk to you."

"All right," she agreed quickly. Too quickly. "Later, please."

She tried to skirt around him, but he put his hand onto her shoulder, stopping her in midstride.

"Why later?"

"Ah... I'm cold. And kids need their dinner."

His reluctance was obvious, but he withdrew his hand. "After dinner, then."

She nodded and all but run into the house.

CHAPTER SEVENTY-NINE

After dinner, Natasha managed to slip unnoticed from the huge dining room where the four of them ate their meal. She excused herself while Dmitry occupied himself with Katia, and tiptoed out. She was near the staircase, poised to run up, when a hand on her shoulder pinned her to the spot.

Startled, she almost lost her footing. Dmitry steadied her.

"I thought you were many things, Natasha, but never a coward." His mild tone rang with accusation.

Immediately on the defensive, she glared at him. "I am not a coward."

"No? Then what are you doing, sneaking away like that? Did you think I wouldn't notice?"

Yes, but damn if she willingly admitted it. Stubbornness, her one and only constant in life, made her chin shoot up.

"I was not sneaking, and I am not a coward."

"Prove it," he countered. "Let's go in the study, and have a talk."

Damn him, he pushed the right button. She never backed away from a challenge. Whether it was the orphan in her still desperate to prove her own worth, or a defense mechanism, she wasn't sure. But as soon as any challenge was issued, Natasha jumped right in. Even if scared half to death.

Like now.

With a curt nod, she strolled toward the room everybody called Elizabeth's study. Always a gentleman, Dmitry opened the door for her, and waited until she stepped inside. Memories immediately assaulted her. How many times was she summoned here for yet another scolding? How many times she marched inside, seething, for yet another argument? Countless.

The last one, especially fresh in her mind, ended with Elizabeth's abrupt collapse. Her expression must have reflected her uneasiness. Dmitry frowned.

"Natasha? What is it?"

"Please, Dmitry, not here. Not in this room."

"All right. Where?"

"Anywhere but here." Hurriedly, without waiting for him, she exited the study.

He caught up with her in the hall.

"Natasha, talk to me. What happened just now? Why are you scared?"

"I hate that room." Calmer, she fixed her gaze on him. "Let's go outside."

He nodded in agreement. Once in the garden, Natasha chose a random path. For a while they walked along in silence. Finally, he stopped.

"Okay. We are outside, no one can hear us. Let's talk."

"All right." Show time. "Let's talk."

"Why?"

Confused, she blinked several times. "Why what?"

"Why did you leave this morning?"

"I should've left earlier last night, but—"

"But you didn't. Instead, you chose to sneak out of my room at the crack of dawn while I slept. Why?"

"I wanted to spare you...You know, the morning after, and all that stuff."

You are an idiot, Natasha. Morning after? Really?

Dmitry pursed his lips, and seemed to ponder her response.

"Oh, I see. You wanted to spare me. How noble of you." His face darkened almost dangerously. Involuntarily, she stepped back. "For your information, Natasha, I don't know anything about 'the morning after' nonsense, because except for my late wife, I've never slept with a woman through the night. "

That shocking admission brought her up short. "You... haven't?"

"That's correct. So, if you'd be so kind to explain that 'morning after' thing, and why were you so anxious to *spare* me, I might understand your motives better."

Unable to look at him, she studied the pattern in the carpet. Inside, she shook with joy. Like a gulp of good brandy, it shot right through her, weakening her knees.

He never slept with any woman through the night. Except me.

He never held any other woman in his sleep as he held her. The revelations made her dizzy.

"I'm waiting," Dmitry's gruff voice interrupted her jubilation. "And while you're at it, explain to me why you were crying while sneaking out of my bedroom."

Like a bucket of ice water in a face, his words chilled her. He was asleep at the time, so how did he know?

"How...?"

"How do I know? Peter told me."

"Petya? He... he saw me?"

"Yes. And seeing you crying, and running barefooted in your robe, he made a conclusion that I hurt you." Ruthlessly, he finished, "Forced you."

"Dear God, no. Dmitry, no." Miserable, guilty, she grabbed his hands. "God, I'm so sorry. So sorry. I'll talk to Petya, I will explain to him..."

CHAPTER EIGHTY

U nable to resist any longer, Dmitry covered her mouth, swallowing her first initial shock, and then her soft, helpless moan. They kissed in plain view in front of the house. That fact held no importance. He shook from waiting for her. She was like a drug, a potent, irresistible drug. If he wasn't careful, he might become an addict. When Natasha melted against him, moaning her surrender into his mouth, Dmitry ceased thinking altogether.

"Natasha, *milaya*..." Breathing fast, he covered her face with desperate kisses.

Her taste, her smell, familiar and unique, drove him crazy. "I swear, my heart almost stopped when Peter told me that you were crying. Did I hurt you that badly?"

"You didn't hurt me at all," she muttered between his frantic kisses. "I wasn't crying from hurt."

"Why, then? Why?" The pulse on her neck trembled like a small, scared bird. Tenderly, he kissed that spot, then laved it with his tongue. "Tell me."

"I was... embarrassed."

Drawing back, he stared at her. Was she kidding? Two scarlet patches spread along her face and neck. Unbelievable.

"Dear God, Natasha, you have nothing to be embarrassed about. You were magnificent. Beautiful."

She framed his face with both hands and looked into his eyes, deep and long.

"You mean it?"

"I mean it."

"You weren't disappointed?"

"No, little one, I wasn't. You are one very passionate woman, Natasha."

"I am?" Tremulous, hesitant, her smile tugged at his heart.

He smoothed the stray locks from her face, and tucked them behind her ears. "You are. Passionate, responsive, generous. And hot as sin. You, Natalia, are every man's darkest, most secret fantasy come alive."

"Don't call me Natalia. Only Elizabeth calls me that. And I hate it."

At the mentioning of his mother's name Dmitry sobered. The sharp and oddly human-like shriek of a bird somewhere up on the tree made them jump apart like a pair of guilty kids. Dmitry swore. Natasha rubbed her arms.

"Elizabeth is awake."

"I know." She became silent. What more could she say?

Her feelings? But she didn't want to lie. Not to him, not to herself. Was she relieved that Elizabeth survived her stroke? Of course.

But a premonition of something dark and inevitable crept into her heart, and made her frightened. And with it, came a sense of urgency. Time was running out. Every second before Elizabeth returned seemed like a countdown. But for what?

She didn't know. She just knew that she teetered on borrowed time.

She couldn't share her eerie premonition with Dmitry. More than likely, he wouldn't believe her, and chalk it up to nerves. And even if he did, what could he do? Elizabeth was his mother. He wasn't the type man to leave her in some institution, crippled and confined to a wheelchair. No, sooner or later, Her Grace Elizabeth Rostoff must come home. And then...

She refused to think about it.

Until that time, she decided to make every single moment count. If she had a matter of days with Dmitry, she'd take them, and enjoy every second. To the fullest.

CHAPTER EIGHTY-ONE

Dmitry noticed the changes in her. From the hollow, empty look in her eyes to the reckless brightness, almost desperation, as if she finally made an important decision. Her impossibly green eyes sparkled almost feverishly in her pale face. An ache in the pit of his stomach bloomed like a poisonous flower. For a split-second Natasha's features seemed to fade like morning fog. Just a trick of the light. Nothing eerie. But for a heartbeat she seemed unreal. Ethereal.

He shook his head and blinked to bring her face into sharp focus.

No, she was real enough, right there, and his. Only his.

How foolish to feel so desperate for a physical connection, but he took her hand, squeezed. She turned, smiled, and air caught in his throat.

She seemed more beautiful than yesterday.

He never knew he possessed the capability to feel so strongly, or need another person more than air. Until now. Until Natasha.

Shaken by the realization, he kept quiet not trusting himself to talk. By mutual agreement, they started to walk, holding hands.

Natasha broke the silence first. "I want to ask you for something."

"Anything."

"Take Katia away from here."

He came to an abrupt halt. "Earlier, at the airport, you protested rather vehemently against my decision to remove Katia from *Zolotoe Selo*. What happened to change your mind?"

"Actually, a lot happened since then. At the airport, I protested not because I wanted her to stay here, but because I wasn't sure *why* you wanted to take her. What's more, neither did you." She bit her lip, then raised her eyes. "Now I know. But most important, so do you."

"Do I?"

"Yes, you do. You love your daughter, Dmitry, and don't even try to pretend otherwise."

Words were lost to him. He nodded, silently inviting her to go on.

"Katia... she is a very special child with an extraordinary talent. But in any other way, she's just a little kid, and she needs a normal, ordinary childhood as much as she needs her paints and brushes. Your mother... she doesn't understand that. Or chooses not to. She keeps Katia under lock and key, restricts her whereabouts to this manor and the companionship of the adults. And the dogs, of course, thank God for them. She forbids her to watch television, to play with other kids, or even go to school. Dmitry, she insists on homeschooling her. Katia is isolated from anyone and anything that's not of Russian descent, be that food or language.

"God knows, I've tried many times to convince Elizabeth that she's making a huge mistake, that Katia needs to play with other kids, and be able to live a life of a normal six-years-old, but," she humped her shoulders, "your mother is unwilling to see the truth."

"I believe that."

Dammit, the picture she painted scared and worried him.

His little daughter was condemned to live a life of a prisoner. And all because of him. Guilt pressed on him like a leaden weight.

Damn Elizabeth. And damn me ten times more.

"Dmitry, that little girl is suffocating here. We love her, Petya and me, and now you. But she needs other children, she needs to be able to run and play and scream for goodness' sake! She must express her emotions not only through colors on canvasses. Do you understand?"

She probably failed to notice that in her desperation to convince him she had clutched the front of his shirt.

"Yes, Natasha, I do." He covered her hands with his. "I agree with you completely."

"Oh, good. Thank God. Thank you."

More amused than annoyed, he lifted his brows. "You don't have to thank me. She is my daughter, too."

"Yes, yes, of course." When Natasha finally noticed his shirt clutched in her desperate grip, her eyes widened and she dropped her hands.

"Natasha." He grasped her shoulders. "I already told you I want to take Katia away from this house. And I will. You don't have to worry about it anymore."

She glanced across the lawn and nodded. "What about Petya?"

"He's a grown man, and if he decides to live with me, I couldn't be happier. And he knows it. But the choice is only his."

"All right. That's good."

God, she was so transparent. A mix of tenderness and anger waged a war in his heart. Did she really think he'd take both kids but not her? Did she think him that inhuman?

He lifted her chin with his index finger, then gazed into her upturned face. It was clouded with misery and acceptance. Clearly, she expected to be left behind.

Her emerald eyes were awash with pain, and his annoyance began to spike. Why on earth did she think he'd walk away from her? That she wasn't important? How could she even think like that after last night?

She tried to avert her face. He edged it back so she had to look at him. A flood of guilt flooded him but he was determined to follow through with his plan no matter.

"No, don't you hide from me, Natasha. I want to look at you, straight into your eyes when I ask you to marry me."

The shock widened her eyes. Unblinking, she stared at him for a long moment.

"Marry? M-me?"

"Yes, marry, and yes, you. Only you."

Tears slipped from her eyes and almost destroyed him.

Good job, Rostoff. So much romance, you stupid bastard.

Here he was, asking the woman he loved to marry him in a manner more appropriate for a business deal. For goodness' sake, could he do anything right with this woman? Softly, he asked, "Do you think I'd leave you again? Do you honestly think I could? My God, Natasha, do you think so little of me?"

A pitiful little sob slipped from her lips. It broke his heart. Framing her face with both hands, Dmitry continued in a gentler voice, "Our family wouldn't be complete without you, darling. *I* wouldn't be complete without you. You, Natasha, are the mother of my children, you are the woman I..."

For a second the words hovered on his tongue. He had no idea why he hedged again, and didn't tell her what was in his heart. Something grabbed him from within, something cold, big and heavy. Fear? Panic?

No clue. But he knew it impossible to step over that last barrier yet.

Natasha stared at him, her shock fresh and clear on her face. For a long time, she remained quiet. Desperate, he leaned closer and looked into her somber eyes. "You are the woman I need the most. The woman I want the most. Please, Natasha. Marry me. Make me complete."

CHAPTER EIGHTY-TWO

H e didn't say he loved her only that he needed her, wanted her, that he wouldn't be complete without her.

As a declaration of love, this was the saddest one... and the most beautiful.

"Yes." Her voice sounded like it came from someone else, someone from a great distance. Same as in Moscow six years ago, when she answered 'yes' to his outrageous plan to adopt Katia and leave her country.

She had never been able to say no to him. From the moment she met Dmitry, she was doomed. Or blessed. Or both.

"Yes," she repeated more firmly, "I will marry you."

But instead of joy, a deep sorrow settled inside of her like a heavy boulder.

A sudden despair chilled her to the marrow.

Dmitry rested his forehead on hers. He smelled like an autumn night—fragrant, intoxicating, and a little sad. Why can't he say what he truly feels?

"Natasha—" he began.

She deliberately cut him off because she couldn't bear to hear him stumble on words he may not mean.

"Dmitry, your mother..."

He uttered a little oath, and lifted his head. "What about her?"

"She'll be mad about it. Us, kids, everything."

"I don't care. She can't win, Natasha, not this time." He let go of her, then took several steps back. "She'll be an invalid for the rest of her life. Confined to a wheelchair. Her doctor gives her a fifty-fifty chance to regain her speech. Elizabeth is a smart woman. She'll realize she can't take care of Katia or Peter anymore. She won't fight me on this. But if despite common logic she takes me to court, then not a single judge in this country will give her custody. Especially, when one of the parents is alive, able and willing to provide for the child. As for us..." He turned to face her again, "She can't do anything to us, Natasha. She won't."

"She can and will make your life a living hell, Dmitry."

"Yes, no doubt about that. So what?" He stepped closer, his somber silver eyes gazed at her with palpable intensity. "Will you fight with me, Natasha? Are you willing to go through that hell with me?"

"Yes." She meant it with all her heart. "I am, and I will."

Dmitry looked at her long and hard, then flashed her a smile. "That's my girl."

He tried to lighten the mood, and she appreciated the effort. Natasha plastered a fake smile onto her face. "I'm my own *girl*, thank you very much."

"That might be," he sent her a flashing grin, and tugged her closer, "but you, honey, are definitely *my woman*."

Only yours. Always yours.

She went willingly into his arms, welcoming his strength and his warmth. She waited for him to kiss her, instead he clasped her hand, and started toward the house. Like a beautiful thick rug, the fallen leaves in all the different shades of gold muffled their footsteps.

"Dmitry?"

"Hmm-mm?"

"Let's not talk to anyone about... about us for now."

"Why?"

She shrugged. "I just want to keep it to myself for a while and not to make it public."

He stopped. "Are you embarrassed?"

"God, no! Just...a bit awkward."

He seemed to ponder it for a moment. Finally, he nodded. "Okay, but with two stipulations."

"And they are?"

"First, we tell the kids. I think they have the right to know, and I'm sure they both will be elated."

Even though she was a little uneasy with the idea, Dmitry was right. The kids have the right to know.

She nodded. "We must tell Petya right away. I still feel guilty about causing a confrontation between you two this morning."

"Confrontation, my boot." Dmitry chuckled. "He barged into my bedroom with murder in his eyes, ready to break every bone in my body."

"Oh, God, Dmitry! I'm sorry! Did he... did you...?"

"Did we pound on each other?" His smile widened as if amused by the idea. "No. Of course not, *milaya*. We talked, and I explained everything to him."

Everything? Oh, my God!

"What did you say?"

"The truth," Dmitry answered noncommittally.

"What exactly?" she persisted.

"Stubborn, aren't you, Natasha? Let's just say, I managed to convince my son that I didn't rape you." Wincing, she bit her lip. "And that I had every intention to talk to you and find out why you were crying. Why?"

"I told you."

"Tell me again, only the truth this time."

"Dmitry, I love you." Not the whole truth, but still.

"Oh, Natasha." He gently drew her into his arms.

Content, she allowed herself a few moments to savor their closeness.

"What is your second stipulation?"

"My what?" He stepped away and studied her.

"You told me you have two stipulations. First, we tell the kids. What is the second?"

"My second stipulation is that we will continue to sleep together. I don't care about propriety. In my heart, you are already my wife." Deep and soft, like an intimate caress, his voice sent shivers along her spine.

"Yes." She accepted the hand he held out to her in silent invitation, and sealed her fate.

I am doomed. Or blessed.

Or both.

CHAPTER EIGHTY-THREE

For Dmitry the following days became a blur of activity. Like a magician in a circus, he juggled the myriad of important matters at the same time. Preparing the house for Elizabeth's return by adjusting it for a wheelchair became the number one priority. Without Vlad's help, who hadn't completely recovered from his accident, Dmitry ran the company single-handedly via phone and computer. He managed to hire a good family lawyer to start preparations for Katia's custody. Even though he knew Elizabeth wouldn't fight him, he still preferred to be ready.

A steady progress on all three fronts left him satisfied. But one thing continued to bother him: his relationship with Natasha.

Dmitry rubbed his neck as he stood at the window of his newly converted impromptu office. Why was he uneasy?

Although they slept together, it seemed that Natasha was becoming more and more distant. Unusually quiet and sad, she lost weight, melting in front of his eyes. He decided to watch over her meals, to make sure she ate enough. Pale by nature, her face became almost translucent. Even the kids noticed. This morning at breakfast Katia asked Natasha if she was sick. Dammit, she really seemed sick. More accurately, she looked almost emaciated. And sad. Dear God, her eyes were so sad, as if she grieved for someone or something. Whenever he asked her, she looked at him with that enchanting smile of hers, and assured him everything was fine.

Fine. He hated that word.

At first, he figured their nights together wore her out, that wild and explosive lovemaking explained her exhaustion. But his instincts screamed at him there's something else, something that try as he might, he failed to identify. Was Natasha keeping a secret from him? Is that why she erected the invisible wall between them?

But that wall existed only in the light of day. By night, they were locked into each other arms, burning with desire that became only hotter and brighter. Consumed by it, drunk with it, he became uncivilized and wild. Night after night, they made love endlessly, tirelessly, coming together like two hurricanes, clashing, fighting, exploding. Their passion became a blazing inferno that refused to be pacified no matter what. But while his feelings were born from the all-consuming need for her, hers seemed covered by a layer of desperation so tangible, he detected it every time. Like she knew that every minute must be accounted for, and she ran against the clock. Dammit.

Dmitry cursed out loud. What was the matter with her? Did she think he might take the kids and leave her behind? Time and again, he made it clear that she was as vital to him as Peter and Katia. Did she doubt him?

God help him, the woman tore him apart. For him to walk away from her was simply impossible. Unthinkable. She was his air, his heart and blood.

His everything.

But what about her? She loved him, of that he never doubted for a moment. Not only because she said that. He *knew* she loved him, *felt* it with every fiber of his being. He *saw* it in her eyes, *heard* it in the undertones of her voice. Ridiculous as it sounded, Dmitry could swear he could even smell her desire for him. Musky and rich, the flavor of her love, like a woman herself, exquisite, sensual, and incredibly generous.

Yes, Natasha loved him. But did she trust him?

That question bothered him. Dammit, he became so vulnerable, it embarrassed him. The shrill ring of the phone cut into his troubled thoughts. He snatched the receiver from its cradle.

"Yes, what?"

"Good day to you, too, *cher*." Marie's lazy drawl made him smile despite his glum.

"Hello, Gorgeous. How are you?"

"I'm well, *mon ami*. The question is, how are you?"

"Good. Or as well as to be expected under the circumstances."

She chuckled. "That bad, huh?"

"You have no idea."

"Is there something I can do, Dmitry?"

His mind turned to Natasha, along with his uneasy thoughts and doubts. "No, Marie. This is something I have to work at myself, but thank you."

"Well, you know if you need something, we are here for you."

"I know, sweetheart, I know. Same goes. How are the kids? How is that Adonis husband of yours?"

"Girls are fine, driving me absolutely insane. As for Vlad, I let you talk to him yourself." She sighed. "Dmitry?"

"Yes?"

"Come home, okay? We miss you."

"I will. Soon. And I won't come alone. I'm bringing Katia with me and... Natasha."

"What? Wait, Vladimir, I'm not finished yet!" she shouted at Vlad who probably lost his patience by now. "Dmitry? What did you say? You're coming with who?"

He chuckled. "You heard me, Marie." Quietly, he added, "I asked her to marry me."

"*Mon Dieu*, is this true? Oh, Dmitry, I'm so happy. Did she agree? Silly question, of course, she did! The woman has been in love with you for ages. And you were just too stubborn and stupid to admit that you were crazy about her."

Taking aback, Dmitry blinked at the phone a couple of times. Trust Marie to take the wind of his sails. "How... how did you know?"

"What? That you are stubborn and stupid?"

"No." Torn between laughter and annoyance, Dmitry asked, "How did you know that she was in love with me?"

"How do you think I knew? Peter, of course. We are friends, you know. And, poor boy, became so disappointed in you for your blindness."

"That *poor boy* better learn to keep his mouth shut," he muttered.

"Don't mind that! Tell me, is she really so beautiful? So wonderful?"

"She is..." How to describe Natasha? Mere words seemed inadequate.

"She is incredible," he managed after a pause. "She is unique. And she is the only one for me."

"*Mon Dieu.*" Marie sniffed loudly. "Oh, Dmitry, I never thought you could be like that. That you could feel like that, *mon ami*. And I'm so happy for you."

"Yeah, I didn't know that, either. And I am really happy for myself."

Right then he was anything but happy, but he preferred not to share that detail.

"When is the wedding?"

Momentarily baffled, he stammered, "Ah... I don't know. Soon."

Shit. He never thought of a wedding. Or a ring.

Nice job, Rostoff.

He made a mental note to contact his longtime assistant Cindy, and have an engagement ring sent immediately. He knew exactly the one he wanted. A square cut emerald encircled by rows of small diamonds. The gem the exact color of her eyes. Yes, that was Natasha's ring, alright.

Grinning, he tried to envision her reaction. Would she be pleased? Stunned? Delighted? Probably, all the above.

"Okay, all right," Marie's voice cut into his fantasies, dragging him back to the moment. "But we will celebrate as soon as you get here. *Oui?* Oh, I can't wait to meet her and your little girl! Come home, *mon ami*, come home soon."

"I will, Marie. Now, where is that vice president of mine?"

"Oh, he's here. I let you talk to him, but promise to call later and tell me everything, you hear?"

"I hear, and I will."

"Love you." Marie passed the phone.

"Well, well." Vlad's amused voice brought a relieved smile to Dmitry's face. Probably still bruised and sore, but his friend sounded his usual dynamic self. Thank God.

"Hi, buddy. How are you feeling?"

"Never mind me, *buddy,* just tell me what is it I hear about bringing home a woman, and all that?"

"Her name is Natasha." Dammit, why was it so simple to talk to Marie and so difficult to his best friend, a man he knew half of his life? Maybe because of exactly *that*, because they knew each other so well Dmitry squirmed, oddly uncomfortable.

"Natasha, huh? Red curly hair, sultry green eyes, firstclass compact body, and knockout mouth with a sexy mole?"

"Watch it, pal. It's my future wife you're talking about."

Vlad whistled. "So, that's how the wind blows."

"Yes." He was riled by Vlad's description of Natasha that sounded offhanded and somehow insulting. "Any objections?"

"Only one: you're in too deep, Dmitry. That means you're vulnerable and in the hostile territory. Watch you back."

He shouldn't feel so dumbfounded. Vlad's perception was legendary and uncanny. Even miles away, he zeroed in on Dmitry's current situation with a lethal precision and accuracy of a missile.

Why I am so surprised?

Vlad knew him, and he knew Elizabeth. And all the embarrassing story that happened few years ago. If not for Vlad, for his help and intervention, Dmitry had no idea how his life might have turned out. They were best friends, confidants. He considered Vlad his brother.

Feeling stupid and ashamed of his ridiculous jealousy, Dmitry frowned.

"Believe me, I am watching my back. Sometimes I feel..." Foolish, that's how he felt right now. And helpless. And afraid. He desperately wanted to confide in his friend, but stopped himself. What's the point?

As usual, Vlad read him like an open book. "I know, Dmitry. Been there, done that. But believe me, the benefits are much higher. And well worth it."

"I'll take your word," Dmitry grumbled.

"I almost enjoyed your current predicament, my friend, being your best pal and all that. But seriously. Don't let your guard down. Finish there as soon as you can, and then run. Grab your woman and your daughter, and just run. You have no business in San Francisco."

"Unfortunately, I do." *Elizabeth.* He didn't say it out loud, but Vlad heard it all the same.

"Dmitry, I know she is your mother, but—"

"Yes, she is, Vlad. Even being my number one enemy doesn't erase the fact that she is my mother."

"What about the girl?"

"I'm shooting for full custody."

Vlad whistled long and loud. "It takes time, Dmitry."

"I know."

"And lawyers."

"Already got one."

"Court?"

"No one could approve of Elizabeth as a guardian in her condition."

"Is she that bad?"

"Worse."

"Well, I'd tell you I'm sorry for her, but honestly I am not. You may pound on me later for that."

"I won't. I'd feel the same if she wasn't my mother."

"Okay. What do you want me to do in the meantime?"

"In the meantime, I want you to concentrate all your efforts on getting on your feet ASAP. I'll need all the help I can get."

"Yeah, tell me about it," Vlad muttered.

For a while, they talked about business. He was relieved and pleased that Vlad followed on the company's day to day operations, taking control bit by bit back into his hands. Clearly his friend wanted to work full time. Knowing Vlad, it was going to happen sooner than everybody anticipated. And that pleased Dmitry. He needed Vlad in operational mode. He needed him, period.

Right before they said goodbye, Vlad stopped him with an unexpected warning, "Dmitry? Be very careful with that bony weasel. I'm talking about your mother's butler."

"Ivan?"

"I have no idea, but I guess we're talking about the same man."

"Why?"

"Because he's slime."

"I know that, but it doesn't mean he's dangerous."

"I wouldn't be so sure. He is Elizabeth's confidant and her spy."

"How did you know that?" True, Ivan was all that, and more, but how on earth Vlad knew it?

"Call it a hunch. Definitely watch your step with him. Did you know he's in love with Elizabeth?"

"What? Are you kidding?"

"I wish."

"Vlad, you must be mistaken. Ivan is a butler, for goodness' sake. You know my mother. The Snob Queen would never get involved with a servant. Period. The very idea is incomprehensible. Impossible."

"I didn't say she had. Only that she knows about his infatuation, and uses it. Uses him. Hell on a man's ego, don't you think? The bottom line is, Dmitry, that butler will do everything for Elizabeth. Absolutely everything. And that makes him extremely dangerous."

"How did you find out about Ivan? About his... feelings for my mother?"

"Never mind that." Impatience crept into Vlad's voice." Dmitry, I have a very bad feeling about all this. Hell, just be careful, all right?"

"Vlad, this is not a war zone." But, dammit, it started to feel like one. "And a pair of seventy-something-year-old people one of which is an invalid in a wheelchair don't make worthy opponents, don't you think?"

Vlad apparently didn't. He made a noncommittal 'harrumph' and left it at that.

"I'm not doing anything illegal, nor do I intend to put anyone in jeopardy, myself included. I just want to take my daughter back home with me and marry the woman I love."

Despite his mood, Vlad chuckled. "You don't ask much, do you?"

They often shared that old joke between them, so Dmitry answered as expected, "No, only for everything."

They both laughed, but their merriment was short lived. Soberly, Vlad added, "Keep on your toes, Dmitry. Especially now when your emotions cloud your brain. Damn, I wish I could be there."

"This is my family, Vlad. My problem. And I'm the one who should deal with it."

With that last statement, Dmitry disconnected the call.

My family. My problem.

Hell, who was he kidding? It was a mess with the capital M.

CHAPTER EIGHTY-FOUR

Ivan loved his mother. Dmitry failed to wrap his brain around it. Damn Vlad for dropping that bombshell. Did Elizabeth know? But of course, she knew. An astute, shrewd woman like her perceived everything. Knowing his mother, there were many times she used Ivan's feelings to full advantage. Dangling her affection like a proverbial carrot, encouraging him, then on a whim snatching it away. How many years of humiliation can one endure before falling into resentment? Talk about a fine line between love and hate.

If Ivan truly loved Elizabeth for so long, he must have learned to loathe her. But still, he stayed in the house, serving his mistress. Loyalty? Devotion? Or sickness? Clearly Ivan was an enemy, and not to be underestimated. Vlad's warning popped into his mind:

...That butler will do everything for Elizabeth. Absolutely everything. And that makes him extremely dangerous.

As always, his friend's instincts were right on.

Must keep on my toes. And leave San Francisco as soon as possible.

Whatever happens afterward, Dmitry vowed to never return to *Zolotoe Selo.*

But first, he must wait for Elizbeth, and make sure she settled in.

A couple of weeks. A month at the most. Surely he can last that long. He had no choice in the matter. For better or worse, Elizabeth was his mother.

Dammit all to hell and back.

She was due to be released from the hospital next week. By that time, he hoped to obtain temporary custody of Katia. And then he'd follow Vlad's advice: grab his girls, and run.

His plane waited on standby for his orders. Maybe a bit prematurely, but he felt better for it. At any time, day or night, the Boeing was fueled and ready for the three of them: himself, Natasha and Katia. Peter chose to remain in California. He decided to stay and finish the school year without transferring. But he promised to join them later. It didn't sit well with Dmitry, but he relented. His son needed time to decide for himself, and choose where to live. For now, Peter started packing and moving his things into a small studio he rented near the campus.

Katia's things were being packed, too. She was delighted with the prospect of living in Paris, seeing the Louvre, make friends with Vlad and Marie's little girls. But especially, she wanted the three of them to live together as a family. The only thing clouding her happiness, the upcoming separation from her brother. They all talked, and explained to her that it was just a temporary thing, just for a few months until the school year finished. Peter promised to visit every chance he got, but still Katia remained devastated. Sometimes she sat and cried without a single sound. That mute bottomless grief scared him shitless, but Natasha and Peter usually managed to quickly pull her out of it. One thing Dmitry hated more than a woman's tears—the tears of a child. It terrified him, and made him feel totally useless. Worse, it made him feel helpless and scared. He, the leading force of the multi-billion-dollar worldwide enterprise who dealt with crises daily and always kept his cool under pressure, became stricken with panic whenever he faced a crying child. And when the child happened to be your own, that panic intensified tenfold.

Katia will come around. Or so he hoped. She'll miss Peter, of course, but she'd get used to living with him and Natasha. He was sure that Vlad's and Marie's twins, Nicole and Michelle, will hit it off with Katia, and make good friends.

She'll be fine. She'll be all right.

Besides, Natasha will take care of Katia. She always has. They all will be all right.

As soon as we leave San Francisco.

And that brought him to the square one: his mother.

Anger overcame him and his hands shook with the fierce urge to break something. Heaving an empty glass against the wall satisfied him. For a split second.

Disgusted with himself, he let out a long string of curses. Only one person in the world had the power to wrangle such a negative reaction out of him.

Only Elizabeth could reduce him to the state of a savage.

Enraged, humiliated, he struggled to keep his infamous Rostoff temper under control. A dull headache that began sometime earlier now pounded in earnest. He squeezed his temples with open palms, pressed as hard as could, but to no avail. A burning sensation in the pit of his stomach brought a wave of nausea. Sour bile surged upward, abrading his throat. Nausea swam over him and he fought the urge to throw up. Damn, that was all he needed.

What he did need right this very minute was Natasha. He wanted to see her, to inhale her unique scent, to touch her. And then he'd be content. That overwhelming constant need no longer surprised him. He accepted it just as he accepted the blue sky and the green grass.

Where is she?

He hurried out of the office. Jumping two steps at the time, and almost collided with Ivan, dressed in his winter fur coat and Russian floppy hat.

"I beg your pardon, Your Grace," the old servant muttered with exaggerated humility. As false as his improbable straight white teeth. It annoyed Dmitry to no end.

The deep bow Ivan executed seemed somehow insulting. It scraped him raw, and set his temper boiling. Repulsed as if he touched something dirty and slimy, Dmitry took a quick step back, not bothering to cover his expression.

"Going somewhere, Ivan?"

"Yes, Your Grace, I'm heading to the hospital, to visit Her Grace Elizabeth. Your dear mama."

My dear mama, my ass.

Dmitry grimaced. He always disliked Ivan, but ignored him like a harmless pesky gnat. After Vlad's warning he changed his opinion of the old butler. Now he grew more suspicious and uneasy around him.

"Well, say good day from me to my *dear mama.*"

Dismissing Ivan with a sharp impatient nod, Dmitry continued up the stairs, all the while he sensed the probing gaze of the old man's colorless eyes on his back.

Bastard, old slimy leach.

So, he chose to visit his mother, huh? How often had he sneaked past them and ran to his Mistress to report the latest gossips? Pathetic snitch.

Since Elizabeth became completely lucid and even began to talk a little, Dmitry's gut told him that she and Ivan have a lot to chitchat about, and undoubtedly plot.

The hell with them. They no longer held the capacity to hurt him anymore. Let them gossip and plot to their hearts content. Elizabeth held no power to stop him taking Katia, or marrying Natasha.

He erased Ivan and his mother from his mind, and walked to Natasha's room. He knocked. No answer. He opened the door to find the room empty. Hell. He turned, and jogged down the stairs. He knew where to find her. Moving briskly, he exited the house, and headed down the path that led to the gazebo.

CHAPTER EIGHTY-FIVE

An incurable restlessness flowed through Natasha as she hid inside her favorite sanctuary. The invisible clock inside her ticked faster and louder with each passing day. They expected Elizabeth to be discharged next week. Her rooms were ready, all stairways and sidewalks modified for the use of a wheelchair. They hired a private nurse just today, a sturdy middle-aged woman recommended by doctor Litowski. Natasha felt sorry for her. Poor thing, she had no idea what she was in for. Natasha kept her ideas to herself, but her fear became harder to deal with. Every time she looked in the mirror her face looked paler, and her exhausted body wanted to do nothing but sleep. Her clothes hung on her, so large they looked like they belonged to someone else. She had lost so much weight, and failed to know why. She looked like hell, and felt like it too. The only thing that kept her going was her family. Without Dmitry and the kids, she would have long ago folded like a house of cards, giving in to the black despair.

Dmitry.

If not for him, Natasha didn't know how she'd survive. Reality intruded on them, keeping them separated most of the day, but the nights belong to them. She threw off her silly fear, and demanded to be treated like a normal red-blooded woman in bed. Having his weight on top of her no longer panicked. On the contrary, she preferred it that way. Instead of being helpless, she reveled in her feminine vulnerability. Craved it.

And she trusted him.

She smiled recalling that memorable moment when she deliberately reversed their positions so his body covered hers. Startled, Dmitry attempted to lift his weight, but she held him tight.

"I want it all. All or nothing."

After a while, he complied. And Natasha's fear eliminated. She wanted it all. Body, mind, soul, and a lifetime together.

Hope, sweet and powerful, made her believe that everything will be all right.

They'd be granted a long life together.

Ignoring her daunting premonition, she convinced herself that Elizabeth held no power or the ability to do anything to separate them.

Like the flame of a candle, hope burned inside her soul, taking hold. She prayed every day: *Dear God, please.*

If there was a God, he already knew her heart's need without any words. He had no use for words. Only people needed them. Words and dreams to keep them warm at night and moving by day.

Dreams are dangerous things.

Svetlana's voice sounded so clear, Natasha spun around as if expecting to see her dear friend beside her. But instead, Dmitry stomped toward the gazebo.

Dreams are *dangerous things, Sveta,* she watched the man she loved, *but without them, life is not worth living.*

As soon as Dmitry noticed her, he stopped. His quick intake of breath made her smile. The strong effect she had on him no longer surprised her. He held the same power over her. One glance, and she burned for him.

And that explained why during the day she avoided him whenever possible. Try as she might, Natasha failed to hide her true feelings, scared all the household might notice. Miraculously, they managed to fool everyone.

Was she unwilling to make their engagement public because she didn't want to share her secret, or because of fear? Probably both.

He never liked pretending, but for her sake he grudgingly agreed to continue their charade. During the day they treated each other politely and cordially, maintaining an employer-employee relationship. But at night their passion ignited. It belonged to the dark and the quiet, and only to them. They completed each other like two halves of a whole. They burned for each other, carefree and uninhibited. They celebrated each other, joyous and drunk on love.

Natasha grew tired of the silly pretense, of hiding her true feelings like they were something shameful and embarrassing.

She wanted to shout, to announce her love to the whole world.

She wanted to be able to touch him and smile at him openly, to laugh and make him laugh. To make him happy not only in bed under the cover of darkness.

She was tired of being afraid and done with that pointless emotion.

CHAPTER EIGHTY-SIX

Dmitry watched Natasha in silence. He hesitated, unsure of how to act. They were alone in the early morning.

She insisted on keeping their involvement a secret during the day. He agreed but intended to humor her for a short time.

So now, outside of the bedroom, he didn't know how to treat her. Pretend to be strangers? And how foolish! They were intimate for days, made love countless times. But still he was uneasy and unsure. Dammit, what now?

As if sensing his dilemma, she smiled. "Make love to me, Dmitry."

What?

Did he hear her correctly?

"Natasha..."

"Now, Dmitry." Her voice held a note of a reckless demand. "Here and now."

He froze in place and stared at her in mute shock. Surely, he hadn't heard right. Or did he? He gazed deep into her emerald eyes, and sucked in air. No, he wasn't mistaken. Her face reflected his own emotions: desire, longing, hunger. She took his hand in silent invitation and held his gaze. He was unable to walk away from her now any more than he had the power to stop his heart. He closed the distance between them in two short strides, then crushed her into his arms. She kissed him. Scorched, stunned by the force of it, the earth shifted beneath his feet.

"Natasha," he rasped into her open lips. "Let's go inside."

"No," she moaned, arching her throat for his kisses, "The kids are in the park for the whole afternoon... servants are... busy..."

Insane with need, he quickly calculated they had roughly an hour of marginal privacy. Only someone in Elizabeth's office might see them, and only from one small window. Impossible for anyone to spy on them.

He spun her around, then propelled them to the farthest corner of the gazebo.

Once there, he took charge. He pinned her against the wall then tugged her blouse and bra out of the way. Her generous breasts spilled into his greedy hands. Swamped with need, lost in passion, he stopped thinking.

They clashed like two hurricanes, heartbeats racing, blood roaring, and sweat blinding their eyes. Sounds of ripping fabric. Desperate groans.

Slaps of flesh against flesh.

Oblivious to the world, they took and gave, begged and demanded, pushing each other toward the first peak which they reached together, plunging from its height with twin shouts of victory. Finesse forgotten, they were driven by the sheer madness of what they brought to each other, blindly fumbling in the haze of that madness, ruthlessly and relentlessly racing to another peak and yet another.

He became insatiable, insane, uncivilized.

She matched him bit by bit, demanding, melting, burning.

When he came the last time, Dmitry emptied himself dry, pumping his seed into her womb. His shout of release abraded his throat.

For a long time, they stood still joined intimately, heartbeats meshed, souls in complete harmony. But then reality intruded.

Dmitry came to his senses first. Bracing on his hands, he jerked away, already feeling cold and bereft. Natasha remained still.

"Natasha?"

His labored breathing interrupted the silence.

Dear God, what have I done?

He treated her like an animal, tearing her clothes, taking her against the wall, plundering like a bull in rut.

At last, she mumbled something incoherent.

"What?" Gently, with shaking hands, he touched her. "What did you say?" She opened her eyes. He expected anything—tears, shock, fear— but not this. Still puffy and swollen from his kisses, her lips curved in a brilliant luminous smile.

Dear Lord, am I losing my mind?

Dumbfounded, confused, he gave her a little shake. "Natasha."

"Hmm-mm." She licked her lips like a cat who just feasted on a plump canary. "I knew it."

"Knew... what?"

"You held something back. Every time. But not today. And it was fabulous."

"Could you... could you please repeat that?"

He leaned closer, afraid his hearing played a cruel game. "What did you say?"

The look she gave him was that of a thoroughly satisfied woman. Not scared, or insulted, or embarrassed. Wearing nothing but that bewitching smile of hers, Natasha stood in front of him like a nymph. Propped against the gazebo wall, her breasts high, her slender legs still apart, the perfect image of an erotic statue came alive. A tuft of fiery curls shamelessly burned on the juncture of her thighs, beckoning his eyes, charging his blood throughout his body.

Dammit, he wanted her again.

"Natasha..." His rasp came out deep and low and tortured.

She had the cheekiness to laugh. The witch. The sorceress. The enchantress.

Mesmerized, he was unable to tear his gaze from her.

"What? Did you think I would be insulted? Hurt? Scared?"

Her rich alto sounded huskier than usual, taunting him. Enflaming him.

Just like that, he became hard as a rock.

He cursed while fumbling with his pants that were somewhere in the vicinity of his ankles. Hastily he managed to pull them up. Not an easy task, considering one part of his anatomy refused to be pacified.

She laughed, leaned forward and put her arms around him. "Relax, darling. You have nothing to be ashamed of. You were terrific. Magnificent. Incredible."

"Out of control," Dmitry supplied dryly, but managed to pull a small smile.

"Mmm-mm," she purred. "And I liked that."

"Did you?"

Enormously pleased, he traced his fingertips along her spine. She shivered in response. God, she was so incredibly sensitive.

"I liked everything," she murmured, nuzzling his nipple.

"Natasha, you're playing with fire." But his warning lacked any heat. Rubbing her lower back, his hands hovered above her buttocks. If he just touched her there, he would be lost. Dammit.

Moving her pelvis in a circular motion against his throbbing erection, Natasha whispered, "Tell me about it."

God have mercy.

"*Milaya,* in case you forgot, we are in the gazebo, and it's still day."

"Yeah?"

"Yes, and... dammit." Dmitry swore and caught her wandering hand just before it cupped his groin. "Natasha, as much as I want to, I can't... we can't... not again."

"Why?"

Curved in a pout, her sinful mouth almost undid him.

"Because the kids will return any moment now. Someone might wander outside."

"So?"

"So? Woman, you are naked as a jaybird. I am hard as a stone. And even the air in this gazebo smells of sex."

"It smells... terrific. Like you, like us."

"Yes, baby, it does," he spoke softly while gathering her into his arms. "It was amazing. You are amazing, Natasha. But it is time to go back."

CHAPTER EIGHTY-SEVEN

Dmitry knew best, of course. Time to return home, to face reality. Natasha didn't want to. The magic of their loving still clouded her senses, but her mind, numb and blind a short time ago, began to stir to life. With a deep sigh, she let go of him and began to look for her clothes.

"Why did you do that?"

"You said it was time to go back."

"No, I mean earlier. Why did you break your own rule? Why did you let me make love to you in daylight?"

"Because I wanted to. Because I love you, and because I'm tired of pretending that I'm not."

"But I thought you wanted to keep it a secret."

"I did. I don't want too anymore. Do you object?"

"Object? Are you kidding?" He let go a bark of laughter. "I never wanted to play this game from the beginning."

"I know. And I'm sorry I insisted on this sham. I don't want to keep it a secret anymore, Dmitry. I'm not ashamed of my feelings or my relationship with you. I love you, and I want everyone to know it."

She watched him closely, tense with determination.

"Are you sure?"

"Yes."

"Thank God!" Dmitry hooted with laughter, and hauled her against him. "Thank you, *milaya*."

"I am sorry, Dmitry."

He frowned and tilted his head. "For what?"

"For hiding my feelings and keeping a distance. God, it was so silly! What do I care what people say? The kids know, and they approve, and that's what matters. Nothing else." She framed his face with both hands. "I love you, Dmitry. And I'm not afraid. Not anymore. I want to be with you. I want a lifetime with you and the children. And I'll fight for it with everything I have, everything I am. If God hears my prayers, we'll be together for the rest of our lives. I'll do everything to make you happy. But if something happens... just remember that I love you. Always have, always will be."

Dmitry clutched her shoulders. "No 'if,' Natasha. Nothing will happen. I swear to you. Everything will be all right. Just hang on a little bit longer, and soon, very soon, everything will be all right. I promise."

"Yes, everything will be fine," she echoed his words.

And desperately tried to believe it.

THEY RETURNED HOME hand in hand, smiling happily at each other, oblivious to the speculative glances and whispers of the servants. Later that day Dmitry officially announced their engagement, taking congratulations and well wishes from the staff. The only one person who didn't join the impromptu celebration and refused a glass of champagne was Ivan. Standing behind everybody, he scowled, sweeping the scene with his colorless eyes. Undoubtedly, tomorrow Elizabeth will be informed of her son's plan to wed Natasha. Dmitry chucked drily.

Either she will have another stroke or drive her doctor up the wall, insisting on immediate discharge from the hospital. He leaned toward the latter.

Knowing Elizabeth, she'd be anxious to return home. And the carefree atmosphere that rooted in the *Zolotoe Selo* during her absence was sure to be ruined forever.

Tomorrow is going to be one hell of a day.

He didn't care. Not anymore.

Smiling at his radiant bride-to-be, he accepted another flute of champagne. And then all the fine hair on his neck stood on end. He turned, and looked at the old butler. Staring back with open malice, Ivan held his gaze. Dressed all in black, tall, and bony, he resembled a skeleton that crawled from the grave. Ignoring his uneasiness, Dmitry made a mocking salute to his mother's loyal servant, and drank to his own happy future.

CHAPTER EIGHTY-EIGHT

Three days later Her Grace Elizabeth Rostoff returned home. As if by a turn of a switch, gloom and darkness settled all around *Zolotoe Selo*. The immediate change in the atmosphere was unmistakable. Subdued and somber, the servants glided silently through the rooms like shadows, taking great care not to make any noise in the tomblike stillness of the house. It seemed to Dmitry that the entire household acted like they were suspended in limbo, holding its breath, and bracing for something bad and imminent.

But most of all, concern consumed with Katia whose behavior changed drastically. Her cheery and carefree demeanor evaporated in a flash, as she became more withdrawn, and guarded. She stayed in her room with the dogs, hiding from everybody. Unnaturally quiet, Katia refused to open emotionally to him or Natasha. Dammit all to hell and back.

Impatient, annoyed, Dmitry busied himself with the legal matters, working from his office all the time. His upcoming confrontation with Elizabeth loomed ahead like an angry grey cloud. In a hurry to cross all the Ts and dots all the Is, he worked like a man possessed.

His mother started her first day at home by firing her nurse. Soon after the poor woman ran away in tears, Elizabeth's trusted attorney arrived, and Ivan escorted him into her suite. The very air in the house seemed to be charged with suspense and misery.

Even the dogs became more alert and tense. Always poised to strike, Pasha and Misha growled ominously at everybody except Dmitry and Natasha.

Since Elizabeth's return, Natasha's life became a constant state of fear. Jumpy and restless, she barely ate or slept. A premonition of disaster hung around her like a wet heavy blanket. It haunted her day and night, disturbing her normal routine, slithering into her dreams. Every time she closed her eyes, the nightmares grabbed her by the throat, plunging her into cold black despair. Even when awake, an ominous, almost tangible shadow of her dream trailed behind her. Dmitry, too, became tense and restless, and seemed constantly on guard.

Cold and remote, a mask of detachment spread across his face once again. She hated it, even as she recognized it for what it really was—a defense mechanism.

Soon we will be far away from here, and everything will be back to normal.

It became her mantra. To her, it couldn't happen soon enough.

Now, in Katia's room, Natasha tried to forget her troubling dreams, but to no avail. Like poison in her blood, her foreboding seeped through her body.

She stole a brief look at herself in the wall mirror, and winced. Her usually vibrant and unmanageable red curls became listless and dull. Her sunken eyes seemed bleak, with two bruise-like circles underneath. Resigned, she drew a broken sigh. Her constant stress played havoc with her appearances.

Soon. Soon we'll be out of here, and everything will be okay.

She dragged her hand through her hair and let it fall onto her lap.

A bright sparkle caught Natasha's attention. The ring. Dmitry's ring.

Mesmerised, she stared at it. Encircled in a double row of diamonds, the huge emerald in the center burst with fire. A magnificent piece. Spectacular. Breathtaking. Despite its size, the ring wasn't heavy. Regal, fit for a queen, warm and somehow... alive. Natasha swore she felt its pulse. Yesterday, he slid that ring onto her finger and made their engagement official.

Smiling, Natasha curled her fingers. Her ring. Her treasure.

The price of it must be exorbitant. He admitted the ring was one of a kind, because he commissioned it just for her. Aptly named *The Green Fire,* it came ablaze every time she flicked her hand. Unaccustomed to wearing any jewelry, except her small cross, she asked Dmitry to put it in the safe for the time being. But he rejected her request.

She remembered asking, "What if I lose it somehow?"

He smiled and tucked a lock of hair behind her ear. "You won't. But even if you do, I'll make you another one."

His offhand dismissal only increased her anxiety. A day after, she still failed to shake it off. Dear God, they were so poorly matched.

Dmitry came from old money, and carried a noble title after his name. And she?

A poor girl from the orphanage, with no background or heritage to speak of.

She didn't know about her parents. Maybe she came from the long line of alcoholics or mental degenerates. Or serial killers. Who knew?

Natasha's true identity and lineage were unknown. It stopped bothering her long time ago, but at rare moments she couldn't help but wonder.

Who were the people that abandoned a tiny helpless newborn near a dumpster? Monsters? Criminals? Was her mother an abandoned young girl without means to take care of a baby? The pregnancy must have been unplanned, or maybe the result of a rape.

Did her mother hate her? Love her? Did she regret abandoning her baby? Or maybe she didn't give a damn?

With a background like that, what could Natasha know about family? Or children?

Annoyed at herself, she fingered the renegade tear, and turned her head to look at Katia. For six years Natasha raised both Dmitry's children like her own. The four of them became a family. A true family. A unit. She knew plenty about family.

I know everything. *Love, loyalty, trust. Those are the most important ingredients. Everything else is irrelevant.*

Natasha gave herself a mental shake to clear away her anger. The heck with backgrounds and noble titles. The heck with parents, his and hers. The heck with money or society. Dmitry and her were meant to be together as if created for each other. And although Dmitry never said it outloud, in her heart she knew he loved her and cared for her. And desired her.

Oh, boy did he ever.

His face swam before her eyes. A hot wave swept up, covering her face and neck. No need to look in a mirror to see her blushing.

She swore silently. Oh, how she hated that curse of a redhead.

She shook her head, then scrutinized Katia. Did she notice? The girl was too preceptive for her age. But no, thank God. Katia was totally engrossed in her painting. It fascinated Natasha to watch her. Katia's complete concentration on the canvas, her eloquent body language, the fluid movements of her brush hand— a dance without music.

Natasha sighed. She sat posing for almost two hours, and her shoulders and back became quite stiff. She squirmed to change her position. Even though the creak of the chair sounded soft, Katia must have heard it.

Without looking at Natasha, she frowned. "Mama, please, keep still. I'm almost done."

Lord, how much longer? But she resumed her pose. After a moment, she asked, "May I look? Just a tiny peep?"

"Not before it's complete."

The little tyrant. Resigned, she winced, but kept still. Natasha's oil portrait was the first serious project Katia embarked on the same day Elizabeth returned home from the hospital. During her grandmother's absence, she spent all her time enjoying life and being a little girl to paint.

But three days ago, Katia's carefree time abruptly came to an end.

Natasha failed to suppress a deep sigh. A pang of regret stabbed at her heart. Bearing down, she tried to convince herself that in no time everything will be back to normal, and Katia will be acting like a little girl once again.

Please, God, let it be soon.

But until then, she must be patient no matter how stressed and restless she became. Posing for the portrait was a blessing, really. For long hours, they both hid in the nursery, away from Elizabeth and her spy, Ivan. She shuddered thinking of the old butler. How ridiculous, but she feared him more than his formidable mistress. The disgusting man. Slimy. Revolting. How hadn't she noticed it before?

Those oddly colorless eyes of his gave Natasha the creeps.

She prayed that soon he, too, became a distant memory. Like Elizabeth, and her spooky grand mausoleum. Natasha couldn't wait to leave everything behind.

The only sadness that swept through her— saying goodbye to her little gazebo, her sanctuary.

"Do you think she will like my work?"

Katia's bell-like voice brought Natasha back to reality. "Who, Kitten?"

"That lady, the French artist." Squinting at Natasha, Katia chewed on her bottom lip, a clear sign of distress. Oh-uh. Time to interfere.

Infusing as much enthusiasm in her voice as possible, Natasha exclaimed, "Of course she will."

Vlad Albrecht's wife, Marie, a well-known European artist, and designer, agreed to take Katia on as her protégé. Since that announcement, Katia grew plagued with uncertainty and worry.

"I'm sure she will!" Natasha repeated more firmly. "How could she not?"

"I hope so." Katia slumped her shoulders, averted her eyes. The forlorn expression on her tiny face tugged at Natasha's heart. In full protective mode, she went to Katia, and kneeled before her precious girl. "I know so, Kitten. Your dad sent her some of your sketches, and she was ecstatic."

"Okay." After a brief hesitation, Katia nodded. "But I just must finish this painting. Sketches are easy, but the oil..." She studied the canvas in progress. "What if she doesn't like my technic? Or my palette? Or—"

"Katia, I'm sure she will love it." Trying to lighten the mood, Natasha winked. "And how could she not, if it's my portrait?"

Katia smiled, then giggled, and for a moment she became a little girl again.

She looked so funny, this tiny midget in an apron several sizes too big for her frame, her long pale hair pulled back with a ribbon, her cheeks smudged with paint. But the burning intensity in her pewter eyes, the manner she held her brush like an extension of her arm, that complete and utter concentration on her face while working bespoke of the pure and unrefined talent that lived inside of her. That talent was so huge it scared Natasha. God blessed her little girl with a wonderful gift. Unique. Distinctive. Magical. Katia's paintings were so mature and masterful, hard to believe that a tiny six-year-old artist created them.

Natasha knew Katia was destined for fame, that she had a brilliant future. Like every parent, enormous pride for her girl filled her. And scared her.

Dear God, you gave this girl such an enormous weight to carry. I know you have your reasons for everything. Please, don't let this talent be a burden for Katia, don't let it become a curse.

Oblivious to everything, her little girl went back to her project. Tilting her head, she examined it, then picked up her brush again. "Mama, please sit. I need to continue." And the little tyrant returned. The silence in the room resumed, interrupted by a faint tick-tock of the old grandfather clock.

CHAPTER EIGHTY-NINE

S everal days passed without incident. Cautiously optimistic, Dmitry almost relaxed, but nevertheless kept on his toes. Yes, the legalities for Katia's custody were met, and yes, the team of attorneys he hired assured him that he will be granted full custody of his daughter. Even without Elizabeth's formal agreement. But still.

He frowned. Was it a mistake that he wanted to talk to his mother first? Was his intention to resolve the situation peacefully an act of folly on his part? Maybe. Probably. Hell, who knew?

If Elizabeth refused to sign the papers, the end result remained the same. Surely, she'd understand that. He hoped so.

Reluctant to drag his ill mother—but mostly his daughter—through the ordeal of a legal battle, he hoped Elizabeth saw the logic, and be reasonable for Katia's sake. After all, they both have the little girl's best interests at heart.

Or did they? He muttered a quiet oath, raked his hair with his hand.

Granted, Elizabeth's interpretation of her granddaughter's interests were quite different from his own. For her, it became an obsession. Something twisted and unhealthy and downright scary. And harmful to Katia.

Clearly, not love. Then again, Elizabeth was incapable of love.

How could he not see it before?

You're blind, you selfish moron.

Did Elizabeth *care* about the girl at all? Even a little? Dimitry sincerely hoped so. Her good feelings were his one and only leverage.

Was it silly of him to try to reason with Elizabeth? Considering their history, the answer was a firm yes. Damn, she almost brought the company to the brink of disaster six years ago in order to destroy him. Her only son. But she couldn't be that cruel toward her only granddaughter. Or could she?

Only one way to find out.

He stole a quick glance at his Rolex.

How long can the stubborn woman keep avoiding him? It's been seven days already, but she still refused his requests for an audience. Locked in her room, Elizabeth only accepted two people inside. Ivan and her attorney, with whom she conferred daily. What was she plotting? And why had she refused to meet with Dmitry? Dammit, that didn't bode well.

He poured a glass of water, then gulped it down. Anything to squelch his fuming. As Murphy's law had it, the liquid went down the wrong way. Spattering, coughing, he deposited the glass on the desk, cursing himself. He should go to her room, and break down the damned door. He ought to demand she hear him out.

And what would it accomplish? You will look like a damned fool. Out of control, out of your mind. Is that what you want?

He struggled with his anger. Damn her. And damn that bastard, Ivan. The slimy weasel never tried to hide his smirk.

Dmitry wanted to smash his fist into that insolent ugly face.

Seething, he cursed out loud. How much longer will she play that stupid hide-and-seek game? Just two hours ago, he requested to see her again. And he still waited.

His patience was fried around the edges. Okay, another three days. If by Saturday Elizabeth failed to grant him an audience, then all bets were off.

She won't like it but the hell with it. I'll start the legal battle. Dammit all to hell and back.

He'd be damned if he let her use him as a blind pawn. Not again. Never again.

He needed Natasha. And Katia. He needed his family around him. To regain his composure. Dmitry yanked open his door then walked out of the office. Impatient, he headed toward the staircase. A sharp cry stopped him cold.

Natasha.

He charged down the staircase two steps at time, then broke into a run. He almost lost his footing when he collided with Natasha. He grabbed her, steadying them both.

"Dmitry! Oh, God, Dmitry!"

Ghastly pale, disheveled, she trembled violently. Panicked, he grabbed her shoulders, ran his hands down her arms and torso to check for injuries. "Are you hurt?"

She shook her head no as she fought for air.

"What is it, then? Katia? Something happened to her?"

He waited for a few moments, but got no answer. Dammit, what the hell happened? He took firm hold of her chin, lifted it, and scrutinized her face. Her wide-eyed stare was flooded with terror. Like a serrated blade, a jolt or recognition went through his gut.

I know that look. I've seen it before.

Six years ago, the last time he saw his late wife alive, she wore the same expression. Chilled to the marrow, Dmitry shook his head in the attempt to erase the image of Polina from his mind.

With an effort, he concentrated on Natasha. "What is it, *milaya*? What happened?" Dammit, he never saw her so frightened. Something terrible must have happened. But what?

"Papers, my papers!" Finally, Natasha found her voice. "Oh, God Dmitry."

He expected anything: a catastrophe of a major proportions, an Armageddon. The fucking end of the earth! Relived that it was not life-threatening, he let out a long loud gust of air. He remained confused, but no longer scared. He gathered her closer, closed his eyes, and rested his chin on her head. " What papers?"

Tense, her small body vibrated in his embrace like an electric wire. "My documents. You told me to find them, and give them to you."

"What about them?"

But God help him, he already knew.

Sonofabitch.

Natasha couldn't find her documents. The chance of her misplacing them by accident – not possible. Neat to a fault, she always kept her things in their appointed places. No doubt someone stole them. And he knew who that *someone* was.

As if she read his mind, Natasha said, "Somebody came into my room. Again. And now I can't find my papers. My social security, my green card, my driver license—everything is gone. Dear God, they even stole my Russian passport, a completely useless document!"

Useless, yes, but it contained a picture of Natasha. By stealing it, they left her without any proof of identity. Dmitry swore silently. Only one person had enough hatred in her soul to do such a thing. His mother. Only Elizabeth was cruel—and desperate—enough to issue that order.

"I knew that something bad was going to happen. I knew it in my heart, but still I hoped—" Her voice broke. Closing her eyes, Natasha shook her head. "So silly of me..."

"Shh-shh, *milaya*. Nothing bad is going to happen." He gathered both her hands in his. They felt like two blocks of ice.

"It already has!" She cried out, pulling her hands free. "Don't you see? It already has, and now I'm left without my legal papers, and I can't travel with you, and...and God only knows what she will do next."

Clearly, Natasha had no doubt as to who ordered the theft. Neither did he. Enraged, Dmitry struggled to keep his emotions under control. He failed. Bitter and familiar, the taste of betrayal surged up, clogging his throat.

So, Mother dear, the war has begun. But you made a mistake, a huge mistake: you attacked the woman I love.

"Calm down, Natasha. Just take a deep breath—"

"Deep breath? Calm down? Are you out of your mind?" She exploded in a fiery flash of temper. "How on earth do you expect me to calm down? Do you understand what happened?"

"Yes, I do. And I'm telling you again: calm down. Let me deal with it."

"How? Just how you can deal with the fact that I'm now left without any identification, any legal paper with my name on it?"

"First of all, the papers could be reissued. Second—and that's more important—you have to stay in control." He punctuated each word, looking straight into her eyes. "We both knew it would be a hell of a fight, and you promised to fight with me, side by side. Don't give up so easily, Natasha. I'm counting on you. Katia's future is at stake." He framed her face with both hands, and softly finished, "Our future is at a stake."

She stared at him, her unblinking eyes bleak and full of misery.

That shook him to the core. He laid both hands on her shoulders, then gave her a firm shake. "Don't. Don't do that. We are in this together. Everything's going to be all right. Trust me, Natasha."

She looked at him, sad and pale and defeated.

He asked her to trust him, but trust must be earned, not demanded. Right now, her complete trust in him was crucial. For both of them.

He held his breath and waited. At first, she remained quiet. Finally, she gave a small nod. It didn't fool him. She still didn't trust him completely.

On some deep fundamental level, Natasha doubted him. Dammit.

He wondered if she knew how deeply she managed to hurt him.

He turned sideways, then thrust both hands into his trouser pockets. His control shredded, his patience evaporated. Adrenalin pumped through his veins, making him alert and energized and quivering. The thunder of his heartbeat bruised his ribcage. If she failed to trust him, he must do something about it. Pronto. He twisted to one side to face her. "It won't do you any good to fall apart like that."

His statement came out curt, almost harsh, but it drew her out of her frozen state.

She jolted, then looked him square in the eye. "Yes, you're right. What will we do now?"

At least she said *we*. Thank God for small favors.

"Now, you are going to pack, and I'm going to see Elizabeth."

"She'll refuse to talk to you."

"I'll insist. She won't refuse today."

"But—"

"Trust me, Natasha. At least, trust me that much."

CHAPTER NINETY

B it by painful bit, Natasha regained her control. Dmitry was right, as always. She couldn't fall apart. Couldn't' afford the luxury. Why had this latest development thrown her for a loop? Why did it shock her so much? For days now she sensed—knew—something bad was about to happen; that Elizabeth won't capitulate so easily.

But hope took deep root in her heart. Against her common sense, she grabbed at the illusion of happiness, holding onto it, closing off her rational mind. She deliberately let herself be seduced by dreams. Impossible dreams. Dangerous dreams.

How did Pushkin phrase it?

Oh, it takes so little to deceive me—I cannot wait to be deceived...

A verse from her favorite poem "Confession" sounded almost like an ill omen.

Did she really think that everything was going to be alright? That it really could?

Silly, Natasha. So silly.

Nothing seemed to be all right. Should've paid more attention to her premonition, and listened to her gut— not her heart. Today's incident with her stolen papers, as insignificant as it might have seemed at first, meted the beginning of the end. Dmitry didn't realize it, but she did. Maybe because Elizabeth was his mother, and he still harbored some illusion of blood being thicker than water. And being a decent man, he failed to comprehend the full extent of his mother's cruelty.

Elizabeth was more than cruel. Evil best described her. Along with twisted, deranged and dangerous.

Like a flame of a candle someone blew on, Natasha's hope abruptly died.

Without that tiny sparkle, she felt untethered. Disoriented. Bereft.

She shivered as cold crept into her. *I wish to be far away from this place. Far, far away.* She failed to realize she said it out loud.

"We will. Soon, *milaya*, very soon. Now, why don't you go up to your room and pack."

She almost laughed. She packed days ago. "Yes, right, pack."

In a burst of hope and excitement, she hugged Dmitry hard. Surprised, he stilled for a second, then returned her embrace. Time stopped. Silence grew.

Oh, how she wished to stay like that forever!

But reality intruded. Stepping back, he squeezed her hands, then dropped a hard kiss on her lips. "I must go."

Don't! Please don't go anywhere.

"Okay." She stood statue still.

"Natasha?" Dmitry frowned. "What did you mean when you told me somebody was in your room *again*?"

"Oh, that. Somebody searched my room for years, regularly. It stopped when you brought the dogs into the house. Now it happened again."

His frown deepened. "Did you say something about it to Elizabeth?"

"Yes, I did. Numerous times. But she insisted I imagined things."

He ground his jaw back and forth, then asked, "Anything taken before?"

"Once. My journal. But a few days after, it magically reappeared, so I had no proof."

His mouth became a razor thin line as his face became a mask of grim determination. "We'll talk about it later." With that, he turned and left her alone.

She continued to stay in place and watched his retreating back. The urge to stop him, to call him back overwhelmed her. The fear that she may never see him again seemed ridiculous. But her premonition that took up permanent residence inside of her gut disagreed. Something terrible loomed on the horizon. Something evil.

Exhausted, Natasha started up the staircase. Defeat and fatigue pressed on her shoulders. She barely managed to put one foot in front of the other. She opened the door to her small room, then dropped onto the corner of her bed, and scanned her domain dispassionately. Strange, she never realized she lived in such a dismal room. No longer mattered. One way or another, she was leaving this house for good.

Her belongings were already in her old suitcase. She only packed the clothes she first came with, and her favorite book, the old distressed tome of Pushkin poems.

Oh, it takes so little to deceive me—I cannot wait to be deceived...

CHAPTER NINETY-ONE

Dmitry fumed all the way to Elizabeth's room. The mix of disgust and rage made him sick to his stomach. He thought he knew the extent of his mother's treachery. Psychological bullying or corporate espionage? Absolutely. But common thievery? He never imagined Elizabeth had the nerve to stoop so low as searching someone's room, invading their privacy. Stealing. Obviously, he was mistaken.

But the fact that she did it—or ordered it to be done—meant two things. First, Natasha held something Elizabeth wanted, and second, she had good reason to be afraid of her. Both scenarios were bad. Dangerous.

Dammit, he'd die before he let Elizabeth hurt Natasha.

Rage consumed him as he hurried toward his mother's study.

Calm down, you are out of control, Rostoff.

Fuck control! Did she think that stealing Natasha's papers could stop him?

Well, Mother dear, think again.

Ivan's job, no doubt about it. Carry out Elizabeth's dirty orders was right up to his scope of talents. Slimy old bastard.

He reached the doors to her bedroom, then paused, then drew in a few calming breaths, but to no avail. His anger churned, his fear blazed, his mind screamed. His body filled with rage to the point of no return. Refused to grant him an audience? Fine. Fucking fantastic.

A single kick to the polished mahogany door, and it flew open with a loud *bang*.

He welcomed the pain that shot through his leg. Ivan jumped forward, arms held high, as if to prevent Dmitry's entry. Face drawn, eyes wide with shock, Elizabeth's butler faced Dmitry and blocked the doorway.

He needed no more incentive. He charged forward, his shoulders hunched, his arms outstretched, drawing a startled cry from the old man.

"Dmitry Nikolayevich! What are you...?" But Ivan's last words stuck in his throat as Dmitry seized him by the lapels of his uniform jacket and hauled him up.

"If you're smart, old man, you're going to shut up and listen. Are you listening?" Dmitry shook him hard. With his face redder by a second, his colorless eyes widening with shock, Ivan tried to say something, but Dmitry gave him another mighty shake so that his false teeth clacked loudly. Ivan nodded jerkily.

"Good. Now, listen very, very carefully, for I won't repeat myself twice. If you make just one more trip to Natasha's room and so much as touch one of her things with your pinkie, I'm going to cut off your stinking fingers one by one and feed them to the dogs. Then I sic those two beasts on you. And after they finished chewing on your bones, there will be nothing left for the police to investigate. Understood?"

Ivan made another jerky nod, his eyes bulged in their sockets.

"Good." Dmitry pushed Ivan out of way. Disgusted, as if he touched something slimy, he wiped off his hands on the priceless gold embroidered drapes.

Ivan's face burned with scarlet patches on his cadaverous cheeks that clashed with the grayish hue of his skin.

"Remember that."

"I will, Your Grace." Narrowed to slits, the old butler's eyes shone with hatred. "As long as I live." Soft and quiet, his voice scraped along Dmitry's nerves.

He recognized the vow hissed at him. Poised for a fight, Dmitry opened his mouth, as a whooshing sound of a motorized wheelchair slid through the haze in his brain. He turned. Elizabeth sat erect in her chair and glared at him in charged silence. So, she witnessed the entire scene. Good. That's even better.

Dmitry waved off Ivan, then addressed Elizabeth, "Mother. I'd say I'm sorry for the commotion, but we both know that's pure bullshit."

He never talked to Elizabeth in that tone of voice or used any kind of profanity in her presence. Her eyes widened, betraying her surprise.

Without giving her a chance to recover, he plowed ahead, "I've requested a meeting with you on numerous occasions, but Ivan told me, time and again, that you were indisposed. My request today went unnoticed, or ignored. Therefore, I decided to spare you the trouble, and came without an official invitation. Hope you don't mind."

And if you do, I don't give a shit.

Elizabeth glared back at him, her indignation clear on her distorted face.

Half of her right side drooped, with one corner of her mouth turned perpetually down. Her once beautiful face became an ugly mask.

Jesus.

After a closer look at this caricature of his mother's former self, he shuddered. More than ugly, Elizabeth was pitiful. Pathetic.

Unable to cover his initial reaction, he averted his eyes.

Get a grip, man.

He shut off his emotions with supreme effort. He deliberately schooled his face into a bland mask. "I wanted to talk to you in private, hoping we can put our differences aside for Katia's sake. I wanted to explain everything, and try to come up with an amicable decision. I thought you might understand and agree with me. But obviously, I made a mistake."

He walked closer, then bent forward and gripped both handrests of her wheelchair. Their faces an inch apart. "Mother, understand this, with or without your approval I will marry Natasha. With or without your consent, I will take my daughter away from this house. You are too old and too ill to care for a child her age, and you know it. Now, push me harder, and I will not only remove Katia from this house but from your life. Forever. You'll never see your granddaughter again. Do you understand?"

Elizabeth glared back at him. Her dark grey eyes seemed almost black. It was like looking into the depth of hell. Pure and undiluted hatred spilled over from her bottomless eyes, from her disfigured face, and that misshapen mouth. The urge to wince grew enormous, but he fought it with every ounce of his willpower.

"Touch Natasha again, and I'll forget you are my mother." He barely recognized his own voice. Straitening, Dmitry stepped back. "Then again, you never gave a flying fuck about that, did you?"

The healthy half of Elizabeth's face flinched. Dmitry nodded, "Now we understand one another. And remember, Mother dear, for better or worse, I am your son. Your tainted blood runs in my veins as well. So, I too can retaliate, and trust me, you don't want to find out just how hard or fast. Now, you have two choices: you will return Natasha's stollen papers immediately, or I'll take my family away from this house right now, and you'll never see Katia again. Do I make myself clear?"

"Y-yess." Like a hissing of a snake, the sound slithered from her deformed lips.

"Good." He kept his eyes glued to her face, and took another step back.

Mission accomplished.

But he couldn't leave just yet. As if riveted by her glaring stare, Dmitry stood unmoving. Had she always despised him? Her only son, her child. She carried him in her womb, gave birth to him. And hated him. Was it his fault? Hers?

"Why?" The years of pain and confusion suddenly burst free. Ridiculously vulnerable, he gazed at the woman who gave him life, who fought him, and betrayed him, and hated him. "Why?"

The deafening silence pulsed with hostility. Hard and unblinking, Elizabeth's stare made his skin crawl. He began to suffocate. His lungs labored for a single breath. Fresh air. He craved a gulp of fresh clean air.

"Dmitry...?"

Every instinct he possessed screamed at him to act, to run away. He bore down, waiting, dreading.

"You... never take her... from me. She's mine."

It took him a moment to understand her laborious speech.

Overwhelmed with regret and sorrow, he watched her for a long moment.

"You don't get it, do you, Mother? You still don't understand."

"She's....mine...mine...and...stay...mine... as long...as I live."

"Listen to yourself! Katia is not one of your possessions. She's a person."

"She's... mine..."

He failed to name what sifted through him. Disgust? Disillusionment? Regret? He stared at his mother, trying to sort his emotions, and came up blank.

His voice, when he finally found it, sounded dull and dispassionate.

"I pity you, Mother. There was a time I would've done anything to make you love me. Even a little. Older, I felt angry because whatever I accomplished wasn't enough for you. Still, I never stopped trying. Even as a grown man, I turned myself inside-out, hoping to gain your approval. Because it mattered. *You* mattered. Six years ago, I finally learned to hate you, and I thought that I stopped caring. But soon realized, I didn't. Not really. Only now, right this very minute, looking at you and not feeling anything, I know you finally stopped to matter. I'm finally free of you, Mother. Talk about irony." Dry and humorless, his chuckle abraded his throat. "Rest assured, *Your Grace*, you have a son no more. Or more accurately, I have no mother."

This time when Dmitry heard his name, he kept walking.

He closed the door to his mother's room, and shut the imaginary lid to his past.

It was over. Finally. He was free at last.

He should feel elated and relieved. Strange, but he felt nothing.

Resigned, he went to his office, then called The Ritz-Carlton to reserve a suite.

They must leave immediately, as soon as he notified Natasha and Katia of the change in plans. He preferred they flew to France right away, but the disappearance of Natasha's papers made that impossible. Not for long. He decided to call his attorney and set the wheels in motion. How long can it take to reissue a green card and ID? A week? A month? Dammit. They had no choice but wait. Elizabeth would never return Natasha's documents despite his ultimatum. Maybe, because of it.

The hell with it. The hell with everything.

He dropped in a chair, then closed his eyes. Bright and joyous, the future beckoned ahead. Today he ventured the first step toward it. But his past still lingered in his subconsciousness, like a thief shrouded in shadows. He gathered his resolve and deliberately emptied his mind, letting the past drain away, drop by slow drop.

CHAPTER NINETY-TWO

Later that night, spooning with Natasha in the Ritz's huge four-poster bed, utterly spent after passionate lovemaking, Dmitry still felt unsatisfied.

And somehow detached. Clouded in dense fog, his brain struggled with the reality of the moment. As to his emotions, they were scattered like the pieces of a giant puzzle. He tried to zero in on his feelings, but came up blank. Like a hollow shell without any substance, his body felt empty and weightless. He heard the strong beats of his heart, watched the muscles flex on the left side of his chest, but he didn't feel it. Odd.

Natasha scooted closer, pressed her naked butt firmly against his lap, and sighed. Dmitry knew a sigh of contentment when he heard one. Looping his arm around her, he drew her closer. Happy to leave *Zolotoe Selo*, Natasha appeared almost giddy. Even more than Katia. As soon as they entered their suite in the hotel, Natasha tore hers and his clothes away. Then she pushed him onto the bed, and proceeded to make love to him with great enthusiasm. A pure wonder they failed to set the sheets ablaze. Thank God, they left Katia in care of her art teacher, who followed them to the Ritz. His daughter will be occupied for some time working on Natasha's oil portrait. Dmitry frowned. So, what was wrong with him? He must be elated, with both of his girls nearby, removed from that dreadful place. Instead, he felt totally empty.

First twinges of uneasiness rooted, spoiling the moment.

Their departure from *Zolotoe Selo* and go to a hotel went surprisingly fast and smooth. The whole process, a spur of a moment decision on his part, seemed to be well orchestrated. And still, something didn't seem right. Out of sync. Even hours later, when they put Katia to bed, and retreated to their own bedroom, he failed to eliminate the strange feeling. Try as he might, he couldn't put a name on it. Now, in a semidarkness of the room illuminated by moonlight, with a naked woman in his arms, he should be content and happy. He was free at last.

Why then was he confused and disoriented, lost? Like his life spun out of its axis, and left him untethered? Damn, what was wrong with him?

The bedsprings creaked as Natasha shifted to face him. He focused on her when she touched his face with her fingertips. Luminous, disheveled, glorious in her nakedness, she stole his breath.

"It'll be all right, my love. It will pass, you'll see."

Full of understanding and compassion, her smile was tremulous, and a little sad.

"Everything will be fine."

"I feel empty, Natasha," he confessed. "I should be delirious with happiness to be finally free, but I..." His voice trailed off.

"But you feel insubstantial and disillusioned and adrift," she finished for him.

"How do you know?" How did she manage to put into words what he struggled to name?

"I love you, darling. I can almost hear your thoughts, feel your pain like it's my own. That eerie void inside of you is almost tangible." She seemed to study him for a few moments. "Give yourself some time, Dmitry."

Time. Yes, he only needed some time.

He glanced down hoping to hide his embarrassment. To be sad and confused was one thing, but to be so vulnerable, quite another.

"You don't have to hide your feelings from me, darling. I love you. More than anything, more than life. I love you so much it hurts. I'll do anything to make you happy. I'll give my life for you. Look at me."

He lifted his eyes, and stared into her bewitching green pools.

"I love you, my darling."

An unexpected anger spiced with a pinch of meanness surged up. "Do you, Natasha? Do you really?"

She jolted as if he slapped her. Immediately, he wished to take his words back, but too late. Dmitry cursed. Why the hell did he question her, doubt her? Hurt her?

After a moment, Natasha answered, "Yes, I do."

"But you don't trust me."

"I do trust you."

"Do you? I wonder."

Really, Rostoff? That's rich coming from you.

Unlike him, Natasha never made any secret of her feelings. Disgusted with himself, he rolled onto his back, then flung his arm across his face. He was his mother's son alright. Mean, a coldblooded bastard.

She sat up, tugged at the wrinkled sheet, then covered herself. "I am not your mother, Dmitry. Or your late wife." Laced with a spark of anger, her voice trembled with accusation. "Even if you push me away, like you tried six years ago, I won't stop loving you." Her voice was thick with unshed tears, damning him. "And I am not Svetlana. I won't accept anything less from you than everything. I'll fight to the end. I'll fight anyone and everyone. I'll fight the devil himself. And I'll fight you, too, if necessary." Rich and deep, her voice gained in strength and volume. "Want to know why?"

He faced her. All the love in the world shone in her misty eyes. He swallowed around the boulder in his throat. "Why?"

She gripped one of his hands, and laid it over her left breast. Strong and true, the beat of her heart reverberated through his fingers.

"Because I love you so much, it rips me apart. I love you so deep, it rooted into my soul. No one before me, Dmitry, and no one after will love you as much. You are the one and the only for me. You are my everything."

Illuminated by tears, her eyes sparkled like two priceless gems. Undone, defeated, he touched her face, then gently traced a path from her eyebrow to her chin.

He wasn't aware that a single renegade tear escaped his control, until Natasha gently whipped it away. Bringing her wet finger to her mouth, she licked it, as if tasting his pain. Pure and innocent, her gesture struck him as highly erotic. His gut squeezed in tight, his throat clogged. In a flash, he grew painfully and desperately aroused.

"I love you, Dmitry." Like an intimate caress, her husky whisper sent shivers along his spine. "Don't you ever forget it, or doubt it."

Of its own accord his hand above her heart slid lower, then cupped her breast. When he leaned forward to kiss her, she placed both palms on his chest, then pushed him away. "No, let me."

Happy to oblige, Dmitry plopped onto his back.

Later, sprawled on top, sated to the point of being half comatose, he heard her soft sniffles. Even without looking at Natasha's face, he knew she was crying. Remorse plunged its blade into his heart, chasing away the euphoria.

He hurt her. Not physically, not now. Earlier, with his words and doubts.

Dmitry shifted, taking some of his weight off Natasha, then pressed his face into her hair. " I'm so sorry, *milaya*. So sorry."

"You don't have to apologize, darling. I understand."

"I hurt you."

"Yes, you did. But that's okay. You were hurting."

"Still, I have no right or excuse—"

"*Miliy*, you're only human, not God."

Bracing on his elbows, Dmitry looked at her tear-stricken face. "Damn, I'm always making you cry."

"No, you're always making me happy."

"Am I? Making you happy?"

"Always, Dmitry."

"Natasha, I..." *Say it. Say that you love her.*

But he hesitated, torn between the wish to confess what was in his heart and his fear to smash the last barrier around it. He'd be totally exposed, utterly vulnerable. So, what? Why was it so hard for him to say those three little words?

"Yes, darling?"

"Promise me you won't leave me. Ever." *A poor substitute for declaration of love, you moron.* "Swear it, Natasha."

"Dmitry..." Biting her upper lip, she averted her gaze.

Scared, desperate, he lifted her face with his hand, peered into her eyes.

"Say it."

He didn't realize he held his breath, until she replied, "I promise, *miliy*."

A mere whisper, her words echoed in his mind in an endless loop. A surge of hope and love burst through in a delirious wave. Overwhelmed, he smiled, then tenderly kissed her swollen lips. "Now it's my turn to show you."

CHAPTER NINETY-THREE

For the first time in her life Elizabeth experienced real fear. Terrified, confined in a wheelchair, she sat in the spacious bedroom that became her prison. Like a wounded bird in the golden cage. Helpless, utterly vulnerable. Impotent.

She fisted her hands and cursed the gods and Universe. A trickle of saliva from the left side of her face brought on angry tears. Her body, the temple she took such a pride in, betrayed her. The ultimate humiliation.

Power, the only thing she ever valued, slipped through her fingers like dry sand. As much as she tried to tighten her fist and hold on to it, she failed.

Totally useless. I have become a useless, broken and pathetic invalid.

Images of giving up and ending her misery became her constant companions.

And that scared her most of all. Her rage, cold, black, and enormous, obliterated every other emotion. It churned like an overflooded river, then surged to the surface, leaving her weak and trembling. A wish to destroy, to tear apart something shook her to the core. Her famous control became almost impossible to hold on to.

The occasional rage spells before her illness were unfortunate, but easily dealt with. She always managed to regain her senses quickly. But not now.

The abyss of madness loomed ahead, threatening to suck her in. She was too weak to fight it. Too old, too damn tired.

Trouble, golubushka, *with a capital T.*

As God is her witness, Elizabeth never allowed herself to play coward. Not once had she buckled under pressure, or surrendered without a fight. She always knew what she wanted, and she always got it, even if she had to go for the jugular. Never a quitter. If one door closed, she squared her shoulders and marched through the other. Granted, she was not choosy in her methods to reach her goal. But everything was fair in love and war, right?

Strong people always survived, using the weaklings. And she considered herself the strongest person of them all. She was Elizabeth Rostoff. The matriarch.

Never had she questioned herself. Until now.

Unthinkable. Unacceptable.

Fortunatelly, the illness that broke her body never affected her brain. It sharpened and honed it to lethal perfection. Confined in the unnatural stillness of her body, her brain became her one and only weapon. Invisible, devious. Deadly.

But her blasted illness seemed to affect her spirit. She frowned.

No way in hell.

She must stay strong to win the battle for Katia. She must be one step ahead of Dmitry. To get what she wanted the most, her granddaughter, the heiress of Rostoff's Empire, she intended to fight to the end. And if her son assumed she presented no danger, feeble and conquered by illness, he'd get one very unpleasant surprise. The hidden weapon in her arsenal was akin to a nuclear bomb.

The bastard took the girl away! As if he had a right! She fisted both hands. Dmitry, that spawn of the pitiful joke she'd married, dared to defy her.

We'll see about that.

Did he really think he could whisk Katia off to Europe? The cackle that slipped past her lips was a pitiful excuse for laughter.

It scratched her throat like sharp talons, but she ignored the discomfort.

The *incident* with Natasha's papers threw a wrench into Dmitry's plans.

An ingenious ploy, she must admit. Her constricted vocal cords produced a sound between a sob and a gargle. She winced and cursed her illness yet again. Good thing she sat there alone so no one witnessed her disgrace. What did it matter? Nothing mattered except revenge. And her retaliation, swift and brutal.

You thought you bested me, son? You thought you won? Foolish man.

She pressed a button and executed a sharp U-turn. Yes, stealing Natasha's documents was a brilliant idea, but just the first step in her intricate vengeful game. She managed to slow the process, but not for long. Then again, she never needed much time. A day or two to finish it all. She plotted her next move without any remorse or guilt. She could almost taste her victory. Sweet, satisfying, triumphant.

Dmitry's impotent fury—an added bonus. Let him rave and rant. Soon he will be writhing in so much pain, he'd barely manage to think straight.

She smiled, determined to curve her misshapen mouth as if all was well. Like a poisonous flower, malice bloomed in her heart.

You declared a war, son, and I accepted. And all's fair in war and love.

Love. The pain that sliced through her heart grew excruciating.

She loved once, helplessly, foolishly. Desperately. She fought it, and at the end she killed it, along with the man she loved.

Alexei.

His beloved face swam in front of her eyes.

Forgive me, darling boy.

With a herculean effort, she slammed shut the lid on her memories. The past belonged to the past. To dwell on it proved agonizing and unwise. Unbearable.

She straightened her spine, and willed her mind to concentrate on the present.

So, Dmitry wanted a war? She was more than happy to oblige. She knew all about war. Thrived on it, excelled in it. Her whole life was one constant war against fate. And she had always beaten the bitch. She'd do it again.

She gathered hate around her like a shield and channeled her mind in the direction of the upcoming events. Eager for step two of the game. Almost time.

But what if I fail?

A sliver of doubt slithered though her heart. She shrugged it off like an irritating gnat. Failure is for fools. She was prepared and ready and two steps ahead of her opponents. Just a little longer until she blew Dmitry's paradise to hell.

Patience, golubushka. *Patience.*

Elizabeth pressed the button on her armrest, and turned the wheelchair around. Her eyes stopped on the grandfather clock that once upon a time decorated her father's office. His Grace Andrei Orloff, God rest his soul, loved that clock. A gift from Her Majesty Czarina, that masterpiece dated back to 1790. It stood over 6 feet tall in all its gleaming glory.

The purpose of such an extravagant gift became a constant subject of speculation in the family. Elizabeth always suspected the Czarina failed to express gratitude for her father's military talents alone. His prowess was legendary. More amused than embarrassed, she smiled. Bittersweet, a pang of sentimental pride warmed her soul. Her Papa was one of a kind indeed. She was proud to inherit his greed and shameless lust for everything forbidden along with his pewter eyes and sinful good looks. Of all his children, her Papa always loved her best. Probably because they were so much alike. She gazed at the clock and mentally saluted her sire. Like a knife through butter, the rumbling chime sliced through her memories, bringing her to the present.

Almost time.

CHAPTER NINETY-FOUR

Natasha woke with a start, alone. She laid her right hand on Dmitry's pillow. Still warm to the touch, but he wasn't there. Where was he? She squinted at the bedside clock. My god, almost ten AM! She jolted upright, blew away the curls that had fallen into her face. She never slept past six. Must be all the stress. But why didn't he wake her? Totally silly for her to feel abandoned. Or scared. She shook off her uneasiness, flung the comforter away, and swung her legs off the bed. Katia must be awake, and wanting her breakfast. Damn, how could she have overslept? Her little girl waited for her, and here she was, lounging in bed, naked and disheveled. She found her robe on the floor, then shrugged into it, and barefooted ran to Katia's room. Empty. Cold fear clogged her throat. Where had they gone? Did they leave without her?

Chilled to the bone, Natasha hugged herself tight. The snippets of her recurring dream bombarded her like shrapnel.

Dmitry and the kids, laughing...She watching them from a distance...

Beating her hands against the invisible wall that separated them...

Alone. Abandoned. Forgotten.

No!

She clutched the lapels of her robe in white-knuckled grip.

They will return soon. They must.

She needed to calm down, and think rationally, and—

A knock on the door sent her heart into overdrive. She spun around, and eyed the closed door with trepidation. Unable to breathe, she stood very still.

Fear coursed through her. Maybe, Dmitry returned. No, he had a key. Someone else was at the door. Room service? Yes, that must be it.

You are acting foolish, Natasha. Open the door already.

She forced her legs to move forward, then flipped the latch.

A young bespectacled man in the hotel uniform met her gaze. Stretching his lips into a polite impersonal smile, he nodded. "Good morning, ma'am. A message for you."

"For...me?"

Natasha's gaze slid to his gloved hand holding a small silver tray. A message? For her? No, it must be a mistake. Probably for Dmitry. The white envelope caught her attention. Her name scrawled in bold round letters sent her pulse skittering. *Elizabeth.* She knew that distinct handwriting. The image of the uniformed boy began to distort, swimming in dizzying circles. Elizabeth found her. Natasha grabbed the door with both hands as her vision narrowed to a dim tunnel. Her ears buzzed. A dark mist threatened to suck her under.

Nauseated, she couldn't tear her eyes from that small envelope.

"I... It couldn't be...Impossible..."

Confused, the delivery boy squinted at her.

"Pardon me?"

She realized she spoke in Russian, and then repeated it in English.

His fake smile slipped a bit. "Ma'am, it's your name on the envelope, isn't it?"

Not trusting her voice, she nodded.

"The gentleman who delivered this message is waiting outside. He said he expects an answer."

"W-what gentleman?"

"How do I know?" Impatient, the young man snapped, then quickly recovered. " I beg your pardon, ma'am. Old gentleman, quite tall and skinny."

Ivan. Dear God...

She swallowed around the rock lodged in her throat. "What... what time is it?"

If the delivery man was surprised by this non sequitur, he never let it show.

"Almost eleven, ma'am."

"Oh, my God!" Natasha closed her eyes.

She covered her face with both hands and choked back a sob. They found her. What did Elizabeth want?

"Where is Dmitry?"

The boy blinked owlishly. "Who?"

"My fiancé. Where is he?"

"Um. I don't know. I'm just delivering a message, that's all. I'm sorry, but if you want more information, you can call downstairs."

"Doesn't matter. She found me." Natasha slumped her shoulders in defeat.

Delaying the inevitable seemed pointless. She finally picked the envelope off the tray. Her fingers stung as if pricked. Her heart slammed into her sternum. Her mind protested.

"I'll be on my way, then. I'll tell the man there won't be any answer." He hurried away.

"Wait! Wait, please."

He stopped, then turned his questioning eyes toward her.

"Just a moment, please."

She dipped her fingers into the envelope, then drew out a folded piece of paper. She braced herself and read the message. A tremor passed through her body like a tsunami wave, then she reread the note.

"Ma'am?"

"Tell the man... tell him to wait for me. Please. As soon as I..." Natasha covered her mouth with her hand to prevent a sob. "I'll be down shortly."

"As you wish, ma'am." He nodded, then stopped. "Are you... okay?"

Such an awkward boy, no older than Peter.

"Yes, I'm okay." She forced a smile onto her face for his sake. "You go on now."

She closed the door, then slowly slid to the floor.

She hugged her knees to her chest, and allowed herself a moment to grieve.

CHAPTER NINETY-FIVE

Petrified, Natasha kept her eyes glued to the chauffer's neck.
Don't fall apart. Don't show your fear.

Inside, she was a jumble of quaking nerves. It took every ounce of her willpower to sit still, and ignore Ivan. The silence inside the car suffocated her. Breathing became a laborious task. Fear like she never experienced before kept her paralyzed. But it also made her strangely detached, as if her body separated from her mind. Even dressed in a warm coat, she shivered, chilled to the bone. Absently, she noticed the vineyards scrolling pass the window. Soon, the imposing golden gate of *Zolotoe Selo* loomed on a horizon.

Did she really think she could escape? Did she really think she ever had the chance to be free?

Silly, Natasha, so silly. Should've trusted your instincts.

She ignored Ivan and the furtive glances he cast in her direction.
Slimy weasel.

As soon as the heavy golden gates started to slide open, the memory of her first arrival flashed before her eyes. She was scared then too, lost and alone and tired, with a tiny baby in her arms. Six years ago already? God, how time flew!

As the car approached the familiar imposing mansion, Natasha's fear intensified. Unlike that first time, now she knew what, and who, awaited her inside.

The imminent confrontation with Elizabeth promised to be ugly. But on some deep level, relief swept through Natasha, glad to finally face her opponent. Openly. With nothing held back. Soon, everything was sure to be over. The emotional roller coaster she rode for six long years finally at its end. Almost giddy with anticipation, she braced herself. Did Elizabeth really think she believed her letter? That the reasons for this meeting that they found Natasha's lost papers or that her bank account couldn't be transferred without her written permission? Really? Warily, Natasha shook her head. Elizabeth held the power to easily resolve everything without requesting her presence. No, it was all about family. Her family. Dmitry, Peter, Katia. Her heart squeezed, then shattered. Somehow, she knew they were the past. Lost to her forever. She squeezed her eyes tight, and sent up a silent prayer.

Dear God, watch over them. Save them. Protect them.

Dmitry's face swam before her closed eyelids. His voice echoed in her ears,

"Promise not to leave me, Natasha. Never ever leave me. Say it."

Like a fist, pain slammed into her, stealing her breath. Lightheaded, she fought a wave of rising nauseous bile.

Oh, Dmitry! If only you had woken me. If only you hadn't left without me! If only...

Pointless to dwell on it now. She deliberately shut the imaginary lid on her emotions, emptied her mind, and stepped from the car.

Oppressive and arrogant, the building in front of her seemed to glow with malice.

Don't show your fear. Don't you dare to show your fear.

The Golden Rule of her orphan's childhood circled inside of her head in an endless loop. Snapping her back straight and squaring her chin, she marched toward the main doors to the mansion. Prepared to confront the resident evil inside.

CHAPTER NINETY-SIX

Dmitry paced the suite that seemed to shrink in size with every step. Fear multiplied by anger bubbled inside him, tearing him apart. What happened to Natasha? Where did she go?

She knew no one in the city. She had nowhere to go. But like a fog, she disappeared during the few hours he and Katia were away. Dammit, to where? The air in the room seemed to hum like an electric current. Suffocating, he marched to the adjoining room and flung the balcony doors open.

Greedily he sucked a few lungsful of air. Rain saturated the air with a faint smell of ozone. When did it start? It was dry when he took Katia out. Dmitry decided to take his little girl to the restaurant, and treat her to a breakfast to give Natasha time to sleep in. Awkward and skittish around people, Katia held on to his hand with a white-knuckled grip. He watched his daughter's reaction to the new environment, and found it almost painful. Everything, from the hotel furniture to the objects d'arte, seemed to fascinate little Katia. The hostess seated them near a bubbling fountain. Katia eyed the starched napkins and fine bone Wedgewood dishes in awe. An order of cold cereal accompanied by a glass of orange juice plunged her into a state of shock. She looked at him with wide terrified eyes, and confided that she never ate such a breakfast before.

"Grandmother wouldn't approve," she explained in a hushed whisper. "It's not the *Russian* way to eat your meal."

She constantly searched his approval before saying a word in her slightly accented English. Dmitry barely controlled his anger.

Only now he realized the full extent of Katia's unnatural upbringing. Confined inside his mother's estate, locked in that oppressive mausoleum like a prisoner, she was socially and emotionally starved. Whenever they meet someone on the way, she hid behind him, acting like a small animal suddenly let out from its cage.

Because of you, you bastard.

Fuming, cursing himself, and ashamed to have been a complete selfish bastard, Dmitry vowed to change her life.

Everything was going to be different. She'd live in a real family, play with kids, go to school. Now his little girl has both parents, Natasha and him. And maybe one day, she'd have a baby brother or sister. Did Natasha realize that he had done his damnedest to get her pregnant? Probably not. Inexperienced, she never noticed a lack of birth control, a deliberate plan on his part. More likely, she'd be carrying their child soon, if not already. He intended to get one of the home pregnancy tests as soon as they arrived in Paris.

Soon, Rostoff. Just a couple of more days.

After breakfast, Katia begged to go to the boarding facility where Pasha and Misha stayed until their departure to Europe. She missed her dogs and worried about them. Understandable since she and the dogs were inseparable all her life. He gladly agreed to the trip.

When they returned to the hotel a few hours later, their suite was empty.

All Natasha's belongings and her books were there, but she seemed to have disappeared. A quick call to the receptionist desk yielded nothing. Dmitry harassed, threatened, and cajoled to no avail. No one saw her. If he knew how to pray, he'd do that too. He'd sell his soul, if only it helped to locate her.

Queasiness rocked him as he dialed Peter's phone number. His son hadn't heard from Natasha since yesterday. Frantic, he called the police, and informed that it must be at least twenty-four hours before the search was officially initiated. Seething, shamelessly using his family name and connections, Dmitry called the mayor who promised to contact the Chief of Police immediately. He itched to call the FBI, but what will he tell them? He has no proof of foul play. Until he had the concrete evidence that Natasha was kidnapped, the FBI undoubtedly must refuse to get involved. Damnation! Deep in his gut he knew that something bad had happened. Natasha wouldn't leave, not willingly. She would never abandon Katia. As far as he knew, she didn't have any money. And all her documents were stolen. She hadn't a single soul in San Francisco to go to.

Except for Elizabeth. Did Natasha decide to return to *Zolotoe Selo?* He considered it for a moment, then shook his head. Impossible.

But what if she was forced to return?

Fear swept through him as he paced the room until two detectives knocked on his door. They introduced themselves, but he failed to catch their names. Quickly, both officers took over, asking him what seemed like a million questions. When did he see Natasha last? How long did he stay away from the hotel? What about her state of mind? Was she upset? And on and on they rattled without doing anything except making a few notes. Ready to scream, Dmitry forced himself to answer the questions as coherently as possible. But enough was enough.

"Why are you questioning me instead of looking for her?"

The older detective met his gaze, his eyes flat and emotionless.

"It's a procedure, Mr. Rostoff."

"The hell with your procedure! My fiancé is missing. You must—"

"Don't tell me how to do my job, sir."

Short of pulling his hair out, Dmitry whirled around, fisting his shaking hands. Dammit, he was unraveling. Fast. Not good.

Control, Rostoff. Stay focused.

Thank God for Peter, who arrived shortly after the detectives. He calmly took the matters of communicating with the policemen in his own hands, shielding Dmitry. His gaze traveled to the little figure sitting on the sofa. Katia seemed to withdraw into herself as she watched the happenings out of bleak dry eyes. She must be scared, but God help him, he couldn't find a single word of comfort for his daughter.

Selfish bastard.

He was going out of his mind. Pictures of Natasha, hurt, and helpless, bombarded his feverish imagination. How much longer did he have to withstand the torment?

Christ, I didn't tell her I love her. And now it might be too late.

That thought brought him to his knees.

No! Impossible! God can't be so cruel.

She must be alive and well, and they will find her. He must believe that.

Otherwise...

A hesitant knock on the door snapped Dmitry back to the moment. One of the detectives went to open it. Accompanied by the hotel's manager, a thin as a beanpole youth in Ritz's uniform entered the room. The boy's troubled eyes scanned the room, until they landed on Katia. Wincing, he averted his gaze.

"Sorry to bother you, Mister Rostoff, but one of my bellboys seems to remember something regarding your fiancé."

With a low growl, Dmitry advanced forward, and grabbed the boy's shoulders in a steely grip. "Where is she?"

"I don't know, sir... mister... I just..."

Dmitry scowled at the boy. "Where is she!"

The kid's eyes filled with terror. "I don't know!"

The older detective laid a hand on Dmitry's arm.

"Mr. Rostoff, let me talk to him." Calm and clear, his voice rang with authority.

The tone and action shot Dmitry's temper sky high. He shrugged the hand away, then rounded on the policeman. "Fuck off. This punk knows something. I can see it in his eyes."

"So do I. You called us to help to find your fiancé. Let me do my job."

A cold hard stare of the darkest eyes he'd ever seen managed to penetrate the haze in Dmitry's brain. Cop's eyes, flat, shrewd, and uncompromising. With a reluctant nod, Dmitry stepped back.

The detective focused his hard stare on the boy. "Your name?"

"Sam, sir, officer. Samuel North."

"Mr. North, your manager here says you know something about Ms. Sokolova. Is that right?"

"Yes, Sir. I..." his Adam's apple bobbled helplessly, before he found his voice, "I delivered a letter to her."

"What letter?" Dmitry surged forward. Quick as a whiplash, the detective's hand gripped his forearm, stopping him in midmotion.

"What time, boy?" he continued his questioning.

"Eleven o'clock, sir. I am sure because she— the lady— asked me, and I looked at my watch. It was eleven sharp."

"Who gave you the letter?"

"A gentleman downstairs."

"What gentleman?"

"I...don't know."

"How did he look like? Young, old, black, white?"

"Old. White, tall, and very skinny. He... he had this accent, kinda funny."

Dmitry tensed.

Ivan. Sonofabitch.

His vicious curse caused the boy to stumble a step backward. With a quick glance in his direction, the detective turned back to the young man. "Okay, what happened next?"

"He—the old gentleman—asked me to deliver a letter. To the lady staying with Mr. Rostoff. He said he'd wait for an answer."

"Why you? Why not one of the clerks? Your position is...?"

"I am a bellboy, Sir. I know I wasn't supposed to, but..." he stole a guilty glimpse at the manager. "The day was slow, and that man gave me twenty to deliver a message, and promised another later, so I thought, why not? It'll take just a moment and... I thought no harm to deliver a letter. I mean, what's wrong with that?"

The manager's angry harrumph made the boy wince. One hard glance from the detective stopped all the noise.

"So, you went upstairs. Then what?"

"I knocked and she, the lady, she opened the door. I told her I have a message. And she looked at the envelope, and then she asked me the time again. I told her eleven. She said "where is D... Di... I don't remember the name, a foreign something, and I said I don't know. If she wanted the information, she should call the desk. Then I handed her the letter because she didn't want to take it. That's all."

"Why do you think she didn't want to take a letter?"

"I don't know, but she looked at it kinda...strange. Like she was afraid, or something. So, I picked it up and gave it to her. That's all."

"You sure? She never said or asked anything else?"

"Oh... oh, yeah. She asked me who delivered the letter. I said an old gentleman, and described him. Then she opened it, and read it, and told me to go downstairs and tell him she'd be there shortly."

The detective narrowed his eyes at the boy. "She said she'd be down shortly? Are you absolutely sure?"

"Yes, Sir, that's right."

"Okay. Now tell me about that gentleman again. Did he give you his name?"

"I... don't know. He didn't tell."

"What did he look like?"

"I told you, tall, skinny, old. Gray thin hair, small eyes. He gave me the creeps."

"Okay, Mr. North. Thank you for the information. I might need to talk to you again. In the meantime, here's my card. If you remember anything else, call me immediately."

"I will, Sir. All right. Sure." Visibly relieved, the bellboy made a hasty retreat.

"Sam?"

Like a silver bell, Katia's voice echoed around the room. Dmitry jolted. Damn, he forgot about her. She stepped forward, gazing at the bellboy.

The boy stopped, then turned. "What, Miss?"

"Was she scared?"

The silence that followed Katia's question became deafening. All eyes focused on Sam except Dmitry's. He stared at his daughter.

"I..." Darting a quick look around the room, the bellboy's gaze returned to Katia. With a deep sigh, he nodded. "Yes. I think so. I asked her if she was okay, but she just said... that she was all right. And then I left."

"Thank you, Sam." Sad and devastating, the smile on Katia's face ripped Dmitry apart.

"Yeah, sure." This time the bellboy ran away like all the bats from hell chased him.

CHAPTER NINETY-SEVEN

"**Y**ou recognized the man who delivered the letter, don't you, Mr. Rostoff?"

The detective's flat voice brought Dmitry back to the moment.

"Yes. My mother's butler. Ivan."

May he rot in hell.

"So, your fiancé willingly went down to meet your mother's butler. It is safe to assume that she left with him."

"And?"

"And your kidnapping theory doesn't fly."

"I don't care. Natasha would never go with him, unless she felt threatened."

Cursing, Dmitry span around, and hurried toward the door.

"Where are you going?"

"To my mother's place."

After a short pause, the older detective nodded. "I'll go with you."

Ten minutes later, they were speeding toward *Zolotoe Selo* in the police cruiser.

The other detective stayed in the hotel with Peter and Katia, just in case Natasha showed up. *Not going to happen.* Dmitry knew that for certain. Grim, he concentrated on the road ahead, silently urging the detective to go faster.

The policeman drove with an experience of a seasoned pilot, navigating the SUV over the speed limit. But it wasn't enough, dammit.

"We don't know if the man was your mother's butler."

"How many tall skinny old men with a funny accent can there be?"

"In San Francisco? Thousands. But let's just assume it was that Ivan guy who delivered the letter." He deliberately ignored Dmitry's murderous gaze. "Your fiancé knew him for ... what? Five-six years? Obviously, he's not a stranger."

"What's your point?"

"My point is, she went with him willingly. She's not in danger, Rostoff."

"Maybe, not in physical danger, but..." He shook his head, and cursed under his breath. "Trust me, Detective, I know my mother. She's plotting something, and that something is very bad. It involves my fiancé, dammit."

The detective mulled it over for a moment. "Correct me if I'm wrong, Rostoff, but your mother has recently suffered a massive stroke. She can't walk or talk." He speared Dmitry a pointed look.

"Yes. But my mother's physical condition is irrelevant. She's capable of..." *Anything short of murder.* Frustrated, he dragged all ten fingers through his hair. "Just trust me on this, Detective. And move this damn car, will you?"

Unruffled, the other man kept his voice neutral, but increased the speed. "Okay, so here's the plan, Rostoff. When we get there, I'll do the talking, and you stay out of the way."

"Like hell I will."

"You will, if you care about your fiancé."

It galled at him that the detective was right. If he wanted to find Natasha, he must do whatever necessary. If that meant stay away, he'd stay away, no matter what the cost. Reluctantly, he nodded. "Alright."

"Good. Officially, I cannot interrogate your mother, or even enter the premises. Unofficially, I can ask her permission to answer a few questions, and hope she'll agree to talk to me."

"Oh, she will, believe me." He fisted his hands until his knuckles went white. Elizabeth would never deny the audience, if only to rub his face in it, the bitch.

"I hope you're right. Otherwise, my hands are tied."

Dmitry's tenuous hold on his temper snapped like a dry twig. "She was the last person who saw Natasha! Does it count for anything?"

Unruffled, the other man countered, "You don't know that for sure until your mother will corroborate that. Or until we find a witness. And even then, what will it give us? Your fiancé willingly went to see her former employee. So, what?"

Dmitry spouted out a single curse. The detective's lips curved in a dry grin.

"Is that Russian? Sounded brutal. What does that mean? On a second thought, don't tell me. I don't think I wanna know." Once again, he grew serious. "I'm not bullshitting you, Rostoff. I won't be able to do anything officially."

"Then I'll do it myself. Unofficially."

"And get yourself arrested? Sure, a big help you'll be then to your fiancé. Or your children."

"Shit."

"An understatement of the century." After a long moment, he asked, "You don't remember me, do you?"

"Should I?"

"We've met before. I was one of the detectives investigating your late wife's case."

Warily, he exhaled. "How kind of you to call it a *case*."

Polina's death was officially ruled as an accident. Running away after the unsuccessful attempt to murder baby Katia, a passing car struck her. The scandal, thanks to Elizabeth, got swept under the rug quickly and efficiently. The case closed within forty-eight hours without a hint of it leaking to the press. A true miracle, considering the Rostoff name. Resigned, Dmitry turned toward the older man. "Sorry, I don't remember you. It was such a...fucking mess."

"You can say that again. The name is Benton, by the way."

"Nice to meet you, Detective Benton. Again."

"Likewise, even though both circumstances suck. Big time."

Dmitry's chuckle lacked any merriment. "You can say that again."

They fell into an uncomfortable silence. Benton broke it first.

"So, what's the real deal here? Why did you say your fiancé would never go to see your mother willingly?"

"It's a long and complicated story. Trust me on this."

"I'm not asking out of curiosity, Rostoff. I have to know what I'm dealing with."

He was right. Reluctantly, Dmitry obliged. "The gist of it is, we have been estranged for the past six years, my mother and I. She hates my guts. After her stroke, I decided to relocate my daughter and my fiancé to France. Two days ago, we left the estate, and moved to the hotel."

"Why? I mean, why didn't you leave for France immediately?"

"That's another troubling story. Natasha's, my fiancé, documents were stolen. To replace them, we must wait a certain period of time."

"Okay, so you moved your family to the hotel. And?"

"And it didn't sit well with Elizabeth. In order to stop me, and prevent our departure, she obviously concocted some scheme. Hence, the letter."

"What do you think was in that message?"

"I don't know. But I am sure some form of blackmail."

"Are you serious? What could she blackmail your fiancé with?"

"Dammit, if only I knew." He racked his brain to no avail. What secret the old witch had in her arsenal? What did she use to lure Natasha back? The offer of money? No, out of the question, even Elizabeth must understand that. What, then? Fear? Did Elizabeth make Natasha afraid of something? Probably. More than likely, afraid for someone. Someone she loved. Him? The children? Only one way to find out.

"Could you floor it?" Dmitry asked for the umpteenth time. Frowning, the detective obliged.

"Are you sure your fiancé wouldn't go there unless threatened?"

"Absolutely. Natasha would never agree to meet my mother otherwise. She was afraid. You heard that boy Sam. She was scared."

Scared enough to go with Ivan without leaving a word for him. Hell.

"Humm." Clearly unconvinced, Benton pursed his lips.

"You don't know what my mother is capable of! You don't know my mother, Detective."

"Can't say I regret it," he muttered, as the large iron gate rose ahead. He whistled. "Some house."

"I call it a mausoleum."

"Looks like it too."

Even before the detective pressed the communication button on the side panel, the heavy golden gates squeaked open. So, they were expected, and allowed the entrance.

The pathway to Hades.

Cold dread settled inside of him like an enormous boulder. He shivered. The time had come. The moment of truth.

And then his resolve crumbled. He realized he was afraid. Petrified.

Whatever answers he found inside that oppressive mausoleum will change his life forever.

How do I know that?

A desperate wish to turn around and run grabbed him by the throat. Dmitry swore.

Coward.

He'd be damned if he showed Elizabeth his fear. Like a predator, she thrived on the weaknesses of others. He'd rather die than allow her the luxury.

Clamping his teeth, he deliberately fanned the embers of his anger until it burst into a bubbling rage.

Better.

"Well, Rostoff, let me remind you that we're here to ask questions, not to demand or attack."

Like a slap in the face, Benton's flat voice jerked him back to present. The detective parked the car in front of the marble steps and killed the engine.

"And I mean it. I'll do the asking. You do not, I repeat, do not interfere. And don't do anything stupid."

"Like what?" With a feral sneer, Dmitry jumped out of the cruiser.

"Like... shit. Hold on just a damn minute!"

But he was already far ahead of the policeman, mounting the steps on a run. Benton caught up with him before he rang the bell. None too gently, he dropped his hand onto Dmitry's shoulder.

"You are a smart man, Rostoff. Think, for Christ's sake! Think of the damage you could do by acting on an impulse."

"That's not an impulse, Detective. Natasha came here. Maybe, she's still in here."

"You don't know that for sure. You don't know that!" He stressed as Dmitry sent him a glowering glance. "All we know is this: your fiancé received a message and, according to the bellboy, decided to meet the messenger personally. That's all."

"That's all I need."

Clearly at the end of his patience, Benton shot him a glare.

"Rostoff, I am the cop here, okay? Let me handle it. If you want to help Natasha, let me do my job. Be a pal, okay?"

"Yeah, whatever you say, *pal*."

CHAPTER NINETY-EIGHT

As soon as the front door swung open, Dimitry charged inside like an enraged bull. A moment later, he snatched Ivan into his hands, then shook him like a sack of potatoes. A rapid string of Russian bounced around the vestibule like pinging bullets. A shade of scarlet spread over his haggard face, a compliment of Dmitry's hands manacled around the butler's throat.

Benton cursed, and stepped forward. He then executed a fast karate strike, dislodging Dmitry's grip. He stumbled back. A new explosion of Russian did nothing to ease the pain in his hands.

Dmitry looked at Ivan. The old man's color was alarmingly high, his breathing came in fast short chops. A prime candidate for a heart attack.

The cop gave Dmitry a look that would kill a lion, then grabbed his badge, and waved it in front of Ivan's face. "Detective Benton, SFPD. I need to ask you some questions."

Trembling from head to toe, the butler gawked. "W-what? P-police?"

Benton scowled. "Your name, sir."

Then he shot a quick glance to his right. A couple of feet away, poised and alert, Dmitry glared at him ready to tackle the detective.

"I don't recommend it, Rostoff," he said in a firm voice, then turned back to the butler. "Name."

"Ivan. Ivan Petrovski."

Dmitry curled his lip. The high-pitched, nasally voice matched his repulsive appearance.

"What is your position in this household, Mr. Petrovski?"

"I... I am the butler of Her Grace Elizabeth."

Pride and arrogance eked through, setting Dmitry's teeth on edge.

"Mr. Petrovski, you've been seen in the Ritz Carlton Hotel this morning by an employee of the hotel. He also informed the police that you gave him a message to deliver for Ms. Natalia Sokolova. Is that correct?"

"Y-yes. I... I was at the hotel, yes. And I delivered the message from Her Grace to Natasha Sokolova." The old reprobate recovered quickly. Still splotched with unhealthy greyish pallor, his face turned indolent. Faded blue eyes darted between Benton and Dmitry.

The eyes of a weasel. Mean, hungry, and unscrupulous.

Benton glanced at Dmitry, then resumed his questioning, "So, your employer gave you a letter to deliver to her son's fiancée. Is that correct?"

"Yes. May I point out that before Natasha Sokolova became His Grace's fiancée, she was employed in this household as his daughter's nanny."

Dmitry itched to bitch slap the smirk on his face.

"I'm aware of that. It also came to my attention that your current employer and her former nanny parted not on friendly terms. Is that also correct?"

"I don't know what you mean, Officer."

"Detective."

"I beg your pardon, Detective. I don't know what you mean. We always treated Natasha cordially."

"Cordially?"

"Absolutely."

"So, there wasn't any animosity in the employer-employee relationship?"

"Not at all."

"What about after she became engaged to Mr. Rostoff?"

"Nothing changed."

"Why do you think Mr. Rostoff removed his family from this house?"

"I cannot say, Detective. Several days after Her Grace came back home from the hospital, Dmitry Nikolayevich with his fiancée, his little daughter, and their two dogs left this estate. I'm not privy to the reason for his decision."

"But you witnessed an unpleasant scene between your employer and her son before they drove off."

Not a question, but a firm statement. Ivan frowned and averted his eyes.

"Yes, I did witness this unfortunate incident."

Benton pounced. "What was that *unfortunate incident* about?"

"She—Natasha I mean—couldn't find her documents, and Dmitry Nikolayevich assumed someone stole them. He confronted Her Grace about it."

"And why would he do that?"

Ivan puffed his bony chest. "You'd better ask *him* that question, Detective."

"Hmm-mm. So, what you're saying is this: after Mr. Rostoff's fiancé lost her documents, he confronted his mother and accused her of...what exactly?"

"He didn't accuse her directly, Detective. Dmitry Nikolayevich mistakenly surmised that someone in this household took Natasha's papers."

"And that his mother was somehow involved, correct?"

"Yes, which is ridiculous at the very least." Ivan huffed, then shook his head.

"I'll tell you what's ridiculous, you old bastard!" Dmitry vibrated from rage, lifted his fists, then stepped forward.

Benton shot Dmitry a warning glare, then turned to the buttler.

Ivan shrugged and arranged his thin lips in a parody of a smile. "Clearly, His Grace is very upset still."

Dmitry's answering growl seemed more eloquent than all his earlier cursing. Benton angled his body, so that he stood between Dmitry and Ivan. "And when did that incident occur?"

"Two days ago."

"Why did Mrs. Rostoff send for Natasha today?"

Dmitry secretly applauded Benton for not saying *Her Grace*.

"I don't know." Ivan raised his bony shoulders, then let them fall. "I just followed orders, Detective. Her Grace asked me to deliver her message and wait for the written reply. Natasha had chosen to deliver her answer personally. Per her request, I accompanied her here. After our arrival, Natasha had a meeting with her former employer."

"Were you present at that meeting?"

"No. No one was present at that meeting, Detective. Only the two of them."

"How long did the meeting last?"

"About twenty minutes, I'd say."

"And after?"

"And after I called a cab for Natasha, and she left."

"In the cab?"

"That's right."

"Why wasn't she driven back?"

"Her Grace offered it, But Natasha refused."

"What time did she leave this house?"

"Oh, hours ago."

"Be more specific."

"Three hours at the most, Detective."

"Did someone besides you and your employer see Ms. Sokolova here?"

"Yes, several people. Boris, the chauffeur, Vera the cook, some other servants. I can make the inquires if you'd like."

"What I'd like is to talk to these people myself," Benton replied.

"Did you say you called a cab for her?"

"Yes, Detective."

"I'd like to have a number for the company."

"Of course, I'll get it for you at once."

"I'd also like to talk to your mistress, Mr. Petrovski."

"I'm afraid, that is not possible, Detective. Her Grace is resting."

"Then—"

"No, she's not." Devoid of any emotion, Dmitry stopped his reply. "Hello, Mother."

CHAPTER NINETY-NINE

B enton turned around and froze.

Dmitry almost laughed out loud at the shocked expression on the detective's face. Her Grace Elizabeth Rostoff seemed to hold him in a trance as if he couldn't tear his eyes of the haggard woman in a wheelchair.

With a passing impersonal glance at Dmitry, Elizabeth then fastened her eyes on Benton.

The detective squinted as if the lights in the room had dimmed. To Dmitry it seemed everything became swallowed by shadows.

She rolled the wheelchair forward, then stopped a couple of inches from Benton's feet, and raised her cold as ice eyes.

The detective shuddered then seemed to stiffen his spine. "Ma'am."

A knowing smile spread across Elizabeth's disfigured face.

"Detective." She pronounced the word slowly, with obvious effort. Flat and emotionless. "What brings you to my home?"

Her eerie vacant voice scraped Dmitry raw. One side of Elizabeth's face drooped lower, lifeless, and frozen. But her dark eyes were sharp, shrewd, and cruel.

Benton cleared his throat. "I'd like to ask you some questions regarding your former nanny, Ms. Sokolova."

She lifted one brow in a perfect arch. "Natalia? You just missed her, I'm afraid."

"Yes, your butler already informed me. Can you tell me why was she here?"

"Because I asked her to come. As you can see," she swept her right hand to demonstrated, "I'm unable to travel."

"Will you explain to me the nature of your meeting with Ms. Sokolova?"

"Of course." Elizabeth manourvered her chair to face Dmitry. She stared at him long and hard before her bloodless lips curled in a chilling half-smile. Keeping her eyes on Dmitry, she resumed talking to Benton, "Two days ago, while living under my roof, Natalia lost all her documents. Obviously, she was very upset. As it happened, today my maid found those papers which she accidentally misplaced cleaning Natalia's room. She brought them to me, confessing her mistake. I immediately wrote to Natalia, offering my apologies and requesting the meeting."

"Why?"

"Why?" Finally, Elizabeth ripped her eyes away from her son, and to look at the detective. He barely managed not to flinch. "Because the woman is soon to be my daughter-in-law, Detective. I wanted to make amends. I admit, for all these years that Natalia lived in my house we weren't...very close. Now that she's about to become family, I wanted to smooth things between us. You know, woman to woman. " After a sideway glance at Dmitry, she finished, "And to present her with a wedding gift."

Dmitry uttered a helpless oath. Elizabeth twisted her lips in a caricature of a smile. Like poison, saliva dribbled from the corner of her mouth in a thin wet line.

"A gift? And what might that be, if you don't mind my asking?"

"Oh, just some trinket, Detective, a small elaborate box with a secret compartment that came from my family."

An almost imperceptible pause at the word 'secret' was followed by a flash of victory in her chilling eyes. A grotesque half-smile transformed Elizabeth's face into something vile and ugly and inhuman. Terrifying.

For a split second, Dmitry swore he looked into the face of insanity.

Elizabeth shrugged with an effort. "Useless thing, really, but beautiful. Just perfect to make a woman's heart...weep."

Her English flawless, her speech, although laborious, clear and coherent.

But the acute impression of double meaning behind her statement galled him.

Being played for a fool didn't sit well with Dmitry nor Benton who frowned and jotted more notes onto his small pad.

"So, you gave Ms. Sokolova her wedding gift. Then what?"

"Then? Why, she thanked me, of course. She was deeply moved. Almost to tears. Wasn't she, Ivan?"

The older butler bobbed his head. "Oh, yes, Your Grace. Almost to tears."

Dmitry uttered a curt word in Russian that made the old man wince but his mother remained completely unruffled. Benton, who didn't miss a bit, continued after a short pause,

"Okay, she was touched. Then what? "

"Then... let me think..." A production of tapping a finger agaist her mishapen lips was worthy an Oscar.

Miserable bitch.

"Oh, yes, then Natalia decided to leave, and I offered her the services of my chauffeur. She refused. So, I asked Ivan to fetch a cab. And she left."

"Are you sure? Are you—"

Elizabeth's icy voice cut through his questioning. "Detective, am I under arrest?"

"No, ma'am."

"Is this an official police investigation?"

Dmitry knew this was coming.

Resigned, Benton replied, "No, not yet, but—"

"Well, then, as far as I'm concern, this matter is closed. I cooperated fully, answered all your questions, although I still don't understand the true nature of your presence in my home. If you'll excuse me." She pushed buttons on the panel of her chair. "Ivan will show you out."

"Ma'am, Miss Sokolova left your house a few hours ago and hasn't been seen since. If she isn't located by early afternoon tomorrow, there will be an open police investigation. I will be back in the official capacity to take your statement, and that of your employees."

"Until then, farewell Detective. And your name again?"

He replied through clenched teeth, "Benton. Detective John Benton."

"Farewell, Detective John Benton." She pushed the button on the armrest and swiveled her chair toward him. "Dmitry? My I have a word?"

Reluctant, Dmitry approached his mother. She switched to Russian and uttered a few words. He stepped back as if she slapped him, then shook his head, and glared at the evil that was his mother.

"*Nyet. Nyet!*"

Elizabeth tilted her head, and added a few more sentences.

Dmitry blanched. His mouth trembled open. She pushed a button on the panel of her wheelchair, then glided away. Frozen, he stared at her retreating back.

Dmitry felt like he had received a mortal blow. Shattered. Lost. Deflated.

"What did she tell you?"

Dmitry jolted, turned, and focused his gaze on Benton. Instead of answering, he walked toward the butler, whose face bloomed with malice, and silently accepted a manila envelope from his hands, then exited the house.

Benton climbed into to the cruiser, and switched on the ignition. Dmitry sat in the passenger's seat with the manila envelope's contends spread on his knees.

"I want to know what your mother told you before we left."

His toneless voice finally broke the silence.

"She told me that she gave Natasha something else besides the trinket."

"What?"

"A check." Dmitry failed to hold back his brittle laugh. "Money, Detective. She gave Natasha money."

CHAPTER ONE HUNDRED

Dmitry's initial shock ebbed away, leaving him strangely calm. Indifferent.

Hollowed out. Numb, as if he was shot with an elephant doze of Novocain, he didn't feel anything. But any anesthetic must wear off sooner or later. And after...

Don't think about after. Don't think at all.

"Why?" Benton's voice cut through the heavy layer of numbness.

"Why what?"

"Why did your mother give Natasha money?"

"Isn't it obvious, Detective?"

"Why don't you spell out it for me?"

"To buy her off, of course."

"You don't believe that, man."

"But I do, Detective. A hundred thousand dollars for a woman raised in the orphanage is a fortune. Obviously, it trumps everything else."

Like love and loyalty.

Benton cursed. "What if your mother lied to you?"

"She didn't. Natasha took the money."

"Are you sure? How can you condemn the woman you love without giving her a chance to explain?"

"I'd give her a chance, Detective, but in case you forgot, Natasha disappeared. And besides, I have proof of that transaction." He tapped the two pieces of papers on his lap. "A copy of the check, and a receipt of acceptance." A dry chuckle scraped his throat as if he swallowed a splintered glass. "Fully executed. In black ink."

Benton's frown made a deep V between his brows. "I still don't think—"

"Then don't." Shoving the papers back into manila envelope, Dmitry leaned back, and closed his eyes. Exhaustion dragged him under. Mercifully numb, detached from reality, as all feeling abandoned him. He no longer cared. "Your investigation is officially closed, Detective."

"Like hell it is!" Benton's angry retort forced him to crack his eyes open. Glaring, the older man held his gaze.

"Oh, it most definitely is, Detective. I'll call your captain as soon as we back at the hotel. And I will mention my sincere appreciation for your help today."

"Shove it, pal. I need your appreciation as I need..." Benton visibly struggled for control. After a long moment, he drew a deep breath.

"Listen, Rostoff. You are a smart man. Think about it. Something's off with this picture. Granted, I never met your fiancé. For all I know, she might be a heartless bitch and a greedy gold digger. But something's just not adding up for me."

"Like what?"

"You are loaded, right? Wouldn't it be more beneficial for Natasha to stay with you? A hundred K seems peanuts compared to your wealth. She'd be smart to marry you, and roll in the mullah for the rest of her life."

A tiny sliver of doubt prickled through his numbness. Was the older man right?

And what if so?

Deliberately, he swept those questions aside. He'd allow Natasha the benefit of the doubt if not for that damning evidence in his hands.

She took the money. She betrayed him. She betrayed them all.

Dear God, and how will I explain it to Katia?

Dmitry cringed. He'd think of something. He must.

Like what? How to tell a six-year-old the woman she loved as her mother abandoned her?

He cursed out loud. "Who knows what went through her mind? Maybe she just—"

"Don't." Benton tore his eyes off the road, and stared at him. "Don't do that, man. You said that your mother probably threatened her, even blackmailed. Remember?"

"I was wrong. Elizabeth just bought her off."

"You don't know that. You can't be sure."

"Oh, but I am." Dmitry lifted the manila envelope, then let it drop.

"Dammit." Benton cursed, then frowned. "Go after her. Natasha won't move far. If you want, I'll give you the name of my friend. He's the best damn PI on this side of the coast. He'll find her."

"No."

"Jesus!" The detective thumped his fist on the steering wheel, then spared Dmitry an incredulous glance. "How could you be so...unmoving?"

"Don't you understand, Detective? My fiancé, or should I say, my former fiancé doesn't want to be found."

"What if you're wrong?"

"I'm not. I know people, Benton. And I know the power of money."

"Do you honestly think that everything has its price? That you can buy anything and anyone?"

"Yes."

Now his gaze shone with open disgust.

"You really are a piece of sh... work."

Under any other circumstances, Dmitry would have bristled. Not now, he no longer cared.

"Yeah, that's me, a real SOB with a macho twist. A quote from my secretary." Void of any emotion, his voice sounded hollow even to himself.

"Obviously, she knows you better."

Without a hint of offence, Dmitry nodded. "Yes, she definitely does."

"But I'm not so sure about *macho* thing."

"You're breaking my heart, Detective." Geez, was he cracking a joke? Moron.

"I don't think so." With a quick glance at his direction, Benton switched his eyes back to the road. "To break it you should have it in a first place."

Score.

Dmitry fought the urge to rub the left side of his chest where his shattered heart struggled to beat.

The rest of their trip proceeded in dead silence.

CHAPTER ONE HUNDRED-ONE

Even though it went against his nature, Dmitry lied to Katia. His explanation that Natasha was called on urgent business sounded lame, totally ridiculous, and he failed to fool Katia even for a second. Her bleak devastated gaze crashed his heart into a million pieces. She never uttered a single word. Not once did she shed a tear. Flattened by grief, Katia all but folded into herself, withdrawn and stock-still. All attempts to draw her out failed. Helpless, he watched his little daughter slowly close herself inside an invisible shell.

No way in hell.

He already lost one person he loved. He'd be damned if he lost his daughter, too. But how to get through to Katia? Dmitry racked his brain for a solution. He paced the floor like a panther but to no avail.

Finally, the answer came in a surge of breathless revelation. The dogs! Almost lightheaded from relief, he called the Ritz's general manager, explained the situation, and wrangled approval to bring the dogs to his suite. As soon as the shepherds arrived, Katia became more animated. Thank God.

At his insistence, she ate half a sandwich, then, accompanied by both dogs, went to her bedroom. He didn't have the heart to stop Pasha and Misha from nuzzling up to her on the bed. He watched Katia from the doorway. She tossed and turned until she finally fell into a fretful sleep. He realized he forgot about her usual bedtime bath ritual. He shook his head. Just for one night. Tomorrow, he'd do better by his daughter. It fell on him now to take care of Katia. Alone.

Tired to the marrow, his body craved rest, but sleep was out of the question. He dragged over the most uncomfortable looking chair from the parlor then positioned it in front of Katia's room. He laid his hands on the carved wooden arms, then sank onto the hard surface, prepared to keep vigil. The silence pressed on him from all sides like a lead weight. Thousands of troubling thoughts hummed in his brain.

What really happened? Where was Natasha? What was she doing right now?

What if Benton was right, and Elizabeth blackmailed her? What if she had no choice but to accept the check? But why?

Dear God, where is she? Is she safe?

She must be scared. Lost in a big unfamiliar city. Desolate. Why not return to the hotel? Where did she go after leaving the estate?

All her possessions were still in the suite. Even if—and that if seemed impossible—Elizabeth gave back all her documents, Natasha still had only the clothes on her back. And no money.

Except that check.

She had no ability to cash such a large sum without identification.

She won't touch that check.

His breath hitched. Of course not! Natasha obviously accepted it under duress, but she will never use this money. She'd never betray him. What was he thinking? He wasn't. He reacted to Elizabeth's shocking revelation. Just as she predicted.

The bitch.

Dmitry jumped from the chair, then paced the room.

He should have listened to the detective, and started searching for Natasha immediately. How could he have been so callous? How stupid for him to have believed Elizabeth?

You are a bastard, Rostoff. With a capital B.

His gut assured him of Natasha innocent. Elizabeth must have manipulated and blackmailed her, otherwise Natasha would never have gone away. She loved him. As for Katia, she loved that little beauty from the day she was born. Natasha would not abandon Katia lightly. An enormous surge of hope left him shaken. He knew she'd come back and explain everything. And then they'd leave this godforsaken city once and for all.

Energized, he went to the balcony, flung the doors open, and gulped in a lungful of fresh air.

What are you waiting for?

Cursing his own stupidity, he walked to the desk, picked up the phone, then put it back. If Natasha was not here soon, he'd call Detective Benton, and ask for the info on that PI guy. He prayed that wouldn't be necessary, and that Natasha came back on her own. And then he paced, worried, and waited.

CHAPTER ONE HUNDRED-TWO

Dawn slowly lifted the curtain of darkness as the first rays of sun illuminated the horizon. And still, Natasha failed to show up.

Dmitry nestled back into the chair to study his sleeping daughter, and brooded.

Somehow, he must have fallen asleep. The insistent calling "Daddy, wake up, wake up," jerked him out of his slumber. Disoriented, he jumped from his chair, and almost tripled over the large body of the dog who planted himself on his feet.

"Dammit, what? What is it?"

"Daddy, I know where Mama is!"

His blurry eyes zeroed in on the tiny figure of Katia, who tugged on his sleeve, trying to catch his attention.

"W-what did you say?"

"I know where Mama is, Daddy."

His heart somersaulted in his chest. His little girl called him daddy. For the first time. Undone, feeling the strange pressure behind his eyelids, he knelt before Katia, and gently put his hands on her shoulders. For a long moment, he hadn't the ability to trust his voice. She stared back at him, her eyes full of hope, her silky hair mussed on one side of her head from the pillow she slept on.

Daddy.

Then the meaning of her words penetrated the hazy mush in his brain.

"You know...what?"

"Haven't you listened to me?" A tiny frown formed between her platinum brows, then cleared, as she beamed at him. "I know where Mama is!"

What? Did I hear her correctly? She knows where Natasha is?

Afraid to move a muscle, he asked, "Where?"

She gave him a pitying look. "In Paris, of course."

"How...how do you know that?"

"She told me."

Oh, Lord.

Either he was dense, or Katia was hallucinating. Did yesterday's event affect her more than he realized? He managed to tame his growing panic and tried not to spook her. "She...told you?"

"Yes. She came to me in my dream, and told me."

"What exactly did she tell you, Pumpkin?"

Tread carefully, Rostoff.

"She said that she will never ever leave me. Not before she has to go to heaven. She told me she's waiting for us."

"For... us?"

"Yes, you and me and Pasha and Misha. She went to Paris, Daddy. She's already there, waiting for us. We must leave right away. We must hurry. Please!"

She pressed both tiny palms together under her chin, her huge eyes pleaded with him. And all he could think of was an angel in an old painting he saw as a boy.

Despite any logic, a new wave of hope surged up.

Was it possible? And why the hell not? Why question the mystery of the universe. The connection between a mother and child went beyond any rationalization. His heart gave one heavy thud, then thundered in his chest.

Was Katia's dream just a figment of her imagination? But he needed to believe it. Coud Natasha have really gone to Paris?

More than possible.

But what about her passport? Just yesterday, her new documents were delivered to the Ritz. Of course! He ran to her suitcase, flung it open, and ruffled through her clothes.

Not here.

Where the hell did she put it? And then he remembered: the desk. She asked him to keep the newly minted passport safe, and he himself locked it in a drawer. He raced to the desk. He tore open the drawer to find that all her documents were missing.

She must've taken them.

Relief swept through him in a huge tidal wave. She had her passport. She can fly to France.

Thank God.

Natasha knew the address of his flat, knew Marie and Vlad's contact info. She had money for the flight ticket, thanks to Elizabeth, if she cashed the check. To make good on her promise to his bitch of a mother, she must have pretended to fold under pressure, then disappeared.

Natasha was smart. She loved him and his children, a concept totally alien to Elizabeth. And his mother's ultimate downfall.

Fail to take into consideration Natasha's feelings, Your Grace?

The longer he considered it, the idea of Natasha thwarting Elizabeth's plan by traveling to Paris became more and more realistic. It was not only feasible, but the only way to fool his scheming mother, and make her believe that she won. Even if Elizabeth called all the airlines none gave out passenger names. Natasha must've been afraid that Elizabeth might order one of her spies to follow her, and that's why she never returned to the hotel.

Of course. How can I be so stupid?

Instead of sitting in his room, going out of his mind with worry and doubt, he should've flown to France immediately. Idiot.

Revved up, blood humming, he drew in a lungful of air and let it out with a loud *whoosh.* He surged to his feet, gave an absent rub to one of the dogs who pressed its furry head to his leg, and grinned at Katia.

"So, what are we waiting for? Let's go to the airport."

"Hurray!" She grinned and jumped up and down. That prompted both dogs to action, barking and running around her in circles.

He laughed and was tempted to join the melee, but the invisible clock in his head ticked loudly. He stole a quick glance at his wristwatch, then calculated how longer before they're packed and on their way. Not soon enough to satisfy him. It only took a moment to decide the hell with luggage. Let the hotel ship their belongings later.

Thank God the kennel saw to the dogs receiving their shots and microchips.

"Okay, my favorite daughter—"

"Daddy, I'm your only daughter!"

Daddy. There's that beautiful word once again.

He glanced down. He was still dressed in yesterday clothes, his shirt wrinkled and probably smelly, but what the heck? He can shower and change on the plane. He looked at Katia, and shrugged. Her Mickey Mouse pjs had to suffice until then.

"Stuff everything you want on the plane into your backpack. You have two minutes because we're leaving now."

Katia raced to her room shrieking with joy. The dogs hot on her heels.

He called to the front desk to have his car brought around. Katia stood at his side when he hung up the phone.

"You have everything?"

She hoisted her backpack over her shoulders. "Let's go!"

He grabbed his sport jacket off the chair, hauled Katia into his arms, and ordered the dogs to follow. They raced out of the door. In a hurry to leave the hotel, Dmitry barely paid attention to the porter who thrusted a small FedEx package at him.

"It was delivered for you earlier, Mr. Rostoff."

"Please ship it together with our luggage to my address in Paris."

"Very well, sir. Your car is awaiting."

Dmitry stepped into the fresh air with Katia in is arms and two eager dogs. His unusual entourage drew a small frown from his chauffer, but he chose to ignore it. The dogs were shooed inside then Dmitry climbed in and set Katia on his lap.

Grinning like a carefree teenager, he called out to his grumpy chauffer, "To the airport."

His little girl patted the dogs on their heads.

"Behave, boys. We are going on an adventure. Soon we'll be in Paris, in our new home." She turned to him, her eyes sparkling with joy. "We'll be a real family, Mama and you and me. And Peter, when he is done with college. And we'll live happily ever after. Right, Daddy?"

Daddy.

His heart swelled, his throat tightened. Even if he lived to be a hundred, he'd never get tired of hearing that beautiful word.

"Right, Pumpkin." He tweaked her pert nose, winked, and unable to hide his own growing excitement, echoed in a gruff voice, "Happily ever after."

Out the mouth of babes.

An hour later, their motley crew piled inside the waiting jet, and flew to the City of Lights.

ABOUT THE AUTHOR

Stella May is the penname for talented author **Marina Sardarova** who has a fascinating history you should read on her website[1] STELLA MAY Author[2]. Click onto About Stella in the header for the details.

Stella writes fantasy romance as well as time travel romance and sagas. Love and family are the two cornerstones of her stories and life. Stella's books are available in e-book and paperback through all major vendors.

When not writing, Stella enjoys classical music, reading, and long walks along the ocean. She lives in Jacksonville, Florida with her husband Leo and their son George. They are her two best friends and are all partners in their family business.

Also by Stella May
UPON A TIME SERIES
'Till time Do Us Part
Time & Again
No Other time
A Twirl in Time
THE ROSTOFF SERIES
New Dawn
New Hope
STAND ALONE NOVEL
Rhapsody in Dreams
COMING SOON
New Life
New Horizon

1.　　https://www.blogger.com/blog/post/edit/19076326/1152448649577793874

2.　　https://www.stellamayauthor.com/

Don't miss out!

Visit the website below and you can sign up to receive emails whenever Stella May publishes a new book. There's no charge and no obligation.

https://books2read.com/r/B-A-COXF-CJSID

BOOKS 2 READ

Connecting independent readers to independent writers.

Did you love *New Hope*? Then you should read *New Dawn*[3] by Stella May!

International playboy and owner of a jewelry empire that spreads across three continents, Dmitry Rostoff holds a memory close to this heart that not even his best friend Vlad Albrecht knows. When Dmitry learns the Russian ballerina he had a passionate affair with died in childbirth, bitterness and hate overrule all other emotions.

Taking the baby out of Russia is an impossible snarl of red tape, but Dmitry gets his way, even if he leaves a trail of chaos in his wake.

Natasha Sokolova planned to turn over the baby to Dmitry then walk away. Instead, she is on a plane to San Francisco with the baby and a cold, emotionless man who makes her heart pound with scorching attraction.

---

3. https://books2read.com/u/4N8wy6

4. https://books2read.com/u/4N8wy6

The family matriarch and evil to her core Elizabeth Rostoff plots to gain control of the baby, no matter what it costs or who it hurts, and will do anything to make that happen. She blackmails Marie Dubois, the manager of their elite Paris store, to seduce Dmitry. But Marie reneges on the deal when former Special Forces officer Vlad Albrecht storms into her life.

Once in America, Natasha finds herself entangled in a sticky web of lies created by the brutally calculating family matriarch. A web that forces Natasha to make a heartbreaking deal with the devil to protect the children—and man—she's come to love.

A vicious circle of malicious deceit and heinous acts weave these people into a web they may never unravel.

Read more at www.StellaMayAuthor.com.

Milton Keynes UK
Ingram Content Group UK Ltd.
UKHW010617250624
444652UK00001B/109

9 798224 207527